for Lissie
x

About the Author

Caroline lives in the Lake District with her husband, small child and two Kune Kune pigs.

She daydreams of one day owning a pair of Louboutin's and having somewhere fabulous to wear them. Until then, she'll be found plodding up a mountain in her trusty hiking boots.

Nearly Almost Somebody is Caroline's second novel. Her first, *#Forfeit* is available from Amazon.

Chapter One

Maggie hung up her coat and pottered upstairs, too tired to bother with the glass of elderflower wine she'd promised herself.

'Night, Hyssop,' she said to the tabby cat curled up on the landing. He flicked an ear.

With the full moon illuminating her bedroom, Maggie padded across the room, humming as she unfastened her pendant and dropped it into its silver bowl. But the pendant hit wood. The bowl wasn't there.

Hyssop, the little imp, must've knocked it off again. Stepping back, she glanced around the floor, expecting to see the bowl, but instead, glinting in the pale light, were the worthless trinkets she kept in her jewellery box. She grabbed the pendant and clutched it to her chest.

Had she been burgled?

Her hands shook as she tugged open the dresser drawer and when she saw nothing more than rifled through knickers, Maggie gulped back a sob. The blue velvet box containing her diamond earrings was gone. A burglar, nothing but a common little thief, had stolen her earrings. They, along with the emerald pendant, were the only pieces of jewellery she had worth wearing, irreplaceable gifts from her only love.

Don't cry, Maggie. Don't let a bloody little hoodie who thinks he can help himself to other people's property make you cry.

She raised her chin and took a slow breath, allowing anger to kick aside the threatening tears. Now, she'd have to ring the police and wait up, just to have them treat her like a doddering old fool and lecture her for not locking the back door. Of course, if they had the odd copper patrolling the streets once in a while, she wouldn't need to. In the hallway, she paused, shaking her head at Hyssop.

And you're a useless guard-cat.

A floorboard creaked. What was that? Maggie's stomach contracted and she held her breath as she turned to the spare room. A dark figure stood silhouetted against the moonlight.

1

Get out. Run. Scream.

But she couldn't. Maggie shrank back against the wall, her heart racing, her legs rigid.

Oh please, no. Take the jewellery.

She held out the pendant, but the burglar stepped forwards, hands on hips, tutting in disapproval. Maggie had made a terrible mistake. This was no hoodie.

'Why don't you just die, you stupid old cow?'

Maggie lurched towards the stairs, treading on Hyssop. He hissed and darted between her legs, tripping her. She screamed, flailing as she tried to grasp at the handrail, doorframe, anything to steady herself but two hands pressed firmly against her back. Maggie tumbled down the steep cottage stairs and landed in an undignified tangle on the tiled floor, banging her head but feeling surprisingly little pain.

How many times had Zoë said not to let Hyssop sleep on the landing? Now that's what I'd call ironic, Miss Morissette.

Maggie closed her eyes.

* * *

After tugging the emerald pendant from Maggie's fingers, the thief paused, watching for signs of life. It was an unnecessary task. No one could survive with their neck at forty-five degrees to their body.

'Ding dong, the witch is dead.'

Chapter Two

Libby's job as the assistant to the North West's most celebrated wedding planner, was to ensure the venue was prepared and the big day ran smoothly. Stupidly expensive Georgian mansion? Tick. Thousands of elegantly arranged deep plum, Schwarzwalder calla lilies? Tick. Groom's tongue down the chief bridesmaid's throat? What the hell? Libby texted the bride-to-be, saying she had something to show her in the wedding breakfast room. Moral code getting the better of Libby Wilde? Tick. Pressing send, she went outside to hide.

Ten minutes later, the North West's most celebrated wedding planner stalked across the terrace towards Libby, who was watching the bride battering the groom over the head with one of the elegant Schwarzwalder calla lily arrangements. The guilty chief bridesmaid hovered on the side-lines, presumably trying to decide if she should step in and rescue the groom or try to apologise to her ex-best friend. The bride shrieked language most lobster fishermen would blush at, while the North West's most celebrated wedding planner hissed the dreaded phrase, Olivia Wilde, you're fired. Libby had heard those words three times in the last five months, making a grand total of eleven times in three years.

'So what if he's shagging the bridesmaid? It wasn't your job to tell the bloody bride. It was your job to make sure the flowers looked incredible and they got married. It was your job to make sure I got paid.'

Seeing little point in arguing her case, Libby welcomed the distraction of the bride-not-to-be throwing open one of the French doors.

'Thank you for saving me from that lying bastard,' she said. 'He said last time was a mistake. I should've known better. People don't change.'

No, they don't.

Libby walked away with her head held high. She might be unemployed again, but morally, she was doing just fine.

The Jumble Bar, a low-key affair tucked away in Manchester's Northern Quarter, lacked Libby's usual boho crowd that evening. Instead the outside tables were filled with corporate types. Women with five inch heels perched at the end of their St Tropez'd pins, sipped agave syrup mojitos, frowning with disdain at the pink dip-dyed ends of Libby's hair. At least a few of the men in striped shirts, all knocking back pints of cutting edge real ale, eyed up her bum as she weaved between their tables.

Inside, another two corporate-type blokes were teaching Zoë, her best friend and flatmate, to play poker. Libby hid her grin as a wide-eyed Zoë flirted blatantly with a guy wearing a Rolex as he explained why a King wasn't better than four sevens. Sucker.

Ordering a glass of Chablis, Libby perched on a stool at the bar and flicked through the *Manchester Evening News* until she reached the job ads. Sales, sales, data entry, sales, care home staff, sales, girls wanted... The *MEN* had sits vac ads for prostitutes? By the time, she'd drained her glass, only three ads were circled. Three. So that was what her life had come to: twenty-four and seriously considering a career in the escort business for lack of other options.

Arse.

'Beginners luck,' Mr Rolex mumbled as Zoë scooped up eighty pounds of his cash.

Luck had nothing to do with it. In between scanning the job ads, Libby discovered he checked his phone every time he bluffed and couldn't help a little smile into his pint when he had a good hand. And if she knew, Zoë knew.

Taking a fresh Chablis and a Bacardi and soda Libby weaved towards their table, raising her eyebrows at her friend who flashed an innocent smile.

'Lib, I've *finally* got the hang of poker.'

'Well, it's a lot easier than it seems,' said Mr Rolex, his gaze slowly running over Libby's body. 'Especially when you have the right teacher.'

Libby, equally unsubtle, stared at the gold ring on his left hand and leant in to whisper to Zoë. 'As much fun as it is to watch you hustle this self-satisfied and unfaithful arse, can we bugger off outside?'

Zoë nodded. 'Fuck, yes. I've had a mentally weird day and I could murder a fag.' She led the way to the last empty table, taking with her two Selfridge bags and a rather lovely looking tan tote.

'What,' Libby asked as she lit a cigarette, 'is that?'

'A Mulberry Bayswater.' Zoë caressed the leather handbag before helping herself to a Marlboro.

'And what are you doing? You haven't smoked since school.'

'As I said, weird day. First, the Dick's texted me to say he's busy tonight, and second, my mum rang, my great-aunt died.'

'Oh God, that's awful. I mean about your great-aunt. Were you close?'

'Are you taking the piss? She was a right miserable cow. She dropped dead a couple of months ago.' Zoë leant forwards. 'But get this. Her and Mum didn't get on, so Maggie only went and left me her house.'

'You've inherited a house?'

'Yep. Mum's totally pissed off. She assumed she'd get it because Mags had no other family. She's already had the place valued.'

'And?'

After leaving a dramatic pause, Zoë's sloe-black eyes glinted. 'The estate agent, some bloke called Jonathan rang me this afternoon. It's only worth two hundred bloody grand.' The two friends squealed. 'Which I reckon totally justifies treating the old MasterCard to a Mulberry handbag.' Zoë tipped her head, looking over Libby's clothes. 'Nice outfit by the way, *bee-atch.*'

The purple mini-dress and denim jacket were both swiped from Zoë's wardrobe. In fact the bangles jangling on both Libby's wrists, the diamante drops in her ears and the aubergine polish were all Zoë's too. Only the black sequin ballet flats were Libby's own.

'Just don't lose those earrings,' Zoë replied. 'They're the only present the Dick's ever given me.'

'And what did Rich text you?'

Zoë pulled out her iPhone. '*Having a drink with our boss. Can't do tonight.* He's sulking because I got headhunted today.'

Libby wanted to throttle Rich for treating Zoë like crap and slap Zoë for putting up with it. Zoë was a five ten, beautiful brunette who cooked like Nigella and earned silly commission from house sales. Which was half the problem; Rich resented Zoë for being better at selling houses than him. But then none of the nine male agents in Zoë's office seemed to appreciate the only female agent regularly pipping their sales targets.

'Headhunted, who by?'

'The estate agent who valued my new house. He basically offered me a senior sales manager's role. I'm not taking it, but there's no reason to let the buggers at Testosterone Hell know that yet, right?' Zoë picked at a beer mat. 'Why are you here, anyway? Don't you have a pre-wedding dinner tonight?'

'Nope.'

'Fired?'

Reluctantly, Libby nodded.

'For God's sake…' Zoë leant forwards and gently, but repeatedly, banged her forehead on the table. 'What for this time?'

Libby explained and handed her the paper. 'But see, I've already lined up the next disastrous employment opportunity.'

'Dental receptionist? I can buy into that because you have immaculate teeth, but youth worker? Really? They'll take one look at your hair and assume you'll sell crack to the kids.'

'Ha, ha.'

'And travel agent? After what happened with the cruise company?' Zoë tossed the paper onto the table. 'You'll be lucky to get another job in this climate. A hundred and fifty people applied for our last admin post, but you could always try–'

'Something will come up. It always does.'

Zoë's forehead creased into a frown. 'Paolo's heading this way. Coincidence?'

Libby took a long drag on her cigarette, determined not to look. 'Yes.'

'Liar. For fuck's sake, Lib. It's been four months. That's the longest you've gone without shagging him.'

'He messaged me, saying hi, but it was just after I'd been sacked.' It was a pathetic excuse. 'I might've messaged him back.'

Standing on the pavement, scanning the outside tables, Paolo de Luca raked his dark hair out of his eyes, seemingly oblivious to the lascivious glances he attracted from the girls at the nearest table.

'Tell him to piss off and take some other idiot home,' Zoë said. 'Move on.'

Zoë's theory, validated by a psychology degree, maintained that a girl only got over a man when she had a new one to distract her. *Move on.* Libby knew she should but Paolo had the sexy, struggling artist act down to perfection and despite being raised near Inverness, he was practically Italian. He stood in front of her, holding out his hand and she stubbed out her cigarette, letting him pull her to her feet.

Not that she'd expected a polite, haven't-seen-you-in-four-months peck on the cheek, that wasn't Paolo's style, but when he hooked his hand behind her neck and kissed her, Libby's knees buckled. *Move on.* Who was she kidding? She couldn't move on while he still had the ability to decimate her defences – it'd be tantamount to infidelity. Resigning herself to the inevitable, short-lived fling she wrapped her arms around his neck. They could never be anything more, not until he saw her as a girlfriend instead of his elusive bloody *muse*. It might seem like an easy occupation to some, but for Libby, sitting motionless while Paolo sketched her every day was akin to sticking pins in her eyes.

'Don't mind me,' Zoë said, standing up. 'While 'dile.'

Libby dragged her lips from Paolo's, vaguely aware of Zoë heading back into the bar. 'Later, 'gator.'

Paolo rested his forehead against Libby's. 'We need to talk.'

* * *

Zoë came back to her apartment at around two in the morning to hear the familiar strains of Tchaikovsky's Dance of the Cygnets tinkling down the hallway. This wasn't a good sign. If Libby was watching the DVD, it was okay. If she were sitting on the sofa with her feet twitching, desperate to copy her onscreen self, then it was bad.

But it wasn't bad – it was worse than bad. Not only was Libby mirroring her younger self on the TV, but she was doing it *en pointe*. Zoë stared. Wearing ballet shoes, a black leotard and long black legwarmers, Libby used every inch of the wooden floorboards as only a professional dancer knew how.

This was worse than Zoë had ever seen.

'It always kills me that I got this bit wrong,' Libby said, adding a smile.

Libby's fake smile – the smile that said *I'm fine.* It was a lie. Libby wasn't fine. Zoë sank into the sofa wondering how to handle the situation. Every morning, Libby would lock herself in the bathroom and perform ritualistic barre exercises using the towel rail. Zoë pretended not to know, they were both happier that way, but when Libby brought her misery into the living room, how could she ignore it?

'You know I've always thought you got it right,' Zoë said. 'It's the other three that have their timing just wrong.'

But they both knew that wasn't the point. Zoë watched in silence as Libby finished the piece and collapsed on the sofa, hugging her knees to her chest.

'Lib, it's been three years. You really need to get back in a class or something. You can't keep doing this.' When Libby leaned down and started undoing her shoes, Zoë knew they weren't going to talk about it. They never did. 'Paolo still here?'

Libby lit a cigarette and nodded. 'I know it's tragic, but he's moving to London. A friend of his has a gallery and he wants to show Paolo's paintings. I know we're not a proper couple but he's leaving, never going to see him again kind of leaving.' Libby flexed her ankles. 'I've not actually lost the plot. He asked me to tell him something, something about me I've never told him before so I... danced for him.' Libby looked at the ceiling trying not to cry, but huge drops tumbled down her cheeks.

'And? Did he draw you?' Zoë asked, suppressing a giggle.

Libby wiped her eyes, smiling as she nodded. A real smile. 'While I danced. He called me his *broken ballerina*.'

Zoë feigned a swoon. 'He really ought to be in Paris, living the perpetually tortured dream. Why don't you run off with him? He might make you happy.'

'He can't replace ballet and he drives me potty.'

'At least he loves you.' *Which is more than I've got.* Zoë picked at her nail polish.

Libby nudged her. 'My life's a mess. I'm jobless, fairly unemployable and my not-boyfriend is abandoning me but right now, you, young lady, look more depressed. Where've you been 'til now?'

'Rich rang about twenty minutes after you left.'

'A booty call,' Libby said, not hiding her disgust. 'He just wanted a shag.'

'He's certainly a dick.' Zoë poured the remainder of the wine into the two glasses. 'I've told him we're over.'

'About time. So now what?'

Zoë took a deep breath. Was she really going to say this? 'How do you fancy moving to the Lakes, to Great-aunt Maggie's cottage?'

Libby's eyes widened. 'You want to leave the city?'

'It makes financial sense. If I live in the cottage for over six months, I avoid a ton of tax.'

'What would I do up there?'

'Well, you'd be rent-free. You could do what you liked. Just think about what you really want to do.'

'Where is this cottage of Great-aunt Maggie's? I'm not sure I can do living in the countryside. I haven't lived anywhere remotely green since I was eight.'

'This is the good bit. It's in a place called Gosthwaite.' Zoë opened her laptop. 'It's a village on the east side of the Lakes so handy for the M6.' Zoë panned around the Google Streetview of a village green. 'There's the King Alfred pub and that's the war memorial in the middle of the green, and that's my new cottage tucked in the corner.'

In a cobbled green mostly edged with smart Georgian places, Maggie's house was the last in a row of small houses. Libby's mouth gaped.

'That's not a cottage. Cottages are cute. That has grey pebble dashing and it's at the end of a terrace. Look at it, it could have been built in the sixties.'

'It's a double-fronted nineteenth century workers cottage and it's directly across from the pub.' Zoë elbowed Libby. 'Well?'

'I can't picture you in the countryside.'

'Me neither, but think how amazing it'll be. Big fish, little pond. We'll be the most fabulous things the village has ever seen.'

'How medieval are we looking? Emmerdale in the Eighties?'

'Gosthwaite's quite cool. There are five pubs, a post office, greengrocer, butcher, baker, arts and craft candlestick maker, two cafés and a couple of restaurants.'

Zoë flicked through Google Images, flashing over pictures of walkers, mountains, and pub interiors. Libby stopped her at a photo of a young girl and pony clearing a jump.

'Horses?'

'You know I hate the stinky creatures, but I think there's a livery yard in Gosthwaite and a riding school in Haverton, that's the nearest town.' Zoë tempered her smile. 'What do you think, ready for a change?'

'I have BHS stage two, but I might need stage three to get a decent job. For the first time I'm actually glad Mum made me go to Pony Club Camp every summer.' Libby didn't take her eyes off the pony. 'That's what I can do next. I'm going to live in the countryside and work with horses. Awesome.'

* * *

The next morning Libby woke to find Paolo gone. On the pillow lay a sketch of her smiling as she stood *en pointe* with her hands on her hips. In his beautifully expressive handwriting, he'd written a dedication: *To my Broken Ballerina, I'll love you forever. Px.*

It was going to take some man to distract her from Paolo.

Chapter Three

At Low Wood Farm, Patrick McBride wandered through the garden, barely registering the borders overflowing with foxgloves or that the lawn needed scything rather than mowing. Like he cared if the Golding's usual quintessentially English standards were slipping – it was a sunny June afternoon and at their annual barbeque the booze supply would be endless. For that alone, Patrick couldn't be more thankful. His pallor matched the grass as he made his way towards the gazebo bar. Hair of the dog time.

'Now then, Vet'nery.'

Bollocks.

The owner of Manor Farm, Tom Ellwood, stood between him and the bottle of Becks that would offer salvation. While Tom rocked back and forth on his heels and remarked on the perfect haymaking weather they were enjoying, Patrick took slow, steadying breaths, trying not to inhale the fumes from the other man's glass of whisky. That really was the animal that bit him on the backside.

Tom moved on to the latest over-officious DEFRA legislation and Patrick scanned the other guests, looking for an escape route. Gosthwaite's social set milled around, clutching glasses of Pimm's – the majority, especially the crag-faced farmers, fidgeting uncomfortably in their smart-cas ensembles. Two of the grooms from the riding school, both layered in fake tans, nails and ponytails, gazed with blatant longing towards the large wooden picnic table where a couple of Patrick's friends lounged around looking infinitely more relaxed in shorts and t-shirts.

Patrick pushed back his mop of black curls as Robbie Golding beckoned him over with an icy bottle of Beck's. Okay, to hell with being pleasant to Gosthwaite's answer to landed gentry.

'Tom, I have to go. Rob needs to talk to me about his new mare.' And without waiting for a response, Patrick pushed past him, collapsing into an oak chair between his two best and oldest friends.

'Liar, liar, pants are on fire. I haven't got a new mare.' Robbie laughed.

Patrick sat down, watching Gosthwaite's hottest blonde, Daisy Golding, saunter across to the gazebo bar. She might look like an angel with her cloud of white curls, but the way she held herself, her pale blue mini-dress clinging to her perfect tits, he bet she'd be absolute dirt. Patrick swore as Robbie's younger brother, Xander, joined her. Why was she married? And worse, why she was so adamant about being faithful?

'She's absolutely wasted on him,' Patrick mumbled.

'That's my brother you're dissing,' Robbie said, gently punching his arm.

Patrick raised a hand as a sincere apology.

'You know you'd kill her if you had to spend a day with her,' Scott said cracking open a bottle. 'Too high maintenance.'

Doesn't stop her being hot.

'Beer?' Scott offered.

'Cheers, fat boy,' Patrick joked, referring to Scott's increasing waistline and earning himself another faux punch on the arm.

With several mouthfuls of cold lager easing his hangover Patrick relaxed, planning to enjoy getting drunk with his friends – a rare occurrence. These days, he had to play with new acquaintances while they went home, walking adverts for married with children. Well, they would be if Scott didn't stifle a yawn every two seconds and Robbie wasn't clenching his jaw in anger. Following his line of sight, Patrick watched Robbie's wife, Vanessa, blushing as a tall, dark-haired guy kissed her cheeks three times.

'Who the hell's that?' Patrick asked. And why was Vanessa tipping her head to the side. Was she flirting?

'The viola player from the bloody string quartet she's in.' Robbie slugged his beer. 'Jason Benoît. French twat. The Argonauts are in tow.' He nodded to a middle-aged man whose girth appeared to exceed his height and a teenager with hair marginally greasier than his skin. 'Those two play the violins while that wanker...' he tipped his bottle in Jason's direction. '...makes a play for my wife.'

'She's playing the cello, not him.' Scott stretched. 'He's got a ponytail, for Christ's sake. As if she would.'

But Robbie still scowled.

Looking for a change of subject, Patrick studied the dark circles under Scott's eyes. 'I went to bed at four. What's your excuse for looking like shit?'

'Work. A telecoms buyout. And Will likes to party as late as you.

He's his mother's son.'

'Don't blame your son, or me. You were watching the cricket.' Scott's wife, Clara, joined them, setting a baby monitor on the table. 'He's finally gone down. If he wakes up, it's your turn.'

Patrick slugged his beer, happily eyeing Clara's long lean legs, capped by tatty denim cut-offs. If only all primary school teachers were five-nine, blonde Scarlett Johansson lookalikes. Fit as, but been there, done that and now she was Scott's wife, strictly off limits.

'Got any paracetamol?' Patrick asked her, praying she would.

Clara perched on Scott's knee and delved into her vast bag, pushing aside nappies and baby wipes as she frowned at Patrick. 'You look like crap.'

'I love you too.' But he meant it when she produced a pack of Anadin Extra.

'And how's my favourite Musketear?' She fluttered her eyelashes at Robbie with exaggerated innocence. 'Ready to whisk me away from all this?'

'You'd run a mile if I asked.' Robbie gave her a wink.

Patrick knocked back two pills with a mouthful of lager. He hadn't heard anyone call them by the old nickname in years. Scott must've confessed. The Musketears – infamous for watching each other's backs and leaving broken-hearted girls in their wake. Those were the days.

Out of habit, he evaluated the females at the party. Amongst the usual village faces, only a few fit the twenty to thirty-five demographic, but he wouldn't want to see any of them in the morning – although, a pretty blonde over by the pond had potential. She seemed a little austere in her prim white dress with her hair in a severe bun, but the way she toyed with her straw, rolling it between her dark plum lips, had him take a second look.

'Who's Grace Kelly?' he asked Robbie.

'Rachel something. She's with Jonty.'

'Don't be fooled by the respectable exterior,' Clara said. 'From what I've heard, she's a ho-bag. She was last year's Miss Haverton.'

'A ho-bag beauty queen?' Patrick nodded. 'I could go for that.'

'What you should go for,' Clara said, giving him her stern, school-teacher frown, 'is a single sexy blonde, not Jonty's or anyone else's. Get a girlfriend of your own. You might like it.'

The hypocrisy of Clara nagging him was almost amusing. She'd spent most of her life shagging around but the minute she got married, she expected him to do the same. Sod that. Patrick concentrated on last year's Miss Haverton as she glanced around, double-backing when she spotted him already watching her. A smile played at the corner of those perfectly pouty lips.

Hello, princess. You might be with Jonty, but maybe I can have you too.

'I bet she would though,' he said to Clara.

'Don't be ridiculous. She's with Jonty.'

'And?'

'You think she's going to ditch him for you? Jonty's twenty-four, a celebrity chef and a millionaire. You're a vet. You shove your arm up cows' bums.'

'And?' Patrick smiled as Clara cast a disdainful eye over his ten year old t-shirt, threadbare, ripped at the knee jeans and battered shell-toes.

She shook her head. 'Jonty looks like he's climbed out of a Dolce and Gabbana ad. You look like a... homeless skateboarder. Honestly, are you so hard up you can't afford a new t-shirt, or is this your tight-arsed Scottish side coming out?'

'He's not even slightly hard up,' Robbie said. 'He just spends it all on mountain bikes. Give it up. You know he's right.'

'Jonty gets his hair cut.' Clara tugged Patrick's hair. 'Have you even brushed yours today?'

Patrick looked her in the eye, smiling. 'And?'

'The only respectable thing about you is your t-shirt has actually been ironed.'

'And?' He raised his eyebrows expectantly. 'Money, table.'

'I'll put twenty on Miss Haverton being a gold-digger.' Scott had his chin resting on Clara's shoulder. 'She'll stick with the twenty-four year-old with too much bloody money.'

Patrick gave a derisory laugh. 'Bitter words from a *very* nearly thirty year-old with too much bloody money. But I'll take your cash.'

'He was born into it. I've earned mine.'

Clara leant away from her husband, her eyebrows raised in mock-astonishment. 'You're a six-figure corporate lawyer who earns immoral bonuses. It's people like you that've brought this country to its knees and stop people like me getting pay rises.'

'Come on, Clara.' Patrick prodded her. 'Who's she going to go for?'

She sipped her wine, refusing to comment.

'Rob?'

'If she is a ho-bag, my money's on you.' Robbie touched fists with Patrick, their old school-yard handshake.

'Clara?'

'Okay, okay. If she has *any* sense, she'll dump him. He's far too slick and you're... well, *you.*'

Patrick glanced at Scott, hoping no inappropriate messages were being assumed. Too much water had almost washed away that bridge, but Scott was smiling; clearly he knew where Clara's loyalties lay.

Over by the pond, Jonty kissed his date and headed into the house, foolishly leaving her unattended. Better still, Miss Haverton wandered to the gazebo, looking to top up her empty glass. Game on.

She innocently inspected the spirits lined up on the groaning trestle table, smiling a polite hello as he joined her.

'You look awfully hung-over,' she said, picking up a bottle of Jose Cuervo. 'Kill or cure?'

He nodded and as she filled two shot glasses, he gave her a once over, not bothering to be subtle about it.

'You do realise I'm here with Jonty?' She sprinkled salt onto the back of her hand and picked up a slice of lemon.

'We all make mistakes.'

Patrick seized her wrist, pulling her towards him. He slowly licked the salt from her hand then downed a shot, never dropping his direct eye contact with her. She would. Her smile grew as he took hold of her other wrist, bringing it to his lips to gently take the lemon from her fingers. Definitely would.

Ten minutes later Patrick returned to the table, where Clara and Scott were still relaxing in the sun, and opened a fresh beer. He sat next to Clara and showed her his phone, displaying Miss Haverton's name and phone number.

'Jonty looks very pissed off,' Clara said, giggling.

Miss Haverton had one hand on Jonty's chest, the other smoothing his shirt as she no doubt tried to explain where she'd been and Jonty shot an accusatory glance in Patrick's direction.

'Are Miss Haverton's tits as fake as they look?' Clara asked, frowning at the beauty queen.

'How should I know?' Patrick asked. 'I just took her to see the horses.'

'Are they fake?' Scott asked.

Patrick nodded, unable to hide his grin.

'Copping a feel behind the stables… d'you remember those days, Scott?'

Scott shook his head. 'They're nothing but dim and distant fantasies that keep me entertained when I'm working away.'

Clara squealed in protest but Scott shut her up with a kiss. Patrick wanted to dislike their loved up PDA but he couldn't. Scott was happy. Knackered but happy.

'Hey,' Clara said, turning to Patrick, her eyes glinting. 'Did you hear you're getting new neighbours?'

Patrick laughed at Clara's blatant gossip-mongering. 'And here's me assuming Maggie left the house to the cat.'

'Can you imagine a worse way to go?' Scott asked. 'Breaking your neck and the only way anyone knows you've died is because your cat pesters the neighbour?'

'Yes,' Clara said, resting her bare feet on the table. 'Bagpuss eats your rotting corpse.'

Patrick didn't laugh along with them. He'd put down hundreds of animals, each time knowing it was the right thing to do, but the sight of Maggie's broken body at the bottom of the stairs… He drained his beer. The least he could do was look after the cat.

'Poor Hyssop.' Scott frowned. 'If Will wasn't so rough, we could–'

'Hyssop's fine with me,' Patrick said, hoping to end the conversation.

'Someone to share the bachelor pad with?' Clara suggested and he threw a cork, aiming it perfectly to land down her cleavage. 'But you might not get to keep the cat. Sheila next door told me the house was left to Maggie's great niece, Zoë.'

'Holiday home?' The last thing the village needed was another holiday home, but if it was they wouldn't want a cat to look after. Patrick picked at the label on his bottle, waiting for Clara's response.

'Lynda from the post office said the niece is moving up here with a friend. Do you remember Zoë? Apparently, these days she's this tall, glamorous brunette. She's going to work at Young & Carr, the estate agents.'

Would she want Hyssop? 'And the friend?'

'Another girl,' Clara replied.

'Hot lesbians moving to the Green?' Patrick asked, flashing Scott a grin. 'Ace.'

'That's right.' Clara shook her head in despair. 'Because when I moved here with Daisy, that's what we were, hot lesbians. Idiot.'

'Scott, you promised me that was true.' Patrick thumped Scott's arm and found himself in a headlock for his trouble. Their laughter was cut short when the baby monitor crackled into life and Will's cries filled the air. Scott jogged away, muttering expletives, and Clara reclined a little further, closing her eyes against the sun.

In an effort to banish the image of her and Daisy, Patrick glanced around the garden. To his left, walking away from the other guests, Vanessa practically skipped along as she spoke to Robbie. They stopped, half-hidden by the rampant honeysuckle draped over the pergola and Vanessa smiled, waving her hands as she spoke to her husband. She looked so excited, Patrick wondered if she might be pregnant again – a fourth kid would explain why Robbie was trying to tear his hair out.

'Are you kidding?' he heard Robbie ask, his voice loud enough to draw the attention of the vicar and Lynda from the post office as they admired the clematis growing up the side of the rickety shed.

Vanessa's smile disappeared as she answered him, quietly so no one could hear.

'No,' Robbie snapped.

She folded her arms, staring at Robbie in surprise. 'What?'

'No,' he said again, folding his arms to mirror her.

Jesus, this didn't look good, and Lynda had sniffed gossip in the air.

'Clara, deal with the vicar,' Patrick said, already psyching himself up to distract the nosiest cow in the village. If Robbie and Vanessa were about to have a marital, they didn't need her within earshot. 'Lynda, how's Boadicea? I had a couple asking about puppies the other day. Have you got homes for yours?'

Lynda lost all interest in the Golding's row as she gave him a simpering smile, resting her hand on his arm. 'Oh, Patrick, I'm so pleased you asked. I wanted to talk to you actually...'

Grinding his teeth, he smiled. *Rob, you owe me for this.* While Lynda rambled on about a puppy's paw, Patrick gave advice he ought to be charging for and kept an eye on Rob. The argument had gone quiet bar the occasional hissed invective, but the arm waving, finger jabbing and clenched fists meant this was an out of character, venomous argument – especially for Vanessa who'd usually never say boo to a gosling.

'... so if you could pop round to look at little Pickle...'

Vanessa turned, tears already falling down her beautiful face and

Robbie stalked away, heading out of the garden.

'... but the cat's never been sick in the house before...'

Patrick glanced back down at Lynda. 'Why don't you ring the surgery on Monday? Grace can book you in for an appointment.' *And I can bill you.* He flashed her a cursory smile and followed Robbie, grabbing a bottle of whisky from the bar on his way.

Around the back of the house, in a small secluded garden away from the party, Patrick stepped over the children's toys littering the grass as he made his way to the large wooden chair swing where Robbie sat, smoking a cigarette and staring at the sky. Patrick sat down and handed him the whisky bottle without saying a word.

'She wants to go on tour with that ridiculous quartet.' Robbie slugged back a mouthful of whisky.

'Be fair, you were always going away with work before you had the restaurant.'

'But she wants to leave the girls for one, maybe two months. Why would she want to do that? Just to play a bit of Mozart? Or is this because of that French wanker?'

'Oh, come on, she's an angel. She'd never–'

'Whose side are you on?' Robbie flicking his cigarette butt across the lawn.

'Yours.' Patrick took the bottle back. 'And never ask me that again.'

'Sorry.'

'Are you going to let her go?'

'Let her?' Robbie rubbed his temples. 'I told her not a fucking chance in hell, but how can I stop her? It's her dream come true.'

'So let her do it. You know she wouldn't shag around.'

'I used to, but these days...' He let out a long slow sigh. 'I'm not sure she even knows what she wouldn't do. Since the restaurant, she's... well, she's always fed-up and the only thing that seems to make her smile is that fucking viola player.'

'She wouldn't, Rob.'

'Even so, how the hell am I supposed to cope with three kids, a restaurant and twelve horses on my own?'

'You could get an au-pair. A hot Swedish girl would help me cope.' Patrick smiled at the thought. 'Might keep Van on her toes and distract you from the drudgery of being a stay-at-home dad.'

'I'm not letting some eighteen year-old look after the girls.' Robbie lit another cigarette. 'Christ, what a bloody mess. Did everyone hear us fighting?'

'No, we distracted the main offenders for you.' Patrick knocked back two mouthfuls of whisky before nodding to the right. 'Look at this, a shining example of modern parenting.'

Scott came over, pushing Will's pushchair with one hand and clutching a six pack of beer in the other.

'Little bugger will only sleep in this.' He left the pushchair ten feet away and sat down next to Robbie. 'Clara told me what happened.'

'I'm trying to talk him into getting an au-pair,' Patrick replied. 'Swiss, maybe?'

'If there was a hot au-pair working here, you wouldn't be allowed on the yard.' Robbie shook his head, smiling.

The buzz in Patrick's pocket alerted him to a new message, the third from Miss Haverton. *Want something to snuggle up against tonight?* The attached photo showed her fake breasts barely encased in a white lace bra, the edge of a nipple peeking out. He thought better of sharing it with his friends. Robbie's jaw was twitching again, his brow furrowed and Scott yawned for the hundredth time. Marriage? Children? Looked a lot of hard work, and for what? From the sounds of things, shagging your wife wasn't one of the bonuses.

Patrick really didn't see the point.

Two weeks later, he sat back, enjoying the buzz of his latest coke hit and Miss Haverton unzipping his fly. Clearly, the girl was a nutcase. They were in the restaurant toilets and the mayor was dining with several local businessmen about twenty feet away. Anyone could walk in but, Jesus, did she know how to use her hands. And tongue.

'Christ, Rachel...'

Patrick clutched at her hair, looking down at her arse as her head bobbed. Her little black dress had ridden up, revealing a leopard print thong, and her shiny black heels were resting against the cubicle door. There wasn't a single classy aspect to Miss Haverton, but since she'd first wrapped her fingers around his dick, rubbing in coke like a pro, he'd cared less about her dubious taste in underwear and more about the toys she had in her bedside drawer. At least he'd persuaded her to stay inside this time. Her penchant for dining al fresco nearly had them collared by the police two days ago.

Sod this. Who cared if the mayor walked in? Patrick pulled her to her feet and moved behind her, smiling as she bent at the waist and wedged her feet against the walls, her hands planted in front of her.

Not a single classy bone in her body. This was the last time he was taking her out. Definitely.

'Baby,' she said, purring as she pushed back against him. 'How do you fancy my friend Emma joining us later?'

Miss Haverton had just earned herself another reprieve.

Chapter Four

A year ago, the tone of the *Haverton Gazette* had taken an odd turn when Michael Wray, an Australian hack and former *News of the World* employee, relocated to the Lakes and took over as Editor-in-Chief. Instead of reporting on crime rates, school fetes and the lack of affordable local housing, Wray focussed his attention on what kept circulation figures high at his last paper – celebrity scandal.

But instead of photographing C-list celebrities falling out of limousines, he turned everyday people into local stars – the vicar and his fling with the verger, the posh kids joyriding in Sedbergh. Patrick and his assistant Grace had devoured every sensationalised snippet – it was all good fun, something to laugh about over a coffee, until one day Patrick became the celebrity.

It started with a drunken brawl at a wedding, escalated when he was spotted with the Cumbrian Business Man of the Year's wife at a boutique hotel and peaked at the Haverton versus Gosthwaite football match last August bank holiday when Patrick was photographed snorting cocaine off his Land Rover bonnet. But it was the blog where he became truly infamous.

The *Haverton Eye* gave the sordid details and revealing photos the *Gazette* wouldn't dare print, and although no one in East Cumbria doubted who was behind it, Michael Wray denied any connection to *the Radar*, the anonymous author of the blog. And the Eye never seemed to miss a moment of Patrick's life – blurry shots at parties, quotes from *friends*. The Radar was always there.

But this time Patrick was in trouble.

He stared at a small photo of himself on the front page of the paper. From his grin he'd been a lot happier when the shot was taken than he was looking at it now. Hardly surprising. It had been taken after a black tie charity event at Haverton Hall where he'd been drinking since midday and had taken a cocktail of recreational drugs. He couldn't remember the photo being taken but since he was smiling in the direction of the camera he must have been aware of the photographer.

But having his photo on the front page wasn't the killer. The content was. His tie was undone and draped around the neck of Miss Haverton – her top was undone and her legs draped around his waist. Whoever had taken the photo would've taken more, x-rated shots the paper would find unpublishable. They'd be on the blog already. Patrick pushed his hair off his face and dared to look at his father.

Malcolm McBride drummed his fingers on his three-hundred year-old desk. 'What is it with you and black tie events? Do you do these things on purpose?'

It was his tone that worried Patrick the most. In previous dressing downs his father had ranted and yelled – he'd even thrown a vase on one occasion. This time his father's voice was steady and his face as hard as Ailsa Craig granite.

'Are you trying to ruin me? This isn't Edinburgh. I know everyone. These people are my friends. They used to respect me. Now I'm Patrick McBride's father and they pity me.'

Patrick knew when to keep quiet. Through the low, leaded window, he watched coal tits on the feeder and waited for the *your mother's so disappointed in you* line that always ended the paternal rant.

The line never came.

'This is it, Patrick.'

This is what? Patrick turned back to his father.

'The affairs with married women are one thing,' Malcolm went on, 'but you come to work hung-over and some days probably still drunk, or worse. You're downright rude to clients and bloody awful to the staff. This is my veterinary practice. You work for me. You're nothing more than a staff member I have the misfortune to be related to. Christ, if I wasn't your father I'd have fired you a year ago, certainly after you were caught with the bloody cocaine.'

'Are you firing me now?' Patrick asked quietly, his heart racing.

'Not yet.' Malcolm shook his head and Patrick's shoulders sagged with relief. 'But this is your last chance. You're nearly thirty, but you're acting like your life is one long Freshers' Week. You need to learn what's really important to you, because sometimes we have to give up what we want to keep what we damn well need. You're on twelve months' probation. Step out of line and I will personally hand you your P45.'

Patrick nodded. 'I swear it won't happen again. Starting now, I'll–'

'No.' Malcolm held up a hand. 'Not starting now. I've heard you swear it won't happen again too many times. You're suspended.'

'Suspended?'

'You're to go to your brother's for two months. Sam's expecting you. I want people to forget this Miss Haverton thing ever happened. When you come back, you'll lay off the booze and no more drugs. There'll be no more flings with married women, no more turning up at Ascot with drunk actresses and absolutely no more bloody newspaper articles.' Malcolm paused. 'Because if I see your face in that bloody paper one more time, you are out of this family.'

'What?' Patrick's face turned cold.

'I will disown you.'

He wouldn't, surely. 'But Dad–'

'You haven't given a second thought to your mother or me for the past eighteen months. Since you came back to Gosthwaite, you've thought of no one but yourself. You're a disgrace to this family.' Malcolm's face reddened as his anger threatened to boil over. 'Go and pack. I want you on a plane tonight.'

Patrick headed for the door, running his hands through his hair. 'What about the surgery?'

'Since it's still my practice, I'll worry about that.'

'But you're retired.'

'Not for the next two months.' Malcolm stood up. 'Patrick, I've never been so disappointed.'

That was a new one. Patrick's stomach churned. He stumbled out of his father's study and into the kitchen where his mum sat at the scrubbed pine table, drinking an uncharacteristically large glass of red wine.

'Mum?'

She didn't look at him as she straightened her back, no doubt strengthening her resolve. 'They call this Tough Love in the States.'

'But Mum–'

'Go to Sam's and when you come back, behave. That's all we ask.' Elizabeth clamped her hands around her wine glass. 'I've booked you on a flight from Manchester. If you get back here at four, we'll take you to the airport. And sort yourself out. You look awful.'

He wanted to hug her, for her to hug him, like she did when he was a kid. 'I'm sorry.'

Finally she looked up, tears glistening in her eyes. 'I really am very ashamed to call you my son.'

No more. He fled, his head reeling with guilt, anger, humiliation. He'd made his mum cry, for Christ's sake. Fumbling, he dropped his keys trying to open his Land Rover door – the six-month-old Discovery that came with the job.

Probation? Suspended? Disowned? What if they meant it? They sounded like they meant it.

He climbed into the Land Rover and pulled away from Braid Hall smoothly and slowly, not slamming his foot down, hoping to release the tension that threatened to compress all rational thought. They'd be watching. He had to show them he could be restrained. He had to. He couldn't lose his job. What other job could he get when he'd been fired by his own parents and had a minor drug conviction?

By the time he'd reached the Green, ten minutes later, the tension had given way to mild panic. What if they really sacked him? He parked outside his house. The end-terrace, three storey, Georgian townhouse that came with the job. If they sacked him, he'd lose more than just his job. The nearest vets was in Kendal and they'd never employ him after he'd accused the practice owner of conducting vastly expensive operations on animals who ought to be put down – an increasingly sickening practice in the veterinary world of putting profits before welfare. He'd have to move away again. He'd have to leave Gosthwaite, and Gosthwaite had everything. Scott and Robbie both lived in the village, he could ride his bike over the fells from his doorstep and his local served decent beer to accompany their award-winning Cumberland sausage and mash.

Jogging up the steps to his house, he glanced to the right, to the front door next to his own. Both painted the blue of the St Andrews flag, the right hand door led to his surgery. *His* surgery. His parents might own the veterinary practice but the Gosthwaite surgery was his. He was his own boss, picking his own staff and largely dealing with the cows, horses and livestock, leaving the dog, cat and budgie owners for Kate and Fergus to deal with at the Haverton surgery.

House, car, job, friends. He had the perfect life.

He slammed the door shut and slumped against it. Hyssop scooted from the armchair closest to the fire to greet him, mewing a hello as he had every day since he'd moved in four months ago. Patrick picked him up.

'Fuck, Hyss, I think they mean it. What the hell am I going to do? And what am I going to do with you? You're about to be abandoned by another human.' Despite the sick feeling building in his stomach, he laughed as Hyssop rubbed his head against his chin, his usual signal. 'Okay, pal. Teatime, it is.'

With Hyssop nose deep in his teatime pouch of salmon in jelly, the same brand Maggie used to feed him, Patrick fell onto the sofa with a mug of strong coffee in one hand and his phone in the other.

He'd had the perfect life so how the hell had it got so fucked up?

When he'd moved back to Gosthwaite eighteen months ago, he'd maybe go to the pub with friends on a Friday night. Now, he woke every morning regretting ever setting foot in the Alfred and vowing to spend that evening at home watching TV. But the next morning it was the same. And the next. He hadn't touched coke since university, but for the last six months, he barely remembered a weekend without it. He barely remembered a weekend. Was it Gosthwaite's fault?

The bottle of Glenfiddich on the kitchen table called to him, promising to take the edge off his hangover.

He flicked through the photos on his phone, looking for someone to blame other than himself. Nina. The photo was taken at a friend's wedding, the only one he had of her, of the two of them. Her dark hair fell in unnatural curls, the red dress subtle but sexy and she held his hand, her fingers linked with his. He smiled, remembering that night in the hotel. But why keep that photo? Because she looked like she most preferred, dressed up rather than scrubbed up? Or because that was the day she'd ruined everything?

We should do this.

Why did she have to say that? They had fun. They got on. Okay, so they slept in the same bed most nights, but they didn't even live together. He'd run a mile, two hundred miles – from Gloucestershire to Cumbria.

Nina: pretty, sexy, clever, a good vet and a good shag.

His problem had been Clara and Vanessa. Scott and Robbie were sledgehammered by those girls. Girls they couldn't run away from. Girls they didn't want to run away from. He'd gone out with Nina for four years and then ran away. Not that Nina wasn't great. Jesus, she was almost perfect. But she was just that. Almost.

He'd escaped a four year relationship. It was normal – understood even – for him to play the field, to have fun, to breathe. But he'd never planned to get hammered every night he wasn't on call and shag coked-up beauty queens. He looked at Nina's photo. Maybe he shouldn't have... He shook his head and pressed confirm. Nina was deleted. Almost wasn't good enough. Almost wasn't a sledgehammer.

Skipping forward through the latest images, he smiled at one of him on his bike overlooking Grasmere, but stalled at Miss Haverton's cleavage. If he wanted to change, it should start with her. She might be an insatiable, moral-free ho-bag but she wasn't a bad person. He should tell her it's over. Surely she deserved that. His thumb hovered over the phone. But she'd cry, swear at him, call him a bastard, tell him she loved him. Just like Nina had.

Man up. He pressed dial and closed his eyes.

'Hey, baby. Did you see the paper? Wow, that brought back some memories.' She giggled. 'What are you up to? I'm bored, naked and about to get in the bath. Come over?'

'Rachel, sorry. I'm going away for a while. This has been fun, but look, it's over.'

She hung up.

He stared at the phone. Well, that was easy.

With his suitcase in the Land Rover, Patrick packed a bag with Hyssop's food and picked up the purring tabby, turning the cat to face him.

'I'll be back soon and you can come home. I promise.'

On the opposite side of the Green, two doors down from the King Alfred pub where she worked three nights a week after her shifts at the surgery, Patrick knocked on Grace's door. Grace, the only person he could rely on. Jesus, if it hadn't been for Grace's treacle-coffee every morning and her willingness to cover for him when he was too wasted to function, he'd have been sacked months ago. How he hadn't killed an animal by administering the wrong drug or dosage was a mystery, though he suspected Grace saved his arse many times.

He smiled, his eyebrows raised hopefully as Grace opened the door. Under her long black fringe, the rest of her hair trying to escape its plastic clip, her frown grew when she saw Hyssop. Patrick had expected nothing less.

'I've got to go away,' he said.

'No.'

'He's got nowhere else.'

'Jack's allergic to cats.'

'Gracey—'

'Don't Gracey me.'

'His coat's only just getting its shine back after Maggie died. Please?'

With an enormous groan, she took Hyssop from him. 'Where are you going?'

'Spain. I've got to work at Sam's for a while. Dad's coming out of retirement.'

'Why? What's wrong with Sam?'

Patrick shook his head. 'Nothing. It's... well, it's complicated.'

'How long for?'

'Two months. I'll be back.'

'You'd better. Your dad's an old fuss-pot.' She kissed Hyssop's head. 'Patrick, are you okay? You look... odd.'

No, Gracey, I'm fucked. He rubbed Hyssop's ears then tugged a wayward lock of Grace's hair. 'Look after him. Please.'

She nodded and he walked away. Thank God for Grace. She might be a gobby cow at times, but she was always there.

* * *

An hour later, as Patrick drove out of the village, Michael Wray received a text: *McBride is leaving.*

Wray swore. Without McBride's weekly antics circulation figures would plummet. He'd have to find a new source of local scandal, and fast.

Chapter Five

Libby hadn't seen anything but dry stone walls, mountains and sheep since she left the M6. The walls were endless, mountains surrounded her in three directions and sheep lurked around every corner – twice she'd had to swerve to avoid running over the little buggers.

But then there it was. Gosthwaite.

She sat a little straighter as her battered Mini followed Zoë's BMW into the village. They crawled past walkers in hiking boots and old ladies chatting outside the post office until finally they arrived at the green.

On Google Maps the Georgian townhouses looked elegant but bland. In reality they were painted pale olives, sky blues and the subtlest of dusky pinks, their facades creating a pastel rainbow around the emerald grass green. Even Great-aunt Maggie's cottage looked passably cute with purple clematis covering half the pebble-dashing.

Was this it, the place she'd finally find a distraction that worked, something to make her forget she was ever a ballerina?

As Libby parked, Zoë hovered at the garden gate. A garden, they had a front garden. Okay, it only came out six feet from the house, but none of the townhouses had one.

'Just so you're aware,' Libby said as they wandered between the fat lavender plants lining the path, 'I've never wielded a lawnmower in my life.'

'I'm hoping there's some fit young gardener we can employ.' Zoë's hand hesitated as she turned the key in the lock. 'God knows what it's like in here. Maggie was a scatty cow, clutter everywhere.'

Libby held her breath. Someone died in this house. 'There won't be any, you know... *evidence*, will there?'

'Lib, she fell down the stairs and broke her neck. She wasn't bludgeoned to death.'

But Libby wasn't fooled by her friend's overly chipper smile. Sure enough, when the door opened into a long hallway, they stood on the threshold, staring at the foot of the stairs, neither of them admiring the black and white Victorian tiles.

'So is that where…' Libby wrapped her arms around herself.

The stairs were wooden, the floor ceramic. She winced imagining poor Great-aunt Maggie's final moments. How long had the little old lady lain there, dying? Minutes, hours? Hopefully, less than a second.

Zoë looked up to where the staircase turned to the right, disappearing from view. 'She had this big, fat old cat and he used to sleep at the top of the stairs. Mum said she probably tripped over him. The amount of times I'd nagged her about him. I nearly broke my neck last time I was here.'

'What happened to the cat?'

Zoë shrugged. 'A neighbour, Sheila, I think, came to feed him after they'd found Maggie, but he'd gone.' With a little shake of her head, Zoë flashed a real smile. 'Okay, maudlin over. Want a tour?' Without waiting for an answer, she opened the door to their left. 'Welcome to the Eighties.'

'Wow.' Libby stared at the flowery sofa, matching curtains and coordinating striped wallpaper, a riot of burgundy and cream. 'I've never seen so much chintz in one place.'

Knick-knacks covered every occasional table, books were stacked against the walls, but Libby just discerned an upright piano from the CDs stacked around it. She squeaked in delight.

'Please, please, please, can we keep the piano?'

'If we must.' Zoë peered at the label on a tassel-cornered scatter cushion. 'Back in the day, Maggie liked quality. This is a Laura Ashley vomitorium.'

Libby cleared the CDs and lifted the lid to stroke the keys. Without hesitation, she pressed middle C. When had she last played? A pub in Cornwall?

'It needs tuning,' she said, closing her eyes, feeling the note as much as hearing it. She hit G-sharp, adoring the melodic ring.

'Don't get started on your Lady Gaga repertoire,' Zoë replied. 'We've got to unpack.'

Through the door on the opposite side of the hallway they found the dining room. It featured no less chintz but at least its blue and white theme was a little less jarring on the eye.

Zoë ducked down, inspecting the underside of the ornate table. 'I reckon that's real mahogany and so going on eBay tonight.'

The kitchen sat at the back of the house. Its magnolia walls were oddly muted compared to the other rooms, though the mustard yellow splash-back tiles featuring the occasional vegetable display made up for it. A gift bag sat on the side, with a card addressed to Maggie.

'*Don't drink it all at once*,' Zoë read before peering inside the bag. 'Wine?'

'Homemade crap.' Zoë plonked a swing-top bottle of elderflower wine on the worktop and took out a pair of tall, beeswax candles. 'Well, they've got *Regift Me* written all over them.'

Libby peered through the window in the kitchen door. At the end of the long garden, edged with tall privet hedges, she could see nothing but fields stretching into the distance.

'Ace, there's a proper herb garden,' Libby said. The multitude of planters dotted around the crazy-paved patio put the window box she'd nurtured back in Manchester to shame. 'I spy... thyme, parsley, mint, rosemary and marjoram, but god knows what the rest are.'

Zoë pointed to the tall, bushy plants growing in a sun-trapped corner. 'It's not all for eating.'

'You're joking. Your great-aunt grew weed?'

'To help with her arthritis, she used to say.' Zoë mouthed, *whatever*.

Giggling, they went back into the hallway and ran up the stairs. The first door led to a peach-coloured bathroom, the second to a striped mint-green guest room and the final door to Maggie's bedroom. Libby hung back in the doorway as Zoë wandered in. The bed was made, no clothes lay strewn around.

'Could you imagine if we died, the state of our bedrooms?' Libby tried to sound light-hearted but Maggie's dressing gown still hung on the back of the door and the room was filled with her photos, trinkets, books, all just as she'd left them. 'People would probably think we'd been burgled.'

Zoë poked through the silver jewellery box, examining a ring as the sunlight dimmed and the room fell into a sudden gloom. Goosebumps covered Libby's arms.

A rain cloud. It's just a rain cloud.

She reached out to the ancient Bakelite switch and with one finger, flicked it down. The light bulb flashed and a loud crack made her squeal. Zoë jumped, knocking the jewellery box to the floor as she span around.

'Ohmigod. I swear I felt that.' Libby's hand shook as she tentatively flicked the switch back up and gave a nervous laugh. 'She's not haunting us, is she?'

Zoë didn't smile as she bent to scoop up the beads and bracelets scattered on the floor. 'Be a BFF and check the fuse box? It's under the stairs.'

'What did your last slave die of?'

'Being eaten by the spiders under the stairs.' Zoë grinned and pushed Libby forwards. 'Please?'

'Like you're *that* afraid of spiders.'

'City spiders, no. You haven't met the rural arachnids yet.'

Three hours later, Libby left Zoë to deal with gas meter readings and a Tesco delivery while she wandered to the Langton Hall livery yard to meet her new boss, Kim Langton-Browne. On paper, it was hardly a career choice. Four days a week, minimum wage, no career prospects and she wouldn't get to ride the horses, but at least it was a job. At the equestrian centre where Libby had sailed through her BHS Stage Three exams, the head instructor had said one equestrian job would spawn another. Fifteen minutes after arriving at the livery yard, Libby prayed the spawning would occur sooner rather than later.

'No music,' Kim barked, marching past a row of inquisitive ponies. 'I can't abide the bloody radio. This is the countryside. I want to hear bird song, not Radio bloody One in the morning.'

The swallows would have to be in fine voice to be heard over Kim's nasal whine, and was a smile actually out of the question? A perma-scowl added ten years to her thirty-five – a *resting bitch face* Zoë would say. Libby tried not to giggle, but focussing on Kim's panty line, perfectly visible under the straining tartan seat of her jodhpurs didn't help. Not that Kim was fat, but those skimpy briefs underneath had to be two sizes too small.

At least Kim hadn't frowned at the purple streaks in Libby's hair. But then Kim's own hair was the colour of a London bus. In fact, in her pristine cream jodhpurs and neatly ironed black t-shirt, Libby felt ludicrously respectable.

'And absolutely no smoking on the yard.' Kim flashed a disapproving frown as Libby paused to stroke the nose of a pretty grey mare. 'Careful, that's a nasty little bugger. Bit me twice last week.' Kim bent down to pet her little Sheltie. 'Not like my little Bublé. You'd never bite mummy, would you? And no feeding the nags Polos. It makes them forget their manners.'

Libby kissed the grey, who blew on her hand.

'The phone in the tack room is for office use.' Kim marched on. 'Yard duties start at eight, not five past. Tea breaks are at ten thirty and three. Lunch, twelve 'til one, not five past. You'll finish at six, not five to.'

Ten minutes later, after berating clients for not stacking buckets neatly and for generally wanting to keep their horses on her yard, Kim thrust out her hand for Libby to shake.

'Nice to meet you, Libby. Now, I have to find my bloody useless excuse for a husband. The stupid man said he'd be grass-cutting by now. Michael's on his way.'

'Does Michael work here too?' Libby delivered her question with utter innocence, but she'd already clocked the flush to Kim's unfortunate high-colouring when she mentioned this Michael. Was she having an affair?

Kim laughed, a silly giggle, as she dragged a hand through her hair, pulling it off her face. 'Good lord, no. He's the feed merchant. I'll see you in the morning. Eight sharp.'

As Kim dashed into the ancient, sprawling farmhouse, Libby saluted. The long days didn't faze her, but the thought of listening to Kim bad mouth the world for ten hours a day made her long for her old job running around after the North-West's most caustic wedding planner.

A month. If she could stick it out for a month, that wouldn't feel like giving up. One month. Or four weeks. Four weeks was practically a month.

'Ow, watch it, Tals,' squealed a voice behind her.

From the little grey's stable, two girls emerged, one nearly as tall as Libby with her dark hair pulled back in a scruffy bun, the other a head shorter and wearing more make-up than Libby.

'I thought she'd never bloody go,' the dark-haired girl said, leaning back against the stable door. She was impeccably well spoken and her huge brown eyes had no need for make-up. 'Are you one of the new girls from the Green? I'm Tallulah. This is Chloe. We're actually the same age but she's a short-arse.'

Chloe gave Tallulah the finger.

'I'm Libby.'

'Are you really a lesbian?' Tallulah asked, tipping her head to the side, studying Libby.

Chloe tutted. 'Lesbians don't wear make-up or have cool hair. They have skin-heads.'

Libby opened her mouth, but hadn't a clue what to say.

'But... so are you a lesbian?' Tallulah asked again. 'Only I heard

Miss Knightmare say she and my aunt Daisy were when they moved to Gosthwaite and that you and your friend are, like, living together so you probably are too.'

'Or not. Zoë and I are most definitely not lesbians.' Libby couldn't help but like Tallulah. 'Aren't you a bit young to be asking about these things?'

Chloe pouted. 'We're not little kids. We're practically twelve.'

Libby focussed on her boots to hide her smile. 'I have to go. Still need to unpack.'

'What's it like,' Tallulah piped up before Libby had chance to leave, 'living in the old witch's house?'

'It's fine.' Libby crossed her fingers behind her back. 'But she's dead so you shouldn't call her names.'

'I'm not,' Tallulah said, as she unbolted one of the stable doors.

'She was a witch,' Chloe said. 'A proper one. Not with a black cloak and broomstick, but one of them white ones.'

'A Wiccan,' Tallulah added, leading out a bay gelding. 'But isn't it weird?'

'Okay, it's a bit weird,' Libby admitted. A Wiccan? That was more than a bit weird. What if Maggie were into Satanic rituals? 'I've never lived in a house where someone died. Well, not knowingly.'

'What about living in a house where someone was–'

'Tal!'

'What?' Tallulah pushed her riding hat low over her eyebrows. 'It's true.'

'What's true?' Libby stroked the gelding, rubbing the brilliant white star peeking from under his perfectly pulled forelock.

'Maggie...' Tallulah's eyes flashed, clearly loving that she had Libby's attention. '...was murdered.'

Libby shook her head. 'She fell down the stairs.'

'Whatever,' Tallulah replied. 'Chloe's sister Lauren said that Becky from next door but one to Maggie, heard her scream. And then Becky saw someone walking down the lane. This is Shakespeare, by the way.' She ran her hand along the gelding's neck.

Chloe's face flushed. 'Well, I'm not sure–'

'Did Lauren tell you that, or not?'

'Yeah, but Becky also said Gary Barlow had moved in down the road.' Chloe made a W sign with her fingers.

'So, what you're telling me,' Libby asked, trying not to laugh, 'is that Maggie was a witch and she was murdered?'

Chloe crossed her arms, shooting Tallulah a smug smile. 'See?'

'Thing is,' Tallulah said as she tightened Shakespeare's girth. 'Maggie was a witch. She made real love potions and chanted to weird goddesses. And she danced around the garden when there was a full moon.'

Libby shivered, remembering the shock from the light switch. 'Seriously?'

Tallulah flashed an enormous smile. 'Aunt Daisy says you should always try to keep an open mind. And Becky swore on her iPhone that she saw someone leave the house. She was having a fag out of her bedroom window. Did you know we're looking for a groom?'

Libby blinked, thrown by the change of topic. 'Who's we?'

'My dad. Mum's going on tour with the band she's in–'

'Oh whatever. It's a string quartet,' Chloe said.

'Bite me.' Tallulah ripped a Pony Club flyer from the tack room door and scrawled a name and number on the back. 'Kim's a complete cow, but you seem cool. Give Dad a ring. He's busy at the restaurant 'cause they reckon it's getting a star or something, so he needs a hand on the yard.'

Utterly perplexed, Libby took the flyer. 'What restaurant?'

'The Bobbin Mill. It's just outside the village,' Tallulah replied. 'It's supposed to be ace, but I'd rather go to Pizza Express.'

'I so want a job at the Mill.' Chloe's face went pink again. 'Tal's uncle Xander is officially the fittest bloke ever.'

'You're so lame.' Tallulah shook her head as she pulled down her stirrup. 'Honestly, ring my dad. I'll tell him you're ace.'

'I've just got a job. I don't need another one.'

'But our place is better.'

'Why?'

'You get to ride my horses.'

Libby stared as Tallulah and Shakespeare trotted out of the yard. Maggie was a witch, a murdered witch and there was another job on the horizon? She shook her head, banishing crazy thoughts. She couldn't switch jobs already, no matter how crappy the current one seemed.

Chloe sat down on an upturned bucket, her thumb blurring as it moved over the buttons on her phone. 'She does have the best horses. Her dad breeds show-jumpers. He's really fit too, but don't tell her I said that.'

Libby stuffed the flyer into her pocket.

Murdered witches, livery yard owners shagging feed merchants, fit men breeding show-jumpers... weren't things supposed to be tranquil in the countryside?

Armed with the local paper and a bottle of champagne, Libby skipped up the garden path, ready to celebrate her new move and get down to some serious unpacking.

'Hey,' she called out as she pushed open the front door. 'So I just made friends with a couple of eleven year-olds.'

'Well, aren't you just living the idyllic rural dream?' Zoë leaned against the kitchen door frame, a mug in one hand and a cigarette in the other.

'You're smoking in the house?'

'Electrics fused twice.' Zoë glanced at the cupboard beside her. 'I needed to calm my nerves.'

Libby took the mug. 'With nicotine and shiraz?'

'Needs must. Who are your new friends?'

'Chloe and Tallulah. They said Maggie was murdered.'

'What the fuck–'

'Witnessed and everything. Oh, and we're lesbians. Cheers.'

'For god's sake, that's all I need.'

'No, you also need an electrician.' Libby ducked into the cupboard and flicked the fuses again. 'God, it's dusty under here. Did Maggie have a dog?'

'No. Just the cat.'

'It's just there are scratch marks on the back of the door. Look.'

'Actually, Lib.' Zoë stood up. 'Fuck unpacking for a bit. I'm starving and the cooker's electric. Pub for lunch?'

'God, yes. It's time to meet the locals.' Libby unfastened her plait and shook out her hair. 'And let them know we aren't lesbians. I'll never find the love of my life if they think I'm batting for the other side.'

The King Alfred, on the opposite side of the Green to Maggie's house, was one of the few double-fronted Georgian buildings. Boxes stuffed with pansies sat in front of every window and hanging baskets overflowed with fuchsias. The Gosthwaite in Bloom winner's plaque was proudly displayed for everyone to see.

Libby pulled open the heavy glass-panelled door as a roar filled the pub. Inside a group of men, all in work boots, stood around the bar, bellowing support as one of the party downed a pint of Guinness.

'Oh god, wrong pub,' Libby whispered, hoping they could back out before they were noticed.

Zoë nudged her forwards. 'No, this is the Alfred. It's okay.'

The first of the men looked round, grinning before elbowing the man next to him, who elbowed the next. The cheering fizzled out until all fifteen men grinned down at them.

'Come and sit yourself over here, love.'

'What you drinking? Bri, you're in the chair, get these lasses a pint.'

The guy who sank the Guinness was the last to turn, his eyes pointing in two different directions as he took in Zoë and Libby. 'Strippers!'

Libby shrank back in horror.

'Get over yourself, Sparks,' said a dark haired girl as she appeared behind the bar. 'As if this lot would pay for a stripper.' She flashed a welcoming smile. 'Come on in. Ignore this bunch of muppets. It's Sparky's twenty-first. What can I get you?'

'Wine, dry white, please,' Libby said, grateful to be rescued. Several of the men still watched them with silly grins, but most had gone back to their pints.

'What size? Pointless, sensible or take a bath in?'

'Bath,' Zoë replied.

At least half of the men watched as the comely barmaid bent down to take the wine from the bottom of the fridge. Libby felt like an ironing board in comparison.

'So, you two must be the girls moving into Maggie's old place. I'm Grace, by the way.' Her chunky black fringe fell just below her eyebrows, shadowing her blue eyes as she half-filled two enormous glasses with a white Rioja and glanced over Libby's jodhpurs. 'I take it you're the one who's got the misfortune of working for Kim. Hideous old cow. Which means you,' she paused to hand Zoë the first glass, 'must be the estate agent, Maggie's niece.'

Zoë nodded. 'She was my great-aunt, but yes. I'm Zoë, this is Libby.'

Libby, overcome with fringe envy, took two huge mouthfuls of the surprisingly good wine, and glanced around. Most of the men looked old enough to be her dad, but at the end of the bar sat a cute guy with light brown hair and a cheeky smile. Was he smiling at her? Libby's cheeks burned and she glanced down at her drink. The countryside rocked.

'She were a fine woman,' slurred a deep voice behind her.

'Oh give over, Stan.' Grace smiled apologetically to Zoë. 'He had a thing for Mags.'

'A fine, fine woman,' Stan lamented.

'I thought you said she was a hideous old witch,' Libby whispered to Zoë.

'She was,' Zoë muttered back, frowning at the ancient old soak now swaying beside them.

'She were a siren,' he fixed his watery gaze on Zoë.

'Leave it, Stan,' Grace warned.

'You two want to watch yourselves,' Stan went on, undeterred. 'Maggie put a spell on that place.'

'A spell?' Libby asked.

'It's a load of nonsense.' Grace leaned on the bar. 'Something Mags and Sheila dreamt up over too much sloe gin. They put a love spell on the house and any girl who slept there would become irresistible to the man she desired.'

'Awesome.' Libby laughed. Seriously, how much fun was the countryside?

'But,' Stan said, bending closer, 'what happens when the siren doesn't desire the man? Lures us in and casts us aside. What then?'

A frown furrowed his already age-creased face as he gazed at nothing, recalling memories. Of what, Libby longed to ask.

'Okay, Stan. Let's not scare the nice girls on their first day.' The cute guy from the end of the bar flashed Libby another smile as he put his arm around Stan's shoulders. 'I'm Jack.'

'Libby, and this is—'

'Zoë Horton?' Jack nodded, shaking Zoë's hand. 'It must be fifteen years ago, but I can still remember you hanging round the village in a tutu.'

Grace leaned on the bar. 'Oh my God, I remember.'

'Fag?' Zoë muttered before she walked out, not waiting for a reply.

Libby watched her friend leave. What on earth? Tutu obsession was something they'd both laughed about in the past. Libby had lived and slept in hers from the age of four to fourteen. Picking up her wine, she smiled at Grace, Jack and Stan. 'It's lovely to meet you.'

Jack shot her a wink. 'You too.'

The door banged shut behind her, but Libby didn't miss his lazy grin through the glass-panelled door. Day one and she'd met a nice guy. The countryside definitely rocked.

Outside, Zoë sat on one of the wooden benches, scowling across at Maggie's cottage.

Libby lit a cigarette and tossed the pack to Zoë. 'And?'

'I'd rather not remember running around the village like an idiot in a tutu.'

'And it's why I hope never to set foot in Brize Norton again.' Libby sipped her wine, settling back in the afternoon sunshine. 'Was Maggie really a witch?'

Zoë still stared at the cottage. 'To me she was.'

That night in the mint-toothpaste spare bedroom, Libby slept badly, her head filled with alcohol-fuelled dreams. A black cat scratched at a coffin, releasing an un-dead Maggie who then waltzed around the Green, swapping partners after every twirl – her suitors the workmen from the pub.

'Libby…' she called, reaching out a hand. 'Libby…'

Libby woke, her heart hammering in her chest as she stared at the ceiling. A floorboard creaked. What the hell? She stopped breathing, trying not to make a sound. A second creak. Slowly, she turned her head, her eyes widening when she saw the woman from her dream, her long grey hair, dark against her white gown.

Maggie.

Libby screamed.

'Fucking hell, Lib,' yelled the apparition.

The room flooded with light and Zoë slumped against the wall.

'Ohmigod, I thought you were her.' Libby sat up, rubbing her eyes. 'What's up?'

'I can't sleep.'

'Bad dream?'

'No. Allergies.' Zoë sneezed. 'The bloody cat's turned up.'

Chapter Six

The next morning, Libby woke in Maggie's old bedroom with sunshine filtering through the curtains and a loud purring in her ear. Reluctantly, she'd switched rooms with Zoë and huddled under the duvet in the dead woman's bed more than a little freaked out. She'd expected to lie awake, fighting off nightmares, but the large ginger tabby cat had padded into the room and jumped up onto the bed, curling up by her feet. Libby, appreciating the company, had quickly fallen into a deep and dreamless sleep.

Yawning, she rolled over to see the cat sitting by her pillow, staring at her. Libby checked her watch. Six o'clock. After the interrupted night's sleep and wine she'd knocked back with Zoë whilst unpacking, she'd expected to wake late.

'You, mister, are one hell of an alarm clock. I've got time for a run.' She turned the silver disc on his collar. 'Hyssop? Nice to meet you, Hyssop. But aren't witches' cats supposed to be black?'

He pushed his head against her hand.

'I'm afraid Zoë isn't going to be your biggest fan. She's allergic to cats.' She kissed his head, smiling when his purr grew louder. 'I wonder if I can keep you.'

He meowed, rubbing his head against her chin.

'Today is going to be a good day, Hyssop. Today, I'm starting my idyllic rural life.'

'Today's a bloody disaster and it's not even half-seven.' Libby leaned against the bathroom door, pulling her socks off. 'Are you going to be long? I'm going to be late for work'

Zoë opened the door, dripping from the shower, her hair still coated in conditioner. 'Heaven forbid I'd be the one to get you sacked. What happened?'

'I got lost.' How, still mystified her.

At the end of the back garden, the little wooden gate opened onto a bridleway, meaning Libby only had to run for fifteen minutes, following the track wherever it took her, turn around, and head back

– the sensible plan for her first day in the area and her first day at work.

Instead, the luxury of running on grass rather than concrete seduced her into running for a little longer, a little further. After twenty minutes, she stopped to size up the valley around her, the wine-blurred memory of the OS map she'd studied the night before giving her false confidence. Surely, she'd thought, if she carried on the same track, it'd take her back to the village.

After twenty-five minutes, she'd realised the track was heading up to Lum Crag, not to Gosthwaite. Her only option was to double back. But that was okay. Until the track started to bear little resemblance to the lane she'd headed out on. Where had she gone wrong? There were no turns, no alternatives, no options. Eventually, she'd clambered a few gates and scampered home across the fields, anything just to get home.

After a hasty shower, Libby pulled on the cream jodhpurs and black polo shirt she'd worn the previous afternoon, before pulling her still wet hair into a scruffy bun and applying three layers of mascara. Ideally she would've had time to put on some eyeliner and dragged a brush through her hair, but she couldn't be late. Not on Day One.

She checked her watch. Quarter to. If she left now, she'd even be a few minutes early. A cigarette on the way and all would be fine with her world. Hyssop sat by the door, watching her like a mother sending her child off to school as she grabbed her jacket, pulled on her boots and threw her cigarettes in her bag.

She stopped to kiss his head. 'This is still going to be a good day.'

He meowed as the doorbell rang.

'Zoë? I'll be late.'

'Naked. Deal with them.'

Libby swore but opened the door, grinning when she saw who was on the other side. Grace. Sadly, she didn't appear remotely pleased to see Libby. Tapping her foot, she stood in an over-sized t-shirt, jersey shorts and Ugg boots, pulling off just-climbed-out-of-bed sexy-chic with aplomb. Libby maintained a pleasant smile.

'I see Hyssop came home,' Grace said, glancing behind Libby.

'Oh, is he your cat now?' Libby stroked him, disappointment coursing through her. 'He came in about midnight. Scared the life out of us.'

Unsmiling, Grace thrust the box forwards. 'His stuff. He's only been with me for a few days because Patrick's gone away.' She nodded to the house on the corner next to them. 'But he'll have him back when he gets home. It's just a couple of months.'

Libby took the box, trying not to grin. 'That's fine. I think he's fabulous.'

'Everyone does.' Grace crouched down to stroke a purring Hyssop as he rubbed his head against her knee. 'See you round, Hyssy. He'll be back soon.' She glanced up at Libby. 'Seriously, please look after him and if you need anything, I work at the vets.' Again, Libby nodded. 'And stay away from my boyfriend.'

'*Boyfriend?*' Libby paled. At the pub, she and Zoë had eaten their goat cheese salads outside, avoiding the drunken men, but twice Jack had come out, blatantly flirting. She's done nothing to encourage a guy she'd just met, but from Grace's wasp-chewing scowl, Libby might as well have hopped on his knee and snogged him.

'Jack and I have been together for ten years. I don't need a peroxided bag of bones–'

'Grace, I'd never–'

'But he would.'

As Grace marched across the Green, Libby picked up Hyssop, turning him to face her.

'That didn't go well. I can't believe she thinks I'm a home-wrecking tramp. At least I get to keep you. Is that okay?' Why was she asking a cat? She checked her watch. Ten to. Bugger. She kissed Hyssop. 'I'm late and Grace hates me. But Hyssop, it's still going to be a great day.'

* * *

The cat sat on the little table in the hallway, turning his attention from the door that Libby had just closed to the stairs Zoë was trotting down. His eyes narrowed. If Zoë didn't know better, she'd swear the mangy fleabag was challenging her, saying *it's just you and me now.*

'And?' Zoë put her hands on her hips. 'This is *my* house and *you're* not welcome.'

Hyssop's tail flicked from side to side, but his condescending air didn't waver.

'You're a bloody...' But Zoë's nose was already tingling. Crap. How the hell was she supposed to outstare a cat when she was about to sneeze?

Three came out in a row, making her eyes water. Round one to the fleabag.

Letting out a frustrated growl, Zoë hit the nearest light switch, but after a heart-stopping crack, the bulb dimmed. Zoë stared up at it, her heart hammering. The stupid electrics. How could they be so appalling? What if Libby was right, what if Maggie was haunting them? Zoë almost laughed. Haunted houses? Really? She shook her head and checked her watch. Shit. It was already eight o'clock and she still had to dry her hair. There was no getting around it, she'd have to reset the fuse box herself.

The door under the stairs was covered with the same revolting peony wallpaper that graced the rest of the wall. Only a ceramic knob hinted at its presence. Zoë tugged it open and tentatively peered inside. In the dank, dark space stood the vacuum cleaner, old wellington boots, several boxes of books and at the far end, the fuse box.

Taking a deep breath, she stepped inside, her heart-racing again. The musty air enveloped her and it still held a lingering spicy trace of Opium, Maggie's perfume of choice. It caught the back of Zoë's throat.

It's so dark.

Cobwebs hung all around. A spider the size of a fifty pence piece watched her, but Zoë couldn't move, her eyes fixed on inside of the door, on the gouges in the wood that looked as if some wild animal had tried to claw its way out. A floorboard creaked upstairs. What the fuck? She glanced up, but something dropped onto her shoulder and Zoë screamed, backing hastily out of the cupboard. The spider fell to the floor and scuttled towards her toes and instinctively, Zoë stomped on it. A sob escaped her mouth as she felt it squish beneath her bare foot.

I hate this fucking house. Hate, hate, hate it.

Tears loomed, but she clenched her fists and glared up at the ceiling. 'Okay, you hideous old cow. When I get back from work tonight, I'm evicting your evil, dead ass. This house is mine and you're not wanted any more than your stupid cat.'

Hyssop's smug attitude faded and after another flick of his tail he slipped through the cat flap.

Ha. Round two to me, fleabag.

Feeling absurdly pleased with herself for standing up to non-existent ghost and a fat old cat, Zoë trotted back upstairs. With the house under her control, it was time to conquer the Carr and Young

Estate Agency.

Forty-five minutes later, Zoë strode through Haverton, her bravado replaced by a knot of nerves in her stomach. First days unnerved her. Working out how to use an unfamiliar photocopier was the easy part. Understanding the other women and how best to manage them was the tricky bit. It took time to understand who needed sucking up to, who wanted reassuring, who craved a BFF.

Mercifully, the men were simpler. They just wanted to shag her. In her last agency, one odious creep actually got caught wanking over her staff photo. Her skin had crawled for a week, but it'd crawled for another two when she'd discovered the incompetent arse was paid twenty percent more than her.

Everyday sexism, baby.

The bright red paintwork around the Carr and Young window framed a multitude of adverts – the cheapest property on display requested offers in the region of four hundred grand. Zoë's smile returned. The commission she could earn working at the North-West's most prestigious estate agency made a mockery of what she'd maxed in Manchester. It'd be worth the sucking up.

She seized the door handle, but staggered backwards as the door was thrust open.

'Like he'd give a–' A guy stared at her from the open doorway.

A fit-as guy.

What was he, thirty? White shirt, ironed. No tie. Some kind of office job, but not too stuffy. Not a solicitor or accountant. She couldn't tear her eyes away to check out his shoes. His eyes were blue. Full on blue, but he had almost black hair. How unusual. And he was still staring.

She smiled.

He smiled back.

'You going in?' he asked, holding the door open.

'I'm going in.'

'You look...' He laughed, shaking his head a little. 'Have a very good day, beautiful.'

'I will.' She stepped inside but paused to glance back. 'Thank–.'

He'd gone.

Fit as, and he'd called her beautiful. He'd called her beautiful and hadn't even glanced at her cleavage. How utterly bloody refreshing.

'You must be Zoë.' A perky blonde dashed over.

And you'd be the one who wants a new BFF. Zoë nodded, smiling. 'I'm Zoë.'

'Come in, come in. Welcome to Carr and Young.'

Within ten minutes, the perky blonde had introduced herself as Jess and twittered without pausing for breath as she made them both mugs of instant coffee. Through the glass panel in the door, Zoë spied on the other employees. Two older women and a girl her own age with glossy long dark hair sat at desks in the open plan office. The two other doors – one marked *Meeting Room*, the other *Mr Carr* – were closed. Mr Carr.

Three phone calls and he'd offered her a job, increasing her salary by twenty-five percent, but she'd yet to meet the guy – and she was dying to. His photo on the company website made him look pretty hot, like Paul Newman in his heyday.

'So where is everyone?' Zoë asked as they left the kitchen, heading to the nearest of the older women.

Jess's brow furrowed. 'Everyone?'

The older woman stood up, holding out her hand. 'This is it. We're a tight knit group at Carr and Young. I'm Barbara.'

Zoë nearly spilled her coffee. *This was it?* Two sixty year-olds, a ditzy blonde and a predatory brunette. Where were the men?

'And this is Nikki,' Jess added.

'Two ks and an i.' Nikki sat on the edge of her desk, undisguised animosity seeping from her pores as she flicked her long dark hair over one shoulder. 'Did Jonathan really give you a job just like that, without him or Maxine ever meeting you?'

Zoë's back stiffened, but she flashed an amenable smile. So this was the office bitch. There was always one. Who the hell was Maxine? 'Is he here?'

'Who?' Jess asked blankly.

'The boss. Mr Carr.'

The remaining older woman hung up her phone, and strode across the room, her black spike heels looking ready to snap under the weight of her cankles. 'Zoë, lovely to meet you, finally. I'm Max, the office manager. Jonathan comes in on Thursdays and believe me, his diary is all about meeting you, but until then, it's just us girls.'

Just us girls? Zoë's stomach dropped. Where were the men she could wrap around her finger from day one? This job was going to be hell on bloody earth.

* * *

'I've had the worst day,' Libby called as she slammed the front door. 'I hate, absolutely hate, hate, *hate* Kim.'

She kicked off her boots, frowning at the boxes stacked in the hallway. Zoë had been busy. In the living room, the curtains and every single knick-knack had gone, and vast decorator sheets covered the sofas. Maggie was being erased. But oddly, Libby missed the clutter.

I'm sorry, Maggie.

Why did she feel guilty? Maggie was dead. She wouldn't care.

Following the aroma of roast lamb, garlic and rosemary drifting from the kitchen, Libby wandered through to find Zoë preparing green beans.

'You've eradicated half of chintz hell *and* made dinner?'

'No. I eradicated half of chintz hell, made dinner *and* made a batch of banana muffins for you. And that was all after work.'

'I love you.' Libby grabbed for an errant walnut half. There was a lot to be said for living with a Nigella wannabe. 'How's Hyssop?'

'Asleep on your bed. I don't think he's moved since I came home.'

Libby frowned at the open bottle of Merlot. 'Wine o'clock already?'

'You're not the only one who's landed a crappy job.' Sighing, Zoë wiped her hands on her tatty, dust covered jeans and picked up a mug. 'It isn't going how I expected, moving here. I hate this house.'

'It's spooky, isn't it?' Libby frowned at the plates displayed in the welsh dresser. 'Like she's still here.'

'That's why I've been evicting the old cow.' Zoë knocked back the contents of her mug and refilled it with a healthy glug of wine. 'So, what's wrong with Kim?'

'Well, I got there at two minutes past eight, but from the look on her face, you'd think I'd arrived at twenty-past.' Libby poured an inch of the red wine into a second mug and slouched against the breakfast bar. 'She's actually lovely to the nags, as she calls them, but fifty percent of the horses in the yard are exercised by their owners and the rest are retirement cases. I don't get to ride. I just get to listen to Kim bitch about the clients, her husband, me and the god who invented all of the above. Horrible, horrible woman. And she's definitely having an affair with Michael, the feed merchant.'

'But it's none of your business. Don't let your bloody morals get you sacked again.'

'It's wrong.'

'It's life.' Zoë sighed. 'They could be in miserable, abusive marriages for all you know.'

'Kim said her husband Pete was a useless waste of space. He's not. He's lovely. He works his arse off and from what I've seen—'

'You've been there for one day. You don't know anything.'

'She married him for his landowner status. She married Langton Hall, not him.' Libby sipped her wine. 'I hate it. What's worse is that Michael is married too. His wife had their second child less than a year ago. Why can't people keep promises and not shag around?'

'Because the human race is inherently hedonistic. And you need to accept that.'

'Sorry. Here I am, whining away. What's wrong with your job? Is your boss an immoral arse too?'

'I don't know. I still haven't met him.' Zoë wandered outside with her mug and the bottle.

Libby followed her and sat on the steps of the crazy-paved patio, wriggling her toes in the overgrown lawn as she lit a cigarette. 'Why?'

'He's only in the office on Thursdays. Rest of the time he's at our Kendal or Kirkby Lonsdale offices. Which leaves me working with *four* bloody women. No men.'

Libby pressed her lips together. 'Oestrogen hell?'

'This morning, all they could talk about was what they were having for lunch, and this afternoon, it was a minute dissection of their salads from the deli down the road and what they were having for *tea*. They're the dullest bunch in the world ever.'

'Oh, give them a chance. I bet they're nice really and it can't be as bad as working in testosterone hell.'

'I know. There's this one girl, Nikki. She seems okay. Shame she hates me.'

'Hates you, why?'

'Who knows? Doesn't like the competition, maybe?' Zoë let out a long frustrated sigh. 'In other depressing news, I got an electrician to come round this afternoon. Remember Sparky from the pub yesterday? It's him. He condemned the electrics. It's going to cost a fortune to rewire the place.'

'Sorry, Zo.' Libby fished into her back pocket, taking out the flyer Tallulah had given her. 'Is it too soon to look for a new job?'

'The only reason I'm going back tomorrow, is so I can make a cup of bloody coffee without getting a dose of ECT.' Zoë sighed at the sky. 'I've spent the last three hours in a pair of rubber gloves.'

'Sexy.'

'Sparky certainly thought so.'

'Bit young isn't he?'

'Didn't stop him trying it on.'

Libby laughed. 'Did you let him ravish you over the fuse box?'

'As if. Nice arse, but you'd need to put a paper bag over his head.' Zoë grinned, elbowing her. 'Ring it.'

Reluctantly, Libby took out her phone, still staring at the flyer. It'd be quitting and she'd never given up on anything in her life – anything other than ballet. But she'd get to ride show-jumpers like Tallulah's horse, Shakespeare. She dialled.

'Hello. Low Wood Farm,' said a woman with vowels capable of etching crystal.

'I'm ringing about the groom's job you–'

'The advert clearly stated the closing date for applications was Saturday.'

'Oh, Tallulah gave me the number. ' Libby cringed. 'I hadn't seen an ad.'

'I can't...' The snooty woman paused. 'The interviews are arranged for Wednesday morning. Perhaps I could take your details. If none of the other applicants are suitable–'

'That would be great.'

'Name?'

'Um... Olivia Wilde.' She'd rather Tallulah didn't know she'd failed to get an interview.

'And number?'

Libby recited her mobile number, desperate to get off the phone, and stared at the dandelion clocks, the flowers already past their best. In one call her hopes had been dashed. There'd be no show-jumpers and no escaping Kim Langton-Browne.

Where was the idyllic rural dream?

The next evening there were no enticing aromas to greet Libby at the door and the dark grey clouds left little sunlight to creep its way into the house. She sat on the stairs and pulled off her boots, sighing at the clumps of dried mud she'd scattered across the tiles. She ought to sweep up but instead she brushed it to the skirting board with her foot. The dirt settled into a previously invisible crack in one of the tiles. Oh god, had Maggie's head caused that?

Goosebumps covered her arms as she rubbed the tile clean with her jacket. Something moved behind her. She glanced up the stairs, her heart racing.

Hyssop.

Libby laughed as he padded down the stairs, meowing. 'Hey, mister. You scared me. But then it doesn't take much in this place.'

He rubbed his head against her chin, purring. He was so content, his purr almost soporific. Why did a silly old tabby cat stop her feeling... edgy?

I have a cat. That's all I have. A cat. I am Maggie. I'm going to end up old, alone and dead at the bottom of the stairs.

'I suppose you want your dinner? Looks like I'll be cooking for everyone.'

After serving Hyssop one of the high end pouches of sardines Grace had given her and spending twenty minutes under the pitiful shower, Libby rifled through the cupboards, searching for gastronomic inspiration. Leftover lamb and... Dried apricots and cous cous? A Moroccan-spiced salad? She set to work roasting red peppers under the grill, slicing the lamb, chopping the mint and parsley from Maggie's herb garden, but it wasn't until she'd finally tossed it all together with a healthy sprinkling of coriander and chunks of apricot that Zoë's text arrived.

Not home for dinner. Nikki on peacekeeping mission. Later gator. Zx

She'd created a Middle-Eastern taste sensation and had no one to share it with. Libby switched on the kettle to make a cup of tea, but plunged the house into semi-darkness.

This house sucked. This life sucked.

Impulsively, she picked up her phone, glancing at Hyssop as she dialled Paolo's number.

Please, don't tell Zoë.

'It's me,' she said when he answered.

'Ach, hello you,' Paolo replied. 'How's the countryside?'

His familiar voice elicited emotions she'd been unaware she'd bottled up, and fat tears tumbled down her cheeks. She didn't speak for a moment.

'Sorry,' she said, sniffing. 'I just wanted–'

He shushed her. 'No apologies. Where are you?'

'The cottage.'

'I...' he started, but a creaking sound suggested he'd shifted, 'am lying on my battered second-hand leather sofa, in my new loft-style apartment in Shoreditch listening to folk music. '

'Why? You hate folk music.'

'I'm trying to incite a cultural riot inside my heart.'

'You're crazy. What on earth does that mean?'

'I miss you,' he replied softly.

'I miss you too. I have no friends and living in the country isn't proving very idyllic.'

'Then come to London. You can share my sofa.'

'Is that all you have?'

'There's a bed too.'

Despite the misery swamping her, she laughed. 'Shame it's in London. You could've picked any other British city and I might've jumped in my car tonight. How can you afford a loft-style apartment in Shoreditch anyway?'

'Remember the Love Triangle?'

'The threesome series?' Libby blushed, remembering the huge oil paintings. 'How could I forget?'

'Sold the lot for five grand.'

'I'm so proud of you. You'll be rich and famous in no time.'

He laughed. He used to run his fingers through his hair when he laughed like that. She closed her eyes, remembering, imagining.

'I still love you,' he said.

Her tears tumbled again and she didn't respond. How many times had he whispered those words – a hundred, a thousand? But they were words she'd never returned. How could she pretend to love him when her heart still belonged to ballet?

'Come here, Lib.'

But what if Paolo was it, the best distraction she'd ever get from ballet? They were friends, good friends, and intense lovers. Who could ask for more than that? Okay, she suspected what he truly loved was sketching the clean lines of her body, but wasn't that good enough?

No.

He was nearly perfect, nearly as good as ballet, but nearly wasn't enough.

'I know,' she whispered. 'But let someone new in.'

As she ended the call, she grabbed a bottle of red from the wine rack. Shiraz? Perfect. It'd stand its ground against the cumin and coriander in the salad. Did she care it cost only four pounds seventy-nine? Not that night.

Still reading the label in the dim light, she groped for the corkscrew but sent it skidding off the counter just as Hyssop came in through the cat flap. The corkscrew narrowly missed his head and he yowled, darting between Libby's legs, almost knocking her over. Only years of dance training kept her vertical and she balanced on one foot, arms outstretched, as Hyssop clawed his way onto the worktop.

Jesus, was that how he killed Maggie? Something scared him, he ran to her for security and she fell? Libby bent down to retrieve the corkscrew, but one arm of it remained on the floor, shattered. She closed her eyes, swearing. She could go to the pub and ask them to open the wine, but what if Grace was there?

Seconds later, she rang her neighbour's doorbell. She'd not seen much of Sheila since they'd moved in, but the fifty-something mother of four sons had dropped off a homemade carrot cake and made Libby promise to pop round if she needed anything. Libby smiled as the door opened but had to stifle a giggle when she saw Sheila's *I ♥ Gary Barlow* t-shirt. That explained why *Back For Good* and *Rule the World* were played on repeat most nights.

'I'm sorry to bother you, Sheila, but do you have a corkscrew I could borrow?'

'Come in, come in,' Sheila said, wiping her hands on a tea towel, 'but excuse the mess. Two teenage boys under one roof and it's a full-time job tidying up after them. And Jack's no better, still treating this place like he lives here.'

Libby followed her through to the back of the house, picking her way over the trainers and cricket bats strewn along the hallway. In the kitchen, Sheila handed her a corkscrew and muted the TV, cutting off the barmaid ranting in the Rovers.

'How are you settling in?'

'Okay.' Libby paused before pulling the cork out. A little company would be lovely. 'Fancy a glass?'

'Oh, go on then. Just a small one.' Sheila winked and took two wine glasses from the cupboard. 'Just *okay*? I'd have thought a pretty young thing like you would be having a whale of a time.'

Blushing, Libby joined Sheila at the kitchen table and poured the wine. *I hate my job, I have no friends and I'm living in a death-trap.*

'It's just different.' She forced a smile. 'Were you and Maggie close?'

'When my husband had an affair with a woman from the butchers

– they live in Haverton now – Maggie got me through it. A true friend.' She stared at her glass for a moment, as she tucked a wayward strand of dark grey hair behind her ear.

'You must miss her.'

Sheila nodded. 'I saw Hyssop came back. I thought he would.'

'He's made himself right at home.' Libby sipped her wine. 'What was she like?'

'Hasn't Zoë told you anything?'

'I don't think they got along too well.'

'It's funny because Zoë's like Maggie. Doesn't fit in around here, too glamorous by half.'

'Maggie was glamorous too?' Libby's mental image of the little old lady disintegrated.

'Oh aye. I mean she was in her sixties when she died, and a bit stooped, but when she moved here, oh, she'd have been about thirty-five. A real looker. Mind you, even in her sixties she still turned heads. Long beautiful wavy hair, steel grey it was.'

'Stan from the pub said she was a siren.'

Sheila laughed. 'Well I don't know about that, but she had one or two men chasing her.'

'Stan?'

'He was just a passing fancy when she had a leaky tap. He's a plumber. Her heart belonged elsewhere.'

Libby leant forwards, smiling, eager for details. 'Really? Who?'

Sheila gently laughed. 'She never talked about him. Just said she'd loved him since the day she met him and she'd love him 'til the day she died. I expect she did.'

'What happened to him? Did he die?'

'No. He's married. Lives in Windermere. Some rich bloke. He's the one that gave her the pendant.'

'What pendant?'

'The emerald pendant. Worth a bob or two. Twenty grand, Maggie reckoned.'

'Crikey, I hope Zoë didn't throw it away with the rest of her stuff.'

'Yes, I saw the skip.' Sheila's accusatory tone had Libby's cheeks flushing.

'So, I heard Maggie was a witch. Grace said you and Maggie put a spell on the cottage.'

'What nonsense.' Sheila laughed, but as she glanced up to her right and scratched her wrist, Libby's mouth gaped. Sheila was lying.

'Oh my god. It's true?'

Sheila paused, looking Libby in the eye before chuckling. 'Now I don't really go for all that mumbo jumbo and it might be real or it might be one of them placebo effects, but I saw some odd things with my own eyes.'

'Did you hear anything the night she died?'

Sheila shook her head. 'Not a peep. She wasn't home when I went to bed. That was at eleven.'

'Why was she out so late?'

'Well, it was Ostara.'

Libby raised her eyebrows.

'It's where they celebrate the Goddess of Spring. Poor Maggie. There she was, celebrating new life when hers was about to end.'

Libby sipped her wine. Dare she ask? 'I heard a rumour she was murdered.'

'That'll be Becky.' Sheila waved a dismissive hand. 'I have Maggie's things. Her Wicca things. The day after she died, after Patrick found her–'

'Patrick?'

'The vet. He lives in the corner house next to yours. I went in, after they'd you know, taken her away. The police said it was okay. I just had a tidy up. Hyssop had made a bit of a mess, knocking things off the dresser and I didn't want just anybody to come across her book and whatnot. Maggie wouldn't have liked that.'

'Her book? What, like a spell book?' Libby couldn't help grinning, imagining some ornate leather-bound tome.

Sheila nodded and delved into the cupboard under the stairs, pulling out a large plastic storage box. 'It's her book and a few herbs. They're... well, I didn't think just anyone should come across them. No matter what you believe in, they can be dangerous.'

Libby lifted the lid, frowning with disappointment at the royal blue lever arch file. That was Maggie's spell book? A little bottle marked Belladonna peeked from under the folder.

'Do you want to take it?' Sheila asked quietly. 'I meant to throw it away but I just couldn't. And it gives me the creeps having it in the house.'

After two small glasses of wine, Libby left Sheila's armed with a box of witchcraft and a half-empty bottle of Shiraz. She devoured the Moroccan salad as she studied the multitude of jars, vials and bottles lining the bottom of the box. Each had a neat label: Coltsfoot,

Hibiscus flower, White Willow bark. Several of the names she recognised as deadly, the rest she'd never heard of. All she needed now was a cauldron.

Utterly absorbed, she flicked through the pages in the folder. Some of the A4 sheets were handwritten in an elaborate cursive style, others digitally printed, but many were photocopies of photocopies of ancient books. They detailed tinctures for headaches and prayers to goddesses but most enticing were the spells: love, prosperity, luck.

A Good Luck Spell? She could totally do with a healthy dose of that.

Libby poured the last of the red wine and picked four candles from the box – white to represent her, plus grey, black and orange. The spell ought to be performed when the moon was waxing. Well it was crescent-shaped, but waxing or waning, who knew?

She lit the white candle.

'This is me.'

She lit the black candle.

'This is the bad luck that has haunted my footsteps. Trouble, disappointment and tears are here. This bad luck now leaves me forever.'

She lit the grey candle.

'All that was bad is neutralized. All my bad luck is dissolved.'

She lit the orange candle.

'This is the energy coming my way, to invigorate my life and speed up change.'

Closing her eyes, she sat, as instructed and visualised the negative energies being whisked into the grey candle and dissolving into nothingness. She tried to imagine the orange candle drawing good energy towards her and the air around her stir with opportunity.

As the stubs of candles finally fluttered out, Libby smiled at Hyssop. 'You believe in this?' She rubbed under his chin. 'Me neither. But the way things are going, I need all the luck I can get.'

Chapter Seven

The next day, Libby headed down the same track she'd run on her first morning, determined to discover where she'd got lost. For fifteen minutes, she pounded along the track, regretting the previous evening's four glasses of wine, but smiling at her daft little dabble with witchcraft.

Or was it daft? She'd thought Jack was cute and then he'd started flirting. *Any girl who slept there would become irresistible to the man she desired.*

Up ahead, the roofs of several houses and barns came into view and Libby slowed. That had to be Gosthwaite Mills, the hamlet to the north-west of the village. She shouldn't be here. How had she missed the bridleway that went off to the north-east, taking her to the common? And where the hell did this track go?

She had to be the biggest failure in the world. She couldn't even navigate the bridleways around the village. She slumped against a dry-stone wall. Obviously, the good luck spell hadn't worked.

But with impeccable timing, a small dog came bounding towards her, a blur of black, brown and white fur. Libby's frustration evaporated as the Spaniel-cross scampered around her, its tail wagging furiously.

'Dylan, heel!' shouted a male voice ahead of her. 'Sorry, but he's harmless.'

Libby crouched down to pet the dog, smiling at the guy jogging towards her pushing a baby in a three-wheel pushchair.

'You must be the new girl in the Green, one of them anyway,' he said before flashing a Colgate-sponsored smile. 'I'm Xander.'

Xander? He was Tallulah's uncle, the *fittest bloke ever.* Chloe hadn't been exaggerating. Tall, with dark blond hair, he had the same fabulous brown eyes as Tallulah.

'Libby,' she said, shaking his hand.

'And this is Evie,' he said, tucking the blanket around the smiling baby.

'Um... hi, Evie.' Libby tentatively wiggled her fingers at the tot, clueless what to say to a child who couldn't talk back.

'My wife Daisy and I live over there.' He pointed to the house behind her on the left. 'No doubt, we'll see you around.'

'Actually,' she said, cringing, 'I'm a little lost. I need to get back to the village but I've gone wrong somewhere.'

'It's easy done, believe me. You've missed the shorter track back to the village. It's about half a mile back the way you came. This track goes back to the village too.'

'Thanks.'

He tipped his head to the side. 'Do you run every day?'

'Usually.'

'I'll pick you up at half-six tomorrow and show you around, if you like?'

She hesitated. After already upsetting Jack and Grace's relationship through no fault of her own, she shouldn't get too friendly with a married man. What if Maggie's spell were real? On the other hand, he wasn't acting remotely flirtatious and she'd be nuts to turn down a tour guide.

'Yes, please.'

Libby jogged away, unable to stop smiling. A running buddy, she had a potential new running buddy. Her first piece of good fortune – was this was the spell at work? She knew for sure when her second piece arrived a few hours later.

Kim had gone to some show with Michael the feed merchant and Libby rattled through the morning jobs, singing along to the radio. With the horses turned out and the yard immaculate, she'd barely sat down with a cup of tea and an illicit cigarette when her phone rang. She half-expected it to be Kim, scolding her for smoking on the yard. It wasn't.

'Hello, Olivia? This is Andrea Golding, from Low Wood Farm.'

* * *

The photos on a full screen were even better than on the phone.

'It's me. I got her.'

'The new girl?' Michael Wray sucked in a slow breath. 'Who with?'

'You're going to love this.'

The expectant pause hovered between them.

'Alexander Golding.'

* * *

As she wandered up the High Street in Haverton, Zoë turned her little silver pine cone key ring over and over between her fingers. Superstitious nonsense.

'It's supposed to bring you good luck,' Libby had explained, blushing as if she'd been caught stealing.

'And I need luck because...'

'You're meeting your new boss. He'll be in your office today, won't he?'

He would be, but Zoë wouldn't need luck to handle him – although, it was nice that her hair had dried like a glossy curtain that morning, which meant she could leave the house on time and not risk the speed camera between Gosthwaite and Haverton for a change. Better still, she'd managed to find a parking spot in the first street she tried so she wasn't running to get to the office on time.

Just superstition, right? She glanced at the pine cone.

'Oh,' Libby had added, 'but be careful. It might boost your sexual power. Like you need it.'

Like I need it? Zoë could live with that risk.

'You're early.' The man's voice came from her left, from the coffee-come-book shop she passed twice a day.

Oh hello. It was the guy she'd bumped into on her first day at work. The fit guy. The fit guy who called her *beautiful*.

Zoë stopped. 'Excuse me?'

'The last two mornings you've dashed past, your heels hitting out this killer staccato beat.' He stepped from the doorway, one hand holding a tiny espresso cup, the other a hand-rolled cigarette. 'But today... you're a chill out tune. You're early. You have time for a coffee.'

His eyes really were stupidly blue, too blue for the dark hair that flopped over his forehead, but Zoë didn't drop contact with them as she slowly walked towards him. Or as she took his coffee, downing it in one. To his credit he merely raised his eyebrows.

'I'm not that early.' And she carried on her way.

'See you tomorrow, beautiful.'

It wasn't even a question. And he'd still never once glanced down at her tits. A girl had to love that.

'Tomorrow?' Zoë glanced at the pine cone key ring. Sexual power? 'Okay. But put more sugar in. I'm not that sweet.'

Five minutes later, she opened the glass door into the Carr &

Young Estate Agency, still grinning, still clutching her new key ring.

'Miss Horton?'

Zoë stalled, her effervescence after meeting Mr Coffee Shop subsiding as she clocked the guy standing beside her desk. Tall, grey and devastatingly hot. Oh, please say this serious piece of ass was her boss. Wrapping him around her little finger wouldn't be a hardship, at all. Shedding her mac, Zoë stalked over, not missing the gold band glinting on his left hand. Or that his eyes dropped momentarily to the lowest undone button on her blouse. Married men were always easy prey. Surreptitiously, she pocketed the pine cone.

'It's Zoë, please.'

Sexual power? Thank you, Libby.

* * *

The next day, with the sun sitting in a cloudless sky, Libby wandered along Market Street, falling ever more in love with Gosthwaite. The butchers specialised in locally-reared meat, the baker's offered to slice their freshly made wholemeal bread and the multi-coloured array of veg outside the grocer's looked like an advert for organic living. It didn't stop there. The café overlooked the River Lum, the village hall had a second-hand book sale complete with honesty box, and the post office sold everything from boiled sweets to Herdwick wool blankets. And more importantly, everyone she passed said hello. This was why she'd left Manchester. This was the idyllic rural dream.

After four days of working with Kim Langton-Browne and a morning weeding the garden, Libby decided she deserved the afternoon off. A roast chicken sandwich, a punnet of strawberries and a jug of iced-tea would accompany her as she soaked up the sun and read a fifty pence copy of *Chocolat*. Or maybe more of the spell book – her top secret, guilty pleasure.

Libby hadn't mentioned the box of Wicca goodies in case Zoë threw it away like the rest of Maggie's belongings. And she certainly hadn't mentioned performing the Good Luck spell. In the cold light of day, she knew there was no such thing as magic but when she lay in bed at night, she couldn't deny her life had significantly improved.

Xander had been good as his word and for the last two mornings, he'd shown her new running routes, threatening to take her up to Lum Crag on Sunday. Libby looked up, frowning at the rocky outcrop to the north of the village. Even on a sunny day, it looked dark, menacing and a long way up, but if Xander thought it was worth it, she'd go. She didn't fancy him, no matter what Zoë's psychoanalysis diagnosed, but a serious case of hero-worship was definitely building.

Better still, Kim hadn't set foot on the yard since Wednesday morning so work had even become bearable. Three days off lay before her, and the forecast said the sun would shine on every one of them. Now, all she needed was for the good luck to spread to the interview at Low Wood Farm in the morning. Libby whistled as she passed the church, swinging her shopping bag and reading the front page of the local newspaper. No gunshot crime, no aggravated burglaries... just a little girl showing a prize-winning pig at a local show. Bliss.

Back at the Green, she spotted a car parked outside Maggie's cottage, a woman with white blonde curls sitting on the bonnet, her scowl worse than Kim's.

'So,' the girl said, standing up, 'you're the one trying to run off with my husband.'

Was that Daisy? Libby's mouth gaped open, but any words fell away as the woman held up a copy of the *Haverton Gazette*.

Running Around, the headline on page twelve screamed and underneath were three photos of her and Xander, one of them running, another showing them chatting in Maggie's garden. The third was the blurriest but largest and in it he was kissing her head.

'Oh my god...' Libby clamped a hand over her own mouth as she skimmed the accompanying words.

Trophy hunting new-comer, Libby Wilde, bags Gosthwaite celebrity. Local girl Grace Newton, confirmed Wilde and Golding run together most mornings. 'I'm not saying they're up to anything, but they do seem very close, and he's not the first man she's tried to lure away from his girlfriend. But I'm sure her and Xander just like running together.'

How could Grace say those things? How on earth could she persuade Daisy that the last thing on earth Libby would ever conceive of doing was having an affair with a married man?

'We're not... this isn't true.' Desperately, she beseeched Daisy. 'I swear we—'

But Daisy laughed, her face breaking into a huge smile as she held out her hand. 'Oh relax. I'm teasing.'

What? Libby blinked, utterly thrown. 'Teasing?'

She nodded. 'Sorry, I couldn't resist. I'm Daisy, fab to meet you at last.'

'But you know it's not true?' Libby asked, tentatively shaking Daisy's hand.

'Of course. Besides, I trust my husband implicitly.' Then, as blatantly as Tallulah had, Daisy looked Libby up and down, taking in the bangles, the purple streaks, the aubergine nails. 'But OMG, you're so not what I was expecting. I thought you'd be all sporty because of the running, but you look like... a Bratz doll.'

Libby laughed. 'Um... thank you?'

'You know Xander thinks you're ace. You've been upgraded to *Wilde.*'

'Yes, I'd noticed.' That morning he'd called her nothing else. 'But seriously, I wouldn't. Have an affair with a married man, I mean. I wouldn't even consider it.'

Daisy waved her protestations away. 'So he said you weren't working today. I'm meeting my friend Clara for lunch. Join us? We'll go as we are.'

Daisy, in a denim mini-skirt, faded black t-shirt and silver Havaiana flip flops, was hardly an example of sartorial style, but Libby glanced down at her own soil-smudged dungaree dress and shook her head.

Daisy waved her towards the house. 'Okay, but don't you dare dress up.'

Fifteen minutes later, Libby walked through the huge glass entrance doors of the Bobbin Mill. A good-looking, dark-haired guy in an immaculate pale blue shirt and dark trousers wandered to meet them – from his rich brown eyes, he had to be Tallulah's dad, the guy she had an interview with in the morning. To her amazement, he looked Libby over with a smile playing at the corners of his mouth and she didn't know if she should be offended or flutter her eyelashes. Thank god she'd changed into Zoë's purple dress.

Finally, he turned to Daisy, frowning at her feet. 'You're lowering the tone of the place.'

But Daisy kissed his cheek, laughing. 'We're young, blonde and sexy. We make the place look cool. Rob, this is Libby. Libby, this is my fabulous brother-in-law, Robbie.'

'Ah,' Robbie said, 'my little brother's running friend.'

Under his very direct eye contact, Libby used every gram of self-control not to blush as they shook hands. Okay, he had the tall and ridiculously good-looking boxes firmly ticked, but this guy had something else and it wasn't just dark hair. And how odd that he hadn't mentioned her interview. Should she?

'Is Clara here?' Daisy asked.

'At the table down by the willow tree. She's brought the thug with her. Seriously, flip flops, Daze?' Shaking his head, he led them to the bar where Daisy ordered wine and dragged Libby to look at the photos on the walls.

'Look, this is me, enormously pregnant at the grand opening.' Daisy stabbed a finger at a photo of herself with a neat bump hiding under her black mini-dress. 'The Golding brothers, how hot? Xander's better looking in a conventional way but Robbie...' Daisy glanced back to him before lowering her voice. 'Clara calls him the sexiest man in town.'

Libby, unable to resist, turned to peek at him. As he gathered up a bottle of white and two glasses, he still watched her. He even smiled. Working at his yard could be the best distraction from ballet in the world.

'And this is his family.' Daisy pointed to a photo of a model-like woman with a glossy dark bob, and three understandably pretty girls. 'His wife, Vanessa, and their daughters, Tallulah, Matilda and Pandora.'

Libby stifled her despairing sigh. Just another bloke who forgot he had a wife when she wasn't in the room. What would he be like when his wife was on tour with a string quartet? Desperate not to risk another eye meet with Mr Golding before her interview, she turned her attention to the *before and after* shots of the Mill.

Someone very clever had taken a three hundred year-old barn, modernised it with cutting edge architecture then stolen the soft furnishings from an interior designer's home. The effect was as über-crisp as it was cosy. Exposed beams and bare stone-work, clean-lined chunky oak tables and simple glass vases – she'd seen those in many restaurants, but in addition to the hundreds of family photos, random pastels of unnaturally coloured sheep hung on the walls along with, in one corner, a framed series of children's finger paintings. Hardly the décor she'd expected for a restaurant inching towards its first Michelin star, but crikey it worked.

'Awesome place,' she murmured.

'Thank you.' Daisy curtsied. 'Xander might get all the plaudits for knocking together the divine food, but I take full credit for making the venue look fabulous.'

'And neither of them care that it's me who makes sure it turns a profit.' Robbie tipped his head. 'Come on, outside before any of the paying guests see you.'

They headed into the garden where rustic oak tables dotted the lawn. Daisy waved to a blonde woman pushing a buggy at the other end of the garden.

'I hear you're working for Kim,' Robbie said, smiling down at Libby.

'Silly old cow,' Daisy mumbled.

Libby nodded, trying not to giggle or pay too much attention to Robbie's spicy aftershave. 'It's quite alarming how much everyone seems to know about me.'

'It's a village.' He held out her chair. 'Everyone knows everything.'

'And what they don't know,' Daisy added, sinking into her own chair, 'as you've found out, the *Haverton Gazette* makes up.'

'Why does it do that?' Libby asked, truly baffled. 'It's not like we're famous, or even Z-list celebrities.'

'It sells papers,' Robbie said simply.

'But why me?'

'You're new.' Daisy sat back, shielding her eyes with a vast pair of sunglasses. 'Have you always worked with horses?'

Libby shook her head. 'But I've ridden since I was a kid.'

'I have a yard, show-jumpers mostly,' Robbie said, handing them menus. 'If you ever want to go riding with Daze, there's usually something handy.'

Libby forced a grateful smile. He didn't know she had an interview. How did he not know? Olivia. She'd told Andrea her given name, not Libby. But then who the hell was Andrea?

He poured the wine, flashing Libby another blush-inducing smile. 'Lucy will be out to take your order.'

Libby sipped her wine, determined not to watch his very nice arse walk away. 'Is he always like that?'

'There are two things you should know about Robbie,' Daisy said, smiling. 'One, as you've already noticed, he's a dreadful flirt, but two, he's utterly faithful to Van. I adore him for it. It gives me hope that Xander will be too. Oh, and three, he'll steal your cigarettes without shame. He used to pinch about ten a day off me when we were doing this place.'

Although a single, or at least divorced dad of one would've been a more appealing distraction, Libby cheered at the prospect of a little, harmless stable yard flirting.

'And four,' said the blonde woman, parking the buggy in the shade of the tree, 'he's the sexiest man in town. Officially. Christ, I love it when he looks you over like he's about to bend you over the sofa whether you like it or not.'

Daisy laughed. 'Clara's chair of the Robbie Fan Club, but she wouldn't. She's married to Scott, one of Robbie's oldest friends. Libby, this is Clara, aka Miss Knightmare, teacher at Gosthwaite Primary School. Sleepyhead over there is Will. Appreciate the peace now, because when he's awake there won't be any. Clara, this is Libby.'

Libby smiled warily at the toddler, grateful he was fast asleep, before turning to Clara. Crikey, standing next to Daisy was intimidating enough. She certainly didn't look like someone who'd had a baby six months ago – skinny in all the right places but with decent, real boobs and a tiny waist that flared to a perfect bum, all in a dinky, five foot two package. And Clara? Libby couldn't help but glance down at her own non-existent cleavage. If only.

'I'm sure you must hear this all the time...' she said apologetically to Clara, 'but you look–'

'Scarlett Johansson?' Clara nodded. 'Not a bad lookey-likey to have. What did you do before you came here?'

'I worked for a wedding planner.'

'Interesting career choice,' Daisy said.

'Well, I have a Performing Arts degree and believe me, you need bloody good acting skills to reassure some brides they're doing the right thing.'

'Performing Arts?' Clara asked.

'Singing and dancing mostly. I do a mean Lady Gaga impression.'

'Clara did a summer as a pole dancer at Pacha, Ibiza.'

'Podium not pole.' Clara threw an olive at Daisy. 'Best pulling season ever. Did you ever perform professionally?'

'A couple of pop videos.'

'Ooh, which ones?' Daisy asked, leaning her elbows on the table.

'None you'd have heard of,' Libby said, waving a dismissive hand. 'So, Xander said you'd been married before, Daisy?'

Daisy smiled as Lucy arrived to take their orders, but tapped her foot, impatient to tell her tale. Libby had yet to meet anyone who wasn't.

'Did he tell you *who* I was married to?'

Libby glanced down, letting her cheeks flush. The actor had graced her own bedroom wall, one of the few males who weren't dancers. 'To Finn Rousseau.'

'Wanker,' Clara spat.

Daisy grinned. 'We don't talk about my bastard ex-husband much, but after I left Finn, Xander came along and we just clicked. You know?'

Libby lit a cigarette, wishing she could answer with a nod. She'd almost had that with Paolo. 'What about you, Clara? Love at first sight too?'

Daisy laughed and Clara raised her hand in defeat.

'No, I was the queen of the deluded idiots. Took me five years to realise Scott was the one for me. We'd been on-off since I was twenty, but I wouldn't let it be anything more than that. My dad was a complete bastard, knocked hell out of my mum and I refused to let anyone boss me around. But Scott... he's like this big, clever, teddy bear. He'd kill me for saying that. Rob might have the looks and Scott's got a broken nose and carries thirty pounds too many, but...' Clara laughed. 'He's a superhero. He sorts everything out for everybody.'

'What does he do?' Libby rested her hand on her chin, loving how misty-eyed Clara had become.

'Immoral corporate lawyer. He earns the big bucks.' Clara's smile grew. 'But you know what? He gave up the really big bucks and left London because this is where I was. Superhero, see?'

I need a superhero.

'Did you leave a hot boyfriend behind in Manchester?' Clara asked.

Libby shook her head, toying with her lighter.

'Why not? You're too pretty not to have one.' Clara's eyebrows raised, her eyes glinting. 'OMG, you're not a lesbian are you?'

'No.' Libby fought a smile, unable to resist a little teasing of her own. 'But Tallulah told me you two were when you moved here.'

'I deserved that,' Clara said, gracious in defeat.

Libby laughed, adoring how different her life had become over the last two days: job interview, running buddy and now, new friends.

'Did either of you know Maggie?' Libby asked.

Daisy nodded furiously. 'She used to make the most amazeballs lip balm out of weird herbs.'

'And my mum bought her dance studio about ten years ago,' Clara said. 'They'd been friends since–'

'Excuse me?' Libby shook her head, certain she'd misheard Clara. 'Her *dance studio?*'

'Yes, the ballet studio in Haverton.'

'Maggie taught ballet?' Why hadn't Zoë mentioned this tiny detail?

'Actually, Zoë and I used to go to class together. Didn't she go to the Royal Ballet School? I hated it, ballet. Street dancing was my thing, which Maggie ridiculed. She always looked down her nose, muttering about in her day at the Royal Ballet–'

'Maggie taught at the Royal Ballet?' Libby asked, her voice wavering.

Clara shook her head. 'No, Maggie was a ballerina, a regular Darcey Bussell until the car crash. It can't be nice to smash your pelvis, but you'd think that woman's life had ended the way she talked. She used to say Gosthwaite's where ballerinas come to die. My mum says...'

Clara twittered on, but Libby stared at the table, only hearing white noise. Maggie had been a ballerina, a broken ballerina. *Gosthwaite's where ballerinas come to die.* Libby stared at her glass, her heart racing.

Don't cry.

'Libby?' Daisy asked, touching her hand. 'Libby, are you okay?'

No, but years of stage performing didn't go to waste and she flashed a practised smile. 'Did you know Maggie was a witch?'

Daisy nodded, frowning. 'But are you–'

'And Tallulah reckons she was murdered.'

'What?' Daisy's frown vanished as she rested her elbow on the table, her chin in hand.

Clara followed suit. 'Why?'

'How?' Daisy asked, her eyes glinting.

Libby sipped her wine, fully in control once more, and explained what Tallulah had told her. 'So whodunit?'

Daisy, giggling, topped up their glasses. 'Surely the favourite has to be the one who inherits.'

'Ah, but Zoë didn't know she was first in line to the throne until after Maggie died.'

'Her parents?' Clara suggested.

Libby shook her head. 'I can't see it. As suburban as they come. What about a jealous love interest? I know about Stan. Do you know him?'

'Of course,' Clara said, 'but he wasn't the only one.'

As Clara sat back, it was Libby's turn to lean forwards, eager for the nugget of gossip. 'Who else was there?'

'Maggie had an affair with Peter, Sheila's husband—'

'But Sheila said he ran off with the woman from the butchers.'

'Maggie screwed Peter before that, about six years ago.' Clara's eyes lit up, eager to pass on her knowledge. 'Not that Sheila knows of course.'

'How on earth do you—'

'Primary school kids hear everything and are gloriously indiscreet,' Daisy explained, 'and Clara's the worst gossip, second only to her mum.'

'And Grace,' Clara added. 'What if Sheila found out and bumped Maggie off?'

Libby laughed. 'No way. They were friends.'

'With friends like that...' Clara grinned. 'What did you do after university?'

Libby, startled at the sudden topic change, knocked her napkin off the table. 'The usual, I suppose. Going for everything and settling for any role I could get.' She ducked down to retrieve her napkin and composure. 'Hey, I inherited something from Maggie. Her spell book.'

Clara dropped her frustrated pout. 'OMG, is it full of love potions and curses?'

While they dined on crab and langoustine ravioli, but only after swearing Daisy and Clara to secrecy, Libby regaled them with a glossed over account of the spell she'd performed and the others she'd like to try.

It wasn't something she'd planned to share, but at least it stopped Clara asking questions and the last thing Libby wanted to do was spoil a perfectly lovely afternoon by discussing her own ruined life.

Gosthwaite's where ballerinas come to die.

Chapter Eight

Libby perched on the herb garden wall, waiting for Robbie. All that stood between her and a job at Low Wood Farm was a quick riding test. Usually a formality, Andrea had said. She turned out to be Robbie and Xander's mother, but crikey, she wasn't like them at all. The woman had a disdainful glare that could wither roses, but after thirty minutes grilling Libby, she'd almost defrosted, and even managed a reluctant smile before she went to fetch Robbie.

Libby had never wanted a job so badly. Low Wood Farm was a dream with its whitewashed farmhouse, cobbled yard and tidy stables. Horses and Herdwick sheep grazed in the fields while chickens pecked at fallen pony nuts and an ancient Labrador lay in the sunshine. Maybe one day, she'd have a place just like it.

The kitchen door opened and Libby fought a smile. Had Robbie worked out it was her already? He came out, studying her CV, but when he looked up, he stopped. Okay, obviously he hadn't realised she was Olivia Wilde. For a moment, he simply stared at her, but then his eyes narrowed and he leaned against the doorframe, his arms folded.

'No,' he said.

What the hell? She stood up, placing her hands on her hips. 'I think there are laws about saying yes or no based on what someone looks like.'

He looked her over, giving a derisory laugh. What was wrong with her? She wore a sensible pink t-shirt with black jodhpurs, her hair in a neat plait. She looked pretty and professional. He hadn't minded her hair or make-up the day before when he kept topping up her glass and pinching her cigarettes. Why did it matter today?

'You want more reasons?' He held up her CV. '*Olivia* Wilde.'

'Libby's an accepted abbreviation.'

'St Mary Magdalene's in Wiltshire? Even Google's never heard of it.'

Bugger. 'It's a tiny independent school. I'm not surprised.'

'You've had five different jobs in the three years since you went to some unnamed university in London, and not one of them had anything to do with your BA in Performing Arts.' He shook his head, but his eyes glinted. 'Even if you didn't have a suspiciously vague CV, you're tiny, too small.'

'I'm five-five, above average height for a girl in the UK.' She rapped her nails against her hips and raised her chin. Was he taking the piss?

'You couldn't handle the horses. Can you even carry a bucket of water?' He waved a hand, dismissing her, but... his mouth was twitching at the corners. He *was* taking the piss.

'I've been carrying water buckets since I was six and I can handle any horse.' Her cheeks reddened as she folded her arms, steeling herself. If he wanted to play that game... 'But maybe not working for an arrogant bastard like you.'

He laughed and looked up to the sky. 'Do you really have BHS Stage Three?'

'I did an intensive course at the Lancashire Equestrian Centre. Give Bridget a call. But I've owned ponies for most of my life and I used to compete at local shows.'

'I suppose you're light enough to ride Lulu's horses.' He simply looked her in the eye for a moment. 'Why didn't you say anything yesterday?'

Because you were flirting and I liked it. 'Felt inappropriate.'

He nodded.

'I didn't mean to lie,' she added quickly, 'about my name. I'd assumed you would've worked it out from the newspaper.'

'Hadn't read it.'

'Oh.'

'Shakespeare's the bay in the end box. The tack room has everything labelled. I'll meet you in the ménage in ten minutes.'

'And sorry. For calling you an arrogant bastard.'

Shrugging, he walked away. 'I doubt it'll be the last time.'

Grateful he couldn't see her flaming cheeks, Libby crossed the yard. Why had she called him an arrogant bastard, even if he had been toying with her? He was a prospective employer – she ought to act accordingly. Relieved at her chance to ride, she crouched down to hug the old dog.

'Thank God I didn't bugger that up, mister. Do you think my run of good luck can last another day? If it isn't over, then maybe there's hope for Zoë and me.'

The night before, Libby had returned from the Mill, tipsy and stewing in Clara's revelation that Maggie had been a ballerina. The second Zoë walked through the door Libby demanded to know why she hadn't told her.

'How could you be so insensitive? You must've known I'd find out.'

'Let it go, Libby. Either join a dance class, or forget it.'

'I can't forget it, and I can't go back to class.'

'You need to move on, or you'll end up just like her, miserable and bitter with just a cat for company.'

'Should I just throw myself down the stairs now?'

'It's better than living half a life.'

It had been the worst argument they'd had since Zoë lost Libby's sparkly black leg warmers in Year Nine, but back then, they'd made up before supper. This time they'd gone to bed, slamming doors, still not speaking, and even Hyssop's purring hadn't lulled Libby to sleep. But she knew why Zoë had omitted a key fact about Maggie. There's no way Libby would have moved to a Home for Retired Ballet Dancers.

'You need a nanny, not her,' she heard Andrea snap, but couldn't make out Robbie's reply.

Hating herself for eavesdropping, Libby tiptoed nearer.

'My wife's leaving in two days and I'm not letting some clueless kid look after the girls. Or some battleaxe who thinks she can boss them, and me, around all the time. I need someone bloody good to look after the horses. The others weren't a day over nineteen and only the stupidest of the lot could actually drive.'

'Robert, be careful,' Andrea went on, 'because she might be twenty-five, well-educated and polite, she might have a full, clean driving license and an actual bloody car, but... she—'

'She what?'

'She looks like she charges by the hour.'

Robbie merely laughed.

Charges by the hour? Thank God it wasn't Andrea who employing her.

Fleeing to the tack room, Libby ran her hand over Shakespeare's saddle, the heady mix of leather, saddle soap and linseed oil reminding her of own childhood stable in Wiltshire. At eleven years old, she'd stood in her empty tack room, ready to leave for ballet school, certain she'd made the right decision. But now? What if horses could've been her life instead? Would she be happy?

What ifs? She shook her head, laughing at herself. Her parents hadn't brought her up to dwell on what ifs; she'd been taught to Just Bloody Do It. And don't bugger it up.

With Shakespeare gleaming after a quick brush over, she slipped on his tack, her fingers fumbling to fasten the buckles. She hadn't been this nervous during her BHS exams. Shakespeare rubbed his head against her shoulder, almost knocking her over as he sniffed against her pocket. She laughed and obliged, sneaking him a Polo mint.

'Please look after me, mister,' she said, kissing his nose.

He stood like granite in the yard, never fidgeting while she adjusted her stirrups, and as he walked on, into the ménage, she relaxed. Thank god, Robbie wasn't waiting already. She'd been twelve minutes by her watch.

Taking it easy, she walked Shakespeare once around the school, before nudging him into a trot. They glided through twenty metre circles. She needed the slightest leg action, the lightest of hands to control him, but his muscles twitched, ready to explode beneath her. Tallulah had made him look like a school hack, but that eleven year-old girl had to be one hell of a rider.

Robbie and Tallulah arrived, perching on the high railed fence, but Libby refused to let their scrutiny faze her. She nudged Shakespeare into a canter and took him through two flawless figure-eights before Robbie whistled her over. Libby listened carefully as he explained the simple five jump course. Nothing was over a metre with the first a tiny warm-up cross pole. She stifled a yawn.

'Late night?' Robbie asked, his face betraying no emotions.

Libby shook her head. 'Didn't sleep well.'

Unwilling to discuss the matter, she squeezed Shakespeare on. Instantly, he moved into a bouncy trot, looking towards the first jump with his ears pricked. They sailed over the jumps, wiping away Libby's fatigue and leaving her itching to do the course again, but with the poles raised another twenty centimetres.

I love this horse.

Slowing to a trot, she patted Shakespeare's neck, grinning like a village idiot, but Robbie didn't appear remotely pleased with her efforts.

'Lulu, get Dolomite,' he said.

Tallulah jumped off the fence, but not before Libby clocked her wide-eyed moment of hesitation. Taking slow, steady breaths, Libby walked Shakespeare on a long rein, utterly aware Robbie still watched her. Minutes ticked by and Libby's apprehension grew until Tallulah led in a beautiful dapple-grey gelding with a near black mane and tail.

Libby spent a minute saying hello, but Dolomite side-stepped, eyeing her with mistrust from under his forelock as she prepared to mount.

'He's strong,' Tallulah said, as she held the offside stirrup. 'Really strong and he falls out on the left–'

'Lulu,' Robbie snapped.

Okay, this was a test. Libby smiled down at her little friend and winked. 'Thanks.'

Ten minutes later, Libby's arms burned and she needed every core muscle she'd ever developed as she fought to keep the bloody grey steam train at a steady trot through ridiculously wonky circles. This wasn't a riding test. It was riding torture.

'Same course as before,' Robbie shouted, his eyes squinting against the sun.

Libby relaxed her hands a touch, letting the gelding move into a canter, but instantly regretted it. He wasn't on the bit and she wasn't in control. They careered toward the first jump, a tiny fifty centimetre warm up, but Dolomite ducked out, shying as if she'd set him up for Beecher's Brook.

Libby landed on his neck, losing her stirrups and her last shreds of control. Somehow, as Dolomite bolted to the far corner of the school, she stayed on, but more though luck than anything remotely resembling ability. She swore. Okay, so he didn't have Shakespeare's natural affinity with jumping. No wonder Tallulah looked so hesitant.

'Okay, baby. You're okay.' She placed a gentle hand on his neck but he flinched as if she'd shocked him with two thousand volts. 'And, God, do I know how that feels. They're just silly jumps. We can do this.'

After a little more soothing, he calmed and she walked him on, remembering the nervy eventer she'd ridden under Bridget's instruction: *Don't fight him. Work with him. You're a team.* Dolomite settled into a trot, and Libby kept up her gentle words, reassuring him while her unrelenting legs and hands kept him going forward.

'You are going over this, mister.'

Come on Good Luck spell, don't fail me now.

Dolomite pulled to the right, trying to duck out again, but she held him. It might've been as ungainly as her first lesson *en pointe*, but he lurched over.

'Three feet. Easy-peasy,' she said, setting him up for the second.

Despite tensing up, he flew over and popped over the third with his ears pricked. Robbie whistled, waving her back, and Libby fought her smile, not wanting to put pride before a spectacular descent into the sand.

Robbie turned to a beaming Tallulah. 'Told you he could do it.'

'What?' Libby frowned but Robbie was already walking away. God, he was hard work.

Tallulah threw her arms around Dolomite's lathered neck. 'That's the first time Dol's gone over anything higher than a trotting pole.'

'You're joking.' Libby dismounted.

She shook her head. 'Dad sold him as a yearling but we heard he was being mistreated, so we got him back. He's getting better but he's still a nutcase. Dad must think you're brilliant to let you ride Dol.'

'Really? He doesn't seem too pleased.'

'He never does.' Tallulah shrugged.

With her legs still shaking, Libby led Dolomite back to his stable, unsure if she should get her hopes up. Exhausted from the sleepless night, a stressful interview and fifty minutes of schooling hell, she untacked Dolomite and leaned against his shoulder, still holding the saddle in her weary arms.

Robbie appeared with two steaming mugs. 'Tea? Lulu's going to walk him around.'

Grateful, Libby deposited the tack and collapsed onto a wooden bench.

'You have the sketchiest CV I've ever seen,' Robbie said sitting next to her, 'but despite that, and my appalling interviewing skills, how do you fancy a job?'

She laughed, resting her head against the wall behind her. 'Really?'

'Got any fags?'

'You are priceless.' But dutifully she took out a pack and a lighter.

'I'd rather smoking was kept nearer the house where everything's less flammable, but never in front of Tilly or Dora. Lulu's seen everything. Come on, I'll show you around.'

He led the way to the far end of the L-shaped stable block, where Shakespeare stood with his head over the door. A little brass plaque declared his name and birth date.

'You bred him?' she asked, rubbing the gelding's ears.

'The first for Lulu. She will hit you if you call her that, by the way. She thinks he's dull.'

'He's amazing.'

'I think so too, but she's head over her half-chaps for Dolomite. Can't handle him, of course.'

'Yes, I can imagine. Thanks for that.'

'I needed to know what you could do.'

'And what can I do?'

'I've no idea yet, but you're more than capable of schooling Dolomite. I want him ready for Lulu in a year's time. She's struggled in the pony classes because she's so bloody tall but at least now she can ride horses that suit her. Shakes will do for now, but I think her and Dolomite will work next year.'

'Why can't she get him ready herself?'

'She's eleven.'

'When I was...' Libby sipped her tea.

'When you were what?'

When I was eleven, I'd taken control of my own life. Why can't Tallulah? 'It's fine. I can school him.'

She followed him around the yard, unable to stop the comparisons with Kim. His arse was a lot nicer to start with, but he introduced her to the horses, never once calling them *nags* as he explained their life stories. Smokey, the elderly grey Shetland was Tallulah's first pony and Ebony, the cheeky Thelwell-wannabe was Matilda's – Dora's had yet to be bought, but Robbie had his eye on a skewbald he'd seen near Lancaster.

He peeked down at her pocket. 'Polos?'

Guiltily, she handed them over. 'I only gave Shakespeare one.'

'Meany.' Robbie fed two to Cleo, a stunning bay brood mare, and took one for himself. 'Max, the stallion goes in the field across the lane. He's quite the gent so you won't have any trouble with him.'

'What is he?'

'Andalusian-cross. My grandmother started the line.'

He pointed to the iPod in the tack room window. 'Lulu's. Bloody awful music but you'll be on your own mostly, so you'll probably need the radio for company. Lulu's back at school for another couple of weeks then she'll be hanging around, getting in your way.'

'She's confident for an eleven year-old.'

'Going on twenty. She'll have shows here and there – can you do early starts? You can have the hours back on Sundays.'

She nodded. 'Though I should warn you, my plaiting skills aren't the best.'

'Fortunately, mine are. You'll have to avoid the pub the night before.'

'I wasn't at the pub. What's the dog's name?'

'Cromwell. The cat's called Mittens. Don't ask. You look knackered.'

'Chickens?'

'They're Tilly's. We'll take care of them. Where were you then?'

'Home. Cromwell or Mittens need anything?'

'No. Make yourself at home in the kitchen. Tea, coffee, biscuits, toast. So what kept you awake at home?'

'None of your business.' She frowned at him, but realised he was trying not to laugh as they headed into the feed room at the far left of the L-shaped block. 'Look, there's no gossip. I had a fight with Zoë. I felt bad and couldn't sleep.'

'It's mostly nuts and sugar beet, but it's all on the board. What were you fighting over?'

'None of your business.'

He shook his head, still fighting a smile. 'Half eight 'til five. Tuesday to Saturday, but next week—'

'Want me to do Sunday and Monday too? First days on your own? Your mum explained.'

His teetering smile vanished. 'Can you?'

She nodded. 'I can't wait to ring Kim.'

'I can't believe you lasted a week. I'd have told her to piss off on day one. The old mare was bragging about how efficient you are. I'd love to see the look on her face when she finds out I've poached you.'

'You didn't poach me. Tallulah did.'

'Christ, don't tell her. It'll cost me another horse. Or worse, getting her ears pierced.'

'She's practically twelve and you won't let her get her ears pierced? You're the meany.'

He frowned down at her. 'I can see you being a bad example. If she starts dressing like you, you're fired. Now, aside from the usual stable jobs, the horses need exercising. And I don't mean a half hour tootle. Jupiter and Storm are up for sale and I want them fit, so plenty of schooling and hour long rides over the common.'

Libby saluted him, trying not to smile. If she did, she might just cry with happiness.

Back at Maggie's cottage, Zoë hovered in the kitchen.

'And?' she asked, blinking furiously, her nervous twitch.

Libby smiled. 'I've got a new job. Yay!'

Zoë laughed, producing a bottle of Prosecco from behind her back. 'And without getting fired from the previous one. Well done.'

The cork popped and Libby held a mug under the bottle as the wine overflowed. On the worktop behind Zoë sat a fat carrot cake, her usual apology to Libby. Heaven forbid she'd ever just say sorry.

'God, I get to ride the best horses in the county. What the hell do you do when you want to quit? Can I tell Kim to piss off?'

'Well I wouldn't burn your bridges but...' Zoë smiled briefly. 'Cake?'

'Please.' Apology accepted.

'I knew you wouldn't have come here if you knew Maggie was a dancer–'

'I know.'

'And I didn't want to do it on my own.'

Libby nodded. 'Why didn't you like her? Everyone else seems to think she was pretty cool.'

Zoë slumped against the kitchen units. 'I bet they weren't subjected to an hour of ballet class every day or getting smacked around the ankles with a walking stick if their turnout wasn't *just so*.'

'Clara said Maggie taught you both ballet.'

'No, she taught Clara. She terrorised me. Every summer from seven to eleven. Mum and Dad packed me off here, thinking they were giving me this great opportunity, but really they were sending me to boot camp. Lesson after lesson, and when I wasn't in class... she nagged me. You shouldn't eat this, you shouldn't eat that. You. Must. Lose. Weight.'

'Surely she wasn't that bad. I mean–'

'One summer, a bunch of us went blackberry picking. When she found out that I'd eaten between meals, she locked me in there.' Zoë glanced to the cupboard under the stairs. 'I was seven.'

Libby wanted to shake her head, unable to believe it, but then she remembered the gouges on the door. 'Oh my god, *you* made those scratch marks?'

'With one of her fucking stilettos, trying to get out. No drink, no food, no light, just me and the spiders. Locked in.'

Who would do that to a little girl? Libby stared wordlessly as Zoë stalked off to the garden. Zoë's anorexia had been the cause of their friendship, the initiating factor at least. When Zoë refused to eat bread at dinner that first day at school, Libby had called her stupid. Good dancers were athletes and athletes ate healthily. It's what Darcey said. And what Darcey said was law. But no one had ever told Zoë what Darcey said. As she had fifteen years before, Libby sat next to Zoë, resting her head on her friend's shoulder.

'When I got into school...' Zoë let out a long slow breath. 'It was over. God, the amount of girls who whined about summer school. It was bliss compared to here.'

'So why move here?'

Zoë shrugged. 'Face some demons.'

'Why didn't you ever mention her?'

'Remember our first day? Holly von Kotze kept banging on about how she'd trained with Tamara Rojo?'

Libby opened her mouth, but paused. Bragging about being mentored by one of the world's greatest ballerinas had caused the rest of Year Seven to blank Holly for a week.

'Are you about to tell me that Maggie was—'

'Margaret Keeley, the ballet legend.'

Libby barely knew what to do with the information. What happened to the provincial old lady she'd first pictured Maggie to be? 'What happened to her jewellery?'

'Jewellery? You mean that hideous jade pendant?' Zoë shrugged. 'I assume Mum kept it. God, it was ugly. Like its owner.'

'Sheila next door said it was an emerald?'

Zoë's eyes flashed. 'Seriously?'

'Sheila next door reckons it's worth twenty *grand*.'

'Get the f—' Zoë laughed. 'Mum, better not bloody have it. That baby's *mine*.'

Libby grinned, loving the return of her friend's smile. 'What about Mr Coffee Shop? How was your breakfast date?'

'I'm not sure the pine cone works. He stood me up.'

No one stood Zoë up. Ever. 'Really?'

'I walked past. Slowly. He wasn't there.'

'What, but you didn't go in?'

'Do I look desperate?'

'But—'

'He had his chance.' Zoë flashed a smile. 'My new boss is okay though. He spent the day with me, discussing my sales strategies, my experience with high end buyers and the possibility of me managing the second home buyers with city bonuses. He's given me three to house-hunt for.'

Libby gave the expected squeal, but she recognised a brave face when she saw one. Over the last week, whenever Zoë spoke of the coffee shop guy, her eyes... well, as cheesy as it sounded, they *lit* up. She seriously liked this guy.

'Now,' Zoë said, topping up their mugs after the bubbles had died down, 'on a scale of one to fuck-me-now, where does this boss of yours feature?'

'About a nine. He might actually be the sexiest bloke I've ever met. Shame he's married to Angelina Jolie's doppelgänger.'

'While the cat's away...'

'Never.' Libby shook her head.

Zoë raised her eyebrows. 'Never say never.'

* * *

Michael Wray picked up his phone. 'I like her. Get me more.'

'She's actually pretty dull. What about her mate? Did you get the photos of her and Jonathan Carr?'

'Ah, forget her, the sheila's too prim. Unless there's a killer angle, makes it too hard to take the mental leap that she'd really do the shit we're suggesting. Olivia Wilde though... she looks like a hell-raiser. All we need to do is hint at bad behaviour. It's too fucking easy, mate.'

'I'll see what I can do.'

Michael Wray hung up, smiling at the photo of Miss Wilde's legs. Shame they couldn't get away with Page Three.

Chapter Nine

The first day at work – she'd had so many first days that she didn't usually feel even the smallest of butterflies, but arriving at Low Wood Farm a swarm appeared to have invaded her stomach. She mustn't bugger this up. This place could be her perfect distraction.

Robbie met her at the door, giving her a blatant once-over, the corners of his mouth twitching as he fought a smile. Libby didn't bother. She'd dithered for ages over what to wear. A black polo shirt and cream jodhpurs would've been the sensible thing to wear, but after his mother's *Charges by the Hour* comment, how could she resist something a little more fun?

The denim jodhpurs were bland enough, but her sleeveless *Fame* t-shirt allowed the straps of her hot pink bra to peek out and she'd layered on more eye make-up than she'd worn to the Mill. Harmless stable yard flirting? Bring it on.

'Morning,' he said, handing her a key, any humour now erased. 'For the tack room. It'll be in the kitchen, on the rack under the mirror. Just knock and come in.'

She toyed with the key. 'Kim's pissed off.'

'Kim's always pissed off.' He held out a list. 'That's the usual routine. I'm taking the girls out for the day, but if you need anything, my number's on the top.'

She nodded, a smile growing as she read the incredibly detailed list – tips on dealing with Dolomite's fragile nerves, which horses went in which paddocks, who she should school in the morning, who she should hack out in the afternoon.

'Tilly,' he called into the house. 'I'll be in the yard for five minutes.'

'Stay here,' Libby said. 'I'll be fine.'

But he came with her, wandering through to the yard, the horses whinnying, eager for their breakfast. As if she'd worked there for years, she headed into the feed room, and flicked on the light. Robbie followed her, watching as she laid the buckets out on the floor. She leaned down to scoop nuts out of the bin but paused, smiling up at him. If she wasn't mistaken, he'd been looking down her top. He really was priceless.

'You don't have to supervise. Stable yards are the same the world over.'

He leant against the wall with his arms folded as she topped up the nuts with sugar beet, following his instructions perfectly.

'It's your first day.'

'Feeding horses isn't exactly rocket science. And you've put everything on here.' She consulted the list. 'Storm will be the one kicking her door.' She paused, listing to the rhythmic thud. 'That'll be Storm, then.' She went back to the list. 'Dolomite will try to bite you when you drop his bucket in. It's all here. Don't worry. I'll be fine. They'll be fine.'

But he didn't leave. He watched her say hello to each horse, his eyes narrowing as she avoided Dolomite's gnashing teeth by opening his half-door and nudging the bucket in with her foot.

'Tallulah said he'd been mistreated.'

Robbie leaned against the door. 'He was in a pretty bad way when we found him. Half-starved and terrified. Christ knows what they did to him.'

Something nudged Libby's hand, but when she glanced down, instead of seeing the old Lab as she expected, a little girl with long black hair and beautiful green eyes stared up at her.

'Daddy told Mummy you were a tramp, but you don't look like the smelly man in town.' The little girl turned to Robbie. 'Is she a pop star like Hannah Montana?'

Libby pressed her lips together as she tried not to giggle, but Robbie laughed, finally letting go of his reserved attitude and she joined in.

'Thanks for that, Tilly.' He picked up his daughter, tickling her. 'This is Matilda, she's nearly four and the munchkin in the sandpit is Pandora, but we call her Dora. She's two. In my defence, you do look like a tramp. Your roots needed doing a month ago.'

Libby laughed, blushing a little. 'I look far too angelic when I don't have roots, which isn't the impression I want to give at all.'

He grinned. 'I doubt you could ever look angelic.'

'Oh, I can, but where's the fun in that?' She winked at Matilda. 'Now go and enjoy your day out.'

'Hey, less of the orders,' Robbie said, trying to look cross. 'Remember who's in charge.'

'Is Libby in charge now Mummy's not here?' Matilda asked.

He walked away shaking his head, telling Matilda off for ruining his attempt to be professional. Libby collected the wheelbarrow, unable to stop grinning.

And she couldn't all day.

By four o'clock, she'd taken to singing along to the radio and an old Beyoncé track had her itching to dance. To her horror, as she hung a hay net for Smokey, a shadow fell over the stable. She turned to confirm her fears and sure enough, Robbie leaned against the door frame, trying not to laugh.

'Oh, so you are a pop star like Hannah Montana.'

'I dance too,' she said, pushing a wayward purple strand off her face. 'Have you had a nice day?'

'Yes. You didn't ring.'

'I said I'd ring you if I needed you. I didn't need you.'

He wandered around, peering into the water buckets she'd scrubbed that morning, checking the hay nets she'd filled ready for the horses coming in, but he frowned when he noticed the cobweb free ceiling in the tack room.

'I hope you don't mind,' she said, 'but I was at a loose end so I tided the tack and feed rooms a bit. Sorry if you can't find anything.'

'But what about taking Storm out? I said–'

'Oh, god, we had the best ride this afternoon. She's awesome. And this morning, Dolomite actually did some half-decent twenty metre circles...'

She twittered on as she tied up the remaining hay nets, telling him about Max almost knocking her over, Ebony pinching the Polos from her pocket and Storm clearing the river on the common. It'd been the best day.

He studied the list. 'You cleaned the tack room *and* the feed room?'

To her surprise, when she nodded his frown deepened. 'Sorry, would you rather... It's just I don't like sitting around.'

He wandered over to the house, shaking his head. 'I knew you'd be trouble.'

How was she trouble? She'd crossed off everything on his list. How could he be mad at her?

Oh, please don't be mad at me.

But then he turned, almost smiling. 'Tea?'

It had to be the best first day at work she'd ever, ever had. Ever.

'Want one?' Robbie asked as he wound a corkscrew into a bottle of Rioja.

Libby hung up the tack room key, stalling. Well, this was new. And surely a really bad idea.

After day one, she'd thought he was easy-going, fun, the perfect boss, but on day two, she'd turned up, wearing a *Little Miss Trouble* t-shirt, thinking it'd make him smile. It didn't. He'd glanced up from his newspaper, taking the time to look her over, scowl and say, *the list's on the side*. Mr Golding, it turned out, could be an utter grumpy arse at times.

At times.

Every morning for the past two weeks he would barely speak to her, a smile seemingly impossible, but when he came home just before four o'clock, he'd make her a cup of tea, steal a cigarette and they'd chat about the yard. He was definitely testing her knowledge, and she could hardly describe him as friendly, but despite being able to ride, jump and school the amazing horses she increasingly found herself clock-watching, eager for their tea and chat.

Oh, he was married and strictly off limits, but was it wrong to want him to like her, to respect her?

But that day four o'clock passed with no tea and chat. He'd called her at three, spoiling her first hack out on Shakespeare by asking if she'd pick up the two youngest of his daughters from the child-minder. He'd been desperate, he'd said please, he'd called her *Lib* – so of course, she'd said, yes. And even though the girls intimidated her to nail-biting levels, she'd even agreed to make tea for them.

When he arrived, not long after six, she'd been sitting in the sandpit, while Dora dictated how she wanted a fairy kingdom to be built. Libby had stayed in the sandpit, hoping to make her point – he couldn't impose on her like this; babysitting wasn't her job. But he'd scooped up his girls, kissing them on the head and apologising over and over for being late. For the last four days, she'd watched his life revolve around those two little girls – which hair band did Matilda want to wear, did Dora prefer chicken or fish for tea? He was such an amazing dad. By the time he'd held out a hand, helping Libby up from the sand, her point had gone blunt.

And now there he was, at the end of week two, offering her a vast glass of rioja rather than the usual mug of Tetley. Arse. Having a drink with him couldn't possibly be a good idea. It was overstepping boundaries. She ought to say no; she ought to say no and leave as quickly as she could.

'Christ, it's been a bloody awful day,' he said. 'The new KP quit before they'd even finished prep and the accountant rang because ten grand had *gone missing*. Turned out he was an incompetent twat and the money's all there, but bang goes my day. So do you want one?'

He was offering her a glass of wine, for heaven's sake, not a dirty weekend in Paris. And she didn't fancy him. 'I do have a life you know.'

'I know. Did you find something to feed them okay?'

Okay? There was half a high-end restaurant in the fridge. 'Ham, cheese and Marmite toasties, with cucumber and grapes, followed by ice cream and raspberries. They chose the menu, not me. Look, they're lovely kids, but I don't get them, little kids.'

He pressed his lips together for a moment, clearly trying not to laugh. 'Then don't see them as little kids. Look at them like really short people. They'll prefer it too.'

'But they kind of freak me out. They stare. A lot.'

'You have purple streaks in your hair. Who doesn't stare at you?' He smiled, offering her a vast splash in a vast glass. 'But thank you.'

Against her better judgement, she took the glass. 'You're welcome, but don't do it again. Please.'

He merely flashed his biggest smile before checking the girls were still engrossed in what Libby now recognised as *Charlie and Lola*. 'Fag?'

'You should buy your own. You must smoke about ten a day of other people's.'

'If I bought some, I'd go through thirty. How was Jupiter?

'Awesome.' She took a sip of the wine. 'God, that's nice.'

They sat on the herb garden wall, where he could keep an eye on the girls through the living room window, and merrily debated Libby's suggestion that it was Sambuca's back causing his reluctance to jump, not a stubborn attitude. But after a minor skirmish between Matilda and Dora distracted them, Robbie suddenly changed the conversation.

'So this life of yours, what are you up to this weekend?'

'Not sure,' she'd replied, a little thrown. He *never* asked about her life outside work usually, and when he finally did, what did she have to reply with? A quiet night in. Alone. Ugh. 'Can't do too much tonight because I'm running with Xander tomorrow. You know he's in training for the Lum Valley fell race? Well, he's daring me to do it too.'

'Christ, you know how to live. Staying in on a Saturday night so you can go running on Sunday?'

Libby cringed. 'I know, but Jack said there was a band playing at the King Alfred tomorrow. Maybe I'll–'

'Jack?' Robbie's eyebrows raised. 'Pulled already?'

'Of course not.' Was it the wine or his suggestion that had her cheeks flushing? 'He's seeing Grace.'

'Never stopped him before.'

'Well, it would me,' she'd replied. 'Cheating's wrong.'

'Ooh, you're a moralistic little thing, aren't you?'

Robbie didn't bother to restrain his mocking smile and Libby's cheeks burned with mortification. The last thing she wanted was for him to think she were some dull-as-dishwater goody-two-shoes.

'Well, be careful,' he went on. 'There are some unsuitable types around here, totally untrustworthy.'

'Sounds interesting.' It was supposed to be a joke, but came out like she meant it. Oh god, time to leave.

'At least remember to play hard to get.'

Flashing a brazen smile that Zoë would be proud of, Libby handed him her empty glass. 'But where's the fun in that?'

And then she fled.

'You're late,' Zoë said, plastering on another layer of scarlet lipstick. 'Boss making you work late?'

Libby's face flushed. 'No. Drink wine actually.'

'Oh, hello...'

'Not like that. I looked after his kids–'

'What the hell? You hate kids.'

'I don't hate them.' Libby picked at her nail polish, avoiding looking Zoë in the eye. 'They just... they're weird. But he was stuck. How could I say no?'

Zoë pressed her scarlet lips together for a moment, clearly fighting her giggles. 'You so fancy him'

'I do not.' Libby shook her head. 'So where are you going?'

'Drunken Duck. Nikki-two-ks-and-an-i has arranged to meet up with some of the blokes from the Kendal office. She says a couple of them are fit as.'

'What about Mr Coffee Shop? Have you been back there?'

'Nope. Are you sure you don't want to come out?'

'Yep.'

'At least go to the pub and say hello to Jack. Wind Grace up as payback for her quotes in the paper.'

Facing up to Grace was the last thing Libby intended to do. She had a better idea. The second Zoë disappeared in a taxi, Libby reached under her bed, feeling for the spell book. Would Maggie have a charm or incantation, something stronger than the pine cone that would have Zoë's Mr Coffee Shop devoted in no time?

The bookmark, a quarter of the way through, marked the point she'd reached with her reading. *Chocolat* she'd devoured in days, but the spell book was heavier going, sometimes requiring Google translations to even begin to understand what the Latin pages contained.

Using random luck to guide her, Libby flicked through the remaining three quarters, landing at a retribution charm. It might be tempting to use against Grace for the newspaper quote, but it wasn't Libby's style and the Wiccan motto was: *If it hurt none, do what you will.* She skipped forward a handful of pages. *Summon Your True Love.* Oh, hello. The spell looked easy enough, a bit of candle burning, some flower petals, a little bag and make a list of your ideal man's traits. Easy. She could do a practice run on herself. At the top of the page, in what she'd come to assume was Maggie's handwriting, was a note: *Imp! Grounding a must before performing.*

Grounding? Hadn't she read about that a few nights ago? Marking the page, she flicked towards the front of the folder, searching for the lengthy Wiccan meditation instructions. If she was going to do this, she ought to do it properly.

Libby showered and changed into a cotton vest and linen trousers then, wearing no make-up, perfume or jewellery, she stood barefoot on the lawn and closed her eyes, recalling the instructions she'd tried to memorise.

Her toes wiggled in the grass and she shifted her weight, focussing on sending her breath down into the ground beneath her, spreading it like roots amongst the bugs and worms. As she mentally reached the core, to the Earth Goddess, she sent down the feelings she wanted rid of – her longing to be a professional dancer again, her attachment to Paolo, her anger at Grace, then she imagined feeling the energy from the Earth coming back up, past the worms and bugs in the soil, rising through her body.

Feeling faintly ridiculous but justifying it as no different to the yoga she'd been doing for years, Libby sent her energy up to the sky. And after a similar ritual swapping energy with the Sun Star, she found herself part of an unending chain. With each in-breath she sent energy from the Earth Goddess up to the Sun Star, and on her out-breath, the energy fell from the sky back through her body and down to the Earth.

A few breaths later, Libby's feet started tingling. Had she hyperventilated? She crouched down, touching the ground, closing her eyes and taking a moment.

'Blessed be,' she whispered.

Well, that was weird. She studied her feet, all fine now. Actually, she felt fine too, but then meditative breathing had always relaxed her.

Assuming she was suitably *grounded*, Libby sat cross-legged on the grass, in the same central spot on the lawn, and lit a red candle. Okay, ideal man traits: *good looks, 25-35, honest.*

She wrote them on a torn piece of chintz wallpaper – more parchment-like than A4 notepaper, she'd decided. That should do it. She burned the list with a handful of red rose petals, tipping the cooled ashes into a small red silk pouch she'd found in Maggie's magic box. Molten wax sealed the bag and the spell.

'Blessed be,' she whispered, again touching the ground.

Hyssop watched from the patio and, if she didn't know better, she could've sworn he was smiling.

Chapter Ten

'Well, this is it, Lib, as good as life gets in the countryside.' Zoë strode across the Green, an amenable but utterly fake smile pasted to her lips. 'Sunday afternoon watching a tribute folk band. Yee-ha.'

Grinning, Libby took off her denim jacket and tied it around her waist. 'Oh, come on. The sun's shining. It'll be fun.'

'Fun?' Zoë raised her eyebrows. '*Mumford and Dad,* really?'

'Give them a chance.' Libby elbowed her. 'And we might meet some hot guys...'

'You just want to prove you don't fancy your boss.' Zoë's smile turned ten times more real as Libby's cheeks turned cerise.

'I don't fancy him.'

'Liar.'

'I just think this might be somewhere we can meet decent guys.'

'*Decent?*' From the rag-tag mix outside the King Alfred, the only blokes ranking over a seven were sitting with their significant others and the below sevens were clearly single for a reason. 'You mean *nice,* don't you?'

'You want more blokes grabbing your boobs?'

'Jesus, no.' Zoë pouted. The night before, her night out with Nikki-two-ks-and-an-i, had started okay when the Kendal boys picked up the tab for dinner, but they quickly expected payment in kind. One arsehole, Adam, had sidled up behind Zoë and copped a feel of her tits. Without asking. The temptation had been to punch him in the face, but she made do with ramming a metal-tipped stiletto heel into his limited edition shell-toes. 'Nice might be doable.'

'Oh God.' Libby wrapped her arms around herself. 'Grace is working. She'll spit in my drink.'

I'd like to see her try. Hell would have to freeze over before Zoë let some yokel like Grace bully Libby. 'I'll get the drinks. You get–'

'Libby!' Clara strode over, her smile huge. 'Daze and I are child free. We've got pink fizz. Come and join us. We're in the beer garden out the back. The band are just getting ready.'

Libby's delight couldn't be more apparent. 'Zo?'

'I'll be there in a sec.'

'Why?' Libby's eyes narrowed and she scanned the bar. 'Or *who?*'

Fighting a conniving smile, Zoë glanced towards Mark #1 – Sparky. The twenty-one-year-old was way below her usual baseline, but he was the only electrician she could even get to come look at the wiring. His six-week time-frame was simply unsatisfactory.

Libby shook her head. 'Don't eat him alive.'

'Never say never.'

Zoë stood for a moment as Libby all-but skipped away with Clara, waving to Sheila from next door and Lynda from the Post office. There was never any doubt Libby would make friends in the village, but Zoë had never expected her to embrace the lifestyle quite so easily. Until a couple of years ago, Libby's world was studded with artists, models and dance megastars; she'd lived in London, Moscow and New York. Was she really happy with this provincial life?

'Bacardi and soda,' Zoë said to Grace, her tone tinged with aspartame, before sidling closer to Sparky. 'How are you?'

He abandoned his chat with that old soak – Stan or someone – his gaze immediately travelling down to her cleavage. 'You alright?'

'I just want to say thanks for coming out so quickly the other week.' Zoë flicked her hair back. There was no point going as far as fluttering her eye lashes – Sparky still hadn't looked up. 'You're *such* a lifesaver. I can't *wait* for the electrics to be fixed.'

'Well, you know it'll–'

'I got zapped again this morning...' It was only a tiny white lie. Libby was the one who'd stupidly plugged the iron in. 'I'll feel sooo much safer when they're done.'

'But I don't know–'

Zoë placed her hand on his arm and let her smile grow. The boy was buff. 'I should buy you a drink. You've no idea how grateful I am.'

Sparky appeared to have stopped breathing. 'Okay...'

'You want to watch her,' mumbled Stan. 'She's a siren. Like her aunt.'

'*Great*-aunt,' Zoë corrected him, her hand still on Sparky's arm. If he suspected she might actually be capable of luring him to a sticky end, he certainly didn't show it. 'What can I get you?'

'Cumberland,' he answered, his ears turning pink.

He'd so be doing the electrics in the next fortnight.

* * *

Poor Sparky. Libby wasn't sure if she should warn him off or encourage him to sweep Zoë off her high heels. He seemed okay. Certainly a lot nicer than Zoë's usual cohorts – Libby had yet to meet one she actually *liked*.

In front of the pub, Libby lit a cigarette and stretched out her legs, loving the gentle breeze circulating the twenty-five degree air. The walled beer garden had been as stifling as a marquee in comparison, which wasn't helping her fuzzy head – though neither was Daisy's refusal to let anyone's glass remain empty for more than half a second. Libby alone must've drank almost a bottle.

'Mind if I join you?' Jack hovered in the doorway, one hand raking through his toffee brown hair.

'No. Of course not.' *I didn't summon you. You have a girlfriend.* 'Is Grace working tonight?'

Jack sat down, but looked away. 'Yes.'

'Do you two live together?'

'Sometimes. Mostly not. It's a bit... And she's... Look, can we not talk about Grace?'

Okay, but at least you won't forget she exists this time. Libby took a long drag on her cigarette. 'You must've known Maggie fairly well. What was she like?'

'Manipulative. Cold.' Jack glanced to the window where Zoë and Sparky were laughing. 'Like her.'

'Zoë's not like that.'

'Oh yeah? What's she doing with Sparky?'

Libby glanced at her feet. Busted. 'She's not cold though.'

'You know you're unbelievably pretty when you blush.'

Surely he wasn't flirting. They'd just talked about Grace. 'Jack...'

He leant a little closer, his eyes twinkling, daring her. 'What?'

'Stop it.'

'Stop what?'

'You have a girlfriend.'

For a moment his smiled faded. 'And if I didn't?'

He smelled so good, so fresh, his woody aftershave drifting on the summer air. No, no, no. He wasn't who she summoned. He couldn't be. Libby's skin crawled. But what if he was? He was twenty-seven, cute as a button with green eyes and was this him being honest? Had she summoned Jack? And what if summoning spells were a two way street? What if the spell worked and the Wiccan magic was tearing him away from his girlfriend and pushing Libby towards him?

Quickly, Libby took the little silk bag from her back pocket and tipped the dusty contents into the nearest plant pot, giving it back to the earth, ending the spell. She'd never willingly destroy a relationship. Never.

'What was that?' Jack asked.

'Nothing.' Libby's cheeks burned. Like she'd admit to casting silly love spells.

'It's just Grace has a bag just like it. Carries it everywhere.'

Grace had a summoning pouch, why?

'Let's get out of here,' he said, quietly. 'Grab a drink at the Black Bull.'

Was he joking? Libby almost laughed, but flashed a polite smile instead as she stood up. 'Sorry, but one night stands aren't my kind of thing.'

'You need to drop a few inhibitions,' Jack said, his threatening smile and twinkling eyes making it impossible to know if he were being serious or just plain teasing her.

Either way, it had Libby slump against the wall and fold her arms defensively. Why did everyone think her such a goody-two-shoes? Was she a goody-two-shoes? Zoë wouldn't give a second thought to a one night stand with someone like Jack.

'I'm not inhibited,' Libby said, her cheeks burning.

Slowly, Jack got to his feet and stepped toward her. 'Then let's go.'

'What, you're daring me? No.' But her stupid nipples pinged into life.

'We'll go back to yours...' His voice was low, his breath tickling her cheek. 'And fuck in the hallway, up against the wall.'

Libby stared at him. The idea of shagging in the hallway, up against the wall on a one night stand with a guy who had a girlfriend appalled her. At least it should have. The reality was that it turned her on more than she'd even admit to Zoë.

A loud beeping brought her to her senses.

'Oh, for...' Jack checked a beeper clipped to his belt and swore. 'It'll be another bloody grass fire.'

Libby stared in horror. 'You're a fireman?'

'I'm a fireman.' He stood up and flashed the cheekiest grin. 'Play your cards right, Tinker Bell, and you might get to see me in the uniform.'

He shot her a wink before sprinting off down the road.

Desire surged through her once again. A fireman? No, no, no. She'd have to perform the summoning spell again, but this time she'd be more specific with her wishes. Wait, when had she started taking this Wiccan mumbo-jumbo seriously? *Maybe the day I stood in the garden and grounded myself with the Earth Goddess and bloody Sun Star.* She had to get a grip. She watched as he disappeared around the corner. It might be mumbo-jumbo, but why did he have to be a fireman?

Slowly, she stubbed out her cigarette and turned to head back inside. Crikey, she needed a very big glass of–

Grace was standing in the window, her arms folded, her mouth set in a grim line. How much of that had she seen? Libby wanted to apologise, to set her straight, to explain that she'd never mess around with someone else's boyfriend, but would Grace ever believe it?

Libby barely believed it herself.

* * *

'Ah... fuck... oh shit, your arse is so fucking sexy.'

Under normal circumstances, Zoë would've been hard pushed not to laugh, but riding the hell out of Sparky she struggled not to mutter a few guttural expletives herself. The boy was ripped, killer abs, but without that paper bag, she'd opted for the reverse cowgirl. He hit places most blokes didn't know existed

'Do you want to touch my arse?' Zoë whispered, knowing it'd trip him over the edge and sure enough, he cried out, his body bucking under her.

'I'm coming, you horny little bitch. I'm coming, I'm coming...'

His thumb pressed into her arse, pushing her down onto his cock and Zoë had to bite back her own screams as she came. He might be totally clueless with his tongue and a girl's clit, but in the end, Sparky wasn't a bad lay. But what the hell was she going to do with him now? For a minute, she stayed impaled on his softening dick. Ideally she wanted him out of the house, but if she kicked him out, he might back out of rewiring the house the following week.

Gingerly, she climbed off and turned to him. 'Sparks?'

He lay spread-eagled, eyes closed and mouth gaping. Shagged into a sex coma. Zoë couldn't help a smug grin. He'd be doing the electrics even if she kicked him out in the morning without so much as a kiss on the cheek. Feeling unusually generous, she peeled the condom off him and dropped it in the bin on her way out of the room.

'Is it safe to come out?' Libby asked, poking her head round the doorway of her room.

Stifling a giggle, Zoë nodded and they fled downstairs.

'You pulled Sparky?' Libby asked she put the kettle on. 'Why?'

'He's got a huge dick?' Zoë offered, but she knew what Libby was getting at.

'Please tell me you didn't shag him just so he'd do the electrics sooner rather than later.'

'Okay.' Zoë lit a cigarette. 'I didn't shag him just so he'd do the electrics sooner rather than later.'

Libby raised her eyebrows. 'Really?'

'But he's rewiring the place next week.'

'Zo...'

'What? It wasn't exactly a one-way deal. He had a lot of fun.'

'I heard.' Libby looked up at the ceiling. '*I'm coming, I'm coming, you horny little bitch.*'

Unable to keep straight faces, they both fell apart, laughing until tears rolled down their cheeks and hissing at each other to shut up. The last thing they wanted was for Sparky to wake up.

'What happened after I left?' Libby asked more soberly.

'Grace and Jack had a fight. He stropped off to the Black Bull.'

Libby groaned, holding her head in her hands. 'How on earth have I wrecked their relationship? All I ever did was say hi to the guy.'

'At least the spell's working for you.'

'Spell? What spell?'

'The one on the house,' Zoë replied, surprised by Libby's defensive tone. 'You fancy Jack – oh, yes you do – and he tries it on. Your boss is offering you wine on a daily basis. Hell, even Paolo still rings once a week, don't think I haven't heard you talking to him. I'd hoped it might work for me too.'

'Er... Sparky.'

Zoë waved the idea away. 'He doesn't count. I don't need a spell to pull him, but Jonathan couldn't be less interested and look at Mr Coffee Shop.'

'Zo?' Libby nervously tucked her hair behind her ears. 'Promise you won't laugh?'

She promised no such thing and did indeed laugh out freaking loud when Libby told her about keeping Maggie's box of witchcraft and the spells she'd done.

'Fuck me, you're a dark horse at times, Ms Wilde.' Zoë stood up. 'Let's do it.'

'Do what?'

'The Summoning Spell. I'll summon my dream guy, and you can summon... well, someone who isn't Jack or Paolo.'

'Really?' Libby wandered, frowning, to her bedroom. 'Well, there's no messing around and you have to do the Grounding thing first.'

Although she was amused by how earnest Libby sounded, Zoë soon found herself sitting cross-legged in the middle of the back garden, no longer worrying if anyone could see them. The whole Wicca thing was nothing more than superstition and fantasy, utter mumbo-jumbo, but under the moonless black sky, the only light coming from the shining band of the Milky Way, Zoë frowned at her blank piece of torn wallpaper, nibbling the end of a pen.

'What are you putting?' she asked Libby.

'Good looks, 25-35, nice eyes, English, honest and single. That should rule out Paolo *and* Jack. Why don't you wish for someone with blue eyes who likes coffee?'

Grinning, Zoë shook her head and wrote: *A great shag with plenty of money.*

* * *

Michael Wray put down his knife to answer his phone, ignoring the disgruntled diners around him.

'Wray.'

'I've got her. In the green.'

'You ripper. Who with?' Michael Wray asked. 'Xander again?'

'No. Jack.'

Wray sighed. 'Not good enough, mate. I want someone that'll rock the local community. Try the blog.' He ended the call and refilled his glass.

'Who're you talking about?' asked the former Miss Haverton, picking at her *foie gras*.

Wray grinned. 'The new you.'

Chapter Eleven

Outside the cottage, splattered with mud and exhausted from running, Libby doubled over, gasping for breath.

'You just couldn't resist, could you?' Grace came down the steps outside the vets surgery, her arms wrapped around herself. 'We've been going out for ten years. Ten years. He's shagged eleven other girls that he's admitted to me.'

'But I haven't—' Libby panted, with her hands still on her knees, and glanced at the cottage. Would her legs get her there?

Grace's eyes were puffy, red and filled with hatred as she stood, hands on hips, her foot tapping. 'Usually, he gets wasted, shags them then buys me flowers to say sorry.'

'But I haven't shagged him.'

'No, you wouldn't, so what does he do? He splits up with me. Why couldn't you just shag him, get it out of his system?'

Jack had split up with Grace? Libby's head swam as she straightened. 'Grace—'

'Don't you dare. He told me about last night. Jack might wander every now and then, but he tells me everything. And he told me about the little red silk bag you carry everywhere with you.'

Libby blinked, the corner of her mouth twitching. 'But how do—'

'Who did you summon, Libby? My boyfriend?'

'No. I...' Her words were a whisper, mortification rising from her toes. She hadn't meant to summon him; she'd deliberately tried to exclude him. *Honest and Single.* Only now it turned out Jack was unfailingly honest and thoroughly single. 'It's just a silly spell. It's not even real.'

'You've got Maggie's book, haven't you? You're messing with something you don't understand. You've come here, a bloody off-comer with your hoity-toity accent.'

'I didn't—' Libby held her cramping thigh. She needed to stretch.

'Look at you. You're knackered. And you think you can do the Lum Valley fell race. In your dreams. You're a middle distance runner at best. You haven't got the stamina for fifteen miles.'

Libby's back stiffened. Stamina? Grace dared question her stamina. She had no idea what Libby could run through, dance through. 'I can do the race. Xander reckons I could go for the women's record.'

Grace laughed. 'I'll see you at the start line and I'll be waiting for you at the finish.'

Libby frowned, looking over Grace's curves. All the fell runners she'd seen had zero body fat.

'You've picked the wrong person to make an enemy of,' Grace hissed. 'You're going to regret this.'

'I haven't done anything.'

'You keep telling yourself that.' Grace stomped back into the vets, leaving Libby unsure whether to cry or scream.

'Libby?' Jack called from his mum's front doorway.

'This is your fault,' Libby snapped, striding up to him. 'Why couldn't you just leave me alone? You're an unfaithful arse. Do you really think I'd go out with someone who sleeps around?'

He folded his arms, scowling. 'I don't remember anyone asking.'

'Just leave me alone.'

'Yeah, well, just so you know, she'll kick your arse in the fell race. She holds the women's record and wins every year.' He ducked inside Sheila's house, slamming the door behind him and Libby fled.

How could everything go so wrong? All she'd wanted was a fresh start, but somehow she'd ended up inciting a feud with Grace and destroying a relationship. Flopping onto her bed, Libby's heel hit the plastic storage box containing Maggie's Wiccan trove.

She pulled out the box and threw in the symbolic candles she had stationed around her room, the sleeping charm from under her pillow, the little red summoning spell pouch and finally the spell book. Maybe it was hocus pocus or maybe it was more real than she'd ever imagined, but either way, Grace was right. Libby had no idea what she was messing with.

As she rammed the lid on, Hyssop padded across the bed to her. He rubbed his head against her hand then batted something shiny with his paw. Libby picked it up. The little silver amulet showed a naked woman holding an offering over her head. It supposedly promoted new beginnings, and as Hyssop's purr soothed her frustration, Libby closed her hand around it.

* * *

'Well, this is different,' came his voice, from the coffee shop as usual.

Zoë didn't stop walking.

'Not the killer staccato beat, or the chill-out tune.' He fell into step beside her. 'You're not late, or not-that-early. You're something else.'

Yeah, struggling to walk, thanks to Sparky. Zoë kept going, refusing to look at Mr Coffee Shop.

'You're not even talking to me?' he said.

Sod it. She stopped, wheeling around to face him. Jesus, he was cute, and those eyes... 'Do you know how many times I've been stood up? Once. By you.'

His eyes flickered, a moment of doubt flashing, but he replaced it with a smile. 'Guess I set myself out from the crowd.'

'No. You blew your chance.' But his lips were ten levels of kissable, despite the fact he'd undoubtedly taste of skanky roll-ups.

'Look, I'm sorry. I got offered a job that I couldn't say no to. If you'd have gone into the shop, Amy would've given you the note I left.'

Zoë folded her arms. 'You're not forgiven.'

'How about you make me pay for it? You can play hard to get until I'm on my knees if you like?' His eyes twinkled as he teased her and Zoë struggled not to smile.

'Sounds like something I'd do.'

'Fancy starting today? Five o'clock when you finish work?'

'Today?' She slowly shook her head. 'Today wouldn't be playing even remotely hard to get. Tomorrow.'

'See you then, beautiful.'

Really, she didn't give a crap about playing hard to get, but she'd promised to be home by six with takeaway pizza and a bottle of Jack Daniels – a depressed Libby's poison of choice. And if she were truly honest with herself, going on a date when she was still saddle sore from shagging Sparky the night before felt... dirty. The odd thing was that, by Zoë's standards, that ought to make it more fun.

So why was it different with Mr Coffee Shop?

* * *

By five o'clock, Libby was still sweeping the yard, her list of jobs far from finished. When Robbie came out of the house, she leant on the brush handle, barely able to look at him. This was it, the moment she'd lose her perfect job. She'd arrived twenty minutes late that morning, hung-over to hell after way too much Jack Daniels and exhausted after a largely sleepless night, most of it spent throwing up takeaway pizza. Since Robbie was usually so bloody grumpy in the morning, she'd expected him to sack her on the spot, but he'd closed the Land Rover door, merely frowning at her as he drove away.

'The yard's clean,' he said quietly. 'Come on.'

The fact he was carrying two glasses of wine suggested he wasn't sacking her – at least, no one had handed her a glass of red with her P45 in the past. Taking a deep breath to summon a little bravery, she hung up the yard brush and followed him.

He bypassed their usual seat on the herb garden wall and led her round to a small, perfectly idyllic, if a little unkempt side garden. Robbie sat on the chair-swing beside the French doors into the living room where he could keep an eye on his daughters who were watching TV and eating berries. One day, Libby would live somewhere like this. Although she'd mow the lawn and the scarecrow wouldn't be at forty-five degrees to the weeds he protected. One day.

Robbie patted the swing beside him and handed her a glass. 'Okay, out with it. What's up?'

She curled up, hugging her knees. 'Boy trouble.'

'Who?'

'None of your business.'

He stretched out his long legs. 'Who?'

'You'll only say he's inappropriate and not to be trusted.'

'Been playing hard to get?'

'I don't play. I am hard to get.' She paused to sip her wine. 'Jack.'

His face darkened with blatant disapproval and the little muscle in his jaw twitched. Why did he look like he wanted to yell at her? Was he protecting her like a daughter? He shouldn't; he was only five years older than her. Or was he... she gave a little shake of her head, dismissing the stupidest of ideas. He was looking out for her. That was all.

'What happened to his girlfriend stopping you?'

'He broke up with her.'

'To go out with you?'

She nodded. 'She laid into me yesterday. She's devastated.'

'Understandable. You've been messing around with her boyfriend.'

'I didn't mess around with him. I told you. Cheating's wrong.'

'But, if you didn't do anything wrong, it's not your fault.'

'I still feel guilty.' A fat tear fell down her cheek.

'Why?'

'Because... I caused a problem in their relationship.'

'If they had a decent relationship, he wouldn't be chasing you.' He fiddled with her lighter, frowning again. 'Now will you listen when I tell you to stay away from unsuitable, untrustworthy types?'

She wiped her eyes. 'Know any suitable types?'

He laughed a little, but didn't offer any suggestions.

'You don't have any single friends?' she asked.

Grinning into his glass, he shook his head.

'Really, not any, half-decent single friends? No chefs at the restaurant?'

'All completely unsuitable and untrustworthy.'

She swatted his arm, smiling for the first time that day. 'Sorry for being late this morning.'

'Obviously it's never to happen again, but under the circumstances, I'll let you off.'

She lit another cigarette and sighed. 'Life must be so much easier when you're married with kids.'

He laughed, but with no humour.

'What?' she asked. 'You have the perfect life.'

His smile fell as he leaned forwards, resting his elbows on his knees. The silence grew, but Libby refused to break it. What the hell was wrong? She sipped her wine.

'I think Vanessa's shagging the viola player in the string quartet. And if she's not, then it's only a matter of time until she does.'

Libby took a slow breath. 'And why do you think she's shagging the viola player in the string quartet?'

'How come you took Shakespeare out today? I asked you to take Storm out.'

'Shakes cheers me up.' She shifted to sit cross-legged, her knee an inch or so from his thigh. 'You're avoiding my question.'

'I am.' He still stared at the grass.

'Hey, misery adores company. Out with it.'

And then he did something that surprised her. He sat back and told her everything. He explained how Vanessa had taken up the cello again, twelve years after she'd stopped playing, and seemed to lose interest in everything else around her. First, the garden suffered, then her friends, and eventually, her family. And when she landed a place in the string quartet, the constant practice, the frequent evenings at rehearsals and the never-ending calls to *Jason* for advice, drove her further and further away.

'The worst of it,' Robbie said, lighting yet another of her cigarettes, 'is how happy she is. It's as if I bore her and only that wanker who plays the viola can make her smile.'

'Have you spoken to her about it?'

He gave a derisory laugh. 'Argued about it? Yes.'

'Then why did you let her go on tour?'

'It's her dream. I'm not going to stop her.'

'But you have no evidence, just paranoia?'

He nodded.

'You should trust her,' Libby said. 'She must be trusting you.'

He turned to face her, his frown growing, and Libby's cheeks burned. Crikey, she hadn't meant herself. Surely, he must know loads of beautiful women. He could have his pick of the single women. And probably most married ones too. The moment passed and he resumed his study of the grass.

'I'm not sure she cares anymore,' he added quietly.

'What's he like, the wanker who plays the viola?'

'One of those talented, good-looking, charming sorts. And he's French.'

'Sounds awful.'

'Yeah well, he has a ponytail.'

'Is it a very long ponytail? Do you think he's compensating for something?' She elbowed him and to her delight, he laughed.

How the hell could his wife be even considering playing around? Robbie was… well, he was perfect. Libby drained her glass, wishing there were another tall, dark, funny, sexy guy in the village – one just like Robbie, but single.

'I should go,' she said, her mood sinking as she handed Robbie her glass. Wouldn't it be lovely to stay and polish off a bottle, drowning her sorrows with him? But they both stood up, the moment over. 'Thanks for the shoulder.'

To her astonishment, he wrapped his arms around her and Libby fought the urge to hug him back, scared it might be taken the wrong way. Wrong way? He was being friendly, not trying anything on. Now, why did that idea depress the hell out of her?

'You'll be okay, Lib.'

The muscles in his arms tensed as he kissed the top of her head and when he released her, she focussed on her boots, unable to look at him. If she did, she knew what she was feeling would be written all over her face. It was official – *I fancy the pants off him.*

'Night.' She walked away, reaching the far side of the garden before she dared to peek back. She'd intended to shout goodbye or thank you, but he was sitting on the swing again, his hands behind his head as he stared at her, frowning slightly. She stared back. Oh god, did he feel the same? Had she done it again, accidentally summoned the wrong man? Robbie was twenty-nine, ridiculously good-looking with the best eyes in the world, he'd been brutally honest and now, if his wife were having an affair, he was bordering on being single.

No, no, no.

Grounding. She needed to do the grounding exercise again and get back in-sync with... well, with whatever had gone so astray because Robbie was married and regardless of what his wife was doing, he wasn't fair game.

* * *

Zoë took a very different view. Quite frankly, Libby had to be insane for not seizing Robbie by his belt buckle and screwing him until he forgot his errant, cello-playing wife. He could give Libby everything she wanted - the idyllic life in the countryside.

She drummed her nails on the steering wheel of her BMW. Her bloody clients were late. People who were selling a house were never late. People wanting to buy a house were never late. People who were too bloody lazy to look for a house themselves, like Jemima and Charlie Harington? They were always late. And tedious.

The week before she'd endured an eye-gougingly boring lunch, but in those hellish two hours of her life which she'd never get back, she'd grilled them on budgets, top lines, dream homes and absolute no-gos. And eventually, she had them nailed. Really, they wanted a house on millionaire's row – the prime stretch of Windermere lake frontage, but their budget was half that of the cheapest property on the market.

It was a tall order, finding them something they could afford and persuading them it was the right property to shell out three quarters of a million on. But if she pulled it off, she'd earn half a percent of the final sale price – the best part of four grand. And Christ did she need it. What with Sparky's rewiring bill to pay, and the repayments on her car, and how the hell had she managed to rack up a two grand Mastercard bill anyway? She'd read the balance twice before poring over every purchase, certain that someone had cloned her card. Sadly, they hadn't. All genuine purchases, all her own work.

Maybe she should've sold the bloody cottage and kept the flat in Manchester. No. Why should she pay stupid amounts of money in tax when all she had to do was live in the middle of nowhere for a few months? It would all be worth it. She just had to keep her head above the poverty line until she was free to sell the cottage. Zoë narrowed her eyes, staring at the Victorian manor house before her. And this was the house that would do just that.

Highfield House is a beautifully renovated Lakeland country home surrounded by three acres of garden and woodland. The house dates from 1861 and has retained its period detailing.

Ideally located between the adorable Lakeland village of Hawkshead and Windermere's West Shore, the property is set amongst the lower fells of the south-eastern Lake District with easy access to M6 and the west coast main line at Oxenholme.

But what really puts this place into a league of its own are its neighbours. To the north is a boutique hotel rumoured to be getting its first Michelin star come January – its clientele reads like a BAFTA guest list. But to the south–

A deep red Jaguar rolled onto the driveway. Jonathan? What the hell – was he checking up on her? Then again, who cared? This was her chance to wow him. And dear god, did she need to wow him. So far, seeking his advice, asking him about *him*, all the usual tricks for making a man feel awesome, had done rock all to earn her anything more than a professional half-smile from him. Would it hurt for him to flirt, just a little? If she undid any more buttons on her blouse, he'd be able to see her navel, and twice she'd caught him checking out her arse. So why wouldn't he flirt back?

As he walked across the driveway towards her, Zoë pressed her thighs together, enjoying the buzzing in her pants. The guy might be fifty, but he was put together beautifully. Perfectly cut grey trousers showed off his long, muscular legs and he'd rolled up the sleeves of his blue and grey striped shirt, showing how toned his arms were. If she ever got the opportunity, she wouldn't play coy like Libby – she'd screw him in his office chair in a flash.

Carefully, elegantly and what she hoped was seductively, she swung her legs out of the car, taking the hand he offered.

'This is a surprise,' she purred.

'I was in the area and the Haringtons are friends. How are you, Ms Horton?'

Smiling, she smoothed her red pencil skirt over her hips. He watched. 'I'm very well. They're your *friends*?'

Laughing, he held up his hands. 'Okay, they're *acquaintances* I try to avoid wherever possible.'

Aside from today. Why was that? But the question would have to wait as the Harington's blue Range Rover trundled into view. Game on.

'Jemima... Charlie...'

Zoë kept the pleasantries to the bare minimum, everyone's eyes already on the house. Disdain dripped from Jemima's Harley Street nose, Charlie yawned and even Jonathan's pleasant smile didn't hide the doubt in his eyes. But none of it fazed Zoë. She confidently delivered her spiel, knowing she'd win them all over. Highfield House had a blinding card in its pack.

'And to the south...' Zoë paused, glancing over to her left where the chimneys of the nearest neighbour could just be seen over the tops of the ancient woodland separating the two properties. 'A certain duchess's parents have a second home. It's not something many people know. It's all very discreet.'

'Do you mean–' Jemima's eyes lit up and she clutched Charlie's arm.

Doing an imaginary power salute, Zoë nodded. 'Apparently, William often puts the kettle on himself when the National Trust people are in doing maintenance.'

As Jemima and Charlie wandered around, enthusing over Highfield's original cornices and the magnificent views from the drawing room, Zoë mentally paid off Mastercard, Sparky and bought herself a celebratory pair of heels. Maybe a pair from Hobbs or LK Bennett? From the flush in Jemima's cheeks, there was a fair chance Zoë could talk them into putting in an over-the-asking-price bid, just to be on the safe side. Four grand commission? LK Bennett it was.

Thirty minutes later, the Haringtons drove away, a sensible offer of seven-eighty sitting with the vendors.

'Well played,' Jonathan said, leaning against a vast gilt mirror. 'Was the duchess part true?'

'Yes. It always pays to talk to the handyman.' Zoë ran her fingers over the hand-carved Mahogany banister. 'They know the flaws of a building and its highlights better than anyone. Did you doubt I'd find them the right house? Is that why you're here, checking up on me?'

He tipped his head. 'I know them. And when I heard you'd selected this house, I was a little... dubious.'

'It's just a matter of finding out what makes a person tick. And the Haringtons are appalling social climbers, right?' Had she wowed him?

Jonathan nodded, clearly fighting a smile. 'We should celebrate.'

She'd wowed him. With her confidence overflowing, Zoë fluttered her eyelashes. 'And what did you have in mind, Mr Carr?'

His smile dropped. 'Let's get one thing straight, Ms Horton. The doe-eyed schoolgirl routine might have other men jerking off over your glorious tits, but it won't work on me.'

Fuck, fuck, fuck. What would he do, fire her? Mortified, Zoë walked up to the mirror and pretended to check her still immaculate make-up. Her hand shook as she opened her lipstick. 'I have no idea what you mean. I'm no doe-eyed school girl.'

'No, you're not.' Jonathan's eyes raked over her body. 'So stop acting like one.'

Hang on, *glorious tits*? Taking her time, Zoë applied a generous coat of Chanel *Pirate* before looking him in the eye. 'What does work on you?'

Finally, there it was, a filthy smile that said he wanted to screw her right there and then. Slowly, he moved to stand behind her, looking her over through the mirror. It was all Zoë could do to keep breathing. What the hell would happen now?

'Ms Horton, you use sex as a weapon,' he said, standing so close, she could feel his heat, breathe his aftershave. 'As a tool to get your own way. You just need to know what makes a person tick, right?'

If he didn't like doe-eyed, flirty imbeciles... She fixed her eyes on his, her chin raised defiantly. 'So?'

'You're a young, incredibly beautiful woman, Zoë. You've a power, a radiance most women don't realise they possess until they're much older, if they ever do. This will go one of two ways. The choice will be yours.'

Zoë stared at him, mesmerised. 'Go on.'

'I could lift up your skirt...' His gaze drifted up from her knees, so slowly he may as well have been lifting her skirt for real. 'What would I find?'

'Black hold-ups. Red silk pants. If you went further, a matching bra.'

His breathing quickened. 'I could rip those pants off and fuck you right here, up against this mirror.'

Oh god, yes.

Jonathan's hand reached for hers, pressing it against her own stomach, pushing her back against him, against his hard cock. 'I could bend you over, and fist your hair while I sink my dick into you.'

She needed to move their hands, for him to touch her.

'Does that idea turn you on, Zoë?'

She nodded, biting down on her lip. If he didn't touch her soon, she'd have to do it herself.

'I could do that, Zoë. I am so hard for you, aching for you, and I have been since you first kept that button undone so I could see your tits.' His hand pushed hers a little lower, making the ache almost unbearable. 'But tell me, Zoë, would you really be happy to let me fuck you, how I like, when I like, where I like?'

Her eyes narrowed.

'Because I see something else in you.' He leant closer, his lips hovering beside her ear, his erection swelling against her backside. How big was that guy? 'How would it feel to get yourself off, to make me watch, to make me stand here powerless and unfulfilled as you come?'

What?

'Does that idea turn you on, Zoë?'   •

Turn her on? Her pants weren't wet; they were soaking. What would it be like to exert that much power over someone, to control their every move? To deny and grant them the permission to come?

'You can lift my skirt,' she said, her voice unsteady, 'and you can undo my blouse. And then... you can watch.'

Through the mirror, he smiled, his fingers tugging up her skirt. 'You're no doe-eyed school girl. You're an Amazon goddess, a queen. I want to worship you, to touch you when you want to be touched, to fuck you when you want to be fucked.'

Oh to have his cock inside her... It'd be good, but not nearly as good as making him walk back into work still hard for her.

'But later?' she said, her breath coming fast, as his fingers brushed over her pants, lingering, pressing. 'You'll fuck me. On Max's desk.'

'Whatever you want.' Jonathan's hands moved up, slipping under her blouse to cup her breasts. 'However you want.'

'I want it hard and rough.'

'If that's your choice, but tell me... have you ever tied a man to your bed and stood over him with a whip?'

Groaning, her head fell back against his shoulder as her fingers slid inside her pants. She wouldn't be keeping her date with Mr Coffee Shop at five o'clock. If it were low to go on a date while you were still saddle sore from shagging a different guy the day before, then to go on a date while you were still dripping with your own come from getting yourself off with a different guy a few *hours* before... that was just immoral.

Even for her.

* * *

A week later, Libby arrived at the Low Wood Farm with no roots, no purple streaks and a new, Grace-like fringe. Thick and long, it fell into her mascara-laden eyes, and when Robbie met her at the door, smiling, she held her hands together in a pantomime angel pose. She peeked out from under the fringe as he looked over her Metallica t-shirt, black denim jodhpurs and dark red nails.

'Yeah,' he nodded. 'You can't do angelic.'

She faux-karate kicked him, but couldn't temper her grin. Since the second grounding exercise, she'd had no inappropriate thoughts about Robbie and their working relationship continued as if the hug had never happened. He'd still be uncommunicative and grumpy in the morning, but at five when she headed into the kitchen to drop off the key, he'd be waiting with a glass of wine. They never mentioned Jack or errant wives, keeping their chat to the health and well-being of the horses, but on her two days off, she'd more than once wished she could pop round for a five o'clock glass of wine. She'd missed him.

'OMG, I totes love your t-shirt.' Tallulah bounded into the room. '*Puh-lease* can we go riding today?'

'I'm not sure...' Libby glanced to Robbie. He was wearing jeans and a t-shirt. 'You're not going to work?'

He shook his head. 'I have three days with her before she buggers off to Pony Club Camp. Thought I'd make the most of it.'

'I'll do the feeds.' Tallulah dashed off.

'Oh.' Libby shifted awkwardly. 'Do you still need me here then?'

'Hell yeah. Your job is to show Lulu that horses are cool. It'll keep her away from boys for another few years.' Robbie looked her over again, shaking his head and fighting a smile. 'Just remember...'

'If she dresses like me, I'm fired, I know.'

'Lib?'

'What do you want?' It was always *Lib* when he wanted something.

'A favour. Pick the girls up tomorrow night?'

She groaned.

'I know, I know. I had asked Daisy, but they really want you to do it.'

'Fine. Just don't expect me to finish the bloody list tomorrow.'

'I never do.'

'What?' Libby stared at him, but he merely looked back, a smile twitching at the corners of his mouth. 'God, you never expect me to do it all, but I always do. That's why the lists get longer and longer, to see how much you can get me to do? You, you...'

She ought to be cross, but how could she be? She loved working at Low Wood Farm. For the first time in three years, she didn't wake in the morning, wishing she were going to class, auditioning, rehearsing.

'You arrogant bastard,' she joked. But to her surprise, instead of smiling at her joke, the muscle in his jaw twitched away. 'What's up?'

'Van's coming back for the weekend.'

'Okay.' So she'd finally meet Vanessa Golding. But why wasn't Robbie looking remotely pleased at the idea of his wife's return?

'Look,' he said, 'I think it'd be better if...'

'I'm not here?'

'I'm taking the weekend off. Family time.'

'Want me to do Monday and Tuesday instead?'

'You can't do seven days in a row again.'

'It's fine.'

'You really are a godsend.'

She struggled to keep her blushes under control. 'Is that why you vastly overpaid me?'

'For the babysitting, the cigarettes.' He tugged her plait. 'And because this place has never looked so good.'

Her blushes were beyond control. 'Can I take Shakespeare out on Saturday, if Tallulah doesn't mind? I'll stay out of the way.'

He nodded as he took a CD from the table. 'Track seven is noteworthy. It's what you should be looking for instead of inappropriate, untrustworthy types.'

She studied the CD, Depeche Mode's *101*. Track seven was *Somebody*.

That evening, she put the CD into her laptop and skipped straight to track seven. *Somebody*. The track, recorded live, featured nothing more than the singer, Martin Gore, playing piano as he sang about what he looked for in a partner. Libby pressed repeat four times, captivated.

This was what she needed, what she wanted. She wanted somebody to share the rest of her life, know her innermost thoughts, her intimate details. She wanted somebody to put their arms around her and kiss her, tenderly.

I want my 'Somebody'.

Chapter Twelve

Strains of Verdi's *String Quartet in E-minor* drifted across the yard as Libby slipped off Shakespeare's saddle. The muted notes Vanessa coaxed from her cello sparked memories of Libby's first professional role for the English National Ballet and the inevitable tears fell. There had to be thousands of classical pieces Vanessa could play, why that one?

'For Christ's sake, Tallulah.' Robbie's voice, loud and angry, obliterated the music.

Libby ran to the tack room, the saddle over one arm as she wiped at her eyes, no doubt smudging her make-up. She couldn't let him see her crying. It sounded as if he was in the garden. She could escape unnoticed.

'Five minutes,' he yelled. 'I asked you to keep an eye on Dora for five minutes, but you're too busy texting Chloe. Go and check in the Wendy house.'

Dora was missing? Libby dried her eyes on her t-shirt, hoping she didn't look too Alice Cooper, and peeked out onto the yard. Dora sat in the sandpit, merrily upending a bucket to create a perfect little castle. The cello music never stopped, so Libby reluctantly broke her promise to stay out of the way.

'Libby!' Dora leapt up, hugging her leg.

Libby took her hand, leading her to the garden. 'Rob? She's here.'

He sprinted over, his face pale as he picked up Dora, kissing her head over and over. He mumbled to his daughter that she wasn't to run off, his relief palpable but doing nothing to diminish his frown.

'Are you okay?' Libby asked, unused to seeing him with stubble or shadows under his eyes.

'Why are you here?' he snapped.

'I took Shakespeare out. You said... What's wrong?'

'Oh piss off, Libby. It's nothing to do with you.'

He stalked away, leaving her with tears once again looming.

The first, distant rumble of thunder filled the valley as she plodded into the village. All she needed now was for god to smite her down with a thunderbolt. The humid air stifled her, like she was breathing through a hot rag. Robbie hated her. She'd interfered, over-stepped the mark. He wasn't her friend; he was her boss. Why did she always cross boundaries at work?

The first drops of rain fell as she walked into the Green. A few fat blobs hit her bare arms, and then the deluge started, but she didn't have the energy to run. Why did Vanessa have to play the Verdi? She'd danced to it at Covent Garden. The *Guardian* had laid praise at her feet, promising a long and world-class career. But here she was, about to be sacked from the only job that had made her happy in three years.

Her t-shirt and jodhpurs were drenched by the time she'd reached the cottage, but she didn't care. Just another disaster to add to the shambles she called her life. Her tears mingled with the rain. A glass of wine. She deserved a vast glass of wine.

As she opened the door, Zoë trotted down the stairs, in a scarlet linen shift, ready for a date with some bloke from work. Why did Zoë find dates so easily while Libby's life was filled with unsuitable types?

'You're dripping all over the tiles.' Zoë peered in the hall mirror, smoothing a hand over her immaculately straightened hair. 'What's up?'

'I'm going to get fired.'

Zoë stopped her preening. 'Why?'

Libby explained, slumping against the wall.

'But he can't fire you for that. He should apologise.' Zoë applied a coat of her usual scarlet lipstick, but didn't let up on the inquisitive frown. 'It's not just a lust thing, is it? You really like him, don't you?'

'No.'

'Liar.'

'What does it matter? He's married. I couldn't have him, even if he didn't hate me.'

'So move on.'

'Who with?'

'Jack?' Zoë suggested, nodding to the drill down the hall.

'Jack's *here*?' Libby hissed. 'Why?'

'He's sorting out the cupboard under the stairs, putting a new door on.'

How could she complain about that piece of DIY? 'It looks done. Why's he still here?'

'He's fixing the dodgy hinge on the pantry door, and pretty much taking all day over it. I'm guessing he's waiting for you to come back.'

Arse. Libby pushed her soaking hair back. 'Why didn't you warn me?'

'Because he's single and he fancies the pants off you.'

'He'd shag around the minute my back was turned.'

'Personally, I'd take the risk. Have you seen his arse?' Zoë checked her watch. 'I can't believe it's pissing down. My hair's so going to frizz.'

'You can't look worse than me.'

'This is true.' Zoë frowned at her. 'Okay, for one, Robbie can't sack you because you've done nothing wrong. And two, there's a rather single, very fit joiner next door, dying to see you. I'm off.'

Libby sighed. 'Later 'gator.'

'While 'dile.' Grabbing her umbrella, handbag and a bottle of red, Zoë headed out into the rain.

Wine. What a great idea, even if she did have to deal with Jack. Libby headed into the kitchen, pointedly ignoring him. Crikey, but he made it hard. In a black sleeveless t-shirt and a toolbelt slung around his hips, he looked straight off the cover of some erotic romance. The fridge was bare. No white wine. She glanced across to the wine rack. And no red. Awesome.

'Hi,' he said quietly.

'Not a good time.' She refused to look at him. She must have mascara halfway down her cheeks by now. 'Bloody Zoë's taken the last of the wine.'

'Sorry,' Jack said, leaning on the kitchen island.

'Why? It's not your fault.' She regretted her snappy tone the second the words came out. 'Sorry, I mean, it's not your fault.'

She wasn't wrong there. He ticked her boxes: good looks, twenty-nine, green eyes, English, single and surprisingly honest. She'd summoned him. This was all her fault.

'Libby—'

She shook her head. 'I'm going for a shower.'

The thunder rolled as she climbed out of the shower, now accompanied by flashes of lightening, some lighting the sky, some forking down to the ground. She stood in her bedroom, wrapped in a towel, watching the storm, Hyssop on the dresser next to her. The black clouds seemed endless. The wrath of the Earth Goddess. You had to admire the power.

There was a knock at her bedroom door. What the–

'You decent?' Jack said from the other side.

She tightened the towel. 'No.'

The door opened a couple of inches and his hand appeared through the gap, holding a glass of white wine.

'It was in the pantry,' Jack said. 'It's Mum's elderflower wine.'

Libby took the glass and hovered by the door, unsure what to do. Well, being polite was a good start. 'Thank you.'

'You didn't fancy starting a fire,' he said, his voice a little further away. 'You know, to see me in the uniform?'

Libby grinned and leaned against the wall. She couldn't see him and he couldn't see her. Sweet that he respected she was practically naked in her bedroom. 'Are there many fires around here? Or is it all dashing off to save kittens from trees?'

'I reckon I've cut more people from wrecked cars than I've carried from burning buildings, but I've never rescued a kitten. There was a tortoise on the church roof once.'

Libby took a mouthful of the wine. The elderflower tasted so crisp and fresh, the acidity level perfect. 'Why on earth was it up there?'

'Well, it had gone up there for the tomatoes.'

'The tomatoes? Why were there tomatoes on the roof?'

'Mrs Barratt at number seven had a greenhouse, one of those plastic Wendy house things. The first decent wind and it ended up on the church roof, tomato plants and all. Stan fetched it down, but he didn't bring all the plants.'

'But how did the tortoise–'

'Ah, well, *Mr* Barratt won the tortoise in the school gala...'

The storm raged while Libby drank her wine, listening to Jack's tales, letting his easy-going charm obliterate her misery over Robbie. Crikey, he was funny. Thunder boomed and her heart fluttered as she pictured Jack's mouth, his tousled sandy hair... running her fingers through his tousled sandy hair, kissing his... Wow, where had that come from and what was he talking about? She shook her head, struggling to pay attention to his words, her vision blurring with a million pixelated lights as she glanced at the empty glass in her hand.

The elderflower wine was potent stuff.

And yet she buzzed with confidence. Okay, her hair had part dried into a bedraggled mess, and she hadn't a scrap of make-up on, but the towel only covered about two feet of her – her legs looked awesome.

As she opened the door, his latest story about rescuing old Mr Jenkins from a portaloo faded away. God, he was so cute. Cute, funny, twenty-nine, with lovely green eyes, English, single and honest – he *was* the one she'd summoned. This was meant to be. And wasn't it the perfect time while the Earth Mother was venting her wrath at the world...

'Hi,' she said, her skin tingling with anticipation.

Jack pushed his hair back, quickly glancing away, before taking a deep breath. 'Libby, I know you don't think too much of me, but I'm trying to do the right thing. I think you're... well, I think you're pretty fucking cool, so I told Grace because I've always been honest with her. I just want the chance to show you I'm not–'

Libby kissed him, her lips lingering against his, but Jack pulled back, surprised. It was a momentary reaction and when she kissed him again, he didn't hesitate. His hand slipped around her waist, pulling her closer. Robbie who?

Lightning cracked and they staggered into the room, tumbling onto the bed. A flicker of doubt flashed in her head, but with Jack kissing his way down her neck, along the edge of the towel, Libby ignored her nagging conscience. She grabbed his t-shirt, pulling it over his head and Hyssop padded out, sending her a disapproving meow.

Jack tugged the towel free and Libby focussed on his sandy brown hair, suddenly seeing it two shades darker, his green eyes turning the colour of molten chocolate. God, she'd wanted this for so long. To kiss her way down Robbie's – *Jack's* chest. She blinked, refocusing on Jack's perfect six-pack. Jack.

His hands trailed up her leg as she ran her fingers through his hair, her tongue toying with his and as his fingers reached the apex of her thighs, she closed her eyes anticipating his touch. It didn't disappoint. Bolts of pleasure shot through her, stronger than she'd ever known. She was as electrified as the storm outside. Every kiss, every caress, sent delicious shivers surging over her skin, making her beg for more. In a blur of kissing, stripping off his clothes, she somehow managed to find a condom in her bedside drawer.

'Your eyes...' He let out a deep groan as she unrolled the condom. 'They've gone all dark and sexy as fuck.'

Libby knelt over him, feeling more alive than she had in years. She was about to have sex with Robbie Golding and he wanted her as much as she wanted him.

'Libby… wake up,' said a girl beside her. 'Libby?'

A sneeze startled Libby. What? As she opened her eyes the light in the room blinded her and her ears hummed with the blood rushing around her head.

'Libby, you need to drink this,' the girl said.

Libby blinked, struggling to comprehend why the girl looked so much like Grace. Oh, because it was Grace. What was Grace doing? She held a mug to Libby's lips. Coffee, really strong coffee. 'I don't want it.'

'Libby, do as she says,' Jack said.

The coffee was warm, not hot, but the acrid flavour made her wince.

Jack. She'd had sex with Jack. They hadn't even been out on a date, never mind the five date rule she usually stuck to. She'd had sex with Jack, so why the on earth was Grace in her bedroom? Libby gulped the coffee, hoping it'd help her think. Her brain was a mess.

'What's going on?' she asked, finally able to focus.

Jack sat on the bed, a frown creasing his forehead as he nibbled at his thumbnail.

Grace knelt by her side, urging her to drink more. 'The elderflower wine you had. It was laced with belladonna – you know, deadly nightshade.'

'You poisoned me?' she said to Jack, wishing she had the energy to move away.

'No.' He sneezed.

'He might've saved your life.' Grace refilled the mug from a cafetière. 'The more you have, the better you'll feel.'

'I don't understand.'

'Well, after you were done fucking my boyfriend–'

'Grace,' Jack snapped, 'not now.'

Grace pouted for a second.

'What happened?' Libby struggled to sit up, wrapping her still naked body in the duvet. 'Why was it poisoned?'

'Poison to one is medicine to another,' Grace said. 'Maggie used to lace her drinks with belladonna to help with her migraines. I doubt one glass would've killed you, though shagging probably pumped it around your blood a lot quicker. That would've been an ironic way to go.'

'After…' Jack sneezed again. 'You went all weird, mumbling

nonsense about work, and your pupils were huge so I got Grace.'

'Why?'

Grace glanced at Jack. 'Because I use it in my eyes sometimes. It looks good. And Maggie told me about her taking it, so that if anything happened I'd know what it was and what it did. Lucky for you.'

'I rang Zoë. She's coming back.' Jack sneezed again, the noise sending another jolt of pain through Libby's head.

'What's the matter with you?' she asked him.

'That cat.' He shot a filthy look to Hyssop, who sat on the bed the other side of Libby. 'It's why I've never rescued any kittens. I'm allergic to the little horrors.'

Hyssop hissed. Jack glared back.

'Oh.' She frowned at him. Jack didn't like Hyssop? Or kittens?

Libby couldn't be more relieved when he went to make more coffee. What kind of person didn't like kittens? She watched Grace, who sat on the windowsill, fiddling with a charm bracelet. And how could Grace, a vet's assistant, *love* someone who didn't like kittens?

For the longest thirty minutes of Libby's life, the three of them sat in silence aside from Grace's occasional instruction to drink more coffee or have a glass of water. The purgatory finally ended when Zoë arrived home and Grace prepared to leave, her charm bracelet jangling as she pulled on her purple mohair cardigan.

Libby took a deep breath. 'Grace–'

But Grace glared at her before striding over to Jack, her chin raised defiantly. She laid her hand on his head, refusing to remove it when he tried to brush her off.

'Whatever influence I hold over thee,' she said, her voice wavering, 'be at peace. I set thee free.'

Was Grace releasing him from whatever spell she'd cast? It wasn't a spell Libby had discovered yet. Jack frowned up at Grace, but she whispered, 'We're over.'

'I'm sorry,' Libby whispered, 'but thank you, for coming to help me, I mean.'

Grace paused on her way to the door. 'Libby, my *ex*-boyfriend is sitting on your bed, there are two used condoms in your bin and I've just had to play nurse maid. I don't think you can begin to imagine how much I hate you right now.'

Two condoms? But they'd only had sex once. Hadn't they? Libby closed her eyes, fighting through the fog in her brain, but then she could see them, both facing the mirror. She was on his lap, her legs hooked over his as he ran his hands over her body, following hers. He'd whispered for her to touch herself, to tell him what she liked, what she wanted. She'd acted like a complete whore and to make things a whole lot worse, the man looking back from the mirror, his fingers sliding inside her, wasn't Jack. It was Robbie. She'd had sex with Jack, but imagined he was Robbie. Her stomach churned, the coffee sitting unhappily with the guilt and shame.

What kind of person had she become?

Tears rolled down Libby's cheeks as Grace left, but she braved facing Jack, as much to punish herself as him. At what point did he realise she was out of it and hallucinating? After the second time, or before?

'Thank you for asking her to help, that can't have been easy, but you should go now.'

'Libby…' His eyes implored her.

'Go, Jack.'

She rolled over, pulling Hyssop towards her, positive she'd never hated herself quite so much.

* * *

'She should be alright,' Grace said, putting the empty cafetière on the kitchen worktop. 'Another of those and make sure she drinks plenty of water.'

Zoë dipped a finger in the deadly-nightshade-laced wine, taking her time to suck off the resulting drips before she answered. 'Will do.'

'But tell her to stop messing around with summoning spells. The craft is not a game.'

'You don't believe in all that burning candles and wishing for your true love bullshit, do you?'

Grace's eyes narrowed. 'You've done it too?'

'Maybe.' Zoë couldn't help a smug smile as she popped the bottle of wine onto the top shelf of the panty. *A great shag with plenty of money.*

'Just be careful what you wish for.'

Chapter Thirteen

On Monday morning, Libby crept into work with trepidation in her bones. Would Robbie still be mad at her, or would he apologise? She opened the door, but he never looked up from his paper. Fine. It'd be easier to have a simple boss/employee relationship if he hated her.

But she didn't want him to hate her. She needed a friend, someone to talk to. Once Libby had recovered, Zoë was bugger all use, finding the whole episode hilarious and saying Grace had got her just desserts for being a jealous cow-bag girlfriend.

'I see you played hard to get on Saturday,' he said.

She stared at her feet, guilt burning her cheeks. How did he know? 'Oh, piss off. It's got nothing to do with you.'

His head jerked up, but Libby grabbed for the tack room key. In her rush, her fingers fumbled and the key clattered to the floor. She crouched down, fully aware Robbie was already on his feet.

'Libby–'

'What? Are you going to yell at me again for trying to help?' She faced up to him, her anger rising. 'I'm sorry if I interfered, but obviously something was wrong, and after everything... I know you're my boss... but after everything that's happened recently, I thought it'd be okay to ask because I sort of thought we were friends. I'm sorry. It won't happen again.'

'Have you finished?' he snapped.

'No,' she said. 'If you ever speak to me like that again, I really will piss off and I won't come back.'

His face held no clue to his feelings, but as she turned to flee, he stopped her, gently grasping her wrist. She refused to face him, too scared she'd cry.

'Libby, wait,' he said. 'I'm sorry about Saturday. It's no excuse, but it was a really bad day.'

The room shifted as relief flooded over her. He didn't hate her. Oh thank God. She closed her eyes, trying to ignore the warmth of his body behind her, the citrusy bergamot in his aftershave, but she glanced down at the hand holding her wrist.

Those fingers... those were the fingers she'd seen in the mirror, the fingers that had brought her to the most intense orgasm she'd ever had. They were fake memories, but she swayed backwards, his shirt touching her back. Had she imagined it, was it another hallucination, or had his thumb really brushed her arm?

'Please don't piss off,' he said, his mouth so close his breath tickled her ear.

Was she still hallucinating? Surely this couldn't be happening. She turned to him, frowning from under her fringe. His face was six inches from hers and his eyes gazed down. She had to be dreaming. With her heart thumping, Libby tipped her head up. Four inches of air stood between them and a kiss. Why wasn't he backing off? The gap shrank. Three inches.

'I should never have given you the job,' he murmured.

Unable to stop herself, Libby kissed him. Or had he kissed her? She didn't know, but when her lips met his, frozen for a second, it was definitely his hand holding her face. Slowly, their lips moved and as the kiss grew, she clutched his shirt, hoping to stay upright.

'Stop it!' yelled a girl's voice.

Oh god, no. Libby pinned herself back against the kitchen units, getting as far from Robbie as possible. He'd stepped away, staring wide-eyed towards the living room where his two daughters were grappling with a pink fairy wand.

'Dora, get off, it's mine.'

Libby sagged with relief. They hadn't been caught, but now what? Robbie turned and slowly, the movement almost imperceptible, he shook his head.

'Daddy, Dora won't give my wand back.'

Libby fled.

The cool feed room did little to calm her burning cheeks. What had she done? She'd kissed a married man and he'd kissed her back. Storm kicked at her door, the other horses fidgeting, eager for their breakfast, but after Libby tipped a bag of Pasture Mix into the bin, she stood, hugging the empty bag, reliving the kiss. His lips against hers. His fingers in her hair. His head shaking.

He'd said no.

She fought mortification and tears as she tried to complete the usually simple task of scooping nuts into buckets. What if he fired her? He couldn't, could he? He'd kissed her too. She had to stop fancying him. What she needed was a distraction from her distraction

– she needed her true love. She'd have to do the Summoning Spell again.

A shadow fell over the room and she closed her eyes, praying he'd go away.

'Lib?'

With a little shake of her head, she pulled herself together and faced him as she faced everything in life – with her head held high. Robbie fiddled with his car keys, glancing at the floor more than her.

'It's fine, a mistake, I know.' She forced a quick smile. 'Sorry.'

'The girls–'

'Let's forget about it.'

He nodded, a huge frown marring his perfect face. 'If that's… I'd better go.'

At least he hadn't fired her.

That evening, under the powerful energy of the full moon, Libby sat on the lawn with her candle, flower petals and a new piece of chintz wallpaper. She had to get it right this time, to choose her words carefully. *Good looks, 25-35, nice eyes but not brown, English, honest, decent morals, single, good with animals.* Then, in a final flourish, she scrawled, *I want my Somebody.*

For two days, she avoided Robbie. Each evening she'd hover outside, waiting until the girls needed him in another room, then she'd hang up the key quickly and quietly, leaving the list on the worktop. The following morning, a new list would replace the previous one, but he wasn't in his usual place at the kitchen table, reading the paper.

Libby's misery grew. She missed him. She missed talking to him. She wanted to tell him about Dolomite clearing four feet, but how could she face him? For two nights, despite working Dolomite and Storm until the horses were more tired than she was, she'd barely slept, her brain and body reliving that kiss. She had to stay away from him.

On day three, with the mucking out finished, she sat down nursing a mug of tea and took the time to light a cigarette before she took out his list. She read his words, stared at his neat handwriting and wished he were with her, kissing her again. Then she read the last item.

Talk to me.

Talk to him. Why, what would he say? Olivia Wilde, you're fired? Or the opposite. She banished the idea. He'd shaken his head. He didn't want her. God, she wanted him, but he'd said no. Another grounding exercise hadn't eased her obsession. All she could do was focus on the routine and turn up the radio to block out inappropriate thoughts.

Lethargically, she dropped the first hay net into a tub of water, soaking it for Smokey's ancient teeth, but the dance track blasting from the iPod stopped. Libby froze, her heart rate tripling. Tallulah had gone shopping to Kendal with Chloe. No one but Robbie would turn it off. Well, to hell with going out there. He could come and find her. Cromwell, who never left her side, lay outside the door, stretched out in the midday sun, giving away her location.

Footsteps approached, but Libby concentrated on stuffing the next hay net, not looking up as Robbie came in and perched on the hay bales.

'Don't you have a restaurant to run?' she said, sounding more cross than she'd intended.

'It's quiet. Laurel can manage.'

Libby pulled the net strings closed and braved facing him. Sitting on the hay, in his pristine white shirt and dark grey trousers, he looked like a model in a high end, arty photo shoot.

'Lib–'

'Can't we just forget it?' *Please, don't fire me.*

'No,' he said, fiddling with a piece of hay, 'because I haven't thought about anything else for three days.'

And just as he did most mornings, he looked her over, but this time she didn't breathe the whole time. It wasn't a mistake. He wasn't going to fire her. He wanted more and the arrogant twinkle in his eyes suggested he wanted more now. Crikey, that was the look Clara had told her about – the look that said he'd bend her over whether she liked it or not. Libby's body pulsed. He could; she would.

No. He couldn't; she wouldn't.

'You're married. It's wrong.'

The arrogant twinkle vanished and he closed his eyes for a moment, his shoulders sagging. 'Fuck, I'm sorry, Libby.'

Sorry for what? Wanting a roll in the hay, or not wanting one anymore?

'What's going on?' she asked.

'It turns out I wasn't paranoid. She finally admitted she's shagging that French wanker.'

Her heart broke to see Robbie's face fill with desolation. 'Did she apologise and beg for forgiveness?'

'Not quite. She wants some time to work out what she wants.'

'A sabbatical?'

He nodded, rolling his wedding band around with his thumb. 'On Sunday... I agreed. I said she could have her free pass.'

'Oh.' What else could she say? She couldn't tell him it'd be okay, that Vanessa would change her mind because she had no idea what his wife might be thinking, but Libby hated to see him so dejected, his ego so battered. 'And do you get one too?'

His hands picked at a piece of hay. 'Why do you think I said yes?'

And he looked at her, his eyes glinting.

'What, are you expecting a quick roll in the hay?' She sounded flippant, but the suggestion of shagging him made her cheeks redden. 'Not my style, I'm afraid.'

'Oh, now you play hard to get.'

'Ha, ha.'

She tried opening the next hay net, but her fingers wouldn't work. Swearing, she threw it to the ground and studied him, her hands on her hips, fingers tapping. Did he really think he could just turn up and shag her? What else could she expect? They could hardly go out on a date. There'd be no relationship, just sex, something to boost his ego, something to distract her. Did she really want that?

'I know you're in a bad place,' she said, 'but I don't want to be the one responsible for wrecking your marriage. Free pass or no free pass.'

'It's wrecked already.' He leaned forwards, frowning at her. 'She said she wants someone to talk to about the thing she loves. Music. He can do that. I can't.'

'But–'

'The thing is, Lib. I get it. I know what she means because...' Robbie took a deep breath. 'Every morning, Dora screams for her. *I want Mummy. I hate you, Daddy.* The amount of times I've almost rung Vanessa, to tell her to come home. Dora misses her so much, but I don't ring her, because if I did... there'd be no more wine at five o'clock with you. And I don't want to give that up because it's the highlight of my fucking day.'

Libby crossed the gap between them in two strides and his arms wrapped around her, pulling her close. Desperate to make him better, for him to make her better, she kissed him, hoping to show him he was wanted by somebody. Wanted? She needed him. *He* was her perfect distraction.

With their bodies pressed together, they kissed, but it bore no resemblance to what had happened in the kitchen. They tumbled backwards onto the hay, his hands holding her face as his tongue tormented her mouth. This time she really was going to have sex with Robbie Golding and he really did want her as much as she wanted him.

'I can't believe we're doing this now,' she whispered, her mouth hovering over his ear. 'I smell like a horse.'

'It's very, very sexy.' He looked her over, smiling as he slowly pushed up her t-shirt.

'But you'll get dirty... I mean...'

'If you're trying to talk me out of it, you're doing a dreadful job.'

Grinning, he slipped her t-shirt up her arms, but used the material to bind her wrists together. Held captive, she squirmed helplessly as his fingers trailed slowly down her arm and along the edge of her bra, his touch sending shivers shooting through her.

'This is so wrong,' she mumbled.

'But inevitable.'

He released her hands and Libby took over, kneeling astride him to teasingly drop kisses down his neck as her shaky fingers unfastened his shirt. The last button opened and she pushed aside the cotton fabric, gaining full access to the torso she'd coveted for so long – the real thing and not some hallucination. Crikey, he was fit.

She glanced up, expecting to see his arrogant smile, but instead he stared, wide-eyed at the ancient beams. Was he having second thoughts? Gently, she placed a nervous hand on his chest. 'Are you sure you want to do this?'

Quietly, he sat up and tipped his head to the side, taking slow, steadying breaths.

'The problem is, Lib...' He tugged the band from the end of her plait and shook out her hair. 'I've wanted to do this since you called me an arrogant bastard.'

They lay on a stable rug, naked, and Libby held him in her arms. They'd had sex. Crikey, they'd had good sex, but his silence for the last five minutes unnerved her. While she scattered kisses along his shoulder, up his neck, he merely stared into space. Was he regretting his revenge shag?

'Are you okay?' she asked quietly.

He nodded.

'Working out how you can run away?'

He shook his head and tipped his head back, kissing her slowly, gazing at her with open affection.

'Can I ask a question?' Reassured, Libby rested her head on his shoulder. 'Is Dora why you're always so grumpy in the morning?'

'This isn't the time–'

'You can talk about her – Vanessa, I mean – if you want to.'

'Not the time, even if I did want to.'

'Okay, question two. On a scale of one to burn in hell, how guilty do you feel?'

'About one.'

Even sitting behind him, she could see him staring resolutely ahead, but his thumb fiddled with his wedding band. Wriggling from under him, she pulled on his shirt, fastening a couple of buttons.

'What are you doing?' he asked, propping himself up on one elbow.

'Telling you the truth so you will too.' A few feet from him, she perched on the balls of her feet for a moment before resting in first position. 'There are two things you should know about me, things that aren't on my CV. Well, they certainly aren't on the CV I gave you.'

She held out her arms and performed five passable fouettés before coming to a halt in an arabesque – hardly her best, but good enough.

'I try not to tell lies in person, only on my CV. You were right. St Mary Magdalene's School for Naughty Girls doesn't really exist. I really went to the Royal Ballet School. I was a professional dancer for five years, but for medical reasons, I had to retire. I'm very rusty, but believe me?'

Robbie nodded, a smile threatening as she dipped forwards, raising her back leg until her face was level with his.

'Secondly, my father taught me to play poker when I was seven. I can spot a tell a mile away and I'd say you are feeling guilty. You have a million tells. I'd say you're the worst liar ever. It's really very reassuring.'

His face said enough, but the eyes flashing to her left gave him away. 'Maybe a five then.'

'I'd rate my guilt at a nine.' Slowly, she lowered her leg, and let him pull her towards him. 'Look, can we be realistic? You need the ego boost and I need the distraction, but despite all the *who's-got-what-*

in-common talk, you love your wife and you want her back.'

He went to argue back, but Libby held a finger over his lips.

'She'll be back,' Libby said.

'What makes you say that?'

'Well, she's married to you. You're easy on the eye, occasionally bloody good fun and the rest of the time you're a massively grumpy pain in the arse. What's not to love? Oh hang on, now we can add a good shag to the list.'

He fought a smile. 'You're one hell of an ego boost.'

'You're welcome.'

'Sorry for dragging you into this.'

'It's okay, but I hope you don't think you can rock up every day and expect a roll in the clichéd, not to mention itchy, hay.'

'Hey, I didn't rock up expecting a roll in the hay, clichéd or otherwise.'

'Oh, really? You were rather well prepared for someone not expecting any rolling.'

'Boy scout. Always prepared.'

'Scouts and Pony Club? Liar.'

'How do you do that?'

'If I told you, then you'd stop doing it—'

'Doing what?'

'And then I wouldn't know if you were lying.'

'Thought I'd better be prepared. Knowing how hard to get you like to play.'

Laughing, she tried to hit him, but he flipped her onto her back.

'You know,' she said, her cheeks heating up, 'I don't normally... I really am hard to get.'

'I know.' Slowly, he kissed her. 'A ballerina, hey?'

'Officially, I was a ballet dancer not a ballerina. That title's reserved for the best of the best.'

'You don't look much like a ballerina.'

'I've spent most of my life wearing baby pink with my hair scraped into a neat bun. When I want to, I can look perfectly angelic, but the rest of the time, I work hard to look like a tramp.'

They grinned at each other.

'But why keep it a secret? I'd started to think you'd spent the last ten years in prison for murdering your family. Where are they?'

'Australia. Rose Bay, Sydney if you need specifics.'

'And why the sketchy CV, the secrecy?'

She took several deep breaths. 'Last time I told anyone about the ballet, I cried. It always makes me cry. It was everything I knew. You can't begin to understand how... and then it was over. I need to obliterate it from my life, move on, but if I put it on my CV, people ask about it. Do you really dance on the ends of your toes? Are you all anorexic? So I took it off my CV and stretched out the jobs.' She wiped at the tear trailing down her cheek. 'Look, can we leave it? And promise not to tell anyone?'

He nodded. 'What other secrets are you hiding, Lib?'

'Full disclosure? I've had eleven jobs in the last three years. Twelve if you include Kim's.'

'Twelve? But—'

'Kim's was the first I wasn't sacked from, hence the sketchy CV.'

'You were sacked from eleven jobs?' He raised his eyebrows.

'Afraid so.'

'I think I'd prefer you to be a reformed serial killer. Sacked for what?'

'Mostly being too honest. My last job as a wedding planner's assistant wasn't bad. I was ace at planning events. I have thought about setting up business here.'

'Really? It's Matilda's birthday in a few weeks. Fancy organising a party for me?'

Her eyes widened. 'What's the budget?'

'It's for Tilly. There isn't one.'

'You're such a pushover. Face paints and a bouncy castle, or is competitive parenting at large round here?'

'I don't give a fuck what anyone else thinks, just make sure it's amazing so it...' He rested his forehead against hers. 'So it makes up for her mother not being here.'

Libby kissed him. 'You know we have something in common other than horses. Neither of us can stand listening to classical bloody music anymore.'

The week before, he'd thrown the iPod across the yard, cursing the French viola player, after a Tchaikovsky piece Vanessa used to play came on.

'Had you been crying on Saturday?' he asked. 'Was that why?'

She nodded, taking a moment to build her courage. 'How did you know about... me not playing hard to get?'

'It's on the blog.'

'The blog?'

He took out his phone, opening a website called *Haverton Eye*. Under a heading of *Saturday Night, Sunday Morning*, were photos of several couples in amorous embraces, and a list of who got up to what and with who. She and Jack were listed at the top.

'Basically, they put online what the *Gazette* daren't print. They email it every Monday morning.'

Local gossip. She was local gossip. She goes running with a friend and it's turned into a torrid affair that half the county can read about. She has drug-induced sex with another guy and feasibly her mother could hear about it in Australia. Libby, dumbstruck, simply stared at Robbie, hoping for... she had no idea what.

'What happened with Jack?' he asked.

She turned her head, avoiding facing him as she explained what had happened after he'd snapped at her on Saturday afternoon. Poisoned, hallucinating, dealing with Grace's help and hatred, but she glossed over Jack's more dubious actions.

'I'm so sorry, Lib. If I hadn't yelled at you...'

'It's not your fault.' She smiled up at him, stroking his hair. 'I really am making a shambles of my life here. It's seems I am trying to find the most inappropriate blokes possible.'

'At least I'm trustworthy.'

'I'd better get dressed and do some work. I have this grumpy arse boss who might sack me if I don't finish his list.'

He gave the expected laugh, but as she nudged him up, trying to escape, he rolled over, pulling her with him. 'Your grumpy arse boss says the list can wait.'

As he unbuttoned the shirt and his lips trailed down towards an already pebble-hard nipple, she relaxed. Mr Golding was the best distraction in the world.

Libby perched on Zoë's bed. 'I need to talk to you.'

Zoë glanced at her through the mirror, but continued applying her eye shadow.

'I had...' Her cheeks burned, as she mimed locking her lips. Zoë nodded. 'I... shagged Robbie this afternoon.'

Zoë abandoned her make-up. 'What the hell... how?'

'We sort of kissed last Wednesday, but–'

'And you didn't tell me because...'

'Because it's wrong and I wasn't exactly proud of it.'

'So what happened?'

Libby explained, flopping down on Zoë's bed, burying her head in the duvet. 'And we've literally spent three hours shagging this afternoon.'

'What's going to happen now?'

'God knows, but he kissed me goodbye, said he'd see me tomorrow.'

At the time, she'd agreed, kissing him back, glad the desolation had gone from his face, but with each step she took down the bridleway, guilt trickled in. He was married. She was having an affair with a married man who had three kids. And it made her feel sick to her stomach.

'So how's his fuck-me rating now?' Zoë turned back to her mirror. 'Fuck me now and keep going forever more?'

And destroy his marriage? 'No. For now. I… think he needs me. He's devastated over Vanessa cheating.'

'So you're doing a good deed? And that's it?' Zoë laughed. 'Whatever. You shagged him because you fancy the pants off him. You know what's going to happen, don't you? You're going fall for him. Hard. He's your new love.'

'No. It's not him.' It couldn't be. She couldn't be the person who split up a family.

Zoë raised her eyebrows, her implication clear. Never say never.

* * *

The full moon hung in a starry sky, but the temperature remained in the twenties. Patrick sat on the balcony, his bare feet on the table, appreciating the breeze.

He'd had a great day off, biking in the Sierra Bermeja mountains, but it left him with a niggle he couldn't shake. For six weeks he'd immersed himself in his brother Sam's ex-pat, Costa del Sol lifestyle – working at the practice in Estepona, hiking, biking, helping with the renovations on the villa, but now? Even the scent of the roses reminded him of his mother's garden.

'The wind's changed.' Sam handed him a beer as he sat down. 'It's coming from the North.'

From home. 'It's better, cooler.'

'You seem restless.'

Patrick stared at the mountains. Like him, they were brown from the incessant sunshine and lack of rain. 'It's time to go back.'

Chapter Fourteen

Three fields away from the farmhouse, shielded from the world by dense oak woods, Libby sat by the river, adoring the warmth of the August sunshine. She ought to put her vest and shorts back on, just in case, but the glorious decadence of being naked in the open was too good an opportunity to miss. She smiled as Robbie, still shirtless, poured glasses of Prosecco. A lazy picnic by the river, what better way to spend their day off?

'A girl could get used to this,' she said, closing her eyes.

Robbie dropped a kiss on her shoulder. 'So could a guy.'

And that was the problem: it was all too easy to get used to.

For the past two weeks Libby's life had bordered on the idyllic rural dream. The sun shimmered in a cloudless sky, Jack was nowhere to be seen, Dolomite's ears pricked when he saw a jump, and she had a thing with Robbie Golding.

A *thing*. A total blissful thing, but a *thing* nonetheless. She didn't know what else to call it.

An affair, Zoë had suggested.

But it was more than that. Or less.

Certainly, there was a lot of sex. Often he'd surprise her by turning up after lunch and they'd end up rolling in the clichéd hay until he had to pick his kids up. If she were honest with herself, she preferred the evenings. With Tallulah at Pony Club Camp, Libby would pop back to Low Wood Farm after Robbie had tucked Dora and Matilda into bed. He'd cook dinner and they'd sit in front of the fire, talking for hours.

All too, too easy.

But they'd never spend the night together or hold hands walking down the street, all she'd get would be snatched moments until his wife came back. But those evenings did something for Libby – she got it now. You were either *Somebody* or a distraction, and now she knew enough to make the distinction. Robbie taught her to expect more.

'Food all set for the party?' he asked.

'Burgers, chicken drumsticks, pasta salads.' Reluctantly returning to reality, Libby lifted a hand, shielding her eyes from the sun. 'Xander has it all in hand.'

'And you reminded him that two of Matilda's friends can't eat dairy?'

'Pinky-promised me the cheese will be a million miles from the meat and rolls.'

'What about the cake?'

'Your pastry chef has designed a fairy princess palace with glitter, sugar work and Smarties.' Libby studied him. Despite the setting, the beautiful day, the spine-melting sex, his usual morning-frown had made a return. 'What's wrong?'

He stared down at his glass. 'I want to tell Xander.'

'You want to tell him what?' But Libby's stomach was already freefalling.

'About us. I don't like lying to my brother.'

'No.' Libby pulled on her vest, guilt washing over her.

'Why?'

He'll hate me. 'Because if people find out, it'll destroy your marriage.'

'Does it matter?'

Libby stared at him. Did it matter? Of course it mattered. 'How did you meet her?'

'Libby, this isn't the time. We've just–'

'How did you meet her?' She buttoned up her shorts, and sat staring at the river, hugging her knees.

For a moment, Robbie merely frowned at her. 'We... we were doing a photo shoot at Oscar's, the wine bar in Haverton? My parents own it and I used to work there. She was the model they'd booked.'

'Did she look beautiful?'

He nodded. 'She has the greenest eyes, like Tilly's, and she was all legs in a little black dress. This is weird, Lib.'

'What happened?'

He lay on his back and lit one of her cigarettes. 'She thought I was the model she'd be working with and just stood there, twittering about the last shoot she did and how she hated waiting around because it made her nervous. All I did was stare at her, listening to her talk. Her accent's adorable.'

Libby tried to ignore the jealousy burning inside her. 'Did you ask her out?'

'I... to begin with I just wanted to get her into bed.'

'You arrogant bastard.'

'In my defence, I was eighteen.' He smiled. 'But when she said she was nervous, I asked if a drink would help and went behind the bar. She realised I wasn't the model and she blushed.' He laughed, gently. 'Christ, when she blushed... that's when I knew.'

'She was your Somebody.'

Slowly, he nodded, his eyes filled with pain and Libby stroked his hair.

'She'll come back, Rob.'

'You don't know that.'

'Oh, I do, because the more time I spend with you the less I understand why she went in the first place. Shagging you is better than dancing at Covent Garden. How's your ego?'

'Boosted.' He kissed the top of her head. 'Do you want to stop this? Us, I mean.'

'No.' She didn't think she could if she tried. 'I need the distraction.'

'From ballet?'

'Yes.'

'Tell me about it.'

She shook her head, flashing a brave smile. 'Maybe one day, but not today.'

* * *

Patrick's return to Gosthwaite got off to a less than auspicious start. He'd got up early, planning a ride out, but his parents had turned up and subjected him to an hour-long meeting on *The Rules*:

- *Practice Hours are 9-5. Monday to Friday.*
- *Monday afternoons are at the Haverton surgery,* pro bono.
- *On call Monday-Thursday, rotating weekends with Fergus and Sarah.*
- *No newspaper articles*
- *No scandal*
- *No hard drugs*
- *No alcohol if working the next day*
- *Must consent to random drug testing*

He wished he could tell them he understood, that he'd changed, but even though his mother had hugged him, telling him it was lovely to have him back, she wouldn't look him the eye.

I really am very ashamed to call you my son.

To make matters worse, once he'd finished with The Rules, he'd gone into the surgery, barely having time to put the kettle on before the phone rang. It was Lynda from the Post office – Boadicea, her Weimaraner had been hit by a car. Leisurely start back into working life? No.

He'd prepped the surgery and had his sleeves rolled up by the time Grace arrived. He hadn't done that in a while – been there before her. At least she'd been happy to see him – throwing her arms around his neck and making him laugh.

Then she cuffed him around the head. 'And don't ever leave me stuck with Fergus again.'

Grinning, Patrick nodded. 'Promise. How's Hyssop?'

'Fine,' Grace said, but quickly turned away to unnecessarily straighten the dressings box.

'Grace... what's wrong with him?'

'Nothing. It's just... her next door is looking after him.'

'I left him with you, not some stranger.'

'What could I do? He moved back in to Maggie's and she wanted to keep him.'

'And since Jack's allergic to cats, you didn't put up much of a fight.' He tried to stay calm, determined not to yell as he would have in the past, but Grace had let him down. Badly. 'Who the hell's her next door, anyway?'

'Don't you get the *Haverton Eye* emails in Spain?'

He shook his head. Grace knew he hadn't paid any attention to that trash since they'd posted the pictures of him and the Cumbrian Businessman of the Year's wife, but when she dug a copy of the *Gazette* out of the recycling box and showed him page five, he had to smile. Xander was messing around with some blonde that wasn't Daisy?

'I'm guessing from the quote,' he said, 'there's no love lost between you two.'

'Payback.' Sighing, she showed him a photo from the blog on her phone.

Jack had been shagging around again – what a shocker. Patrick peered at the image, focussing on Olivia Wilde, who was wearing a tiny red dress. Nice arse.

'Who is she?' he asked.

'Zoë, Maggie's niece, the one who inherited the house? It's her mate. Six weeks ago she was in the paper getting up close and personal with Xander, next minute she's all over Jack.' She tried to sound as though she didn't care, but her eyes filled with tears.

'Gracey, you've always been too good for Jack.' He held her face and kissed her forehead. 'You need to move on.'

Blushing, no doubt at persevering with Jack for so long, Grace nodded. 'Lynda's pulled up outside.'

In a blur of activity, Grace comforted a sobbing Lynda, while Patrick opened the back door. Boadicea lay whimpering, blood seeping from a gash across her side, her two front legs clearly broken and her face an unrecognisable mush. Shit. With Grace's help, he carried the dog into the surgery, gently laying her on the table.

'Hey, Boadicea,' he said quietly. 'You're supposed to chase cats, not cars.'

'It's not like her,' Lynda said, 'but she just ran out into the road. Brenda from Inglenook couldn't stop in time.'

Once he'd sedated Boadicea, Patrick did a gentle but thorough examination. It wasn't good news and he frowned at Grace, an unspoken communication she'd understand: the dog needed to be put down.

'Will she be okay?' Lynda asked.

He hated this part of his job. 'I'm afraid she has two broken legs and from the sounds of her chest, a punctured lung.'

'But you can operate?'

Patrick gripped the table. 'Yes, but–'

'Then do it. Please, just make her better.'

'Lynda, she's sustained a nasty head injury. I'm not sure there's anything–'

'Please?'

Grace put her arm around Lynda. 'You're talking about expensive–'

'She's my baby. I don't care about the money.'

'...and invasive surgery,' Grace went on. 'You have to think what's best for Boadicea.'

'I'm not sure it's in her best interests, Lynda.'

Lynda looked up at him, her eyes pleading, tears tumbling down her cheeks. 'She's all I have, Patrick. I can't lose her.'

Jesus Christ. When did he become a soft-touch? 'I'll treat her, see what we can do, but if I think we're prolonging her suffering... I won't have her in pain if it's not going to make her better.'

'Thank you.'

'Lynda,' he said, his voice grave. 'I'm serious. I will make that call.'

Grace led her away. 'Why don't you go home, have a cuppa, Lynda? There's nothing you can do here. I'll ring you when we know more.'

With a sobbing Lynda gone, Patrick set to work. 'Grace, make some coffee and get me the cat back.'

The green track beneath his wheels improved Patrick's mood with each passing minute. Biking in Spain had been challenging, but the brown, dusty trails weren't a patch on his familiar route across the common and down through woods. It had to be the only good thing about coming home.

Get the cat back.

It wasn't a lot to ask, but at six o'clock after he'd informed Lynda that Boadicea was moderately stable, Grace reluctantly admitted that Olivia Wilde wouldn't answer her calls. Irritated, he kept an eye on Maggie's cottage, planning to ask for Hyssop back himself, but he saw no sign of Zoë or her friend. In the end, he'd gone home to an empty house. And it sucked.

Patrick stood up on his pedals, punishing himself up the hill towards the woods, but already smiling in anticipation of the next descent – the best downhill for miles around. Pedalling hard, he turned into the woods, his knees soaking up every bump in the track. He flew over a bank, turning hard right to avoid a vast Douglas Fir. He still had it. The first time he'd taken the jump, he'd ploughed straight into the trunk, dislocating his shoulder, but never again.

Trees flew past. He ducked to avoid a low branch, but kept his eye on the track, lining up the next bend, spotting the apex, mentally preparing for a brief burst of effort before a huge rolling left–

Shit.

Someone was on the track.

He yelled as he swerved, but his back wheel clipped the runner and Patrick slammed into a branch. The bike fell away and he slid down the hill, dirt and stones dragging against his bare arms and legs.

Jesus Christ.

Winded, he sat up, the skin on his arms and legs stinging, but looked for the runner. She was lying under a tree, holding her right leg in the air. He ignored the stabbing pain in his knee as he jogged up the hill, hoping she wasn't badly hurt.

'Are you okay?' He crouched next to her, waiting for his sunglasses to react to the dim light in the shade of the tree.

'I think I've twisted my ankle, nothing serious.' Not a local girl. She sounded posh, not upper-class posh, but well-spoken. She touched her face, flinching.

Finally, his sunglasses adjusted and he turned her chin, examining the graze on her cheek. Was this Olivia Wilde? Pretty. And her skimpy, skin-tight running gear covered little, but showed off how toned she was. No wonder Jack had been tempted.

'It's a wee graze,' he said. 'You won't be scarred for life.'

She winced as she sat up. 'Are you okay? You're bleeding.'

He lifted a hand to his forehead and frowned at the drop of blood left on his finger. That explained the axe ripping his skull open. 'I'll live.'

He held out a hand and helped her to her feet, watching as she tentatively put her right foot on the ground. She swore and he tried not to smile. Was this fortuitous? Olivia Wilde needed his help and she had his cat. One good deed...

'Oh god, that bloody hurts.' She closed her eyes for a second, before taking a deep breath. 'Old injury. It'll be okay, just needs a couple of days to recover.'

'Think you can walk?' He hoped not. Helping Ms Wilde would hardly be a hardship.

She frowned, peering down the track, then shook her head. 'But it feels a bit melodramatic to ring the Mountain Rescue for a swollen ankle.'

'Wait here.' He scooted down to collect his mercifully still intact bike.

Her frown grew as he returned. 'I don't like bikes.'

'It's this, or walking.'

She swore several times, but perched on the crossbar and clutched the inside of the handlebar. 'Please, be careful.'

Instead of going down, he pushed the bike back up the hill, detouring out of the woods as soon as he could onto the smoother, grassy bridleway down to the village. He couldn't help smiling. Despite his banging head and the burning coming from his grazed arm and leg, the morning was already a hundred times better than the day before. He had a damsel-in-distress on his crossbar.

'Okay, hold tight and... just don't do anything stupid.' He climbed on the bike, trying not to grin as he put his arms either side of her to take hold of the handlebars.

'Oh God,' she groaned, cowering into him.

A pretty damsel-in-distress who smelled of... roses. How could she smell of roses when she'd been running? As he changed gear, his face next to hers, he took a deep breath. Not just roses, roses and sweet peas, like the roses and the sweet peas his mum grew. She smelled like a god-damn flower garden, a Wilde flower garden. And this flower garden would owe him a favour.

Like giving me my cat back.

He peeked round at her, trying not to laugh. 'Why've you got your eyes shut?'

'Because this is terrifying. I haven't ridden on a crossbar since I was about twelve.'

'You run half-naked through the woods at seven in the morning and you think this is dangerous?'

He laughed, loving the way she leaned against him. Should he seize the opportunity of a captive audience and ask for Hyssop back? Plenty of time for that.

'Open your eyes,' he said, his lips brushing her ear. 'It'll be less scary. We're really not going that fast.'

She opened her eyes and squeaked, cowering against him even more, her head against his shoulder. 'Oh god, we are. I really hate bikes.'

'Tough, I'm not carrying you back to the Green.'

He took another sneaky peek at her as they coasted down the track. Christ, she was small, skinny small, and he didn't think legs like that existed outside of air-brushed adverts – long, trim and very toned, the body of an athlete. Okay, her tits were underwhelming, but better that than the fake things Ms Haverton had stuck to her chest. Overall, Ms Wilde was a very nice package.

'How do you know where I live?' she asked.

'You're Olivia Wilde, aren't you? The girl who's been misbehaving with Jack and Xander.' He regretted his piss-taking when she straightened her back, putting an inch or two between them. 'Sorry. I don't really know anything. Just rumours.'

But she didn't relax, making it a very bad time to ask about Hyssop. She might say no, just to be obtuse. He leaned forward to give his most sincere smile, to show her he wasn't a bad guy, but she looked away, her eyes shining. Why did girls always cry?

'Don't worry about the paper,' he said. 'Everyone knows they make up half of what they print.' Unless it was about him, then it was usually true.

She didn't speak for the rest of the ride down, though after an unavoidable cattle grid made her shriek with pain, she did at least lean against him again.

Roses and sweet peas.

Carefully, he stopped outside her house and helped her off the bike. 'Do you need a hand to get into the house?'

She turned, hopping on her left foot, and smiled.

And when she smiled, pretty became angelic.

Jesus.

* * *

In the woods, with his back to the light, all she knew was he looked tall, had curly hair and a slight Scottish accent. On the bike, she'd discovered he was fit. She'd ogled the thigh muscles, admired the arms, and couldn't resist leaning back against his shoulders, but the rest was a mystery. A mystery until she turned around and he lifted his sunglasses.

Ohmigod.

A mop of black curls, hazel eyes, great cheekbones... Crikey, he even had an adorable smattering of freckles across his nose.

'I'll be fine, thanks,' she said, trying not to stare.

He flashed a smile as he held out his hand. 'Nice to meet you, Olivia–'

'I only get called Olivia when I'm being fired,' she said, shaking his hand. Rough hands, nice. 'It's Libby the rest of the time.'

'Then it's nice to meet you, Libby. I'm Patrick.'

Patrick? She glanced to the corner house next to hers. 'You're Patrick, the vet?'

He nodded, still smiling, but preparing to leave. 'I'm Patrick, the vet.'

Aware she was definitely staring, but too bemused to do anything else, Libby watched him peddle away, heading for the lane between their houses.

'Oh, and Libby?' He paused. 'I want my cat back.'

Bemusement vanished. 'He's not your cat.'

Smiling up at the sky, Patrick circled around, cycling back to her. Crikey, he had something about him and not just a fit body. The irritating thing was she knew from his easy-going smile he only wanted one thing: her cat.

'How is Hyssop?' he asked.

'Healthy. Happy. At home.'

Patrick laughed. 'I want him back.'

'Not happening.'

He glanced at his watch. 'As much as I'd like to debate this now, how about we discuss it tonight? Seven o'clock, the Alfred? I'll buy you a drink to say sorry for nearly killing you.'

Libby faced up to him, with her hands on hips. 'The Alfred's a bit tricky. As I'm sure you know, Grace and I don't get along.'

'Yeah, she mentioned why.'

Libby folded her arms, desperate to flee. She had to walk away. Now.

'I wouldn't worry about it. I've been telling her to dump him for years.' Patrick leaned on his handlebars, his eyes twinkling with amusement. 'Grace won't say anything if I'm there. Tell you what, I'll call for you on the way then you don't even have to walk in on your own.'

'Wow, you're almost making it sound like a date. Will you bring flowers? I adore peach roses.'

'It's not a date.' He grinned, blatantly looking her over. 'It's a custody battle.'

'Planning to ply me with booze until I say yes?'

'Will it work?'

She shook her head.

'Then I won't rely on booze.' He shot her a wink then pedalled away again. 'Seven o'clock.'

Seven o'clock. She had a… custody battle with Patrick the vet. It wasn't a date, but guilt swamped her as she hopped into the house. Hyssop, as ever, padded down the stairs to meet her, mewing a hello. She sat on the bottom step, stroking his head.

'Do you want to go back to Patrick?'

He mewed again. Was that a yes or a no?

'I mean, because, if you want to, then I'd understand. You've probably known him for longer, but…' *I don't want you to go.*

Hyssop rubbed his head against her chin before plodding back upstairs to curl up as he usually did, on her bed. It was as if he'd said, don't worry, I'm staying. No way was Patrick taking him, no matter how much he fluttered his fabulous eyelashes.

She'd tell Robbie, of course. When she got to work, she'd tell him. It wasn't a *date* after all. He wouldn't mind.

But despite plenty of opportunities, she hadn't told Robbie. He'd come back in the afternoon and helped her round the yard, good-naturedly telling her off for over-using her ankle. After work, he poured her a glass of wine, but when he asked if she was coming round later, she'd lied. She'd told an outright lie and said Zoë wanted to go out for a drink. He'd nodded, his disappointment clear. Why hadn't she told him the truth?

It wasn't a date.

Chapter Fifteen

Libby checked her cheek in the hall mirror. The graze wasn't too bad and an icepack had taken the swelling down, but even copious layers of concealer couldn't hide the bruise. Not exactly the best look for a non-date. She glanced down at her multitude of bangles and pushed them off, not wanting Patrick to think she'd made an effort. Bugger, why was she so worried?

Okay, she'd admit Patrick was good-looking. Not at Robbie's supermodel level, but certainly an eight out of ten, maybe a nine. What was he, about thirty? Plus he was a vet and being a vet made him good with animals. To cap it all he didn't have brown eyes. Hazel eyes couldn't be classed as brown, could they? But was he single and was he honest with decent morals? Could he be the one she'd summoned?

'Is it me,' Zoë said, pausing as she painted her toenails her usual scarlet, 'or are you a little nervous about your date with the vet?'

'It's not a date. It's a custody battle.'

'There's no battle. He can have the flea-bag.'

Libby stroked Hyssop's head. 'Don't listen to her.'

'I'm allergic to him. I have to take Clarityn every bloody day.'

'You get hay fever. You'd take it anyway.' Libby checked her watch.

'Why are you so twitchy? Worried he'll stand you up?'

'No. He wants Hyssop too much.' Libby kissed the cat's head. *But he's not having you, mister.*

'I can't believe you're going on a date with Patrick McBride. I must've been ten when I saw him last. He was always nicking Maggie's weed and she used to call him the *Wee Scots Beastie.* I used to fancy him, of course. God knows why. He was this gangly fifteen year-old. What's he like now?'

'Oh, you know… fit.' She'd forgotten the Scottish accent. 'And it's not a date.'

'Fit, as in mountain biker fit, or fit as in…'

'You would.'

'Miss Wilde, is that why you're so twitchy? Wow, what if he's the one?' Zoë turned to her, wide-eyed. 'The one you summoned.'

Libby shook her head. 'He's not.'

'But he could be.'

'He's not. He's Scottish.' To avoid summoning Paolo, she'd added English to her list of desired traits. 'Bugger, he's here. You sure I don't look too try-hard?'

Zoë frowned at her. 'You're wearing a denim mini-skirt and black t-shirt. You're as bland as can be.'

Bland wasn't good. Libby pushed several bangles back on and hopped to the door.

'Hi,' she said.

'Christ, it's good to see you.'

Libby blinked in surprise, but Patrick wasn't speaking to her. He crouched down, reaching out to pick up Hyssop. After a thorough examination, accompanied by several chin rubs, Patrick set Hyssop down, then slowly straightened. He fought a smile as his gaze travelled up her legs, but when he reached Libby's face, his eyes widened and he recoiled, laughing.

'Wow,' he said. 'Didn't expect–'

'What?' She folded her arms.

'Aren't you a little old to be dressing like a misunderstood teenager?' He headed back down the garden path. 'You coming?'

A misunderstood teenager? Libby straightened her back a little more. This wasn't a date. It was a custody battle. Grabbing her bag, she followed Patrick, deliberately hobbling slowly. If she'd aimed not to look too try-hard, he'd outdone her. His jeans looked threadbare through use rather than some designer's whim, and that faded t-shirt would be rejected by the homeless. But crikey, he looked good.

No.

Patrick slowed, glancing back at her. 'Hyssop looks well.'

'He said, begrudgingly.'

'His eyes have been okay?'

'I got Zoë to get the drops from Grace.' *Oh god, the Alfred. Please don't let Grace – or worse Jack – be inside.*

For the first time, Patrick gave her a smile. 'Don't look so worried. Yes, Grace will be in there, but honestly, she won't dare say anything in front of me. Grab the table over by the window.'

'Can't we sit outside?'

'I'd prefer to sit inside.' He held the door open for her.

'I might want a cigarette.'

'Feel free to go outside for one. It's a disgusting habit. Drink?'

'The white Rioja,' she said, already wishing she hadn't agreed to the non-date.

Grace didn't hide her displeasure at Libby's arrival, and Jack sat at the bar, staring straight ahead. Why had she let Patrick boss her around? She didn't want to sit inside. She didn't want to be sitting in the same pub as Jack or Grace.

She darted to the left, taking refuge in the window seat hidden from the view of the bar. Her ankle started throbbing again. She could be getting ready to go and see Robbie. What had she been thinking? She could just leave. Walk out. Longingly, she glanced across to the cottage. Hyssop was sitting on the war memorial in the middle of the Green, watching her. Keeping an eye on her?

Her chance to flee passed as Patrick sat opposite, pushing a bath-sized glass of wine towards her.

'Sorry for almost killing you this morning.'

'Apology accepted.' She took the wine, trying to force a polite smile.

'You really don't want to be here, do you?'

'Nope.' She took a mouthful of the wine. 'So you've been away. Nice tan.'

'My brother has a practice out in Spain.'

'Practice?'

'He's a vet too, family thing.' He had his head tipped slightly, studying her. 'My dad's a vet, my mum's a vet, my big brother's a vet. Why was Xander hugging you?'

'Trying to unearth a little scandal you can use in the custody battle?'

'Maybe. You didn't answer me.'

'He's my running buddy.'

'And he was hugging you because...'

'He's nice like that?' Libby grinned. 'He hugged me because I said I'd think about doing the fell race.'

Patrick sipped his beer, leaning further back in his seat. 'Why'd you come here?'

'The irresistible lure of a free drink.'

He glanced out of the window, trying not to smile. 'To Gosthwaite, I meant.'

'Zoë and I were sharing a flat in Manchester. She inherited the cottage and moved here to avoid capital gains. I came too.'

'What really happened with Xander?'

'We're just friends.'

'Can I have the cat back?' he asked, looking her in the eye.

'His name is Hyssop. And no, you can't. He's settled.'

'He's not yours.'

'He's not yours either.' She kept up eye contact, fascinated by the odd mix of green and brown in his irises.

'Maggie said that if anything happened to her, I should look after him.'

'I've seen her will. Your name wasn't mentioned.'

'He was happy with me.'

'What, until you buggered off and left him? He needs a home, not someone who lets him down.'

'And you're going to stick around forever? Grace said you and Zoë were planning to move on when the renovations are done. At least I own my house.' He glanced up to his right.

'Liar,' she said, without thinking.

'What?'

'You don't own that house, you're lying.'

He frowned at her for a second, before shaking his head. He was clearly irritated, but his eyes were twinkling. 'Okay, okay, so my parents own it. That's not the point.'

She sipped her wine, trying not to smile. 'Ding, ding, end of round one.'

'Bitch.' He gently kicked her ankle under the table.

Libby winced. 'Ow.'

He sat up, his eyes wide. 'Christ, sorry.'

She couldn't stop her huge smile. 'It's okay. It was the other ankle.'

'I'm really starting to dislike you.' He threw a beer mat at her, his smile growing.

'Careful, some might call that flirting, like pigtail pulling in the playground.'

'Don't flatter yourself. You look like seventeen year-old trailer trash.'

'Crikey, you know how to charm a girl out of her cat.'

He knocked back several mouthfuls of beer, never taking his eyes off her. Robbie had some serious competition for the sexiest bloke she'd ever met.

This isn't a date. Don't get carried away. He only wants Hyssop.

'I hear you used to pinch Maggie's weed,' she said, trying to keep things a little less flirty.

'She gave me permission to help myself when I was eighteen. Can I still?'

'You just said smoking was a disgusting habit.'

'Weed's different.'

'Hypocrite. I don't think being a regular drug-user is going to help your custody case.'

'And inflicting second-hand smoke on Hyssop is helping yours, is it? Ding, ding, end of round two.'

Libby pressed her lips together, trying not to laugh. 'What was she like?'

'Maggie?' He turned to the cottage. 'She used to be ferocious. Christ, the amount of times she whacked me with her walking stick. She changed though, softened up in her old age. I liked her.'

He still stared at the cottage, his frown growing. Libby could feel his sadness. She wanted to comfort him, hold his hand. Hold his hand? Run her fingers through his hair, more like. She gently nudged his ankle.

He turned to her, smiling. 'Ow.'

She smiled back, glancing up at the cut that was showing from under his curls. 'How's your head, by the way?'

'Fine, but my helmet's knackered and my bike's scratched to hell.'

'That was the scariest twenty minutes of my life.'

He laughed, leaning forwards, his elbows on the table. 'You were hilarious. I can't believe you had your eyes closed.'

Libby blushed as he smiled and his legs stretched out under the table, accidently brushing against hers. He did fancy her. A bit at least.

'Isn't he a bit single for you, Libby?' Grace said as she wiped down a nearby table. 'You want to watch yourself, Patrick. Her reputation's worse than yours.'

Libby clutched her glass, mentally screaming at Grace's departing back.

'Turns out, you were wrong,' she said, looking up at Patrick, hoping for some reassurance, willing him to reprimand Grace.

He didn't. He stared back. 'I've got to go, sorry.'

'You are not walking out on me in front of her.'

He stood up, abandoning the last quarter of his pint. 'I'll try not to run you over again.'

Her cheeks burned with mortification and anger. 'Damn right. That was a public footpath, not a bloody cycle route.'

He left.

Libby downed her wine before hobbling to the bar where Grace stood with her arms crossed, grinning.

'You want a war?' Libby said, keeping her voice low. 'You've got one. You have no idea what I can do. I will take you on in the fell race and I'm going to win.'

Grace blew her a kiss and Libby strode off across the Green, refusing to limp. She wouldn't give Grace or Mr McBride the satisfaction of watching her suffer.

'Matilda, can't you play in the bloody house?' Libby manoeuvred the wheelbarrow around the collection of teddies having a picnic in the middle of the yard.

'Tilly, take the bears nearer the sandpit, please.' Robbie waited until Matilda was out of earshot. 'And you're in a bad mood because?'

'None of your business.' Libby dragged a half-full bag of shavings to Max's box.

'Libby?'

She stopped, looking up at him.

'Don't ever take your bad fucking mood out on my daughter again.'

He headed back to the house and she kicked the shavings bag, sending a bolt of agony into her ankle.

'I went for a drink with Patrick the vet last night,' she said, flopping onto the bench. 'I shouldn't have said yes. I feel bad.'

Robbie looked up at the sky for a moment before joining her on the bench. 'Lib, if you want to go out with someone... Not that I want you to, but under the circumstances, it's not fair to stop you.'

'I lied. I'm sorry.'

'You did. Why?'

She shrugged.

'And what happened when you went out with Patrick the vet last night?

'The utter bastard walked out on me.' She pulled a face then braved looking up at him. *You're ten times the person he is.*

'Sounds like you got off lightly.' Robbie ran a hand though his hair. 'He's my best-friend but–'

'What?'

'You didn't realise? Have I not mentioned him?' He laughed. 'I suppose there's some irony there. Look, I wouldn't trust my sister with him, if I had a sister.'

'Why on earth are you friends with him?'

'I've known him since I was nine and... he reminds me of who I used to be.'

Oh. 'I am sorry.'

'It's okay.' He glanced across to the girls who were merrily feeding the teddies sand, before dropping a kiss on her head. 'Just promise me, if you do meet someone else, don't lie.'

She nodded.

'And stay away from Patrick.'

Happily.

* * *

Zoë sipped her tea, watching as Libby walked up the garden path. 'She's not going to be happy.'

Patrick didn't respond. He rubbed Hyssop's head, showing no emotion.

'Is it wine o'clock yet?' Libby called. She stopped and stared when she stepped into the living room but then turned, glaring to Zoë. 'What's he doing here?'

'I've come to take my cat—'

'He's not your cat,' Libby said, her voice a vicious hiss.

Zoë sat back, nursing her mug, intrigued by the drama unfolding in front of her. Patrick had rocked up, casual, confident and utterly persuasive. Not that he needed to persuade her. Hyssop had trotted down the stairs to meet him, hissing at Zoë along the way. The cat hated her and she hated the mangy fleabag right back. She hadn't said as much to Patrick, but she'd already decided it made sense for Hyssop to move next door.

What she hadn't appreciated was just how attached to the furry lump Libby was. Hyssop jumped off Patrick's knee, sidling up to Libby, purring away, and Libby's eyes filled with tears. She was crying over something that wasn't ballet. How very interesting. And even more interesting, Patrick had sat forward, frowning, his casual confidence crumbling. But was he concerned over Hyssop's defection, or Libby's tears?

Libby scooped Hyssop up, kissing him. 'Can't you get another cat?'

'Look,' he said, taking a deep breath. 'I know you like him, but he means a lot to me—'

'He does to me too.' She looked at Patrick, tears pooling again. 'Hyssop's my friend.'

Zoë almost choked on her tea. Patrick and Libby both glared at her. 'What? It's just a cat.'

Patrick shook his head before turning back to Libby. 'He's not just a cat.'

'No, he's not.' Libby shook her hair back, composing herself. 'But anyway, he's Zoë's cat officially and she'll let me keep him. Won't you?'

No. I don't want the bloody cat here.

'Zo, come on.' Patrick turned to her, flashing that terrific, flirty smile. 'We've known each other for years. We used to go blackberry picking. Remember when your tutu got stuck in the brambles?'

'And for mentioning that, Libby gets full custody.'

Patrick swore, taking a few moments to stare at the floorboards, but finally he stood up, towering over Libby, to say goodbye to Hyssop. Libby looked up at him, her eyes apologetic and Zoë again struggled not to laugh. These two were bonding over a stupid cat.

'Look after him,' he said, his voice quiet.

'I promise,' Libby whispered.

Oh, this was fabulous. Patrick's jaw twitched away, but he spent more time gazing into Libby's big blue eyes, now framed by smudged mascara, than he did looking at the cat he so desperately wanted back. He was as smitten with Libby as Libby was with him. Priceless.

He headed for the door, glancing one last time at Libby.

'But…' Zoë said, stopping him. 'You can have visitation rights.'

'What?' Patrick and Libby asked.

'Feel free to visit on weekends and evenings. You know, to make sure he's okay.' *And let's see what develops between you two.* Zoë pottered through to the kitchen, leaving them to it, but hovered outside the closed door, listening in.

'I might take her up on that,' he said.

'I hate you. Get out.'

'You won, princess. I'm not too fond of you either.'

Zoë grinned. A match made in heaven. And if she wasn't mistaken, Patrick fulfilled every single one of Libby's Summoning Spell criteria. But she'd let Libby discover that for herself.

* * *

Annoyed, irritated, and coming home to an empty house, Patrick slammed the door, cursing girls who cried. How could he fight back and persuade Zoë when Libby had got all... weepy. Christ, why did girls cry so much?

His phone rang. Robbie. Thank you. It was Saturday night. He could go round there, drown his misery. 'Hi Rob—'

'Stay away from Libby.'

'Fucking hell. *Droit du seigneur?*'

Robbie hung up.

Jesus. He'd broken his parents *rules* by drinking on a work night to win that girl over, and for what? Still no cat. He'd lost Hyssop and now Robbie was pissed off with him. Libby Wilde was quickly ruining his life.

Chapter Sixteen

Trundling his bike down the Low Wood Farm drive never failed to cheer Patrick. The place almost felt like home. Shame he'd had to waste a day's holiday so he could drink on a Sunday – no booze when he was working the next day had been the hardest rule he'd agreed to. It ruined his usual Sunday bike ride with Robbie, but there was no way Patrick could endure a four year-old's birthday party without a beer or five.

In the yard, Cromwell the fat Lab lay in the sun, the cat spread out next to him. Nothing had changed. Except the place was a damn site tidier. Not that Robbie kept a sloppy yard, but the stable doors gleamed under a coat of fresh stain, the windows sparkled and hanging baskets filled with petunias and nasturtiums hung from the roof beams.

Would Ms Wilde be here? Yes, she was. Patrick paused by the yard gate as she led Harmony, Tallulah's old gymkhana pony, out of a stable. Jesus, Libby looked more like seventeen year-old trailer trash than she had when they went to the Alfred. Her pale blue eyes, what you could see of them under her fringe, were caked with more black eye shadow than he'd seen most girls wear on a night out in Haverton and what was she wearing? Denim jodhpurs and a purple ACDC t-shirt that hung off one shoulder displaying a turquoise bra strap. He much preferred the girl he'd crashed into. He much preferred angelic.

As he opened the gate, Robbie came out of the house. Patrick approached him, offering an apprehensive handshake, but it quickly evolved into a back-slapping hug. Christ, it really was good to be home.

'This place looks good,' Patrick said. 'Van's been busy.'

'She's still away. Libby's done all this.'

Robbie smiled in her direction, but she was too busy grooming Harmony to notice, and unless Patrick was mistaken, there was a definite edge to Robbie's voice. Was he still worried about Vanessa and the bloke from the quartet?

'How's Van getting on?'

'She's in Yorkshire, at some music festival.' Robbie led the way to the garden. 'So how come you buggered off to Spain? You didn't call, you didn't write...'

Robbie was clearly passing idle chit-chat, settling the ground after the terse phone call the previous week, but how much should Patrick tell him?

'Dad blew up after the Miss Haverton story,' Patrick explained. 'Had to keep my head low for a while, let him calm down.'

'I don't blame him. Shagging in the park?' Robbie shook his head, trying not to laugh. 'You're lucky you weren't arrested.'

'Seemed a good idea at the time.'

'If you ever fuck anyone in my restaurant again, I'll have you arrested.'

Patrick swore, his stomach bottoming out. 'You know about that?'

'We have cameras.'

'You're joking?'

'Yes. Laurel saw you go in.'

And this is what he got now, why he didn't need any rules. The days of pulling stunts like that were long gone. That wasn't who he wanted to be.

Patrick stalled at the garden gate. 'Jesus.'

If Vanessa had planned Matilda's party, he might've expected bunting hung around the garden, a bouncy castle at one end and pass-the-parcel at the other, but the bouncy fairy palace, vast paddling pool filled with bubbles and a giant rabbit performing magic tricks to one of Matilda's enthralled friends seemed way beyond the usual Low Wood Farm soirée.

'Did Libby do all this too?' Patrick asked, eyeing up a stilt walker dressed as a ballet dancing fairy. 'Where the hell did you find her?'

Robbie laughed. 'Fantastic, isn't she?'

Without question, Patrick knew they were both referring to Libby not the fit as girl on stilts who'd given them a cheeky wink.

'It's official, I'm in love with Libby,' Scott said as they joined him at the picnic table. 'She used to work for a phone company and the little beauty's unblocked my phone. Will managed to do Christ knows what with it this morning. Clara's free to a good home if you're interested, Rob.'

Robbie laughed, but they all turned as Libby led Harmony into the ménage. What was it with that girl? Patrick didn't get it.

'How's she working out?' Scott asked, handing them both beers.

'She's a godsend,' Robbie replied. 'She knows her stuff, works her arse off, does what she's asked and never complains.'

'And happens to look like a St Trinian's Sixth Former.' Scott grinned.

'Which doesn't hurt.' Robbie laughed. 'That's actually demure for her, most days she looks like she'd get kicked out of St Trinian's.'

'I don't get that whole trashy look,' Patrick said. 'She looks better in her running kit.'

'Never seen it.' Robbie slugged his beer, frowning.

'You should,' Patrick said.

'If you don't like how she looks, why did you ask her out?' Robbie asked.

'To get Maggie's cat back.'

Libby crouched down, talking to the first of Matilda's friends clamouring for a pony ride. The little girl laughed and Libby's face broke into that huge smile. Even the trashy make-up couldn't hide pretty Libby. Maybe he shouldn't have walked out of the pub. He shook his head. No, she'd been sensationalised in the paper, outed on the blog, and if he wasn't mistaken, that meant Michael Wray had a new obsession. Patrick felt for her.

'Libby seeing anyone?' Scott asked, looking suspiciously innocent as he raised his eyebrows at Patrick.

Christ, don't go there. Patrick picked at his beer label as Robbie said no. They'd not discussed Robbie warning him off and Patrick was happy to leave it that way. Libby Wilde had caused enough trouble.

* * *

The last of the party bags had been handed out, Matilda's munchkin friends waved off and the entertainers paid – a party perfectly managed, even if Libby did say so herself. At five o'clock, she ducked into the house to change from her jodhpurs into a denim mini-skirt and when she returned, only Robbie's closest friends remained: Scott, Clara, Daisy, Xander, their kids and unfortunately, Patrick. He and Robbie were on the chair swing, laughing and knocking back bottles of beer.

Considering how nervous Robbie had been to have the party in Vanessa's absence, Libby hadn't expected to see him so chilled. In t-shirt and shorts, he'd milled amongst the guests, the parents of

Matilda's friends, topping up glasses, laughing, smiling. Of course, that was all part of his Mr Restaurateur persona, but when he joined his friends, his smile relaxed into something entirely more natural.

'Libby,' Daisy said, 'please tell me you'll do this for Evie's birthday?'

'Oooh, and Will's?' Clara beamed. 'Where the hell did you find stilt-walking fairy princesses?'

Libby laughed, trying to ignore Clara's bare feet, the evidence of corns and bunions almost as obvious as on her own. But where Libby had her toes hidden in ballet flats, Clara had her feet propped up without any sense of shame. If only.

'Unbelievably, Libby still doesn't have a hot boyfriend,' Daisy said.

'What happened with Jack?' Clara tipped her head to one side, studying Libby's feet, as usual in third position, her habitual resting stance. 'He's cute. I would.'

'I can hear you,' Scott called across the lawn.

Libby reluctantly sat at the table, as uncomfortable with the scrutiny as she was the conversation.

'How about Jonty?' Daisy suggested. 'He's adorable, good-looking, half-Italian.'

'Rich too,' Patrick added.

'Money doesn't make you happy,' Libby replied, tucking her hair behind her ears. What did Robbie think of this? She daren't look at him.

'He's far too nice,' Clara said. 'I wouldn't.'

'Ignore her.' Daisy swatted her friend's arm. 'Xand and I can come too. We'll do tapas and cocktails in Haverton. It'll be fun.'

Libby stared at her feet, desperately to get out of saying yes. 'Look, I don't want to go out with Jonty, whoever he is.'

'Why?' Daisy asked, sitting up. 'Oh my God, it's true, isn't it? You and Xander—'

'No,' Libby said, appalled Daisy could even consider it.

'Fitzgerald.' Xander shook his head. 'You've had too much wine. Trust me, please?'

'But you two are...' Tears tumbled down Daisy's face.

Libby looked to Robbie and he stared back. She couldn't let Daisy think this. They had to tell them. They had to. Matilda and Dora were merrily jumping in the bouncy castle and with Tallulah at Chloe's, there was no one to overhear. Libby opened her mouth.

'Xander's not having an affair with Libby,' Robbie said, standing up.

Libby closed her eyes as he walked over and didn't open them, even when he put his hands on her shoulders. Oh god, no.

'I am.'

'Wow, Rob,' Clara said. 'If I knew you were going to shag around, I'd have formed a disorderly queue.'

'Clara,' Scott hissed, 'not the fucking time.'

* * *

What the actual fuck?

Patrick stared at Robbie, still not believing what he'd just heard. Okay, it'd been his suggestion for Robbie to get an au-pair while Vanessa was away, but he hadn't actually expected Robbie to shag her. Robbie was a romantic. He wasn't the unfaithful type, not these days. But it certainly explained Robbie warning him off Libby.

Jesus.

So why did Libby go out for a drink with him? He'd assumed she fancied him, but she obviously didn't. He'd flirted with her. What an idiot. Hang on, she'd flirted right back. Maybe she did fancy him. Was that the kind of girl she was, shagging one guy then going for a drink with his mate? Nice. Thank Christ he'd walked out.

'What about Van?' Patrick asked, unable to keep the anger from his voice. 'Is this why she's not here for her daughter's birthday?'

Robbie didn't answer, but turned to Libby. Whatever their unspoken communication was, she understood it.

'I'll bring the horses in,' she said.

Patrick folded his arms as she walked away, her shoulders sagging. Was this her fault? On first impressions she hadn't seemed the sort, she seemed a nice girl, but throw Jack then Robbie into the pot, and Miss Wilde was looking far from angelic.

'Vanessa's having an affair,' Robbie explained, kicking Patrick's world off its hinges for the second time.

'What? Who with?' Scott asked, leaning forwards.

'That French wanker,' Robbie replied and filled them in on the viola player.

From the subsequent silence, clearly no one knew what to say. The six of them sat staring at hands, picking at beer labels, sighing at the sky.

Robbie forced a smile towards Clara. 'Will you check on Lib?

Make sure she knows you don't hate her. This isn't her fault.'

Clara, who'd do anything for Robbie, obediently nodded and led Will off to the yard.

Xander stood up, pulling Daisy with him. 'I can't believe... We have to get Evie home. Can we talk tomorrow, Rob?'

It had to be whisky o'clock. Patrick went to the bar, cracked open a bottle of Macallan and poured three hefty shots. Robbie hugged his brother, apologising, but Xander shook his head, holding him in a tight backslapping hug. Patrick sank back into his seat, not knowing what to say. Scott, as ever, was the first to man up.

'Van'll come back,' he said, swirling his drink in its glass.

'Maybe,' Robbie replied, watching as Libby, Clara and Will headed off to the fields to bring in the horses.

Patrick couldn't stop himself. 'If she does, will the plaything be out on her ear?'

'Libby's not a plaything. She's...'

'Jesus, you really like her, don't you?' Patrick leant on the table, trying to fathom Robbie out, but his friend was staring at his glass, his face unreadable.

'Look, Libby's not trying to take Van's place, she's just... she's doing a bloody good job of keeping my head together. We have a lot in common, but if... if Vanessa comes back, then yes, Libby will be out on her ear.'

'Does she know that?' Scott asked.

'Yes. My daughters need their mother. Van has no idea how much they miss her, Dora especially. She'd come back if she did.'

'Then tell her,' Scott said.

'She needs to come back because she wants to, not because she feels she has to.' Robbie pushed his hair back, watching Libby jog behind the Shetlands. 'And then there's the other what if. What if Vanessa doesn't come back? What if I've caught the luckiest break of my life?'

Was Robbie seriously considering ending his marriage? Patrick downed his whisky. 'Does Libby know you're thinking about this?'

'Do you think she'd have gone out with you if she did?' Robbie asked. 'She's an amazing girl. If you can get her to speak to you again, you'd like her, but she's... Look, I can't stop her, but she's *Off Limits*.'

Scott mouthed an exaggerated *Wow* and Patrick let out a slow breath. This was more complicated than he'd thought. Calling *Off Limits* was reserved for special girls, girls you didn't want your best mate to go out with even after you broke up with them. Only two women had earned *Off Limits* status in recent years: Vanessa and Clara. Why Libby? Patrick didn't get it. Yes, she was pretty when she wasn't dressed as trailer trash. Actually, she was quite hot when she wasn't dressed as trailer trash and he'd admit she was fun – she'd made him laugh on several occasions, but leave your wife material?

As if he'd read his thoughts, Robbie turned to him. 'Seriously, you don't know Libby.'

No, but it's time I got to know her.

As Scott and Clara prepared to leave, Patrick followed Robbie into the yard. Libby was sitting on an upturned bucket, clutching a mug and smoking a cigarette. Her mini-skirt and wellies combination elicited a brief pang of jealousy from Patrick. *Off limits.*

'You have to head off?' Robbie asked.

Patrick shrugged, glancing to Libby. 'I don't fancy playing gooseberry.'

Robbie laughed. 'It's fine. Tallulah will be back soon. Stay. I have to ring Van so she can speak to Tilly. Please make friends with Lib. You can start by saying sorry.'

Reluctantly, Patrick agreed and while Robbie rounded up his daughters, walked towards Libby, not missing the wary frown that flashed over her face. Did she think he'd give her a hard time? Would he?

'How's Hyssop?' he asked, a half-hearted effort at peace-making.

'Go away. I hate you.'

Sod peace-making. 'You're trashing my friends' marriage. You're not exactly at the top of my Christmas card list either, princess.'

'Have you any idea how humiliating it was to be dumped in the pub?'

'It's probably up there with how Rob felt when you told him you'd gone out with someone else.'

She stubbed out her cigarette, becoming fascinated by her boots. 'It's not like it was a date.'

He shifted uneasily as her cheeks turned pink. It had been a date and they both knew it.

'Look, Rob's my best mate, so... how about a truce?'

'You run me down on a footpath you shouldn't have been on, make me look like an idiot in front of Grace and play dirty to get Hyssop back. Not a chance.'

Fine. If she wanted an apology, she'd get one.

When Patrick was thirteen, infatuated with Melody Lawson, Robbie had let him in on a secret he'd discovered reading chick lit. An overblown romantic gesture never failed to win a girl over. It'd surely work in non-romantic situations too. Patrick plucked a nasturtium from the nearest hanging basket and dropped to his knees before her.

'Libby, I am very sorry for walking out of the pub. I had my reasons, but you're right, it was bloody rude. And I'm sorry for going to Zoë about Hyssop. Please, *please* forgive me.'

She had the makings of a smile as she took the flower.

'Think of the cat,' Patrick said. 'He hates to see us fighting. Friends?'

The angelic smile grew and she shook his hand. 'Friends.'

He sat back on the bench, surprisingly relieved. 'He's been coming to visit me, by the way.'

'Hyssop?'

'A few nights last week, he's turned up about eight, knocking at the window—'

'Oh God, I love how he does that, tapping his paw against the glass 'til you let him in. He's so clever.'

'Then at about eleven, he'd sit up, listening for something. Let me guess, you coming home.'

'Thursday is Pilates.'

'And the other days?'

She blushed. 'Tallulah spends most evenings at Chloe's.'

'Handy.'

'It's wrong, I know.' Guilt flooded her face for a second before she looked up at him. 'Did you know Tallulah's convinced Maggie was murdered?'

'Really? Why?'

Patrick leaned forwards, amused, as she explained how Becky from next-door-but-one had sworn on her iPhone that she heard Maggie scream and saw someone walk out of the house. No one had mentioned this before. The police hadn't thought anything remotely suspicious had occurred.

'You found her, didn't you?' she asked. 'I think that's what Sheila said.'

He nodded. 'Hyssop came round the next day, meowing. I didn't think much of it. If Maggie went away for a few days, Sheila would feed him. But after a couple of days...' He ran his hand through his hair. 'He just kept hanging around, driving me mad. In the end, I went to Maggie's. She didn't answer and she never locked the door, so I went in to make sure he had food.'

And there Maggie was, cold and grey, her head facing the wrong way.

'That must've been horrid.' Libby lit another cigarette. 'It gives me the creeps just looking at the bottom of the stairs. There's a cracked tile....'

Patrick looked up as Tallulah came into the yard. 'Lulu, why didn't Becky tell the police about seeing someone coming out of Maggie's?'

She looked up from her phone. 'She did, but like they believed her. Jack said his mum didn't hear any screaming so basically they all ignored Becks.'

'Patrick...' Libby paused, her brow creasing. 'Was Maggie wearing her pendant?'

He shrugged. 'But she wore it every day. Why?'

'It's missing,' Libby replied. 'Zoë doesn't have it, or her mum.'

'Murdered,' Tallulah said, still texting.

Libby's frown deepened. 'Did the house look like it'd been burgled?'

'Maggie had so much junk it'd be hard to tell.' Patrick laughed. 'Why are you so interested in Maggie anyway? You didn't even know her.'

'I want to make sure that whatever happened to her doesn't happen to me.' Libby flicked her hair off her shoulder, smiling as Robbie came out.

'Does anyone fancy a margarita?' he called.

Tallulah's face lit up. 'Me.'

'In your dreams,' Robbie said, his post-Vanessa scowl easing as he tickled her.

Hours later, after several margaritas, more burgers, and a surprisingly good time with Robbie, Libby and Tallulah, Patrick waited in the yard while Robbie and Libby said their goodbyes. Understandably, they both looked very uncomfortable. It was so wrong. Patrick did all he could to look busy, checking his phone. Eventually, she jogged over and Robbie waved, clearly happy to see them all friends again. Still wrong.

Patrick pushed his bike as they headed down the bridleway, determined not to ask her the question screaming in his head. Why was she shagging Robbie? Vanessa would come back and Libby would be out on her ear. Why would she do that to herself?

'I could give you a lift.' He nodded to his bike.

'Not a chance, mister.' She looked up at the black sky, dotted with stars. 'It's a nice night. I like the walk.'

'So you run most mornings, Pilates on a Thursday, walk to work and back, ride twice a day… do you ever sit still?'

She smiled, shaking her head. 'Rob's glad you're back. Did you and Scott talk to him?'

Patrick nodded, hoping she didn't ask what was said.

'He only confided in me because he didn't have anyone else to talk to. This might not have happened if you'd been here.'

No, it bloody wouldn't, because I'd have got in there first. Rob wouldn't be messing around with you. I would be.

'Rubbish excuse. He could've talked to Scott.' He glanced at her, unable to stop himself. 'You know you'll end up with nothing, no job?'

'Yes.' She focussed on the ground and tucked her hair behind her ears. 'He loves her and they have three daughters who need them to be together. I'm just something for now, to make him feel better. It's not ideal, but worth it for the distraction.'

'The distraction?'

She flashed a brilliant smile. 'I have my reasons.'

He shook his head, laughing. 'Which are?'

'What are yours?'

'I asked first.'

'None of your business. You don't have to escort me home, you know. I'm quite capable of looking after myself.'

'With a potential murderer on the loose?'

She laughed. 'A good point, well presented.'

'Actually, you have got me thinking.'

'Careful. Don't hurt yourself.'

He faux-punched her arm. 'I was thinking if the place looked burgled.'

'And?'

'While I was waiting for the police, I went into the kitchen to feed Hyssop. There was a card and gift-wrapped box on the side, unopened. If you were robbing the place, wouldn't you open it?'

'I wouldn't bother. It was a couple of scented candles and a bottle of wine from Sheila.'

'But a burglar would've at least opened it.' He shook his head. 'So, no. I don't think the place had been burgled.'

'But where has the pendant gone?'

'Maybe Maggie lost it at the Ostara festival. I'll ask Grace on Tuesday.'

'Why would Grace know?'

'Because she went with Maggie to the Ostara festival.'

'Are you telling me—'

'Grace plays witch too.' He smiled down at her, loving her bemused expression. 'Nuts, isn't it? Grown adults believing in *magic*.'

'You don't think there's anything in it?'

'Of course not. I mean, okay, some of the herbal remedies Grace knocks up are pretty effective, but spells and amulets? Whatever.'

'What about fate and luck?'

'I prefer to control my own life.' He studied her, watching as she nibbled her thumbnail. 'What, do you believe in all that crap?'

'Maybe.' She shrugged and he'd bet his life that if the light were better, he'd be able to see her blushing. 'Just sometimes it's like everything happens for a reason.'

'Bullshit. That's just what people say to excuse their own crappy behaviour.'

She stopped, her face looking up at him, unsmiling. 'Is that what you think I'm doing?'

Bollocks. He hadn't meant that. Then again... 'Is your affair with a married man for a reason?'

'No.' She set off again, her arms wrapped around herself. 'And I hate myself for it.'

Oh, so everything happens for a reason, does it? And what possible reason could fate have for making Libby hate herself?

Chapter Seventeen

Why the hell did the weather have to finally break on her lunch hour? Mercifully, Zoë's heels had a centimetre platform that shielded her toes from the puddles. Jess had offered to pop to the bakery down the road for ham and egg rolls, but Zoë would rather stick pins in her own eyes than sit in the office with them all as they flicked through *Heat* and *Grazia*, wittering on about the latest celebrity reality show. Instead, she claimed the need for fresh air and a trip to Boots, but then headed the opposite way, to the coffee-slash-bookshop.

It was ridiculous. It wasn't like she owed him anything. He'd stood her up first. Yet she scurried under the awning, shaking out her umbrella. This was Libby's fault. Or Patrick's – the way he'd looked at Libby... The windows were steamed up but the door was open, and from the buzz of voices inside, it was clearly busy. Would Mr Coffee Shop be there? Taking a deep breath, she pushed open the door and stepped inside.

He wasn't there.

Fuck.

A table at the back was free. She could sit and read at least. After shedding her mac and taking out her book, Zoë folded herself onto an oak chair and sank back against a purple velvet scatter cushion. All credit to Mr Coffee Shop, the place was a little oasis of boho class. Zoë smiled at the three blackboards hanging side by side on the wall: Eat, Listen, Ponder. Under the first were the day's specials, under the second was a playlist of the eclectic music they'd be playing, and under the third a quote:

We accept the love we think we deserve
– Stephen Chobsky

'What can I get– oh, hi.' The waitress held up a finger, as if Zoë were about to dash off. 'I have something for you.'

She returned from the counter with an envelope. The one Mr Coffee Shop had left two months ago no doubt.

'I'm sure you've seen him since then,' the waitress said, 'but it's still here. What can I get you?'

'Coffee, American, black and...' Zoë glanced up from the envelope to the specials board. 'The morello cherry and chocolate fondant, please. With vanilla ice cream.'

The envelope was thick, quality and he'd written her name in blue ink. It'd smudged under what looked like coffee.

I have Jonathan. I don't need this guy.

But then there he was, coming in from the side door marked *Staff Only*. He didn't say a word, but sat down at her table, looking her in the eye. What was it with him? And why after six weeks of walking the long way round to get to work, had she suddenly decided to go and see him? Okay, she itched to rake her fingers through his hair, to push it out of his stupidly blue eyes and drag him to bed, but he was a waiter in a bloody coffee shop-come-bookstore. He wasn't her type. She liked corporate men in suits; he had a silver chain holding a bow and arrow hung around his neck, and three leather thongs on his wrist.

And why did he look so familiar? Someone famous, an actor maybe? Whoever it was, it wasn't *the man of her dreams* as Libby suggested. Zoë didn't buy into that true love bullshit.

Yet here she was about to utter the one word she aimed never to say. 'Sorry.'

His eyes twinkled as he stretched out his legs. 'What was it, payback?'

'No. Something came up at work that I couldn't say no to.'

'Cocktails with Jess and Nikki?'

'Friends of yours?' And which had he shagged?

'Nikki,' he replied, answering her mental question. 'A long time ago.'

Zoë's coffee was placed on the table and Mr Coffee Shop ordered a double espresso, but the whole time, they never dropped eye contact with one another. Obviously he wasn't too pissed off with being stood up. Eventually, he smiled and glanced away.

'Virginia Woolf?' he asked, nodding to her copy of *Orlando* on the table. 'You're a lipstick feminist?'

Refusing to rise to his mocking tone, Zoë smiled back. 'Not particularly. It's a waste of time in this world.' She turned the book in her hands. 'But it's good to see the world through other people's eyes.'

'I'm Ed.'

'Zoë.' As they shook hands her heart rate increased. How good would it feel to have those hands undoing her blouse, slipping her bra straps off her shoulders? 'So, *Ed...* you work here?'

He shook his head, his eye contact again unwavering. 'But I help out since I'm here all the time.'

'Why are you here all the time? Don't you have a job to go to?'

'I'm a writer.'

Penniless, no doubt. 'What do you write?'

He shrugged. 'Whatever needs writing. Exposés of oil companies leaving wildlife to die on a beach, a novella about date rape, a four hundred page sci-fi tome decrying heartless capitalism.'

'Ah, you're a do-gooder journalist.'

'And you're a soulless estate agent.'

'The most heartless of capitalist occupations.' She tipped her head, unable to hide her grin.

'Good job I'm a ghost writer then. I write whatever I'm paid to. I'm as soulless as you. We've still got a chance, beautiful.'

Zoë blushed. *Blushed.* When had that last happened?

For forty minutes, over coffee and a side order of palpable sexual tension, they discussed her move from Manchester, his desire to move to Paris, her penchant for chocolate puddings, his disgust over Amazon deforestation.

'Ah, so you *are* a do-gooder.'

He grinned. 'You got me.'

'Do I?' She leaned forwards, resting her elbows on the table, mirroring his pose so their faces were merely inches apart. She could smell his aftershave, the coffee he'd drunk, the cigarette he'd had earlier.

'You do.' He brushed a strand of her hair off her face. 'Hooked.'

Her chest rose and fell with each increasingly unsteady breath. *I want to kiss him. I want to kiss him more than I've ever wanted to kiss anyone in my life.* Surely, if he looked down, he'd be able to see her heart hammering in her chest. If he looked down? The whole time they'd been talking, he never so much as glanced at her tits.

Five past two? Shit. How had she lost track of time?

'I have to go,' she said. What would she give to stay? 'Walk me out?' *And kiss me goodbye?*

Laughing, he stood up and grabbed a paperback from the shelf behind the counter. 'Here. So you can see the world through my eyes.'

She took the book, unable to see the title, or the cover image. All she could see were the two words proclaiming his name: *Ed Carr*. Bile rose to her mouth, her stomach contracting. This couldn't be happening. She needed to dissolve into a shrieking puddle like the wicked witch of the west.

'You're... Jonathan's son.'

'I'm Jonathan's son.'

'I've got to go.'

'But—'

'Bye.' She dropped a twenty on the counter and fled into the rain.

How could he be Jonathan's son? How? How could she look him in the eye ever again when the previous night she'd tied his father to a bed and sucked his dick, tormenting him but never letting him come?

'Zoë?'

She struggled to put her umbrella up, the rain now torrential. Stupid, bloody—

'How long have you been fucking him?' Ed stood before her, his white shirt already turning transparent.

'I have no idea what you're talking about.'

'Don't give me that bullshit. I knew it. I knew it the minute I saw you. You look just like that bitch.'

Zoë abandoned the umbrella, blinking away the water coating her eyelashes. 'I look like who?'

'Why else would he give you the job?'

'Because I'm good at selling houses?'

Ed laughed, but any of his early eye twinkling was long gone. 'If Dad believed that, he'd have you in the Kendal branch with his real sales team. Face it, he employed you to be his latest whore.'

Her hand struck his cheek before she even knew she wanted to hit him.

Twenty minutes later, Zoë's hands were still shaking with barely restrained rage as she pushed open the door of Carr & Young's Kendal office. Somehow, after leaving Ed standing in the rain, his cheek red, she'd got into her car, letting out a scream of frustration before she'd calmly pulled her hair into a neat bun and repainted her lips the most Chanel of red.

The *real sales team*?

What the fuck was she? Okay, it was weird the Haverton branch only employed women, mostly ineffective ones at that, and the Kendal branch appeared *manned* by the go-getting boys. But she merely assumed the boy branch would be as lazy-assed as the girl branch. Although, when she met a few of them on that night out with Nikki, they did seem to be pretty on top of their game. And her tits.

Was Ed right?

The second she'd seen the glass and steel front of the Kendal office, the cutting edge monitors on the sleek wooden desks, Zoë knew he was. She'd been sectioned in some façade of a Head Office, shuffling paper, sweet-talking the tricky high-end customers and letting the Kendal staff handle the bulk of sales, earn the real commission.

'Can I help you?' the girl on reception asked.

'It's Casey, isn't it? I'm Zoë Horton, from the Haverton office. I'm here to see Mr Carr.'

'Oh, okay, but he said–'

'He's expecting me,' Zoë lied.

'Oh, I guess you should go on back. Last door on the left.'

Stupid girl.

Zoë stalked to the back of the office, smiling pleasantly at the *real sales team*. Jonathan's door was open and he sat on his desk chatting to Adam, the one who'd copped a feel of her tits. Without asking.

'Mr Carr?' she said, smiling for Adam's benefit.

'Excuse us, Adam.'

The second Adam did as he was told, Zoë kicked the door shut with her heel, glaring at Jonathan.

'Maybe I should have explained this a little clearer, Miss Horton. There's a time and a place for you to–'

'My name is Zoë and this is the time *and* the place to discuss my *job*. I want to know why I'm rotting with those dimwits in Haverton, using past-it PCs while your little boy's club here has touch screen monitors and bloody iPads?'

'What is it you want?'

'To work here. To be treated as an equal. To be a *genuine* member of the sales team, not just your god-damned mistress.'

'Are you my god-damned mistress?'

'That depends on how the rest of this conversation goes.'

Jonathan nodded. 'It'd be a longer drive to work.'

'I'll set my alarm clock that little bit earlier.'

'The sales quotas will be higher.'

'I'll deliver them.'

'I still want you to do the searches for customers.'

'Happy to.'

'Then it's a deal. Martin is leaving at the end of the month. You can take his desk.'

Two weeks. Survivable. Slowly, she walked towards him. 'And you'd better re-evaluate my pay. If I discover any of the misogynistic arseholes out there earn a penny more than me, I will take you to the cleaners.'

'You really are absolutely magnificent,' he gently held her chin before he kissed her.

Jesus, she loved this whole dom/sub thing. The control it gave her. The power. It radiated from her skin.

'I know.' She gently bit his bottom lip, just how he liked it. 'Now, why don't you introduce me to my new colleagues?'

Chapter Eighteen

From across the street, Zoë could see Ed sitting at a table in the window, his laptop open. She glanced at his book in her hand. *The Orphan*. She adored the sketch of the cuckoo, but then she adored the typeface used to show his name and every single word he'd written inside. Ed, it seemed, held more thought, could wield more compassion with a mere word, even one as seemingly insignificant as *the*, than anyone she'd ever met. But this was over.

His brow furrowed when she walked in, but he sat back and looked up at the Quote of the Day.

Mistakes are the portals of discovery
– James Joyce

'How apt,' she offered.

'I picked it. Yesterday's was a little more bitter and Thursday's... it pretty much offended everyone. How are you?'

Still shagging your dad.

She dropped his book on the table. 'You have serious issues with your parents.'

He nodded, his burning gaze never leaving hers. 'And you haven't even met my mother.'

Seriously, why did he never check her out? She'd worn her favourite red dress, a sleek bodycon number that pulled in her less favourable bits and showed off her curves. What was the point if he never looked?

Slowly, he slid the note he'd left her across the table. 'You never read this.'

What was the point now? 'I've been relocated, to Kendal.'

He nodded again, folding his arms. 'What did you have to do to earn that?'

'Stay away from me.'

Most definitely over.

She strode away, bouncing between wanting to hit someone and

162

bursting into tears. Time to get shit-faced. But as she reached her car, her mobile lit up. Jonathon. Was he changing his plans for the night? He was supposed to be going to some tedious golf club soiree with his frigid wife, leaving Zoë to watch a village bloody football match with Libby.

'Hello,' she purred.

'Is that Zoë Horton?' asked a posh woman.

Oh, holy… Was that Jonathon's wife? Had she found out? Had Ed told her?

'It is.'

'This is Fee Carr, Jonathan's wife.'

Shit, shit, shit.

'Is awfully unprofessional to call out of the blue, but I was a friend of your great-aunt…'

Didn't see that coming.

'…thought it would be lovely to say hello. Would you like to come for lunch next Thursday?'

Or that.

She'd said yes partly because she couldn't think of a genuine excuse not to, but wouldn't it be interesting to understand why the hell Jonathan didn't just divorce the woman. And why her son hated her so much.

* * *

The village football match, a grudge game between the two Kings, the Alfred of Gosthwaite and the George of Haverton, was an annual fixture, which the Gosthwaite Eleven had lost 1-0 for the last two years. This year, Robbie had informed Libby, they were determined to win – Scott had even rallied the troops for three training sessions. Libby had her doubts. Scott, Xander, Patrick and another six guys stood in the beer tent, pints in hand. Not a winning attitude in her book.

'I don't like this,' Libby said, frowning up at Robbie. With her holding Matilda's hand and him carrying Dora, they looked exactly what they weren't – a happy little family. 'People will talk.'

'Stop worrying.' Robbie set Dora down, smiling as she and Matilda skipped off to the bouncy castle stationed in the corner of the field. 'Half the people here know anyway.'

'And the half that don't know think I'm shagging your brother. I'd rather be at work.'

'I'd rather you were here. I'm half-tempted to kiss you right now.'

She elbowed him, knowing he was teasing her. 'Where the hell's Zoë? She promised me she'd be here for moral support. Oh God, there's Jack.'

'Relax.' Robbie placed a hand on her back, guiding her towards the bar. 'Drink?'

She smiled hello to his friends, the people she knew, but pointedly ignored Grace. 'And it's fair to say your mother knows.'

'She does not. What do you want, jug of Pimm's?'

'Please. Your dad was looking at me very suspiciously before we left.'

'My dad was checking you out.' He dropped a twenty on the bar, looking over her denim shorts and silk halter neck top. 'Understandably.'

'Oh, there it is.' She took four plastic cups from the barman and walked away.

'Oh, there what is?' Robbie lay out a rug at the side of the pitch nearest the bouncy castle.

'The look.' She smiled at his raised eyebrows. 'Like you're about to bend me over the sofa, whether I like it or not. You're infamous for it, but for the record, you can and I would.'

'Takes the fun out of it, if I have permission.' He dropped to the rug, glancing over to his daughters bouncing merrily away. 'But that's not what I was thinking.'

She sat cross-legged, holding out her cup for him to fill. 'So what was it?'

He popped a strawberry from the jug into her mouth. 'I want to wake up with you tomorrow.'

Libby stared at him and he stared back. 'Really?'

'Mum and Dad are there to look after the kids. It won't make any difference to them.'

They could go to bed, fall asleep, wake up. Talk, kiss, shag whenever they liked. Unrushed. Turning away, Libby watched the other players jogging onto the pitch. Why wasn't she thrilled at the idea? Because she knew he really wanted his wife back? Was he closing his eyes and thinking of his wife? Had he always been doing that?

'You're really going to stay the night?' she asked, her cheeks flushing with shame as Patrick ran by.

'I hope you're not planning to get much sleep.'

'OMG, Daze, look. A picnic rug and Pimm's, is this a romantic date?' Clara wandered over with Daisy in tow, both pushing sleeping tots in buggies. 'Oh, the kids are here too.'

'Playing happy families?' Daisy asked, barely able to look Libby in the eye.

With her worst fear confirmed, Libby's blushes increased. People did think she was trying to get her feet under Low Wood Farm's kitchen table. She knocked back her drink as Clara sat down. Where the hell was Zoë?

'So, Ms Wilde,' Clara said, helping herself to the Pimm's. 'Shall I sign you up for the fan club, or pencil you in to be guest speaker at the AGM?'

Robbie pulled Clara's ponytail. 'Leave her alone.'

'You're no fun.'

'Rob,' Scott called from the pitch, beckoning him over.

Robbie checked on Matilda and Dora, still bouncing. 'Lib—'

'I'll keep an eye on them,' Daisy offered.

'They'll be fine with me,' Libby said, and as Robbie jogged away, she turned to Daisy. 'I'm not trying to take her place if that's what you're worried about.'

'You couldn't. She's their mother.'

Libby stared at her empty cup.

'Daze, pack it in. It's Van's fault as much as anyone's. Besides, Libby's only human. I'm not a hundred percent sure I'd say no.'

'I'm just... if Robbie would, what if Xander would too?'

Libby hadn't a clue what to say. Would sorry cut it?

'I'm going to the bar.' Daisy strode away, pushing baby Evie towards Xander who was already grinning, clearly delighted at their arrival.

'Xander never would and she knows it,' Clara said, turning to watch the other men warming up. 'You and Rob explains a few things though. I couldn't understand why Patrick didn't have his hands in your pants already. I'd started to think he'd either found God or caught HIV. If I were you, that's who I'd be doing.'

From the safety of her sunglasses, Libby watched as the boys started stretching, Patrick laughing with Scott.

'He's not my type.'

'Why? He's the classic Byronic hero and sexy as fuck. And OMG, does that guy know how to party. There are three days of my life I can't remember. All I know is we got the train to Paris and I couldn't walk when we got back.'

'You and Patrick...' But wasn't he one of Scott's oldest friends? Well, that was his decent moral values box left unchecked.

Clara waved a dismissive hand. 'It was yonks ago, before Scott and I got together. Well, we were kind of on a break. Scott's the settle down and marry type, but Patrick's more likely to get you fucked, fuck you then fuck off.'

'Definitely, not my type.'

'He's fun. Last year. Gosthwaite would've won the football, but he got hammered, punched the Haverton goalie and got sent off. Scott was furious, but it really kicked off after the match. Patrick got busted snorting coke off his Land Rover bonnet. I thought it was hilarious, but PC Andy wasn't so amused. You should so go out with him, Libby.'

Not a chance. Whatever his reasons were for walking out of the pub, Libby had to admit she'd had a lucky escape. Clara was right; Patrick was hot, very hot, but the last thing Libby needed was to get involved with someone who slept with his friend's girlfriend.

'O... M... freaking G.' Clara pointed to the other side of the field.

The Haverton team stopped their knee-raises as Zoë walked into the park. One-by-one the Gosthwaite players slowed to a halt, watching her hourglass body, perfectly encased in a sleek red dress, killer heels in hand, wiggle past. Jack and the Haverton goalie even managed to walk into one another. But if Zoë knew she'd literally brought members of two football teams to their knees, she appeared oblivious, merely flicking her glossy black hair over one shoulder, bee-lining to Libby.

'Bit over-dressed for a football match, aren't you?' Libby filled a cup, offering it to her. Zoë downed it in one then held it out for a refill. 'Bad day not-at-work, dear?'

'That's one way to put it. Jesus, there's no shade. I'm so going to get freckles sitting here. Hi, Clara.' Zoë hitched her skirt up, flashing more shapely thigh.

Libby frowned at the linked Cs on the arms of Zoë's sunglasses. 'Are they Chanel?'

'Yes.'

'You can't afford—'

'They were a gift from a guy at work.'

'Ooh, who?' Clara asked. 'Adam's pretty hot.'

'And a total dick,' Zoë said, her head tipping to the side as the

Gosthwaite team began stretching. 'Jesus, Patrick's put together pretty bloody well.'

Libby nibbled a slice of cucumber, determined not to answer, and thankfully Clara's little boy woke up, distracting them.

'Oh for...' Clara groaned. 'I'll be back in, well about twenty minutes if I'm lucky.'

'It's a shame he's a vet,' Zoë said, suspiciously casual.

'Patrick?' Libby hated herself for biting. Zoë knew all her soft spots. A vet had to be the hottest profession around, even surpassing a fireman. Rushing in, saving kittens, puppies, ponies – all completely heroic to Libby.

'Might do it for you, Lib,' Zoë said. 'And okay, they do earn a fair whack, but it's a bit... grubby.'

Libby glanced again at Patrick. His grubby side wasn't his job, it was his rather dubious morals: rude, backstabbing and willing to sleep with his friend's girlfriend. She sipped her wine. Thank God he wasn't English. Thank God she hadn't summoned someone like him.

'What's going on?' Libby asked, topping up Zoë's cup. 'You've a face on you like someone's cut up all your credit cards.'

Zoë let out a long sigh. 'Remember the hot coffee shop guy? He's a no-fly zone.'

No fly zone? But Zoë didn't have rules; she thrived on breaking other people' rules. 'Why?'

'He's...' Zoë's guilty blinking was so obvious the partially-sighted lady collecting money for guide dogs outside the WI tent could see it. 'He's Jonathan Carr's son.'

'Your boss?' Why would that matter? Unless... Libby folded her arms. 'You're shagging him?'

'Don't you bloody dare?'

'What?'

'Don't give me that *why-can't-people-be-faithful* crap.' Zoë pinched one of her cigarettes. '*You're* shagging your boss.'

'That's different. Rob's in a difficult place.'

'And what if my boss is in a difficult place, does that make it okay?'

'Is he?'

'As a matter of fact, yes. His wife, Fee, had a car crash years ago and has permanent back pain. Total cripple. They have a very open marriage.'

'She *knows*?'

'She even invited me for *lunch*.'

Libby worried the polish on her thumbnail. 'Why didn't you tell me about him?'

'Why do you think? You wouldn't have *approved*.'

'Sorry.' Libby glanced across at Robbie. Pots and Kettles. 'But you're choosing your boss over his son, even though–'

'He's just some guy.'

'Who you like a lot. Admit it. You loved his book... Zo, you could LOVE this guy.'

'Ha ha.'

'Why are you choosing his dad?'

'Because he's a god-damned silver fox.' Zoë took a long slow drag on her cigarette. 'And he's totally loaded.'

'He won't be if his wife divorces him and takes him for everything he has. What's wrong with having a normal boyfriend?'

'Oh, like you've got?'

'Why not choose the son?'

'The penniless writer?'

'You fancy him. Is Jonathan's money really that important?'

'Of course not. But if there are two equally hot guys, one rich, one poor, which would you do?'

'The one I liked the most.'

'Or the one who could give you control of your own life?'

Control? Why did it always come down to control?

'You're insane. Going out with Ed, who's *single,* is sensible. It could be a long term thing. That's what you should be doing.'

'Really?' Zoë asked. 'If that's what you really think, why are you shagging your *married* boss when you could be doing the sensible thing with the hot vet?'

Libby lay down and closed her eyes. 'There's nothing sensible about that vet.'

'I rest my bloody case.'

The gentle English afternoon of Pimm's had given way to a beer tent filled with flashing lights and Lady Gaga booming from speakers. Laughter came from every corner, but Libby sat outside, curled up on a bench. This had to be in her Top Ten of situations she never wanted to find herself in. Ever. Zoë currently had some farmer friend of Scott's wrapped around her finger and Robbie still hadn't come back from taking the kids home. Clara and Scott were laughing at the bar, but Grace and Jack's close proximity meant Libby couldn't join them. At least the smoking gave her a valid excuse not to be in the marquee.

She lit her second off her first. She could just go home. Robbie would come over and they could spend the evening together, not just the night. That idea had a lot going for it, but it didn't give Robbie the chance to get drunk and hang out with his friends. And he needed that.

Distracted by the strobe lights, Libby didn't notice the shadow fall over her, but the aroma of the barbeque gave way to the more enticing smell of fresh sweat on a fit guy.

'The white Rioja,' Patrick said, handing her a glass as he sat down.

'Thank you,' she said, sure she'd never been so grateful for a drink or a goodwill gesture in her life.

'Enjoy the match?'

'I'm guessing you did, Mister Hat Trick.'

Patrick had been named Man of the Match after Gosthwaite cruised home three-one, thanks to his goals.

His grin was like a child's at Christmas, unashamedly happy. 'I don't know if you heard about last year—'

'Clara couldn't resist.'

'She never can.' He gazed across the deserted pitch, still smiling. 'Christ, I feel like...'

Libby's mood lifted – his happiness infecting her. 'What?'

He shook his head. 'Anyway, I've made up for it.'

'And when their back took you out, you didn't hit him.'

He laughed softly. 'I nearly did.'

'But you didn't.'

'I didn't.' He turned to her. 'Are you hiding?'

She nodded.

'Come inside. Scott's just bought a bottle of tequila.'

Libby shook her head.

'Why?'

'Grace.'

'She won't bother you, not really.'

'You've said that before and she did.'

'She was just mouthing off. Sticks and stones.' Patrick wafted her smoke away.

'Sorry.'

'Since you're not putting it out, you're not forgiven. Look, you can't avoid her forever.'

'I can try.'

'She's behind the bar, but I promise if she even looks at–'

'You didn't last time.'

'I told you. I had my reasons.'

All too aware of how his post-football body felt so close to hers, Libby shifted on the bench, trying to distance herself from him, but as she crossed her legs, her knee touched his, the skin-to-skin contact making her flinch. He stared down at their knees.

'How's Hyss–'

'Did you–'

Libby tucked her hair behind her ears, blushing. 'Did you ask Grace about Maggie's pendant?'

'Yeah, on Monday, but she got all... so I didn't push it.'

'She got all what?'

'Well, she and Maggie were friends and she got all upset. I hate it when girls cry.'

'Ohmigod, you soft touch.' She elbowed him, laughing, and they both relaxed. 'Go ask her.'

'Tell you what. I'll man up and ask Grace, if you man up and come inside.' He stood up, taking her glass. 'Come on.'

Reluctantly, she followed him into the marquee, but he led her to the furthest end of the bar, beckoning Scott and Clara to join them.

'Why are you being nice?' she asked.

'It's my job to look after you when Rob's not here.'

'Excuse me?'

'I've got his back. It's a Musketear thing.'

'A what?'

He looked away, grinning. 'Can't say anymore.'

'I'll cry...' She smiled up at him, fluttering her eyelashes.

'God help me.' He leaned on the bar, his elbow resting against hers. 'Scott, Rob and I went to school together. They used to call us the Musketears, tears spelt the boo-hoo way. We broke a lot of hearts apparently. And I say they, I think Scott started it.'

Libby laughed. 'I'm guessing he's Athos?'

'He's your traditional sporting hero, academic, alpha-male, captain of all the teams.'

'And from what Clara told me, you'd fit the wine, women and song role of Porthos.'

'Christ, what did she tell you?'

Libby mimed locking her lips.

'It'll all be true.'

'You sure? Even sleeping with your best friend's girlfriend?'

His grin faltered. 'Yeah.'

'But you and Scott are still friends?'

'We are now. Took about a year.'

Libby had her chin on her hand, intrigued. How could someone have so few moral values that they'd do something like that? 'Why did you do it?'

He sipped his pint, turning to where Clara and Scott were chatting. 'I don't trust her, never have. We get on, she's fun, but she screwed Scott around and I don't like that.'

'You've got his back?'

'Absolutely. It was a stupid idea, but I was wasted and I wanted to show him that she didn't really care about him. Christ, after we'd, you know, she sent him a picture. Nice, hey?' He shook his head. 'But he forgave her and one day, she just asked him to marry her. And now look at them.'

Libby turned, watching Clara and Scott gazing at each other. 'So is Rob Aramis, the romantic hero?'

Patrick nodded. 'He's going to kill me for telling you this, but he spent most of his time pulling anything in a skirt and he was bloody good at it.'

Libby sipped her wine, trying not to show her shock.

'He'd have a girlfriend, one on the side, and another waiting in the wings.'

'I thought he was Mister Faithful.'

'Back then, he wasn't.'

'What happened?'

'Vanessa. I take it you've never met her?'

She shook her head.

'If you had, you wouldn't be shagging him, because she's the nicest person in world.'

'Don't make me feel any worse.' Libby sighed. 'So he changed, just like that?'

'Scott and I came back for Christmas and Rob was shacked up with her. We couldn't believe the change. He said he knew the day he met her that she was the love of his life.'

'She still is.'

'Why are you messing around with a married man who blatantly loves his wife? Habit of yours?'

'No. I have huge issues with infidelity. This is different.' Libby nodded to Grace, who'd left the bar to collect glasses. 'Ask her now.'

'But–'

Libby pushed him away. Cursing her, and not under his breath, Patrick went over to Grace. The sound system pounding out the Weather Girls prevented Libby from hearing anything they said, but at least she had an unobstructed view. As Grace spoke, she glanced over at Libby, loathing in her eyes, and Patrick's body language changed. He had his back to Libby, but he folded his arms, his shoulders stiffening. This wasn't chit chat about Maggie. More interesting was how Grace glanced down, her nod full of contrition. Unless Libby was very mistaken, Patrick had just given Grace a telling off, and she'd taken it. That girl hero-worshipped him.

The next time Patrick spoke, Grace's bottom lip wobbled, and his shoulders sagged. He really was a sucker for tears. Man up. Was he still speaking or was Grace struggling to compose her answer? Hard to tell, but when Grace did speak, she twiddled her hair, looking down at her feet, anywhere but at Patrick. And in response to his last question Grace's right hand hovered over her mouth. Ashamed of her words. What on earth was she lying about?

Libby leant on the bar, eager for the news as Patrick joined her back at the bar. His frown intriguing her. 'And?'

'Maggie was wearing the necklace at the Ostara festival. And she left early because of a migraine.'

Libby's eyes widened. 'So where did the necklace go?'

'No idea, but Grace said she thought it was odd that the elderflower wine you were poisoned with was in the gift bag.' He leant on the bar, his frown worsening. 'You were poisoned? How?'

Libby stared at him, shock and shame bouncing around her head. 'I thought she told you what happened with Jack?'

'She just said you messed around with him. Jack *poisoned* you?'

'No. I mean, yes, but not intentionally.' With mortification seeping out with every word, she gave him a glossed over account of the horrific night four weeks ago.

Patrick leant back, open mouthed. 'Jesus Christ, that's practically date rape, Libby.'

'No. It wasn't his fault.' She forced a smile. 'How often does she use the waterworks on you?'

He raised his eyebrows. 'Grace?'

'I think she's playing you, putting on the tears to avoid the situation. You really don't react well to girls crying. Soft touch.'

'How the hell do you...' Patrick glanced across to Grace, who now laughed with Clara at the bar. 'Really?'

Libby nodded. 'And... she was lying.'

'What about?'

'I don't know. You were talking to her. All I could hear was *It's Raining Men.*'

'How do you know she was lying?'

'Body language.'

'But that's—'

'An art form I happen to be bloody good at.'

'How?'

'If I told you that, I'd have to kill you.'

'Get over yourself.'

'My dad used to be an expert for the MOD. Interrogations, diplomacy, but seriously, I'm not allowed to say anymore.'

'Rob said he thought you were a compulsive liar. I think he might be right.'

'Can you read me, tell if I'm lying? I doubt it.' She smiled as Robbie headed over, swiping Scott's bottle of tequila along the way.

'She's really been playing me?'

Libby elbowed him. 'If it makes you feel any better, she's very good.'

'What doesn't make me feel any better, is that I've given her a bloody pay rise every time she's cried.'

'What was the last thing you asked her about?'

He thought for a moment. 'I asked why someone might want to steal the necklace.'

'What did she say?'

'She said, she hadn't the foggiest.'

Libby watched as Grace moved back behind the bar. 'But she was lying.'

If Sheila knew the emerald was worth a fortune, surely Grace would too. So why lie about it?

* * *

On the doorstep of No.4, Libby stood in her running gear, the skimpiest vest and shorts, with her arms around the neck of Robbie

Golding. His hands were on her arse and in one shot, she almost looked naked. Together with the snaps of them knocking back tequila after the football, this was pure gold.

'It's me. You're going to love this.'

'Libby Wilde?' Michael Wray asked, the pitch of his voice rising with repressed excitement.

'And Robbie Golding.'

'You beauty. Send them to me.'

She hung up and kissed her phone.

Pure bloody gold.

Chapter Nineteen

On Wednesday, Libby almost skipped into the yard, planning to make a cup of tea before she fed the horses. What she hadn't planned on was World War III breaking out. Tallulah's screaming quietened to a low sobbing, but Libby approached the house with caution. Had Robbie denied Tallulah another pony, or was this about getting her ears pierced again?

In the kitchen, when Tallulah turned, her hands clenching and unclenching, Libby knew the tears and shouting weren't another petulant pre-teen demand.

'You were supposed to be my friend, you fucking whore.'

'Lulu!' Robbie snapped.

'Fuck off,' she spat back at him. 'You and Mum were special. Now, you're just like everyone else, a fucking divorce statistic.'

Libby stared at Tallulah, unable to defend herself, or her actions. 'I'm sorry.'

'I fucking hate both of you.' Tallulah ran out, slamming the door behind her.

Robbie stared at the door, his face emotionless. 'I think it's fair to say she's mastered the use of the word *fucking*.'

Libby slumped against the table. 'I hadn't thought about Tallulah. How it'd affect her, what she'd think. Who told her?'

'You haven't seen it?' Robbie looked up to the ceiling, before pointing to the newspaper on the table. 'Christ, I'm sorry, Lib. It's worse than that.'

She picked up the paper, already open to page three. *Lock Up Your Husbands*. Two photos, side-by-side dominated the page. The first was of her and Robbie, kissing on the doorstep, the second a blurry snap of Libby and Robbie arriving at the football with the kids, looking every bit the happy family. They'd even dragged out the photos of her with Jack and Xander. She didn't read the words.

How had everything gone so wrong with her life? Once, she had everything. Now, even her morals were unravelling. Thank God her parents wouldn't find out.

'It's about now that people generally say, *Olivia Wilde, you're fired.*' She wrapped her arms around herself, her stomach churning. 'I'm so sorry.'

'What for? It's not your fault.' He sighed and after a glance towards the living room where Matilda and Dora were still engrossed in cBeebies, he pulled Libby to him, hugging her. 'I'm the married one.'

'I'll keep an eye on them, if you want to go after Tallulah.'

'Why, so my eleven year-old daughter can tell me to fuck off again? I really ought to curb her language, but she got it all from me in the first place.' His arms tightened as he kissed her head. 'I'll give her ten minutes to calm down.'

'Should I go and never come back?'

'No,' he said, taking her face in his hands. 'Maybe this is for the best.'

'How?'

'If it's out in the open, it can be… real. What if my marriage is over?'

Libby closed her eyes for a second, to compose her thoughts. She knew what he was getting at, what he'd hinted at several times. He wanted to know what would happen if Vanessa didn't come back.

'Look,' she said. 'Sometimes, a lot of the time, I daydream about what it'd be like if you were single and… didn't have kids.'

His face clouded over.

'Sorry,' she said, knowing the mere suggestion would horrify him. 'I love your life, the house, the yard, the horses, but it feels borrowed and I'm not sure if it'd ever feel like mine. You have three kids. She's their mother and… I'm not.'

His already dubious expression grew darker. She knew she was denting his ego, effectively rejecting him.

'Don't look like that,' she said, gently kissing him. 'If things were different, I'd fight like a wildcat to keep you. When you're not being a grumpy arse, you make me laugh more than anyone and you're… we're friends, right?'

He nodded.

'The thing is, you've raised my expectations, Mister Golding.' She blinked away her looming tears. 'I'd have loved you to be my Somebody.'

'You really did listen.'

'Of course I did. But you love her. She's your Somebody and you know it.' Libby sighed. 'And maybe I want more. Maybe I want to live in the whitewashed farmhouse and have kids of my own.'

'Would that be the ultimate distraction?'

'Maybe.'

He held her tighter 'I'm sorry for everything.'

She forced a smile for him. 'I'll do the horses and carry on as though I've not been outed as a home-wrecking tramp.'

'Stay away from Harmony's box. It's where she always goes when she's upset.' He kissed her head again. 'I don't regret a thing.'

I do. Libby closed her eyes, sheltering in his arms. 'You need to speak to Vanessa. Find out what she wants. We can't... You can't move on until you know.'

This was it, the end. Vanessa would find out, come to her senses and Libby would lose the only real distraction she'd ever had. For the first time, Libby hoped Vanessa had fallen in love with the French viola player.

* * *

Vanessa. Patrick read the name of the caller and swore. Why was Vanessa ringing him? He flipped over the paper, sighing at the photos of Robbie and Libby. Had Vanessa found out?

'Hello, stranger,' he said, trying to sound as though her husband hadn't been caught shagging the staff.

Vanessa sniffed. 'Please, tell me it's not true. Tell me you're the one who's shagging her and he was just giving her a hug.'

A hug? In one photo Robbie had his hand on Libby's arse. Did she think Robbie regularly copped a feel of Patrick's girlfriends? 'Van...'

'Is it true?'

'Come home.'

'I can't.' She broke into fresh sobbing. 'Does he love her?'

'No, he loves you.'

'Then why's he shagging her?'

Because you're shagging the French bloke. 'Come home.'

'What if he doesn't want me back?'

'He does. Do you want to come back?'

Silence sat on the line.

'Van?'

'I don't know,' she croaked. 'I mean all the things that were wrong aren't suddenly fixed by him shagging Livvy.'

Patrick couldn't help himself. 'What, you thought shagging that French wanker *would* fix things? And her name is *Libby*.'

She hung up.

Bollocks.

Time to call in the cavalry.

Scott, the undisputed leader of the Musketears arrived at six, still suited and booted from the office, and Patrick started the Land Rover, filling him in on Vanessa's call. At Low Wood Farm, everything was quiet, but Robbie met them in the yard with a six pack in hand, his forehead furrowed.

'Where is everyone?' Scott asked, loosening his tie.

'If you mean Libby, she's gone home,' Rob replied and handed them beers. 'I take it you've seen the paper. Tallulah's being a little... vicious.'

'Do you blame her?' Scott asked

Robbie lit a cigarette and shook his head.

'How is Libby?' Patrick asked, refusing the proffered beer.

'Devastated.' Robbie frowned. 'Are you ill or something?'

'No, driving,' Patrick said, dismissively. 'Look, Vanessa rang me earlier.'

Robbie stared at the sky, swearing under his breath. 'She knows?'

Patrick nodded. 'She was upset, crying, asking if it were true.'

'She hasn't come home though, has she?'

What the hell could Patrick say? He sat back, leaving the cavalry to come up with something.

Scott sighed. 'This has to end. Mate, Libby's not for you.'

'Why?' Robbie asked.

'Is she ready to play the wicked step-mother?'

Robbie took a long drag on his cigarette.

'I'll take your silence as a no,' Scott said. 'You need to get Vanessa back before it's too late.'

'What if it already is?' Rob stared at the table.

Scott smiled. 'When I thought all was lost with Clara, what did you tell me?'

Why did they have to bring his fuck-up with Clara into this? Patrick held his breath, unsure what his friends had discussed behind his back.

'It's never too late if it's the love of your life.' Robbie drained his beer.

'So how are you going to get Vanessa back?'

'For fuck's sake, she walked out, Scott.'

For a few minutes, they sat in silence. Robbie chain-smoked, Patrick tapped his fingers, wishing he could drink but finally, Scott sat up.

'She did. She left. The question is, why?' Scott sucked in a deep breath. 'Van's not the sort to suddenly have her head turned by some French viola player. Why did she really leave?'

'She said...' Robbie leaned forwards. 'Originally, she wanted to go away to be her, Vanessa Jones, not Vanessa Golding. She was sick of being my wife. She hated that all she'd ever done was get her face on Marie Claire and have three children. That everything she's done was for me, but I take her for granted and she's fourth on my list. Girls, Horses, Restaurant, Wife. It's like the last thirteen years have been a waste.'

'Have they?' Scott asked, quietly.

Robbie shook his head. 'And she's not fourth on my list.'

'But that's how she feels,' Scott said, opening their second bottles. 'Now, what the hell are you going to do about it?'

'I don't know.' Robbie stared up at the sky. 'It's not just that. She said we had nothing in common. She's right. She loves music. I don't get it. She wants to talk about Mozart and I want to talk about breed lines. And she wants a life in music. She can't have that around here.'

'Yes, she can.' Patrick frowned. 'Haverton has an orchestra. It might be small, but it's an orchestra. My mum loves going to see them. Or Van could play in Lancaster, and Manchester's only an hour away. Or if it matters that much, move.'

'Move?'

'What matters more, her or here?' Patrick asked.

Robbie sat back. 'Her.'

'Then why the fuck are we having this conversation? Go see her.' Scott laughed.

'But she's right. We don't have anything in common. Libby and I do.'

'*Breakfast at Tiffany's,*' Scott said, holding his hands in the air as if he'd scored a goal.

'The film?' Patrick asked.

'The song. Clara loves it. You say we've got nothing in common, no common ground to start from, and we're falling apart. She says it reminds her why she puts up with me when I'm watching cricket, or buggering off to Twickenham.' He smiled at Robbie, knowing he had the answer. 'So you're overly obsessed with horses and couldn't give a damn about Beethoven, that doesn't mean you don't have anything in common. Think about all the other stuff. You've been together for thirteen years. Something worked.'

'*Breakfast at Tiffany's*? That's your motivational talk? You're slipping, mate.' Robbie laughed a little, before picking at his beer label.

'Think about it,' Scott said, still looking pretty smug.

'I suppose...' The despair had gone from Robbie's face, instead he sipped his beer, his forehead furrowed in thought. 'It's a bit... but we both liked it, the film. Actually, we generally like the same films. We always said we'd rather watch a Disney DVD with the girls than anything with subtitles.'

'Well, that's her and Frenchie screwed.' Patrick grinned.

Scott patted Robbie's back. 'I think it's time for an overblown romantic gesture.'

'I don't think a bunch of flowers will cut it.' Robbie shook his head. 'Besides, I can't drive to Grassington. I'd be over the limit.'

'I'll take you,' Patrick offered.

Scott smiled. 'Excellent. I'll babysit. Cricket's on.'

'What if Van won't come back?' Worry etched Robbie's face again.

'She will,' Scott said, 'but you'd better make it a bloody good gesture so she knows the last thirteen years weren't a waste of time.'

Robbie nodded, his face set. 'I'm going to need a bucket, a clean one.'

A bucket. Patrick pulled into the car park at Grassington Town Hall and frowned at the silver pail on the back seat. The seventy minute journey had been mostly silent with Robbie staring out of the window, tapping his foot.

'What's the bucket for?' Patrick asked as he turned off the engine.

Robbie's frown worsened. 'The day I met Van, I asked her what she'd like to drink. She said a vodka and tonic, but that she'd need a bucket of the stuff because I made her so nervous. I never understood how someone so confident in front of a camera could be so shy.'

Patrick smiled, picturing Vanessa shifting from foot to foot when she had to chat to someone who intimidated her.

'She finally agreed to meet me that night and when I met her in the bar, I had a bucket. I'd put a glass of vodka and tonic inside. Months later, she admitted that's when she knew she'd love me forever.' Robbie hung his head back. 'What the fuck am I doing?'

Patrick's smile grew. Robbie was the king of romantic gestures.

The Town Hall was filled to capacity, but the lady on the door had said since it was half-nine and the concert would finish soon, it'd be okay for them to sneak in if they stood at the back of the hall.

Vanessa was on stage, in a long black dress, her hair swaying as she played, her face down, eyes closed, immersed in the music. Robbie slumped against the wall, staring with blatant pride at the talented, beautiful woman on stage.

'I should've gone to more of her performances,' he whispered, still watching her. 'I haven't seen her play for well over a year. She's right. I have taken her for granted. What the fuck was I thinking, agreeing to the free pass?'

'Because you wanted one too?'

Finally, Robbie turned his head. 'Yeah. I wanted to see if the grass is greener.'

'Is it?'

Robbie turned back, frowning. 'I'd say it's just as green, but this is Van.'

The applause was rapturous, but always uncomfortable with too much praise, Vanessa dashed through the audience, clinging to her cello case for support. They waited, watching her until eventually she saw Robbie. Aside from stopping mid-conversation and abandoning the woman she was speaking with, Vanessa didn't show any emotion, but she at least headed their way. Sadly, Jason Benoît wasn't far behind.

'She's seen the paper,' Jason said.

'*Va te faire foutre, branleur de français,*' Robbie said.

Patrick suppressed a smile, his French rusty, but the bad language he'd learned as a teenager didn't fail him.

'*Je t'emmerde,*' Jason replied.

'Stop it. You know I don't understand a word you're saying.' Vanessa crossed her arms, frowning at Robbie, but she'd not even glanced in Jason's direction.

'*Tu ne la mérite pas,*' Jason said.

'Undoubtedly,' Robbie replied. 'Now piss off.'

Once Jason had flounced off, Patrick stepped away, but leaned against a pillar, hoping to eavesdrop.

'Why are you here?' Vanessa asked.

'To remind you.' Robbie shoved his hands in his pockets, still leaning against the wall. 'How are your fingers?'

'Bloody sore. Remind me of what?'

'Green olives, unpitted, are far superior to black ones. King prawns kick ass over tiger prawns, but we'd rather have langoustines cooked on a fire on the beach. Rioja in La Rioja equals heaven. We hate the smell of vanilla unless it's in ice-cream. Sunday morning lie-ins are the best bit of the week, especially when we get an hour to ourselves before the bed's invaded by kids.'

'Go on,' she said, lifting a hand to her mouth, trying to hide her smile.

A sudden jolt of jealousy surprised Patrick. Not that he wanted Vanessa, he'd known her for so long she was like a sister, but the way she gazed at Robbie, Patrick couldn't help wishing for... something.

'Sunsets, walks in the woods, never relaxing until we get to the airport, but once the bags are checked the holiday starts. You might hate horses and I may not love classical music, but we have thousands of other things in common, including the day we fell in love.' Robbie picked up the bucket by his feet. 'For my nerves this time. I'm sorry about Libby, but I'm more sorry I ever made you feel you were fourth on my list. You're not. You're the most important person in my life.'

Tears were trickling down Vanessa's cheeks, and a small crowd had gathered. Patrick shoved his hands in his pockets, not wanting to leave, not wanting to go home to his empty house.

'I love you,' Robbie went on, 'and we can find a way for you to have a life with me and with music. I always planned to open a second restaurant. We could open it somewhere near an orchestra, Covent bloody Garden, if you like.'

She wiped her eyes, but still didn't speak.

'When you're ready, I'd like you to come home. We can talk about what you want and how we can make it work.' He handed her the bucket. 'You were amazing tonight. That Debussy piece you played was beautiful.'

Then without kissing her, as Patrick expected, or even saying goodbye, Robbie walked away, a bold move, but one that visibly shook Vanessa. Patrick followed, dropping a kiss on her cheek as he passed.

'Thank you,' she whispered, still staring at the door Robbie had disappeared through.

In the foyer, Robbie stood with his back to the wall, his face pale. 'What's happening?'

Patrick hovered beside the reception desk where he could still see inside the hall. Jason was speaking to Vanessa, but she hugged her cello case, putting a barrier between them.

'It looks like she's telling the French wanker to piss off, in her very polite and apologetic way.' Patrick smiled as Vanessa, clearly desperate to follow Robbie. 'Sit tight, she'll be here in about ten seconds.'

Robbie took a deep breath. 'Thanks.'

Patrick nodded. 'And the plaything?'

'I'll speak to her in the morning.' Robbie glanced at his feet. 'Do me a favour?'

'Name it.'

'Keep an eye on her for me.'

Shit. Patrick didn't expect that. He needed to stay away from Libby Wilde and her knack of getting in the paper, but then again, she didn't deserve this. 'Okay.'

The wait seemed interminable, but then Vanessa ran through the door, cello case in one hand, the bucket in the other, her eyes wide when she couldn't see Robbie. Patrick nodded behind her. She turned, dropping the cello and the bucket. Vodka and tonic spilled onto the parquet floor as she threw her arms around Robbie's neck. Patrick's work here, was done.

'Ohmigod that's the most romantic thing ever,' said a female voice beside him. 'I can't believe he came all this way for her.'

Patrick looked around. A pretty and curvaceous blonde in a short velvet dress stood gazing at Robbie and Vanessa, nibbling her thumbnail. 'You know Vanessa?'

The girl nodded. 'We play together sometimes. She was telling me about him, how much she loves him, but she didn't think he felt the same anymore. He does though, doesn't he?'

'Yeah.' Jealousy nipped at Patrick again. 'He does.'

'Bit of a pain though,' she went on. 'We're supposed to be going to the party at the hotel together.'

'I think she might be otherwise engaged tonight.'

'Are you?'

She didn't look around, but Patrick hadn't missed the sexy, suggestive tone in her voice. Grassington – forty-five miles from

Gosthwaite and Michael Wray's prying eyes. Maybe his work here wasn't done. How good would it be to get totally wasted, score a gram of coke and screw her senseless? It'd beat the hell out of going home alone again.

But regretfully, Patrick turned to the girl.

'Sorry,' he said. 'I have to get home. Have fun though.'

He had a point to prove, and not just to his father.

Chapter Twenty

How could it be such a perfect day when she felt so hideous? Not a single cotton wool cloud dotted the sky, and the forecast promised a twenty-two degree afternoon. What she wanted was grey and miserable with perhaps a little drizzle. A dreadful night's sleep hadn't helped her hangover and her hangover hadn't helped her mortification over the previous day's newspaper article.

Libby shook her head, dismissing her melancholy. She didn't want to look depressed when she saw Matilda or Dora, and besides, she could take Shakes out in the morning and school an ever more responsive Dolomite in the afternoon. And she needed to see Robbie, to have a hug, to give a hug.

In the yard, he stood by the Land Rover, wearing a t-shirt and jeans. He wasn't going to work? Someone else was strapping the girls in. Oh god, no. Robbie was too busy laughing, smiling, looking exactly like the love of his life had come home to notice Libby, but when Vanessa straightened, her ridiculously glossy black bobbed hair blowing in the breeze, she spotted Libby and her smile disappeared. For the longest time, the two women stared at each other, their eye contact only broken when Robbie kissed his wife's head, whispering something.

Libby held onto the gate, needing its support. Vanessa was back. Libby was sacked.

Run. Turn and run.

She clutched the gate. The Land Rover drove away, leaving her and Robbie staring at each other. Did she love him, was that what had happened? Is that why this was hurting so badly?

Run.

But she didn't run. She opened the gate and faced him with her head held high and and knowing she'd walk away looking exactly the same.

'So how does this work?' she asked when she was six feet from him. 'Do I make it easy and quit, get made redundant because you don't need a babysitter now the mother of your children is back, or am I fired for shagging the boss?'

'I'm sorry, Lib.' He closed his eyes for a moment, his hands in his pockets.

Three days ago, he'd wanted to spend the night with her. They'd spent the night together. He'd said *what if*. What if, what if, what if...

She couldn't do this.

In the yard, Storm kicked at her door, demanding her breakfast, and although Libby already knew she was no longer employed at Low Wood Farm, she prepared the morning feed buckets, using the routine to pull herself together.

This was her fault. She should never have got involved with a married man. She should've stuck to being his friend, an ear to bend, but instead she'd welcomed the ultimate distraction, and now she'd have nothing. She should've listened to Patrick, to her own bloody conscience.

By the time she dropped the last bucket into Shakespeare's stable, Robbie was already sitting on the bench with two mugs of tea. She paused, watching Shakespeare, her equine best friend, as he hoovered up his nuts and sugar beet. No more Shakespeare, no more Dolomite. No more distraction.

And that's what hurt. She didn't love Robbie. She'd miss his friendship, but it was the job she loved, the horses. What had she done? With a bravery she didn't feel, she joined him on the bench, taking a tea, offering him a cigarette. He shook his head.

'I promised to quit,' he said.

'I should too,' she said, lighting one, 'but not today. So when did she get back?'

'I went to see her last night.'

'Why didn't you warn me?' They'd been too busy kissing and making up, no doubt.

He leant forwards, resting his elbows on his knees, staring at the floor. 'They were supposed to be gone by the time you got here. You were early. Would you have preferred a text?'

She pulled her feet up, hugging her knees. 'Are you okay? Happy?' He nodded.

'Did you tell her about me?'

'She'd seen the paper, some kind soul emailed her a link to the paper's website, but yes, I told her all about you.'

'She's very beautiful. I can see where the girls get it from. I mean, Dora and Tallulah clearly take after you–'

'The stroppy, grumpy pain in the arse?'

'Opinionated, confident, outspoken. Matilda really looks like her though, doesn't she? Is that why she's your favourite?'

'It's because Matilda's a bit of a miracle.' He sipped his tea, taking his time. 'There were three others between Lulu and Tilly.'

'Miscarriages?'

He nodded. 'The first was a little boy at eight months. Van nearly died too. The second got to twenty-two weeks, but the third didn't even make it to twelve weeks. I'd started to think it wasn't meant to be, but then Tilly came along. And survived.' He smiled up at her. 'So yes, there may be a little favouritism, but to be honest, she's much sweeter than her sisters.'

'She is and from what I hear she's very like her mother.'

Again he nodded.

She elbowed him, forcing a smile. 'Oh, don't look so depressed. We knew this would happen.'

'Fuck, I'm sorry.' He wrapped his arm around her shoulders, pulling her to him, kissing the top of her head. 'This is my fault. I never should have dragged you into my messed up marriage.'

'It's fine.'

'No it's not.' His lips were buried in her hair. 'The thing is, I love her, and I mean really love her. I'd forgotten… But, yesterday, I had to make a choice and, I had to choose her. It was the scariest thing I've ever done, because yesterday, you were the safest, most secure thing in my life. If she hadn't wanted to come home…'

'I know…' She looked around, smiling down at Cromwell. 'But I'm glad you're back together, honestly I am, even though I'm going to miss this place. It's the only job I've had that helps me forget.'

'You never did tell me what happened with the ballet.'

'Today's not the day, sorry.' She stubbed out her cigarette and relaxed back against him, his arm around her so familiar. 'I'm going to miss the horses, but I won't miss your bloody lists though.'

'I'm going to miss you.'

'You'll just miss having a tidy yard.'

'I'll miss you.' He removed his arm to take a piece of paper from his pocket. 'I know it's not… here, but it's better than the livery yard.'

'You've organised me a job?' *Haverton Equestrian Centre.* She hated it already.

'Give Helen a ring. She's okay. I promised her the best groom in the world, plaiting skills aside, and in return I get some numpty sixteen year-old.' He stroked her hair back, frowning. 'I really am going to miss you. Maybe in a few months when things have settled down, then maybe she won't mind—'

'Don't make promises. She might be the nicest person in the world, but really, you think she'd let me come back?'

'No.'

'I'd better go.' She tipped the last half of her tea down the drain, and stood up, tears pricking her eyes.

'Come here,' he said, already pulling her to him, wrapping his arms around her, holding her tighter than he ever had.

'You will be okay, won't you? Because I'd hate to give up all of this only to have you two get divorced in another six months.'

His head nodded against hers. 'Thank you for looking after this place... and me.'

'You,' she said, blinking to keep her tears at bay, 'are most welcome.'

'If you ever need anything, ask.' He kissed her head, ending things the way they'd started. 'I mean it.'

'Got any other brothers?' she laughed, wriggling out of his arms, facing him with a smile. This is how she'd walk away. Happy. 'Now, don't forget, put in the effort to spend time with your wife like you did with me. Give Dora more attention so she doesn't get jealous of Matilda and stop yelling at Tallulah.'

She stood on her tiptoes, kissing his cheek, then walked away, still smiling. When she was certain she was out of view, she collapsed in a gateway, sobbing as she'd only cried for ballet.

* * *

Stonerigg House. Wow. Zoë climbed out of her car, shielding her eyes from the sun. The place was more Georgian mansion than country estate. *I could so live here.* She laughed at herself. What, as the new Mrs Carr? Bit soon to be imagining Jonathan popping the question, especially since he was already married. With two kids. On cue, he appeared from the vast doorway, the incumbent Mrs Carr at his side.

Still, imagining life as lady of the manor wasn't a bad daydream to have.

'Zoë, congratulations. I hear contracts were exchanged on Highfield.' Jonathan politely kissed her cheek, before he whispered,

'You could've said no when she rang.'

She grinned. 'Where's the fun in that? Shall we celebrate later?'

'Lovely to meet you,' Fee said, seemingly oblivious to her husband's hand drifting down Zoë's back and cupping her arse. 'Come in, come in. Lunch is almost ready.'

This is going to be so weird.

Sure enough, the lunch of salmon with minted new potatoes and fresh peas, was stilted and awkward, not helped by Jonathan barely dropping eye contact with Zoë, and Fee necking Chablis at an unsociable rate. The second she put her knife and fork together, Zoë ran through plausible excuses to get the hell out of there. Sadly, Fee had other ideas.

'Jonathan, would you mind clearing the table and fetching dessert?' Fee said, pushing away her barely touched plate. 'It's all prepared, but my back...'

'Of course not,' he said pleasantly, even if his scowl suggested otherwise. 'Relax.'

Very, very weird.

The second they were left alone, Fee flashed the most saccharine of smiles. 'Do you like gardening, Zoë?'

'Not really.'

'Your aunt had some marvellous plants. She had offered me cuttings, but sadly... If you're not interested, perhaps I could just take the originals.'

Zoë sat back. 'My friend Libby *is* a little green-fingered. I'd have to check with her. Which plants are you after, the wisteria?'

This time, Fee's smile was much less sweet. 'I'll be honest, Zoë. I have a debilitating back condition, constant pain.'

Oh hello. 'Which plants?'

'The *hemp* plants,' Fee replied, brushing her hair back. 'Do you still have them?'

'I do.' Zoë's eyes narrowed. 'But they're valuable. You can't just *have* them.' *Not without some negotiation.*

'I see.' Fee nodded, any hint of a smile evaporating. 'Yet you think you can just *have* my husband?'

What the hell... 'Then perhaps we can come to some arrangement, Mrs Carr?'

* * *

Grounding in the early evening sunshine didn't work. She needed darkness, a full moon, even twilight would add a bit of atmosphere, but Libby held her cross-legged position in the middle of the lawn and persevered. Bloody Zoë hadn't helped. The day Libby had her idyllic rural life at Low Wood Farm snatched away from her happened to be the day Jemima and Charlie Harington signed the deal on Highfield House and Zoë pocketed just shy of four thousand pounds. After lunch with Jonathan and his wife, he'd whisked Zoë away to a swanky Ullswater hotel.

'On a scale of one to weird,' said a familiar, slightly Scottish voice, 'you're heading up the weird end. What are you doing?'

Libby opened one eye and took a drag on her cigarette. A mud-splattered Patrick sat on his bike, leaning against the garden fence, clearly amused.

'Bugger off,' she said closing her eye again. 'I'm meditating, not your cup of tea, I'm sure.'

'I pride myself on having a very open mind.'

She refused to look, but the clattering noises he made didn't sound like him pedalling away, more like him getting off his bike. She could do without him right now. From the scent of fresh sweat, mud and the remnants of his aftershave, she guessed he'd sat down opposite her.

'Now, I'm no expert,' he said, 'but I'm fairly sure meditation isn't usually done with a fag and a glass of white wine.'

'Bad day.' Again, she opened one eye, peeking at him.

'I heard.' He sat about three feet away, mirroring her pose, hands resting on his knees.

'I'm guessing Robbie sent you.' She closed her eye, focussing on the sending her negative thoughts to the centre of the earth. 'You've got his back, right?'

'Right.'

'You can go home. I'm fine.'

'Really?'

'I've lost my job. What do you think? But you should go, I'm liable to cry and I'd hate to push your fraternal loyalties to breaking point.'

'I'll man up.'

Libby looked up, revealing her red-rimmed, puffy eyes in all their glory. Patrick pressed his lips together, clearly trying not to laugh.

'At least tears have washed away most of that hideous black crap.'

He took her glass and tipped the wine into the grass.

'What the hell–'

'That's not going to make you feel better.' He produced a little plastic bag of grass, a joint already rolled. 'From your garden, so it's only right to share.'

'I don't like weed.'

'If you drink a shed-load of booze, you'll just cry all night. This might make you smile.' He lit the joint, taking a long drag. 'And you need to lighten up.'

'I do not.'

'Oh come on, you're so hardworking and earnest. Do you ever let your hair down, get wasted?'

'You're such an arse. I was trying to tonight, but you threw my wine away.'

'I call bull. You're all smoke, a front. I reckon you wear the black crap and dress like seventeen year-old trailer trash because you want to look bad. You want to look bad because really you're nice but you don't want to be nice. You'll smoke this...' He held out the joint. 'Because it's bad and it'll prove you're not nice.'

'Stop trying to psychoanalyse me. I hate you.' She took a drag on the joint, trying to be cross, but Hyssop padded towards them. He stood on his back legs to rub his head against Patrick and Libby found herself smiling for the first time that day.

'Hey, pal.' Patrick's smile grew to a huge grin, as he petted Hyssop. 'There's nothing wrong with being nice.'

'I'm not nice.'

'Yes, you are. I wish more of the world was nice. I wish...'

'What?' She took a second, longer drag, the effects of the first already hitting her.

'There's nothing wrong with nice.'

A happy buzz enveloped her and she lay back on the grass, smiling. 'Oh god, I'm going to be wrecked.'

He lay alongside her, a couple of feet away, Hyssop curling up by his side. 'Me too. I haven't smoked in months.'

She turned her head to him. Patrick. He couldn't be her somebody – he was Scottish, so he couldn't be the one she summoned, but God, he could be... something.

'Did you see the paper?' she asked.

He nodded.

'Do you know, until I came to this bloody village I'd never so much as flirted with another girl's boyfriend and now I'm talk of the town as a home-wrecker. The ironic thing is I constantly persuaded Robbie not to give up on Vanessa, I've never touched Xander and Jack was perfectly single when we... you know, so no scandal there. Yet read all about it and I'm the village whore.'

'Not nice, is it? At one stage there used to be some crap about me in there every week.'

'How did you cope?' She lay on her side facing him, propped on one elbow.

'I'd go out and get drunk, which would usually make things worse. There was a lot of coke involved. At least you'll be safe hiding here. I reckon you can only see into this garden from the air, so not much danger of being papped.'

'Papped?'

He nodded. 'Okay, sometimes I was too wasted to know if someone was taking photos, but at other times... there were photos... someone had to be watching.'

'That's weird. You're not a celebrity. You're a vet.'

'It's what Wray's done with the paper. Neighbours are selling out neighbours. I've heard he pays them for gossip shots he can use to back up his stories.' Patrick rolled onto his side, mirroring her position. 'And it looks like he has you in his sights.'

'So lesson one, when your name has been trashed in the local rag, don't go and make things worse by getting wasted with unsuitable types who have a reputation worse than your own.' She took another drag on the joint. 'Oops. What's lesson two?'

'Don't do anything in public. There's a law which stops the press invading your privacy. They can only take photos in public places. I sued over the first story they did on me using that. They settled out of court and that pissed Michael Wray off. He hounded me and I was stupid enough to keep getting drunk and up to no good in very public places.'

'What was your worst story?'

'Definitely the... there was this beauty queen, Miss Haverton... it was messy.'

A beauty queen? Oh.

Patrick put out the joint. 'But getting nicked for coke at the football last year wasn't great.'

'I heard PC Andy wasn't impressed.'

'He was just pissed off because he couldn't turn a blind eye. Or have any of the coke later.'

'What?' Libby stared. 'But he's a police officer. He can't…'

Patrick grinned. 'Earnest, hardworking *and* naive.'

'Oh bugger off.' Libby stuck her tongue out at him. 'What happened with Miss Haverton?'

'No comment.'

'Was everything they wrote true?'

'Pretty much, I gave them so much material they didn't need to sensationalise it.

'So, *Porthos*, at the football Jack, Grace and a few others were doing coke. Why didn't you?'

'Aren't I allowed a night off?'

Despite the fug of dope enveloping her brain, Libby didn't miss his tell, the twitch in his right eye. It was tiny, and would be barely noticeable on anyone else, but unless Patrick was smiling, his emotions were buried, his face impassive and that made his tell all the more obvious to her.

'You had a few beers,' she said, 'a few shots of tequila, and I heard you walked back alone. From what I've heard, that wasn't your style at all.' She poked a finger in his ribs. 'You, don't match your reputation. It seems to me that since you came back from Spain, you've turned nice. What happened?'

In response, he lay on his back and stared at the sky with his hands behind his head. 'I went to my brother's to sort myself out. I just wanted to work, relax and – well, not be here.'

'Why did you need to sort yourself out?' she asked, trying not to stare at the patch of torso peeking between his t-shirt and shorts. Or touch it.

'Things had got a little wild. Charlotte, my sister-in-law, decided I needed some therapy so they cold-turkeyed the house, no booze for anyone. There are no TVs at their place so they talk, a lot. It drove me insane to start with.'

'And what did the therapy reveal?'

'Charlotte decided I'm a hedonist.'

'Zoë reckons the entire human race is made up of hedonists.'

'According to Charlotte, I don't know where the off-switch is. I'm a danger to myself.'

'And what about according to Patrick? Do you have an off-switch?'

His face softened into a smile. 'Actually yeah, I do. The football proved that. But Charlotte's Google-informed psychoanalysis did make me realise I'm used to getting my own way. Mum says I never liked being told no.'

'So you're an overindulged, selfish arse?'

He laughed and shook his head. 'No. I just like getting what I want.'

'Like Hyssop? You must be losing your touch.'

'He visits every day. I've still got it.' Patrick grinned, finally turning his head to face her. 'Why were you meditating in the garden?'

'I've just lost my job and a very good friend.'

'I meant why the garden.' He sat up, preparing to roll another joint. 'Maggie used to sit in the exact same spot and channel Mother Nature, or something.'

Libby opened her mouth, wanting to lie, but how could she when he'd been so honest about Spain? So as Patrick skinned up with practised ease, sticking the papers together, crumbling the dried weed, his long fingers rolling it all into a neat joint, she told him about inheriting Maggie's spell book and the Good Luck spell which had kick-started her life in Gosthwaite. Patrick didn't even bother to restrain his amusement.

'I can't believe you're getting sucked into that crap,' he said.

'Don't you dare tell anyone, especially not Grace.'

He lit the joint, his eyes still twinkling. 'Think you're the nice white witch and she's the evil one?'

'Something like that.' Libby's cheeks heated up.

'You two really ought to be friends. You'd like her. You both run, you're both into this Wicca nonsense, Christ, you even look the same, with your ridiculous fringes.' He twirled her lighter through his fingers. 'Libs, I've been thinking about the elderflower wine.'

Libby's hand paused as she stroked Hyssop. 'Why?'

'It was something Grace mentioned. She couldn't understand why the wine had belladonna in.'

'But she said Maggie laced her drinks with it to get rid of migraines.'

'Look, this might sound a bit... Grace reckons that it could be because you're skinny, but the way you reacted after one glass was fairly full on. Maggie used to knock back a bottle of that at a time. Grace thinks it was too strong for Maggie's usual dose. She doesn't think Maggie put the belladonna in.'

'So who did?' Libby frowned. The wine had still been in the gift bag when she and Zoë arrived.

'Sheila,' Patrick suggested.

'Okay… maybe she thought she was doing a good deed, but got the dose wrong.' Libby liked the neat explanation. 'It was an accident.'

'Accident or attempted murder?'

'But why would Sheila want to murder Maggie? They were friends.'

'You know Maggie had an affair with Sheila's husband?'

'Does Sheila know?'

Patrick nodded. 'Last Christmas, Jack and Sheila had an almighty row on the Green. He hated Maggie because he found out about it at the time. He blurted it out. Half the village heard.'

'Do you think Jack might've poisoned the wine?'

'Would he have given you wine he knew was poisoned?'

'I hope not.'

'Sheila it is, then.'

'You know this is ludicrous, right?'

'Yep.'

'We're just guessing, making wild allegations based on the assumption that Maggie didn't lace the wine herself.'

Patrick nodded. 'But what if we're right?'

'Do you think Sheila took the emerald pendant too?'

* * *

He'd only meant to stay for an hour, to make sure she wasn't going to go nuts, but Patrick stayed for three. They made cheese on toast, smoked some more and eventually wound up on the sofa listening to music, talking about Robbie's horses. Libby lay curled up at one end of the sofa, nursing an empty mug, her eyes half-closed.

'I should go,' he said. 'You'll be okay?'

She nodded. 'I liked him and the stables. It was the best distraction, but I'll survive.'

'The best distraction from what?'

'Being bloody miserable.' She yawned. 'Now I just need a distraction from my distraction.'

He played with the Fatima's Hand attached to his keys, a little talisman Maggie had given him to promote honesty. He'd mentioned, in passing, how much it irritated him when people wouldn't 'fess up to doing something that resulted in an animal winding up in his surgery. The dishonesty often slowed the diagnosis. Not that he believed in the whole Wicca thing, but he still carried it with him, just in case.

'And why are you bloody miserable?' *Come on, Fatima.*

She didn't answer, but curled up a little more.

'Libs?' Was she asleep?

'You'd be a good distraction,' she mumbled.

He sat frozen for a moment, not having a clue how to react, but her mug slipped as her hand relaxed. She'd passed out and relief flooded over him. He could pretend he hadn't heard her, or that she hadn't even said it. The last thing she needed was to be rejected again. Once in a day was enough.

Carefully, he took the mug and covered her with a throw. Asleep, she seemed as angelic as she did when she smiled, and how much prettier did she look without all that hideous black crap? He sighed, still crouching beside her.

It didn't matter how angelic she looked, or that she made him laugh – Robbie had called her *Off Limits* and she was Michael Wray's new target. Even a harmless trip to the cinema with Libby Wilde could lose him everything.

'It's not going to happen, Libs,' he whispered. 'I can't be your distraction.'

But the dope-high made it irresistible for him not to take the opportunity and he dropped a brief kiss on her lips.

Chapter Twenty-One

As the assistant to the head girl at the Haverton Equestrian Centre, Libby's job was to ensure the yard and horses were immaculately prepared: hooves oiled, tack spotless and yard hay-free. None of that bothered her, but the attitude of the riders did. At weekends and evenings lazy kids moaned their arms ached if she asked them to carry their Welsh Mountain's saddle, and on weekdays, yummy mummies climbed out of their Range Rovers, expecting their Thoroughbred Crosses to be stood waiting. Why did no one want to groom and tack up their own horses? She'd begged to do it when she was a kid.

She hated Haverton Equestrian Centre. Helen, her boss, was work-shy, quick to delegate and far too soft with Kayleigh, her overweight, spoiled ten year-old daughter. Kayleigh, the worst *it makes my arms ache* offender, felt she was within her rights to order Libby around like a slave, a habit that quickly caught on with Melanie, the head girl.

Libby longed for her days at Low Wood Farm. Hell, she'd started to long for her days with the North West's most caustic wedding planner.

But that wasn't all she longed for.

It'd been over two weeks since she'd lost her job and Patrick had come to check she wasn't going bunny boiler. She hadn't seen him since, but she hadn't stopped thinking about him. She didn't know if she'd dreamt it, or if it really happened, but she seemed to have a memory, or something, that he'd kissed her and said he couldn't be her distraction.

It had to be a dream. He made no secret of disliking how she looked – of course he hadn't kissed her. If only she could dismiss other memories so easily – like the one of him stretching, revealing that patch of perfect torso, the hair leading down to the good stuff.

The only thing keeping her sane was Xander's amped up running regime. He'd turned up the morning after Patrick got her stoned, announcing fell race training had begun. And God, did he mean it. Four times a week, he pushed her harder than most dance instructors had. She hadn't had abs so defined since she left the ballet.

In ménage, Kayleigh was putting her pony Ferrero over the jumps. Libby watched with mounting annoyance as Kayleigh's legs remained resolutely still, but the crop in her hand bashed the little Fell pony's flanks.

'Kayleigh,' she called. 'Less whip, more leg.'

Kayleigh pulled up Ferrero, scowling at Libby. 'I do know how to ride.'

'No, you know how to sit on your arse and hit that pony around the course. You're fat, lazy and a woefully ineffective rider.'

Libby wanted to regret the words the second they came out, but she didn't. And when she realised an apoplectic Helen stood six feet away, she regretted them even less.

'Olivia, how dare you—'

'Tell the truth?' Oh, what the hell... 'If you weren't such a fat, lazy and woefully ineffective riding instructor, you'd already know that I'm right.'

She walked away as Helen spat out the dreaded four words: *Olivia Wilde, you're fired.* At least Robbie's three month guilt money meant Libby wouldn't starve while she looked for a new job.

A new job? She ambled up from the post office, *Gazette* in hand, scanning the situations vacant ads. Care worker, care worker, domestic staff – all required qualifications she didn't have. The escort ads in the Manchester Evening News were looking promising. Maybe she could get a job in a hotel – being a receptionist at one of the high end boutique places around Windermere might be nice. Would Robbie fudge a reference for her, say she worked at the Mill, not the yard? Oh, a hack on Shakespeare would cheer her up. Libby sighed, folding up the paper.

What was the point? Even a job at the swankiest hotel wouldn't distract her. It wouldn't distract her from Low Wood· Farm and it certainly wouldn't distract her from ballet. She had to leave. It wasn't working. Gosthwaite, the countryside, wasn't working. What did she have left to try? Australia with her parents, or London with Paolo.

Her feet itched as they always did at times like this, begging to be laced into satin. Her toes wanting the familiar pain of being *en pointe*. If she moved the sofa, she'd have the whole living room, twice the space she had in Manchester. And real pitch pine floors, not three millimetres of laminated oak.

No. She had to put dancing behind her.

'Afternoon, Libby,' Sheila called, pausing as she washed her windows.

Did you try to murder Maggie? If you did, I can't be your friend. Libby smiled, possibly the most insincere smile she'd ever given, and hated herself for it. What if Patrick was wrong? What if Maggie had laced the wine?

'Sheila,' Libby said, as she stood by her own filthy bay window, 'I was wondering how that bottle of elderflower wine came to have belladonna in it.'

No one needed to be the daughter of a body language expert to see Sheila's guilt. She dropped her chamois leather, blinking furiously as she paled. Libby wanted to be sick. It was true. Sheila had tried to poison Maggie.

'Maggie hadn't even opened it,' Libby said, sitting on the windowsill, 'so she couldn't have put the belladonna in.'

'I don't know what you're talking about.' Sheila wrung out her cloth before going back to her windows.

Seconds ticked away, but Libby didn't care how long they kept this up. This was for Maggie.

'Sheila, did you put the belladonna in?'

'Maggie fell down the stairs. She broke her neck.'

'I know you didn't *actually* poison her. I'm asking if you tried to.'

Sheila swallowed hard as she rinsed her cloth. 'You should do your windows. My mother would turn in her grave if she ever thought I'd let mine get into that state.'

'When she didn't appear for a few days, did you wonder if it'd worked? Did you go in to see if she'd drunk any? Did you see her body? Did you walk away and leave her there for someone else to find?'

Sheila's cloth paused and tears rolled down her face, her shoulders sagging, her eyes downcast.

'And did you take her pendant, Sheila?'

'I'd never steal from anyone,' she said, moving onto the second bay. 'And especially not her.'

'Really?'

Sheila made broad strokes over the window, creating a soapsud rainbow that glinted in the sunlight. 'Maggie was my friend.'

'With friends like you...' Libby walked away.

London or Sydney? Whichever, she had to leave. The heart of

Gosthwaite had turned black.

The ballet clothes remained in the box under her bed until nine o'clock, but after half a bottle of wine her resolve collapsed. Hyssop was out, at Patrick's no doubt, and without the tabby's calming influence she needed to dance. She pulled on a spaghetti-strapped black leotard and her favourite long black legwarmers – they were so old they'd frayed at the heels, but she'd never throw them away. As usual, she left the shoes until last, flexing her feet, stretching her hamstrings, laying her forehead on her shins before she slipped padding between her toes and eased on her lucky black satin shoes.

In her head, the music had started, the opening strains to Swan Lake, but this time her role wasn't a cygnet. This time, she'd take on the role she was born for, the role she'd never got to dance on stage – Odile, the black swan. She'd watched Tamara Rojo claim the role, turning through thirty-two fouettés and Libby knew, one day, she'd do the same, but she'd be better. She'd be better, because she'd be England's own prima ballerina.

But instead of ruling the Coliseum, here she was, performing substandard, rusty turns in a cottage in the Lakes. In the home of Margaret Keeley, another dancer who should've been a prima ballerina but had it ripped away from her.

The imaginary music ended, but Libby shook her head and moved into first position, ready to start again. Her ankle throbbed, unused to the punishment after only a brief warm up. This time, she'd do it perfectly.

Halfway through, with sweat pouring down her back, a knock on the kitchen window stopped her dead. Was it Patrick, coming to check she was okay? Patrick? Why was he her first thought? She unfastened her shoes and kicked them under the sofa, hiding the evidence.

There was a second round of knocking. A persistent caller – not how she pegged Patrick. Robbie maybe, was something wrong?

Libby hovered by the door to the kitchen, peeking to see who it was, but the efficient LED lights under the wall units meant she could see nothing but her own reflection and the silhouette of a male. What if it were Patrick? She stepped forwards, as did he. It wasn't Patrick. It was Jack.

'Let me in, Libby,' he said, his voice low.

'Why?' *Because I accused your mum of murdering Maggie?*

'I want to talk to you.'

The door wasn't locked, left open for her to pop out for a cigarette later, but if the key were in, she might have chance to lock it. She glanced over. No bloody key.

'Libby...'

Her phone was in her bag sitting on the kitchen table, too near the door for comfort, but there was no way she could make a run for it. Maybe she could fake it, calmly walk over but then call the police. The police? Oh, ha ha. PC Andy, Sheila's eldest son? Well, she could call the cavalry, at least.

With all the nerve she could muster, she headed across the kitchen, as if she were going to the kitchen door, but when she reached the table, she picked up her phone, grateful she'd not taken Robbie off speed dial. She stared at Jack through the glass pane in the kitchen door, his face turning seven levels more angry as he stepped towards her, reaching for the door handle.

Please answer.

'Libby?' Robbie said.

'Remember you said if I ever need anything, I should call you? Jack's turned up.'

Robbie swore. 'I can't–'

'I have no idea why he's here, but I might need rescuing. Please.' She hung up, needing both hands free.

Her mother had trained Libby for moments like this. She could fell someone Jack's size with a leg sweep, break a few ribs with a well-placed kick, incapacitate him, but if she missed her chance he could easily overpower her.

She backed away, towards the other side of the kitchen as he came in, keeping an escape route behind her. Sadly, that exit involved a deadlock on the front door. Five minutes. The cavalry could be here in five minutes. She just had to manage Jack for five minutes.

'What do you want?' she asked.

'To talk.' He leaned against the sink, his jaw twitching, his arms folded.

'About...'

'You know what about. My mum rang me tonight, crying.'

'And?'

'And she said you accused her of murder.'

'No, I accused her of *attempted* murder.'

'Maggie died of a broken neck. There was an autopsy. Mum didn't kill her.'

'When did she find out about Maggie and your dad?'

He studied her. 'Who did you just call?'

'Robbie.' Her heart raced too much to have any chance of hiding her tell. 'Hardly much point in ringing the police.'

His arms relaxed, undoubtedly after calculating how much time he had, and his fingers tapped out a repetitive beat on a cupboard door. 'Shagging the boss, hey? Was he why you kicked me out?'

'No.' Libby edged nearer the door, ready to flee. She could hide in the bathroom. The lock was pathetic, but it might buy her a little time until Robbie arrived. Would he arrive? 'I kicked you out because you took advantage of my incapacitated state. When did you realise I was out of it?'

'When you called me Robbie.'

'You bastard.'

'It was a mistake. I'm sorry.' The drumming stopped as he looked her over. 'A big mistake.'

Feeling naked and vulnerable, she wrapped her arms around herself. 'Please go away.'

Jack moved towards her, but a little to her left, creating a triangle between the two of them and her escape route. She'd never make it upstairs. Stupid, stupid girl.

'I don't want to fight with you, Libby. I like you, a lot. You know that.'

How could she get out of this? Libby's stomach churned as Jack reached out, his thumb brushing her shoulder, and she turned to the window. Patrick stood on the other side of the glass. Her heart jumped, but her relief was short-lived as Jack toyed with her strap, caressing her skin. She implored Patrick with her eyes.

Please, help me.

Patrick darted across the patio, catching Jack's eye and Libby seized her opportunity. She raised her hands to Jack's shoulder as her right leg smashed his left from under him. Using his momentum and her body weight, she toppled him just as she'd learned. Jack yelled, hitting his head on the worktop on his way down, but Libby didn't look back as she jumped over his flailing legs and ran behind Patrick.

'Why are you here?' she asked.

'Rob couldn't make it.' Patrick glanced back at her. 'What the hell's going on?'

'Fucking bitch…' Jack lay on the floor, winded.

Libby peeked out, clutching Patrick's t-shirt. 'Go home, Jack.'

Jack looked up, rubbing his head. 'Oh, I see.'

'You don't see anything,' Patrick said, his voice a menacing growl. 'Get the hell out of here.'

Jack laughed as he stood up. 'She doesn't hang around, does she? She hardly drew breath from fucking Xander, to me, then Robbie, and what, a couple of weeks later it's your—'

Patrick grabbed him, shoving him up against the wall. 'Shut your mouth. Libby and I are friends. What are you doing here?'

'I just came to talk to her.' Jack held out his arms, laughing, showing he had no intention of retaliating. 'Calm it, man.'

'He wanted to shut me up,' Libby said.

'About what?' Patrick frowned back at her, still restraining Jack.

'I spoke to Sheila this afternoon,' Libby said. 'You see, Jack, it's not just me who's asking questions. Patrick is too, and I bet Grace won't be far behind. I'm ringing the police. And not your brother.'

Jack closed his eyes, slumping against the wall, his fight gone. 'She didn't kill her.'

'But she tried to?' Libby asked.

Jack nodded.

'Jesus Christ.' Patrick backed away, running his fingers through his curls. 'She really poisoned the wine.'

'And what's the bets that PC Andy knows all about it,' Libby said.

Patrick sat on the table, next to her. 'Sheila tried to kill Maggie?'

'No... well, yes, but half-heartedly.' Jack stared at the ceiling, fiddling with his watch strap. 'When Maggie hadn't been around for a few days, Mum freaked and rang me. She thought she'd killed her. She wanted to go to the police, but then you found the body and it turned out Maggie had broken her neck. Mum hadn't killed her.'

'Liar,' Libby whispered. 'Your mum went in, she found the body, didn't she?'

Jack paled. 'What, no...'

'Or did you?' Patrick asked.

The silence grew as Jack stared at them both. Libby felt for him. He was protecting his mum, a noble aim, but he had to make things right.

'Yes.' Jack sighed. 'The next morning, I came in to see if... well, to see if she was okay or not. She was dead, but the bottle was on the side.'

'Why didn't you tell anyone, or phone an ambulance?' Patrick asked, his voice quiet.

'Mum was a mess. She would've confessed and what good would that have done? She didn't hurt Maggie.'

'And your brother,' Patrick said, 'I'm guessing, did a half-arsed investigation so no one would find out what your mum nearly did. Brilliant.'

Jack hung his head in shame. 'What now?'

Patrick sighed. 'Look, I don't want your mum to get into trouble any more than you do. I've had tea at her house nearly as much as my own.'

'But the necklace is still missing,' Libby said. 'Someone took that.'

'What necklace?' Jack said. 'Mum didn't take anything.'

'A green pendant,' Patrick said, 'Egg shaped, with some inscription engraved around it.'

'No idea.' Jack headed for the door.

'Wait.' Libby bravely approached him, laying her hand on his forehead as Grace had done in August. 'Whatever influence I hold over thee, be at peace. I set thee free.'

Jack shook his head, giving a hollow laugh. 'You know that's all bullshit, right?'

'Maybe.' Libby shrugged. 'Or maybe I had no idea what I was messing with. We're over.'

Jack simply nodded and disappeared into the night. Libby turned to Patrick, wanting to thank her new superhero, but found she couldn't speak, her head filled with the memory of Jack stroking her shoulder. What if... what would he have done? Had she created this monster with her summoning spells? She stared at Patrick.

'You're okay.' He pulled her to him and wrapped his arms around her. 'He's gone.'

She clung to him, never wanting to let go. With her cheek against his shoulder, she could smell the woody tang of his aftershave. This was... home. Bugger him being a distraction, why couldn't he be her somebody, the one she'd summoned? Because he's Scottish, and she'd wished for someone English. Arse.

'Life's never dull with you around,' he said, his head resting on hers. 'Now, what shall we discuss first, how you took Jack down like that or why you look all... *Flashdance*?'

She laughed, as tears rolled down her cheeks. 'Thank you so much.'

'Are you crying?'

She nodded. 'Sorry.'

'It's okay. I'm impervious to tears now. No more pay rises.'

'How about jobs? I need one. I'd make a great cow castrating assistant.'

'If you think cows get castrated, you don't even make it to interview. What happened to the riding school?'

'I got sacked today, which makes fourteen jobs in three years.'

He held her at arm's length, his mouth gaping. 'Fourteen jobs? You're definitely not making it to interview.'

She pushed him away, smiling. 'Like I'd really want to work for you. You'd be grumpier than Rob.'

Patrick's phone buzzed in his pocket. 'Speak of the devil.'

Libby dug out a cardigan, painfully aware how flat her chest looked in the leotard. *Flashdance*. God, he must think she was an utter weirdo. Was that why he couldn't be her distraction? Or was it because she looked awful? Without asking him, she poured two glasses of the red she'd started earlier, trying not to stare at his arse as he chatted to Robbie. Why did she have a knack for fancying sexy-as-hell blokes she couldn't have?

'Libs?' He handed her the phone, swapping it for a glass. 'Christ, I need this.'

They sat on the rickety bench outside, and after Libby spent five minutes reassuring Robbie she was fine, she lit a cigarette.

'Why did you get sacked?' Patrick asked, wafting her smoke away.

She explained, smiling when his body shook with repressed laughter. 'It's not funny.'

'Oh, it is. Fat, lazy and woefully ineffective? I would've paid to have been there.' He sipped his wine and stretched out his long legs. 'What are you going to do?'

She hugged her knees, resting her chin on them. 'I don't know. Maybe it's a sign I should move on.'

'Where would you go?' He moved his glass in little circles, swirling the wine.

'I don't know. Sensibly, I should go to Sydney or London.'

'Sydney Australia? Bit extreme.'

'It's where my parents live.'

'Why don't you?'

'A long story.'

He laughed. 'And London?'

'Paolo.' She hoped he couldn't see her reddening cheeks. 'My ex.

He moved there just before I moved here.'

'Why didn't you go with him?'

'A long story.'

'You are priceless.' He elbowed her.

'So who do you think took the necklace?' she asked, desperate to change the subject.

'Beats me.'

'Sheila mentioned that Maggie had a few flings. Maybe there's another homicidal wife out there? What about the rich guy who gave her the necklace in the first place, maybe he has a wife hell-bent on revenge?'

'What, you think she came in, pushed Maggie down the stairs then ripped the pendant from her body, taking back what was rightfully hers?' Patrick shook his head. 'There would've been fingerprints, footprints—'

Libby laughed. 'Do you watch far too much CSI, by any chance?'

'Far, far too much.' He nudged her, grinning back. 'But I can't really see Lucinda Doyle bumping anyone off. She's more likely to have them excommunicated socially.'

'Who's Lucinda Doyle?'

'Seamus Doyle's wife.'

'Seamus Doyle, the poet?'

'He has a house near Windermere. He's why Maggie moved up here in the first place.'

'How on earth do you know that?'

'Because I went to a black tie shindig with his daughter, Tabitha, last New Year.'

Libby laughed. 'I can't see you in black tie.'

'I wear it very well, actually. Anyway, Maggie was there too. Tabitha really didn't like seeing Seamus and Maggie together and it was so obvious they were having an affair. Did a valiant effort at ignoring each other, acting like strangers, but the second they were alone, thick as thieves.'

'Recognise the signs from your own sordid affairs?'

'Actually, yes.' He smiled, chinking his glass against hers.

'So it was still going on, even this year?'

He nodded. 'I asked her about it when she came to get eye drops for Hyssop. She'd been shagging Seamus for over thirty years.'

'Patrick, what does Lucinda look like?'

'Tall, blonde—'

'Like the ghost of Maggie? Do you think Becky next-door-but-one was telling the truth?'

He fought a smile. 'If you do move to Sydney, do I get full custody of the cat?'

When Patrick had left, making her lock the door behind him, Libby took out the spell book, flicking through, looking for inspiration. Good luck, grounding, prosperity? A spell for Inner Power and Spiritual Guidance? Perfect. She longed to go outside and sit on the lawn, but what if Jack were still lurking? Instead, she ducked out to collect a few sprigs of thyme, then double checked the door was locked before sitting in the middle of the living room.

The purple, lavender-infused candle sitting on a ceramic dish inscribed with a pentagram would supposedly help clarify her thoughts, while the thyme she held in its flame would increase her psychic powers. Libby watched the herb smoulder.

What do I do, stay in Gosthwaite, go to London, or go to Sydney? I need a sign.

'Divine power within, bless and guide me on the path of my destiny.'

She repeated the mantra until the thyme was nothing more than ash dotted through the molten wax.

I need a sign.

Chapter Twenty-Two

Going to his parents' house always felt just that to Patrick – *their* house. Kiln Howe, an ancient, sprawling farmhouse, was a great place, but aside from Christmas holidays, it held few memories for him. The family home, the place he grew up, was his house on the Green, but the McBride's had moved out the year he went to university.

He knocked on the door but went straight in, laughing as the pack descended on him – Flynn and Jess, his parents' flat-coat retrievers, scurried around, while Baxter, Patrick's old sheepdog, limped along at his heel, his hips clearly no better despite the latest meds.

In the kitchen, his dad stood at the Aga, cooking bacon and eggs and his mum sat at the table, reading the papers – a Saturday morning tradition in the McBride house.

'Morning,' Patrick said, dropping a kiss on his mum's cheek.

'Morning, darling. Coffee's fresh.' She glanced up from the Guardian's *Weekend* magazine, just long enough to give him a warm smile. It was always the same when she became engrossed in an article. Years of burned bacon had prompted his dad to take over Saturday morning cooking, leaving his wife to her newspaper. Patrick suspected she'd done it on purpose, just to gain a little time off.

'You look tired,' his dad said, wagging a spatula at him. 'Late night?'

'Nothing outside of the rules. I was at Rob's for dinner.'

'How are they?' his mum asked. 'Has Vanessa forgiven him?'

Patrick clenched his teeth, having promised Robbie that, for the sake of the kids, Vanessa's little holiday would never come to light.

'They're fine. What are you reading?' he asked, pouring a coffee.

'It's the most marvellous piece about an artist. He's from Lochaire. It's an hour from where I grew up.' She folded the pages back to the start of the article. 'He's about to be an international success, but what's fascinating is that he exhibited two paintings of a ballerina. He sold the painting of her dancing for fifty thousand pounds, but turned down another fifty for the second painting, *The*

Broken Ballerina. The price was upped to seventy-five, but he said he regretted showing it and he destroyed it. They're beautiful paintings.'

She handed him the paper and Patrick almost choked on his coffee. Looking back at him, immortalised in oils, was Ms Olivia Wilde.

Or was it Libby? By seven o'clock that night, Patrick had persuaded himself he was being ridiculous. Or was he? The rough style of the artwork generalised the ballerina's features, and certainly the girl in *The Happy Ballerina* could be anyone, but in *The Broken Ballerina...* Was that Libby? The dancer sat on the floor, tears rolling, hugging her legs, her head resting on her knees. The same position Libby had been in when they'd sat on the lawn eating cheese on toast at Maggie's cottage and she'd told him how much she'd miss the horses at Low Wood Farm. And the artist was Paolo de Luca. Her ex, the one who buggered off to London, was called Paolo.

It had to be her.

Patrick laughed. If Libby was a ballerina, it'd explain a few things – the perfect legs, the super-skinny body.

It definitely had to be her.

But so what if it was? Why did he care? She was just some girl. She looked bloody awful most of the time, yet he'd showered, put on a half decent t-shirt, jeans that weren't falling apart and, for Christ's sake, he'd even combed his hair. Properly. He didn't even fancy her, not really. Well, not the majority of the time, but when he'd walked past a florist's earlier, the heady scent instantly reminded him of hugging Miss Olivia Wilde. How come she always smelled like a rose garden?

This was stupid. For two weeks, he'd avoided her, trying to forget he'd heard her say that he'd be a great distraction. Why the hell had he kissed her? Then Robbie begged him to check on her. Christ, when Jack went to push the strap off her shoulder... If he closed his eyes, Patrick could still picture the fear on her face. He'd never wanted to kill anyone or anything in his life, not until that moment. It terrified him.

But he'd promised to keep an eye on her and a couple of times since then they'd had coffee. A couple? Okay, four. Patrick stared at the paper again.

Sod it.

Clutching the paper, he headed round to Maggie's cottage, walking as casually as he could to the back garden gate. She might not be in. She might have a date.

She was in.

She and Zoë were sitting at the rickety old table. As ever, Zoë looked like she ought to be gracing the fuselage of a WWII bomber, her scarlet lipstick perfectly matching her cleavage enhancing top, but it just didn't work for him. Maybe it was because he could remember her as a kid, running around in a tutu.

Tutus, *Flashdance* – it all made sense. Libby had to be the Broken Ballerina.

'Welcome to the Gin Terrace,' Libby said with a perfectly clipped, fifties heroine accent. 'You've arrived in time for cocktails. G and T, darling?'

He laughed as he crossed the lawn. 'Why the hell not?'

Zoë stood up. 'I'll get it.'

As he sat at the table, he looked Libby over with a mixture of amusement and horror. In ripped-at-the-knee jeans and a simple black t-shirt, with no hooker-esque bra straps on display, she lacked her usual trailer trash styling but made up for it with twenty black bangles on each wrist, near black polish on her nails and pink hair. Christ, it really was pink – a pale, candyfloss pink with six or so black streaks scattered through it. She'd gone even more rock chick. Why? It was all a front. He'd already discovered she preferred R&B.

'Nice hair,' he said examining one of Libby's new pink locks. And the silly fringe still covered half her eyes.

'It's for my new job. Cool, hey?'

'Not even slightly. It's *pink*. What's the job?'

'Oscar's Bar and Bistro in Haverton. Rob sorted it. I'm sure it'll suck, but it's a job. This might be the last Saturday night I ever have off and so we're having a girly night in. You can be an honorary girl, if you like.'

'An honorary girl? My weekend's made.' He leant on the table, still holding the paper. 'Libs, your ex… Paolo, is he an artist?'

Libby's frown told him enough, but when she pulled her graceful legs up onto her chair, hugging her knees, he knew it was true.

She nodded. 'Why?'

'And is this you?' he asked, dropping the paper on the table, already open at page twenty-five. 'Are you the Broken Ballerina?'

Libby stared at the paper, her hand shaking as she gulped her drink.

* * *

The words were a blur, but she stared at the photos. Two large oil paintings, one of her doing a rather good arabesque and the other showing her in tears as she told Paolo how once upon a time she used to be a ballet dancer. Oh, Paolo. Libby's fingers brushed over the photo of him. He'd had his hair cut a little shorter. She preferred the way it was before.

'You're a ballerina?' Patrick asked.

'No, I'm a broken ballerina.' She held the paper up to her face and screamed before taking a deep breath and facing him. 'Sorry. Shock.'

'What's going on?' Zoë asked, dashing out. Her accusatory scowl evaporated as she spied the paper and snatched it from Libby. 'Fuck me. He finally painted you.'

Libby rested her forehead on the table. Oh god, Paolo had painted her, not just painted her, but made her famous too. Okay, he hadn't named her, but Patrick had recognised her, what if others did? 'How could he do this to me?'

'They're quite good.' Zoë peered at the photos. 'Not at all chocolate box considering they're of a ballerina. I never realised he was actually talented.'

'The article's not about him being talented,' Patrick explained. 'He turned down seventy-five grand and then burned the painting to protect Libby.'

Which would be Paolo's style. Libby closed her eyes. Oh Paolo. Why couldn't she have loved Paolo?

'I bet he regretted it,' she said, picking up her phone, 'because he knows I'm going to kill him.'

Paolo answered instantly.

'Ach, I'm sorry,' he said, his familiar voice like molten chocolate for her soul. 'I've just been thinking of that time we went to Devon in Mikey's campervan. You were so angry, but remember how I painted you? Need me to do it now?'

God, he'd promised not to sketch her for a week, but she'd found his pad and threatened to walk all the way home. She didn't. Under a starlit sky, they'd built a fire on a deserted beach and he'd painted her. Literally. With his watercolours, he painted elegant swirls and flowers over her arms, legs and torso, until she lay naked but decorated from the neck down. They'd washed it off, shagging in the sea. It was no wonder he'd talked her back into bed so many times. He knew how to break down her defences: a knee-weakening kiss, an erotic endearment whispered into her ear, a hand brushing over her neck. It didn't take much. Patrick watched her. She couldn't weaken. Not this time, Paolo.

'Sorry?' she snapped. 'I trusted you to keep a bloody secret, not plaster it all over page twenty-five of the bloody Guardian.'

'It got a wee bit out of hand.'

'A *wee bit*? You could've bloody warned me—'

'I rang you last week. Twice. You didn't answer.'

'Well you should've rung a third time. Of course I'm going to ignore your calls. I'm trying to move on with my life—'

'Me too. Painting you is part of that. I'm trying to let go.'

Libby sighed. 'Why didn't you sell the painting?'

'I said I'm trying to let you go. I haven't yet.' His voice softened. 'Come to London.'

'Sofa still free?'

'And the bed.'

Was this a sign, to tell her to move to London? She closed her eyes, refusing to look at Patrick again. *I want more.* 'I can't.'

'I love you.'

'Let it go.'

She hung up, staring at the sky to banish the tears.

'And how is our perpetually tortured artist?' Zoë asked. 'Still pining for you?'

'So what if he is?' Libby strode along the patio, trying to ignore Zoë's amused smile and Patrick's growing frown.

'You should've told him years ago,' Zoë said, picking up her beeping phone. 'He might've made you happy.'

Maybe he would. As Zoë headed into the house, Libby began dead-heading the faded chive flowers. She ought to change the subject before Patrick started asking questions.

'God, I could kill the Scottish fuckwit. Bloody untrustworthy men.' Libby flashed Patrick a smile. 'No offense meant to any Scottish non-fuckwits present. Although I expect you're just as untrustworthy.'

'Absolutely,' Patrick replied. 'But I'm not Scottish.'

Libby's fingers hovered around a purple flower. 'What?'

'Technically speaking, I'm not Scottish. My mum and dad are both Scottish and I went to Edinburgh University, so the accent's inevitable, but I was born and bred here.'

'You're English?' Libby's heart had stopped.

'I'm English.'

Oh god. 'I… have to… check the potatoes.' She ran inside and slumped against the kitchen units, waiting for Zoë to finish her call. 'It's him.'

'What's him?' Zoë asked.

'Patrick. He's the one I summoned. He's twenty-nine, good-looking, single, and despite his appalling behaviour, he has decent morals. He's a vet, for god's sake. You can't get better with animals than that. He's got hazel eyes and now, it turns out, he's bloody English.'

Zoë pressed her lips together, trying not to laugh.

'Oh, you cow.' Libby threw a tea towel at her. 'You knew.'

'I wanted to see what would happen when you found out.'

'I swear you only keep me around as some kind of psychological case study.'

'I could get a PhD out of you. You don't really believe this Wiccan nonsense?'

But surely, this was her sign; she should stay in Gosthwaite. 'What am I going to do?'

'Shag him?' Zoë suggested.

As if. Libby dug around in her bag, searching for the little red pouch containing her summoning spell. She'd stopped carrying it, doubting its effectiveness, but Patrick fit everything she'd wished for. And more.

Oh please, let him be my Somebody.

She tucked the pouch into her back pocket as Patrick came in, frowning at her. Sticking to her potatoes ruse, Libby opened the oven, poking at the dauphinoise with a knife.

'Almost done.' Libby closed the oven door, her face composed.

'Change of plan,' Zoë said, putting her barely touched drink on the table. 'I'm going out.'

'What about our girly night?' Libby put her hands on her hips, her nails tapping.

Zoë glanced at Patrick. 'Er, there's a boy present. It's not a girly night.'

'Whoa, don't blame me,' Patrick said. 'I'm an honorary girl. Where're you going, booty call?'

Zoë flashed her coyest of smiles. 'Something like that.'

'With the silver fox?' Libby asked.

'Older, by how much?' Patrick asked, clearly warming to his honorary girl role.

'Sugar daddy kind of older.'

'You're a very bad girl, Ms Horton.'

'And what about dinner?' Libby asked, despising the way Patrick smiled at Zoë.

'Patrick looks like a red meat kind of guy,' Zoë said before heading out of the room.

Oh, the stirring cow. Patrick sipped his drink, trying not to smile. And what was he after? Clearly, he didn't fancy her. He couldn't have been more disparaging about her new hair.

'Are you hungry?' she asked.

'Starving.'

'Would you like to stay for dinner? Steak with dauphinoise potatoes and green veg.'

He nodded, looking her over. 'You don't strike me as the steak and dauphinoise type.'

'It's all part of my fell race fitness regime. Saturday. Red meat and carb night. I'll run it off tomorrow.'

He grinned at her. 'Ob... sess... ive.'

'Bite me.'

'There's more meat on a potato. I'll pass.'

She handed him a bottle of red. 'Here, make yourself useful.'

Although she did a sterling impression of sounding pissed off, Libby struggled not to smile. Patrick didn't bother.

'So, little miss ballerina, I have a million questions.'

'You can keep them to yourself. I don't want to talk about it.' She stood on the opposite side of the kitchen island to prepare the vegetables. 'Any of it.'

'Dinner's going to be fun. What's in your back pocket?'

'None of your business. Broccoli and French beans okay?'

'Fine. Why did you go all weird when I said I wasn't Scottish?'

'It was a surprise.'

'Were you a professional ballerina?'

'Did you get out for a ride today? Awesome day.'

He laughed. 'Oh come on, Libs. There's a big fucking elephant in the room and it's wearing a tutu.'

She banged her head against a cupboard door.

'Okay, let's start easy,' he said. 'If Paolo's so in love with you, why did he go to London?'

'None of your business.'

'Libby...'

She sighed, lacking the energy to distract him. 'He said he wanted to become rich and famous. Really, he went because I didn't love him. God, he's actually done it, become rich and famous. All I've done is become slightly infamous.'

Patrick studied the paper, peering at Paolo's photo. 'He's good-looking, talented... what's wrong with him? Rubbish kisser?'

Despite everything, she smiled. 'No. He's pretty fabulous in every way. I actually questioned my attraction to men when I didn't fall in love with him.'

'How seriously?' He leant forward, his elbows on the worktop, his grin infectious. 'Any girl on girl action?'

She laughed, flicking her hair back. 'Sorry to disappoint you. I didn't question it for long. He's hot.'

'He can't be all that hot. You're here. He's there.'

'He's a good friend, but he just... he was nearly perfect, but just not quite, if you know what I mean.'

He nodded. 'Nearly isn't good enough. What wasn't perfect with Paolo?'

'He's too emotional. We fought a lot. Mostly over his obsession with painting me. I met him the first week I moved to Manchester and we went out for a year. I actually thought I could just fall in love with someone...' She checked the potatoes, fussed over the vegetables.

'But?'

'He ticked all my boxes, but he literally spent all the time we weren't in bed sketching me. It's actually quite draining to be stared at that much, to sit still for that long.'

As Patrick laughed, Libby relaxed. God, it was nice to talk to someone about Paolo. Zoë only ever mocked her for sticking with him for so long.

'We split up, but for the last two years neither of us went out with anyone else. We've had more absolutely never again last nights than I've had my roots done.' Libby gazed out of the window, smiling. Bloody Paolo. 'When he told me he was leaving for London, I told him I used to be a ballerina and he drew me. He said he finally understood me. I guess he understood me enough to paint me, the bugger.'

'You spent three years with the guy and you didn't tell him until he said he was leaving?' Patrick's eyebrows had disappeared under his black curls. 'Why?'

'I don't see why people need to know everything about me.'

'Well it helps them get to know who you really are.'

'What if I don't want people to know who I really am?'

'Then you'll never be happy.' He rested his chin on his hand, still leaning on the island. 'What is all the secrecy about? You were a ballerina, so what? Or are you in some ridiculous witness protection program?'

'It's not even remotely exciting,' Zoë said, tottering in wearing a skin-tight black dress and the five-inch Louboutin heels. 'But good luck trying to talk any sense in to her. I've failed on many occasions. I'm off. While 'dile.'

Libby kissed Zoë's cheek. 'Later 'gator.'

'Careful you don't give him a heart attack,' Patrick said, frowning at the metal studs on Zoë's heels.

'But surely that's the point of a sugar daddy,' Zoë called as she walked down the hallway.

Patrick appeared to be unable to take his eyes off her arse.

'You're not old or rich enough for her.' Libby frowned at him, holding up a sirloin steak. 'How do you want it?'

'I'd be scared she'd eat me alive afterwards. Medium rare, please.'

This would be a disaster. She'd never be able to cook, not with him watching. His t-shirt was snugger than his usual tatty efforts, and it showed off his perfect body. She could see the muscles in his back working as he pulled the cork from the bottle. God, what must he look like with his kit off. Her cheeks burned.

'I'm not promising it'll end up that way,' she said, 'but it's something to aim for at least.'

Somehow she held it together and ten minutes later, they sat at the kitchen table with pretty perfect-looking steaks and potatoes that made her mouth water from the mere aroma. He poured the wine and held up his glass.

'Thank you, it looks great.' He chinked his glass against hers. 'The elephant's doing pirouettes, by the way.'

He wasn't going to let this go and she couldn't go through the entire meal deflecting his questions. She took a deep breath.

'Look, I was a ballet dancer, but talking about it makes me cry, so I don't talk about it.'

'Everything makes you cry. I'm used to it.'

He sliced into his steak and Libby smiled. Medium rare, miracles do happen.

'So this is why you need the distractions?'

She nodded. *Don't cry.*

'What happened?'

Maybe she should've told Paolo the truth years ago. Maybe Patrick was right. Maybe she'd never be happy until people knew who she was. The *Somebody* song popped into her head. She'd wanted somebody to know her innermost thoughts, know her intimate details. Was this her chance?

Chapter Twenty-Three

Saturday night. He could've done anything, gone anywhere. He could've got drunk, got stoned, rang Miss fucking Haverton and got laid. Instead, Patrick had chosen to visit Ms Olivia Wilde and now he sat willing her to speak.

Come on, Libs. Talk to me.

Libby opened her mouth, no doubt to voice her usual *none of your business* response, but instead she ate a forkful of potatoes, never dropping her eye contact with him. What was going on behind those pretty grey eyes?

'I grew up in Brize Norton.' She took a sharp breath, as if the admission shocked her. 'It's honestly not that interesting.'

Oh, it is. 'Go on.'

'My mum was a senior officer in the RAF, my dad did god-knows what for the MOD. I learned not to bother asking.'

'Brothers or sisters?'

'Two brothers, Lucas and Connor, but they're ten years younger than me, so I was an only child for ages. Originally, I wanted to fly planes, like Mum used to, so she taught me to toughen up. Judo, kick-boxing, generally how to take someone down–'

'Like Jack?'

She laughed a little. 'Like Jack. But she didn't want me to grow up a tomboy, so she picked girly hobbies. Horse-riding, Brownies, piano lessons and ballet. I was eight when I saw my first professional ballet. *The Nutcracker.* I took one look at the Sugar Plum Fairy and decided to be a ballerina rather than a fighter pilot when I grew up. I worked hard, took it seriously and got into the Royal Ballet School.'

'Is that where Zoë went too?'

'We met on the first day and we've been best friends ever since. God, I missed her when she left London, but we stayed friends. She went to university and I turned professional. I joined the corps of the English National Ballet.' She sipped her wine, smiling at the ceiling. 'It was like some kind of fairy tale and I was starring in it. They paid me to dance and by the time I was twenty-one I was a senior soloist, well on my way to being a principle.'

'What happened?'

She dug into her steak, her frown deepening, but she wasn't crying and after several mouthfuls she carried on. 'One day we were rehearsing, and my dance partner... he dropped me. I landed badly and fractured my ankle in three places.'

'Ah, the ankle that hurt when I mowed you down. Surely they pinned it?'

'Yes, but it was never the same. When you're in a company, you work hard. Class, rehearsals, performances. It adds up to eight hours dancing a day.'

'Jesus. So you quit?'

'For about a year, I tried so hard to keep going, refusing to admit it was killing me, but the black cloud on the horizon kept getting bigger and bigger. In my last ballet, I was a cygnet in Swan Lake. My ankle was agony, plus I had a broken metatarsal and two stress fractures in my right shin.'

'You danced with a broken foot?'

'I had to. I wasn't letting some corps wannabe steal my place.'

'You're certifiable.'

She laughed. Finally. 'One night I'd taken so many painkillers, my head was fuzzy and I missed my cue. I mean, ninety-eight percent of the audience wouldn't have known, but I buggered it up and I have the DVD to prove it. I'd rather not dance than be second best, so I quit. One day I was understudy for Odette, the next I wasn't a dancer anymore.'

'But why just abandon your whole life?'

'Because I was Olivia Wilde, the ballerina. I doubt I would've been the next Darcey Bussell, but that kind of talk got bandied around me at school. But oh look, I'm not a principal ballerina. I failed.' She forced a smile. 'I don't do failure very well.'

'Ob... sess... sive.'

Her smile grew. 'I don't like making mistakes.'

'You have very high expectations of yourself.'

'Oh come on. Your mum's a vet, your dad's a vet and your big brother is a vet. You wanted to be one too. How would you have felt if you'd failed?'

An excellent point. Christ, this could be him if his dad sacked him. What would he do if he couldn't be a vet? Somehow he doubted he'd be dealing with it even half as well as Libby. And she wasn't dealing with it at all.

'Why don't you teach ballet?'

'And why would I want to teach ballet? Every day I'd send a mini-me off to live my dream. Every day I'd be reminded I was a failure.'

Her bitterness surprised him.

'You had an accident,' he said quietly.

'I should've found a way to carry on. Tamara Rojo broke her foot. She dances through it. I wasn't tough enough.'

'You need to give yourself a break.'

'But it was my own stupid...' She knocked back her last half a glass of wine in one.

'How was it your fault?' He leaned forwards, resting his elbows on the table.

She shook her head as she moved to sit cross-legged on her chair, picking at a French bean. 'I haven't had enough to drink for this conversation.'

He topped up her glass. 'Don't let me stop you, princess.'

Libby defiantly glugged her wine.

'Feel better? Now, spill.'

'The guy who dropped me was Tristan, my boyfriend. I should never have got involved with my own dance partner. It's too distracting, especially when things go wrong. He thought he'd teach me a lesson. It went a little further than he intended.'

'Nice guy. What was he pissed off about? Aside from being called Tristan.'

She didn't smile, but turned her head, staring out of the window. 'He expected me to love him more than ballet. To skip class for him. Basically, he was pissed off because he loved me, but I didn't love him back.'

'I'm seeing a theme here. Tristan, Paolo.' Patrick sat back. 'Little ice maiden, hey?'

'Piss off. I'm not an ice-maiden. I just loved my job. The routine, the perfection, the pain. God, the adrenalin rush of being on stage, under the lights, hearing the music... I miss it, but I'd sacrificed too much to waste time missing class to go to Paris for the weekend.'

'Sacrificed what?'

'My family.'

'Why aren't you in Sydney?'

'I don't want to give you the satisfaction of getting full custody.'

She kicked his ankle and for a moment they grinned at each other.

Jesus, they'd be flirting next.

'My family emigrated when I was sixteen. I refused, point blank, to leave the Royal Ballet School so they went and I stayed.'

'You could've gone after your accident. Think how big a distraction a whole new country would've been.'

'Don't take the piss.' Sadness filled her face.

'Sorry.' He meant it.

'I can't face my mum. I rejected them for ballet and I can still see the disappointment in her face. I failed in my dream and I failed my family.'

He closed his eyes, knowing the same shame she was feeling. 'Sorry for calling you an ice maiden.'

'You're forgiven.'

He was a coward. Here he was giving her a hard time for keeping things to herself, but he had no intention of telling anyone that he had a noose hanging over his head. Failed? Libby hadn't failed. Patrick was the one who'd failed. He'd let everyone down. But no more.

His plate was empty, hers almost as she put her knife and fork together.

'Man, that was fit as, by the way,' he said. 'The steak was perfectly cooked and the potatoes... actually, can I have the rest of yours?'

She laughed as he switched their plates and began hoovering up her leftovers. 'Zoë taught me. She still says I'm rubbish, but I think my paella rocks.'

'A bold statement you'll have to prove.'

Her answering smile definitely crossed the flirting border.

'I can't help noticing that you're not crying,' he said, trying not to grin.

'Yes, I'd noticed that too. I suppose, things have changed.'

'Why?'

'Moving here. This life.' She paused, toying with her glass. 'Rob.'

He drained his wine. 'You're not still likely to go bunny boiler, are you?'

'No. He just raised my expectations. He...' She pressed her lips together, staring at her fingers as they tapped against her glass.

'Do you think your dad being so secretive made it impossible for you to be open?'

'I hate you,' she said, blushing a little.

'Rob raised your expectations and...'

'I don't want to have this conversation.'

'For god's sake.' He pushed his empty plate away, laughing. 'Let me guess, Mister Romantic has shown you that you can love something more than ballet.'

Her cheeks turned another three shades pinker.

'What would've happened if Vanessa hadn't come back? Would you've played happy families?'

'Probably. I liked the life.'

'Marriage, kids, dog, cat, tumbledown farmhouse?'

She nodded.

'Why do all girls want the married thing?'

'What's wrong with it?'

He shrugged. 'I ran two hundred miles from the last girl who suggested it.'

'Commitment-phobe.' She tucked her hair behind her ears and gathered up their plates, but he didn't miss that her smile had fallen.

'Hey, your dream is to have what Rob has. This is the guy you were shagging while his wife buggered off with a viola player. What's so great about that set-up?'

'Who was she, the girl you ran away from? The one who scarred you for life.'

'Nina. We met at vet school.' He cleared the table, putting the peppermill and placemats away as she quietly directed. 'But she hasn't scarred me. I still don't get what's so great about persevering with the same person forever.'

'Commitment-phobe.' She flashed him that angelic, shy smile. 'How are they, Rob and Vanessa?'

'Happy. Very happy. More so than I've known for a long time.'

'I'm glad.' She nodded, looking genuinely pleased.

Together they pottered around the kitchen. He washed the griddle pan as she stacked the dishwasher. He liked that she got on with it, not needing to fill the silence with inane chatter. Nina used to hate silence. He left the pan on the draining board and dried his hands, watching as Libby wiped down the worktops. She even managed that with effortless, graceful movements.

He'd come to assume she'd didn't possess anything other than jodhpurs and mini-skirts, but jeans worked on her. Okay, they covered her perfect legs, but they were tight and low cut, showing off her trim waist as she reached up to put things in the cupboard. In fact, Libby looked hot in jeans. Shame about the bloody awful black stripes in her pink hair. Seriously, pink hair...

'So,' he asked, 'is the rock chick look part of denying you were ever a ballerina?'

'No. Seventeen year-old trailer trash has always been my off-duty style. I've always hated being *nice*.' She stuck her tongue out at him, but then laughed, flicking her hair back.

He couldn't imagine her not falling in love. It was so easy to picture her holding hands on walks through the woods, having easy conversations over dinner in the pub. Now, he just had to stop picturing himself doing it with her. She was *Off Limits*.

'You don't look much like a ballerina, aside from being so thin.'

'Don't say it like that. I've never been anorexic in my life, or come close.'

'I can't see you in a tutu, looking pretty.'

The dish cloth hit his shoulder. 'I'll show you, mister.'

She ran upstairs and he half-expected her to come back down in a tutu. Instead, she returned with a thick photo album and they headed outside with the wine. In the fading light of the late September evening, he sat on the rickety bench as she opened the album near the back, pointing to a photo of a Libby he'd never seen before – maybe he'd seen a hint of it when she was in her running gear. In a pink and purple dress, stood on the tip toe of one foot with the other leg lifted behind her. She looked... beautiful. Jesus Christ.

'See? Me in a tutu, *pretty*.'

He poured the wine, trying not to show how floored he was.

'*Passable*.' *Perfect. Fuck. Don't get hung up on her. Not her.* Robbie was too good a friend to break the *Off Limits* rule. And Michael Wray would be on them like a rash. 'Christ, you were even thinner then. You're just sticks with muscle. And you can see your chest bones. That can't be right.'

'I was a ballet dancer. It's what we look like. Do you have to focus on the fact I have no tits?'

Without bothering to be subtle, he glanced down to compare now with then, making her laugh. He shrugged, trying not to smile. 'Not so bad now.'

'Try admiring my fabulous legs and perfect arm positions. This is when I was the Sugar Plum Fairy, my dream come true.' She gulped her wine. 'You've no idea how much I miss it, but hey, I couldn't drink bottles of wine back then.'

'It's a whole different world.' He shook his head and flicked back to the start of the album. 'Can I?'

She nodded.

He absorbed himself in her life, smiling briefly at the snaps of little Libby in her first tutu, laughing at the stick insect teenager. In one photo, she stood with an equally stick insect girl with dark hair and bad skin.

'Christ, is that Zoë? I never knew her when she was a teenager. She's thinner than you.'

Libby took a long drag on her cigarette. 'I know you think I'm too skinny, but that's just the way I am. I eat well and exercise a lot. Zoë's different. Thanks to Maggie's hideous influence, Zoë's had a hard-core battle with food since she was seven.'

'Maggie, why?'

Libby explained how those long summers that little Zoë Horton had spent in Gosthwaite were really six weeks of bullying hell, and guilt swamped him. He'd have been twelve the day he, Zoë and a few others went blackberry picking. With purple fingers and faces, they'd eaten until their stomach's hurt. When Zoë's tutu got stuck in the brambles, he'd rescued her, but she'd started crying, upset over the shredded netting. A soft touch for tears, even then, he'd walked her home to explain to Maggie what had happened. But Maggie hadn't cared about the tutu, only the evidence of the blackberries around Zoë's mouth. Her first question wasn't for her great-niece's well-being. It was, *what have you been eating?* Poor Zoë.

He skipped forward and smiled at a portrait of Libby dressed in a black and purple tutu. Her poker straight hair was white blonde, her lips bare, her eyes coated with the usual black eye make-up. Stood on her toes, hands on hips with the nonchalant attitude he knew so well, she looked about twenty and just the kind of girl the twenty-five year-old him would've quite happily shagged.

But his favourite photo was taken in rehearsal. She sat with a friend against a mirrored wall, wearing a leotard and legwarmers like she'd worn the night Jack hassled her. Her hair was pulled back, her face make-up free and her smile... That was her, the real Libby, the one he'd seen when she wasn't hiding behind the black crap and fringe.

She leant in, looking at the photo and her subtle floral perfume filled his head.

'You actually look very pretty when you're not wearing the black crap,' he said, unable to stop himself.

'We had to attend grooming classes, to make sure our eyebrows were waxed, our complexions flawless. It took a lot of effort to look that perfectly natural, I can tell you. I rebelled against it.'

She flicked over the page, flinching at the photo of her lying in a hospital bed with her foot in plaster. The girl in the photo smiled, the one next to him looked to be on the verge of tears for the first time.

'You okay?' he asked, his voice quiet. *Don't cry, Libs.*

'I had no idea my life was ruined at that stage. I thought I'd be out of action for a few weeks, then back at class.'

Patrick nudged her. 'It's not ruined. It just needs to be different.'

The last photos were of her in a white tutu. 'Then it was over.'

'Your life's not ruined. You'll see.'

She closed the album and picked up the empty bottle. 'More wine?'

Without waiting for his answer, she ducked inside, taking the album with her. Christ, he had to be careful. A few glasses of wine would be okay, but they shouldn't get pissed because if they did... He'd seen the signs: the smiles, the gazes. He'd probably given enough himself. She might be recovering from Robbie, but Libby so would. And he would too. Thankfully, when she returned, her smile in place once again, she lit the patio heater and they sat in separate chairs at the table. Safer.

'God, everyone's going to know, aren't they? What if Lynda asks me and I cry in the middle of the post office?'

'I'd be surprised if anyone else recognises you. I only did because you mentioned Paolo the other week and... you sit like that a lot.'

'No, I...' Libby lifted her head off her knees, glancing down at her arms hugging them. 'Oh.'

'You know, I think you're going about this distraction thing all wrong. You can't just pretend the last twenty years of your life didn't happen. You'd been dancing when Jack came round, hadn't you?'

She nodded.

'You need to get it back in your life.'

She shook her head.

'You believe in Fate. Don't you think it might be for a reason that you've ended up in Maggie's cottage?' He waited, but she shook her head. In denial. 'Clara's mum used to be a ballerina too.'

'I know.'

'She has a dance studio in Haverton.'

'I know.'

'You could go there. To dance.'

'No. What I need is a decent career.'

She forced a smile, her lip wobbling and he knew to shut up. He didn't want to ruin a perfectly good evening by making her cry.

'Okay, a new career,' he said. 'A is for... Artist? Architect? Air Hostess? Actor? Anaesthetist? Do you have any GCSEs?'

'Bugger off, of course I do. I also have Dance, English and French A-Levels, all As, and a First Class degree in Performing Arts and Dance. Not sure if that'll get me into medical school though so forget Anaesthetist. And we can skip B. I'm starting my barmaid life tomorrow and as we've already discussed, I don't have the boobs to be a beauty queen.'

He laughed along, loving how she didn't take herself too seriously. 'C... Clown? You already have the make-up skills.'

She punched his arm and they settled into an easy routine mocking one another. Although a lingering regret of a missed opportunity didn't abate, he kept his distance. She was Michael Wray's target and *Off Limits*. Besides, he liked spending time with her. If he shagged her, it'd be over. He'd fuck her and fuck off. It's what he always did.

Being friends was better.

* * *

The following morning, Libby stared at the orange leaves on the ground, trying to focus on her stride, her breathing, the next bloody big hill, but her mind kept flitting back to the night before, to Patrick. She'd bared her soul to him, told him everything, and yet he'd gone home without even kissing her cheek. From what Clara had told her, Patrick ought to have tried to shag her by now. Oh, he'd made it perfectly clear that he hated how Libby looked, but he'd also said she was very pretty.

She shook her head. She should be concentrating on the fell race, not Patrick. In six weeks, she'd have to run fifteen miles over some bloody big hills and despite the training, the idea still terrified her.

She and Xander regularly clocked up fifty or sixty miles a week – running long, varied terrain circuits, short steep uphill repetitions, sprints, jogs, all of it with little regard for the weather. She'd learned two things: always carry extra layers and just keep going, no matter how much it hurts. Just keep going. She jogged next to Xander, wishing she'd never said she'd do the bloody race, let alone that she'd beat Grace.

'You're quiet today,' Xander said.

'Too tired to talk.'

'It's been an easy run.'

'Late night, too much wine.' She held up a hand. 'I know. No lectures.'

Too much wine with Patrick. Oh god, there he was. Outside the vet's, Patrick leaned against the railings, talking on his phone. He'd been mountain biking and had the mud splatters to prove it. Xander pointed to the police car and they jogged over, curiosity piqued.

As they neared, Patrick hung up, giving Xander a terse hello and Libby a small smile. This really wasn't how she wanted to look when she saw him: red, sweaty, hair scraped back and make-up free. In an effort to hide her face, she stretched her hamstrings.

'What's going on?' Xander asked.

'Burgled last night. A load of drugs gone. Ketamine mostly.' Patrick ran his fingers through his curls. 'Grace is adamant she put the alarm on on Friday night, but it was off when I came in to sort some paperwork. Not what I needed this morning.'

'Hangover?' Libby asked, trying not to show how badly she wanted to run her fingers through his hair too.

He nodded.

Xander looked from her to Patrick, but didn't say anything, just smiled at the floor.

Libby frowned at the alarm box on the wall. 'Zoë and I got burgled last Christmas in Manchester. They took the usual: laptops, iPads, but it was our bloody passports that was the worst. We were going skiing a few weeks later and had to get new ones. Zoë couldn't find her birth certificate, so we ended up not being able to go. The buggers had turned the alarm off. It's so easy to override them these days, especially older systems like yours.'

Patrick and Xander both raised their eyebrows.

'What?' she laughed. 'I worked for an alarm company for a while. Only the engineers should have override codes, but you can get them off the internet. You need a better system.'

'Point noted, Safecracker Barbie.' Patrick smiled, tugging her ponytail. 'Did you do it?'

Libby didn't laugh. Grace came out of the surgery and Libby wrapped her arms around herself, needing the reassurance. As she did, Patrick and Xander stood either side of her. Flanked by her superheroes.

Grace looked Libby over with disdain, but smiled at Xander. 'Good run? I did the Crag Loop last night.'

It'd been over three months since Libby and Jack... but if Grace's animosity hadn't lessened, her bodyweight had. She had to have lost at least a stone and her fell-running capabilities suddenly seemed a lot more realistic.

'You managed the Loop yet, Libby?' Grace asked flashing a saccharine smile.

The intimidating Crag Loop made up half the race circuit and as yet, Xander wouldn't let her attempt it. Libby stood a little straighter. 'I will beat you.'

'Oh, for Christ's sake,' Patrick snapped. 'Will you two pack it in?'

Xander took Libby's arm. 'Careful,' he said as they walked away. 'You've got a way to go before you can beat her.'

Libby glanced back, just catching Patrick's comment to Grace.

'I don't know, Gracey. She's bloody determined.'

Libby jogged beside Xander, heading to the back garden.

'Well, this explains a few things,' he said as they did their usual cool down stretches. 'Daze sulked all night at the football because Patrick didn't hit on her once. I know she wouldn't, but she does like the attention.'

Libby frowned at him. 'What are you talking about?'

'You and Patrick.' Xander's smile grew. 'I wholeheartedly approve, by the way, because if you can keep him away from Daze, I'd owe you. Big time.'

'I'm sorry to disappoint you, but we're just friends. I'm not his cup of tea.'

'Doesn't look that way to me,' Xander said. 'Maybe he just needs a nudge. You should have a party. He loves parties.'

Libby sat on the grass, stretching down to put her head over her shin. A party? Would that be the answer?

Chapter Twenty-Four

'What do you think?' Zoë stood back, admiring the carved pumpkin lanterns arranged in the fireplace.

'You've missed your calling.' Libby sat on the windowsill, summoning the enthusiasm to prepare for the Halloween party to end all Halloween parties. 'The courier picked up your parcel.'

'Thanks. How was work?'

'Just awesome,' Libby replied, sarcasm dripping from her voice.

Three weeks. Twenty days, if she was being precise. Twenty days she'd survived at the bar. How she'd managed that was a miracle. If she'd had one friend at work, just one, it would help, but every single member of staff hated her. They were jealous. She'd shagged not just one Golding brother, but both of them. It didn't matter how many times she told them she hadn't touched Xander, because they'd seen the photos in the paper; they knew the *truth*.

The job itself was surprisingly okay. Oscar's Bar and Bistro was set in the old magistrate's court, kitted out with ornate mahogany tables and ancient chesterfield sofas. In keeping with the classy setting, they served decent wine and addictively tasty tapas. Libby proved to be a great barmaid, but then she'd done it so many times in between other jobs that she ought to be a bloody expert. Actually, if she included the temporary bar jobs, her employment tally over the last three years had to be well over thirty. An incredible feat.

'What happened?' Zoë handed her a staple gun. 'Cobwebs on the beams, please.'

Libby dutifully stapled stringy nylon threads to the ceiling while she explained how at ten past eleven, Oscar Golding, her über-boss and father of the Golding brothers, had walked into the bar. Inevitably, he'd asked why she was working there and not Low Wood Farm, but before Libby could answer, she'd glanced around to see Steve, the chef, taking a photo on his phone.

Without hesitation, she'd taken Steve down with the defensive leg sweep her mother had taught her and, as he lay on the floor groaning, Libby deleted the photo. Of course, then she'd had to explain to Mr Golding Senior not only why she'd lost her job at the farm, but why she'd floored the chef. *I fort she were goin' for an 'at trick,* Steve had said. Sadly, the ground hadn't swallowed her.

'It's a job,' Zoë said, 'and for Haverton, not a bad one. Don't bugger it up.'

If Libby could just keep her head down at the bar, the rumours would die down and she'd make friends. Or, more likely, the very dishy Mr Golding Senior would see she could run the place better than Greg, give her the manager's job and the staff would resent her even more.

Libby sat on the windowsill again, staring outside. 'Do you think he'll come?'

'Paolo or Patrick?'

When Libby had mentioned throwing a party, Zoë leapt at the idea. A Halloween shindig, Zoë said, would be the perfect excuse to dress in porn-worthy costumes and pull hot guys – exactly what she needed to keep Jonathan on his toes, so they'd emailed everyone they knew, in Gosthwaite and Manchester, with the majority saying yes. Friends were crammed into holiday cottages throughout the village, even Robbie and Vanessa were coming. Libby had been astonished when Robbie emailed to say yes, but he'd explained how it'd show everyone that things were okay. The only person who hadn't responded was Patrick.

Four o'clock. Libby frowned towards the veterinary surgery. His Land Rover still wasn't there.

She didn't get him. A few weeks ago, he'd persuaded her to bare her soul. He'd totally taken an interest in her life; he'd said she looked pretty. But since then, *nada* and the other day he'd posted eye drops for Hyssop through the letterbox. Patrick was avoiding her.

What if he didn't turn up – or worse, copped off with someone else? Where was he?

An ancient MG pulled up and Libby's heart made an involuntary leap. Paolo. He'd really come all this way. After a quick check for smudged make-up, she ran outside to meet him. Okay, her lust cravings were purely for Patrick, but she still longed to see her old friend.

Paolo climbed out of the car, raking his hair out of his eyes. It'd grown back to dishevelled perfection. God, it was good to see him. She ran down the pavement, straight into his arms and he held her tight, muttering how much he'd missed her, how much he loved her. She held his face, gazing up at him.

Had she been an idiot? This was Paolo – a talented, truly lovely person. He'd never walk out of the pub, embarrassing her in front of Grace. His fingers gently pushed aside her fringe as he looked into her eyes. She should kiss him. She should. She should kiss Paolo and make it work. Surely, she could love him back.

With the worst possible timing, she spotted a dark green Land Rover in her peripheral vision. Patrick. She glanced round, catching his eye. She smiled. He didn't. Arse. She rested her head on Paolo's shoulder.

At least you're here.

Paolo frowned, taking in the Green. 'Ach, it's great to see you again, but did you have to move to the middle of nowhere? It's an artistic wasteland.'

'Hey, I like it.'

'You're insane,' Paolo said, finally letting her go. 'I have a present for you.'

From the car, he took out a large canvas covered in a dust sheet. Oh god, had he painted her again? Libby sat on the garden wall as Paolo propped the canvas against Zoë's BMW. When he lifted the sheet and Libby saw herself, she stifled a sob. It was *the Broken Ballerina.*

'You didn't burn it?'

Paolo sat next to her. 'Of course not, I struggle to throw a sketch of you in the bin. I'd never burn it, but I can't keep it or sell it. It's too personal, so it's yours.'

She sat for a moment, taking in Paolo's rough style. It was too personal, her heartache in oils for the world to see. But Patrick was right – it'd be a miracle if anyone recognised her.

'Thank you.' She leaned against him, kissing his cheek. 'I love it.'

Paolo nodded over her shoulder. 'You have company.'

She turned to see Patrick sauntering over with his hands in his pockets, peering at the painting. Was this the hot or cold Patrick? God, he looked hot in his Arran jumper and jeans.

'It's *the Broken Ballerina*,' he said, nodding to the painting. 'You must be Paolo.'

They shook hands as Libby formally introduced them, but she didn't miss the wary look in Patrick's eye. He didn't like Paolo. Was he jealous? Libby's hopes soared.

'It is very good,' Patrick said, again focussed on the painting. 'Very Libby.'

'Are you coming to the party?' she asked.

He shrugged. 'Not sure. Depends on work. See you later.'

Will you? Libby watched him head back to his house.

Paolo scowled. 'And he would be?'

'A friend. He lives next door.'

'A friend you happen to be in love with?' Paolo sighed. 'It's stupid, I hoped—'

'I'm not in love with him.'

'Yes, you are. It's written all over your beautiful face.'

Maggie's cottage, the spiritual home of witchcraft in Gosthwaite, had been transformed from country cottage to kitsch Halloween extravaganza. A cauldron filled with a vodka and blackberry liqueur punch, complete with floating lychee eyeballs, sat at one end of the living room, while orange pumpkin balloons, huge plastic spiders in faux cobwebs and furry black bats dangled from the walls and ceiling. In the garden, a gazebo over the lawn stood festooned with orange fairy lights and creepy witch silhouettes knocked together by Paolo out of bin liners.

Cheesy Halloween tat? Tick. Porn-worthy costumes? Tick. Two drinks already downed to get in the party spirit? Tick. Paolo cutting up lines of coke? Arse.

'It's a party.' Zoë lifted the bodice of her Queen of Hearts dress, raising the hem another two inches to reveal frilly red knickers. 'I'm up for it.'

Libby shook her head as the doorbell rang. No way would she risk her chance of pulling Patrick by becoming some itchy-nosed, self-centred cow. She'd rely on her sweet-but-kinky Alice in Wonderland outfit and copious shots of vodka-based self-confidence.

It would be a great night.

An hour later, zombies, witches and superheroes filled the house. Even Grace turned up. Wearing a tiny black PVC witch's dress and fishnet stockings, she'd brazenly handed Libby a bottle of Sheila's elderflower wine. Refusing to bite, Libby took the wine and politely asked if Jack was playing out. Grace's response was to introduce herself to Paolo. Not that Libby cared.

Xander and Daisy, dressed as a zombie pirate and his undead wench, were knocking back shots of tequila, while Morticia and Gomez Addams, aka Robbie and Vanessa, were snogging in a corner and had been for twenty minutes. Libby tried to ignore them as she weaved through the bodies dancing in the living room. Sheila waved her fairy wand, winning the most inappropriate costume award as Glinda the Good Witch, and Jack winked at Libby, assuming he looked hot in his cowboy get up. Brokeback Mountain, more like.

But her friends in ridiculous costumes couldn't distract her from the absence of the one person she'd had the bloody party for in the first place. Patrick hadn't turned up. And, since it was getting on for ten o'clock, she guessed he wouldn't. It was anything but a great night.

On the patio, Zoë and Clara were comparing their cleavages, not a game Libby wanted to join in, so she lit a cigarette and poured a shot of Blavod.

'Are you sulking?' Zoë asked, pinching a cigarette.

Libby downed the shot. 'No.'

'He's not here, is he?'

Libby shook her head. 'The party's rocking and he hasn't come.'

'Who?' Clara asked, straightening her Wilma Flintstone wig.

'The boy next door,' Zoë said, earning a swat on the arm from Libby. 'Oh, it's hardly a secret. You fancy him; he fancies you.'

'Or not.' Libby pouted. 'If he did, he'd be here.'

'But he does like you.' Clara's eyes lit up. 'Scott thinks so anyway.'

Libby stared at Clara. 'Why?'

Clara shrugged. 'But Scott's never wrong.'

Zoë took a long drag on her cigarette. 'If you want him to come, go get him.'

Libby frowned but Clara nodded.

'Have you looked in a mirror, Lib?' Zoë turned her around, facing the kitchen window. 'You look incredible. Sexy as fuck. How could he turn that down? Now get your arse next door and tell him to get his over here.'

* * *

Standing on Patrick's doorstep had to be the sexiest Alice in Wonderland any man could hope to see. Jesus Christ. The low cut, little blue dress showed off her cleavage, but the skirt crucified him. Incredibly short, it grazed the top of her legs leaving a foot of perfect naked thigh between the fluffy net underskirt and top of her stripy over-the-knee-socks. Tottering in very high heels, her legs looked longer and better than ever.

'You've got to be kidding,' he muttered, but grabbed her arm, pulling her in before anyone saw her.

This was exactly what he didn't need and worse still, when she stood in the living room, the lights showed her glazed eyes. She flashed him an overconfident smile and he groaned. Pissed, or getting there at least. He needed her to leave, but she wandered over to say hello to Hyssop who'd taken refuge from the party.

'What do you want, Libby?'

'I came to see if you were ever going to come to my party. We've got canapés, cocktails... coke. Right up your street.'

Coke? Shit. Grace would have a gram he could scrounge. He itched for a line, imagining the high. No. 'I'm on call.'

Her smile grew and the look in her eyes turned from mischievous to downright dirty. Slowly, she walked up to him, all legs, cleavage and blazing confidence, until she stood with her body inches from his. Oh Christ.

'I don't believe you,' she whispered.

'Libs...' But he didn't back off. Instead, he looked down at her, his heart thumping in his chest.

'Why don't you come out and play? I'd guarantee you'd have the best time ever.' She smiled up at him, peeking through that suddenly sexy fringe. 'Say yes.'

He opened his mouth to tell her not a chance, but found himself staring at her. The shoes made her five inches taller, nearer his height, and her mouth was only a couple of inches below his. *Don't kiss her.*

Kiss her? He wanted to fuck her. Probably more than he'd ever wanted to fuck anyone. He wanted to do a couple of rails, neck a few shots and spend the rest of the night in bed with Libby Wilde. Sod the bed. The sofa would do. He doubted they'd get as far as the stairs anyway. He buried his hands in his pockets, desperate not to touch her.

'What happened to Paolo?'

'He's just a friend.' She took hold of his t-shirt, tugging him toward her. 'Are you coming out to play?'

Oh Christ, she was right there, on a plate and dressed like Alice in fucking Wonderland. His hands left his pockets, one to hold her tiny waist, the other to hold her face. He rested his forehead against hers, fighting the almost overwhelming urge to give in, to go and party with her. If she kissed him, he would. But she didn't. She waited, expecting him to kiss her.

Taking a deep breath, he leaned away, making sure she was paying attention. He wanted no misunderstanding between them. 'Libby, you need to leave. Please.'

It took every ounce of restraint he had, but he gently pushed her away and put his hands back in his pockets, closing his eyes while he took control of his senses. He couldn't be seen with Libby Wilde and he certainly couldn't party with her. If he did, he may as well write the article and email the photos himself.

'Are you really on call?' she asked, her voice quiet.

He looked her in the eye and, knowing the reaction it would have, that the lie would make her leave, he shook his head. 'No. Now please go.'

It was her sharp intake of breath that made him regret it. She straightened her back and shrugged, putting on a brave face, but he'd hurt her and he felt sick for doing it. He wanted to hug her, kiss her until she smiled again, but he couldn't.

I'm sorry, Libs.

She mumbled goodbye and he watched through the window as she walked with an arrogance he knew she was faking. Surely he could join the party. Surely he could have one drink. He didn't have to get wasted or end up in bed with her. They could just have fun. Okay, maybe one line. He almost caved in, about to run after her, when the phone rang.

A sow with six dead piglets saved him from making a very big mistake.

Chapter Twenty-Five

Monday afternoons sucked. Four hours of unpaid do-gooding in the Haverton surgery. Hannah, the RVN, made appalling coffee. Fee, the practice manager, could simper for England. And the clients... Christ, this was penalty enough for the Miss Haverton story.

Patrick pushed open the office door, having already ignored the people in the waiting room, and scowled at Grace who was sitting at Fee's desk, working on her PC. She didn't look up, but from her reddening cheeks, she obviously wasn't comfortable. He'd given her a bollocking for being late that morning, still coming down from the party. Hannah hovered beside him, smiling, giggling, making it patently obvious what she wanted. He ignored her. Twenty-two year-old veterinary nurses weren't his cup of tea. He didn't even like tea.

A fresh pot of coffee sat on the machine and he helped himself, giving Grace the chance to explain her presence in the Haverton surgery on her afternoon off. She didn't. He added a drop of milk, scowling at the pale brown colour.

'Hannah,' he said, 'electricity and water are precious resources. So you shouldn't waste them on piss-poor coffee.'

'But that's how Fergus likes it,' she said, her argument weaker than her coffee.

'Is Fergus working this afternoon?' he asked.

Hannah's face turned an amusing shade of red as she found the staff notice board suddenly fascinating. He'd have felt guilty, but she'd almost managed to kill a dog the previous week because she'd been too busy fluttering her eyelashes to check the sedative dose. The ruder he was, the quicker she'd get the message. Not interested, so get on with your job. He never had any of this crap from Grace. Christ, he hated working at the Haverton surgery.

'It's Monday,' he said, perching on the desk beside Grace. 'It's your afternoon off.'

'It is.'

'So what are you doing here?'

'Wages,' she replied, not looking up. 'Fee's off sick again.'

'But why are you doing them?'

'Because I want to get paid and that prescription drug junkie hasn't been fit to do the payroll for months. But no one here...' Grace glanced over at Hannah. 'Knows how to do them, or has the balls to tell you or your dad that Fee's a liability. I've been doing it for five months.'

He took a slow breath, trying to control his building anger. 'We'll talk about this later and you can explain why you haven't had the balls to tell me that Fee's a liability. Now, show Hannah how to make a pot of decent bloody coffee.'

He strode through to the treatment room, his hands on his head so he didn't lash out at anything. If Fee was screwing up and had been for months, why had no one said anything? For Christ's sake, Grace didn't normally hold back. If he couldn't trust her, who could he trust? He slumped against the door, trying to calm down.

'Ohmigod,' Hannah said, her voice muted from the other side of the door. 'Have you seen the paper, about the orgy in Gosthwaite?'

'Are you having a laugh?' Grace replied.

'There was this mental party in the Green—'

'I was there, but it wasn't an orgy. Libby's too uptight for anything like that.'

'Who's Libby?' Hannah asked.

'Blonde cow who lives in the Green.'

'Is this her?'

Patrick frowned at the pause in conversation, unsettled by the rustling of paper.

'Oh my God,' Grace whispered. 'Yes, that's her.'

'Is she really a prostitute?'

What the... He strode back in. The two girls were leaning over the table, eyes wide at the *Haverton Gazette* in front of them. He grabbed the paper, meaning to scowl at Hannah, but his mental vow to make her life a living hell every Monday afternoon vanished as he read the headline. *The Libertines.* Christ, poor Libby.

He took in the first picture, of her in her Alice in Wonderland costume, sat on Jack's knee. Or maybe not poor Libby. She'd copped off with Jack?

'Grace, coffee!'

He couldn't read fast enough. The general insinuation was that Zoë and Libby were running a brothel from Maggie's cottage. The paper had churned out the old photos of Jack, Xander and Robbie, plus a new face – Zoë's silver fox, Jonathan Carr. Not only was he Zoë's boss, the owner of the estate agents, but he was also Fee's husband. No wonder she'd called in sick. But Libby a prostitute? Utter crap. That said, there was no denying she'd got up to some pretty out-of-character behaviour with Jack. In one shot, he was doing what looked like a line off her cleavage, and in the next they were laughing, utterly wasted, as they walked out of the Alfred after being *barred by the landlord for behaviour reminiscent to that of Patrick McBride and Rachel Holloway six months ago.*

Shit.

And there was an old photo of him and Miss Haverton being evicted from the Weir Wine Bar in Haverton.

'I'm going out,' he said.

'But surgery's due to start in–' If Hannah finished her sentence, he didn't hear it as the door slammed behind him.

Monday afternoon, she would be at work. Still holding the newspaper, he almost ran down the road to Oscar's Bar and Bistro. Through the window, he could see Libby behind the bar, restocking shelves. The place was deserted except for her and a couple of women drinking at the far side of the bar. He threw open door, his jaw aching from clenching it so tightly.

Libby turned, her initial welcoming smile faltering as her eyes flared under her fringe.

'Go away,' she snapped and went back to restocking the fridge with Smirnoff Ice. 'I'm busy.'

He leaned against the bar, watching her, waiting for her apology. It never came. He held up the paper. 'What's this all about?'

'Well, apparently, I've been shagging all the men in Gosthwaite for money. Why, are you looking for mates' rates?'

He swore, mostly under his breath. 'I don't give a rat's arse what you get up to, but don't drag my name into it.'

'Not my fault.'

'Yes it is. What the hell did you think you were doing, Libby? This is pretty much what happened with Miss Haverton and I'm guessing you know it. Jack, for f–' He shook his head. 'Have you forgotten the night he threatened you?'

'This was on my terms.'

'Can you stop for a minute?'

'I'm at work. No.' But she paused, taking a deep breath. 'It's my life.'

'Well, don't involve me in the mess you're making of it.'

'Please, piss off.'

The desire to slap her grew, but he merely shook his head and watched as she walked out from behind the bar with a cloth. The tables were already clean, but she wiped them anyway, probably to avoid facing him.

He strode over, grabbing her arm. 'Just stop it, Libby.'

For a second she gazed up at him, her face teetering between anger and tears. From her pale skin, red nose and constant sniffing, he guessed Jack hadn't been the only one doing lines at the party.

'I thought we were friends,' he said.

She snatched her arm away. 'Whatever.'

'Fine, but next time you want rescuing, ring someone who gives a fuck.'

'I don't remember ringing you anyway.'

'No, you risked Rob's marriage to save you from someone you're fucking again. I'm sure Rob's over the moon.'

'It's nothing to do with you.'

'You're right, but you've no idea what this might cost me.'

She folded her arms, refusing to face him. 'Get out.'

'I'm going, but don't you ever turn up at my house like that again. Whatever you're imagining in that pretty little head, it isn't going to happen.'

'I hate you,' she whispered, her cheeks turning red.

'Right now, princess, the feeling's mutual.'

He strode out, kicking the door open, but stopped outside. Shit. He watched as she hung her head, her shoulders shaking, but he couldn't relent. She'd done this, not him. After a minute or so, she dried her eyes and went back to wiping the tables. He took out his phone as he walked back to the surgery.

'Dad?'

'If you're ringing to ask if I've seen the paper, the answer is yes.' Malcolm clicked his tongue, his standard pause before a telling off. 'This is the same wee lassie that nearly destroyed Robbie and Vanessa's marriage, is it?'

'Yes, but it's not–'

'More than a dram of trouble in that one.'

'Dad, half of the article is made up. Libby's not–'

'It's not about what's true. It's about what people read.'

'But this doesn't count, right? I mean, I've not done anything. I can't stop Wray digging up old stories.'

'Let's class it as your first and last warning. You'll be docked two week's pay.'

'That's not in the rules.'

'Strictly speaking, there's a newspaper article about you. That's in the rules.'

'Fine, two weeks.'

Patrick managed a polite goodbye, before hanging up. He had to stay away from Libby. He had to, absolutely. No more popping round to see how she was, no more shoulder to cry on, no more Olivia Wilde. He returned to the surgery in a worse mood than when he'd left. That coffee had better be ready.

* * *

Libby sat curled up in an armchair with a mug of honey and lemon, staring at the TV. She hurt. Her bones ached, her head throbbed, her skin tingled. Flu was taking over her system, but it was nothing compared to the pain she felt thinking of Patrick's disgust. He was right. They were friends. *Were*. Past tense.

Whatever you're imagining in that pretty little head, it isn't going to happen.

Mortification burned through her. She'd thrown herself at Patrick and he'd turned her down. If he turned her down when she'd looked hotter than she'd ever done before, how had she deluded herself into thinking he'd want her on a normal day?

And Jack. She cringed, curling up a little tighter. When they were kicked out of the Alfred, had she really just laughed as he gave her a piggyback across the Green? Had she really just shrugged when the police turned up at the cottage, telling them to turn the music down? It seemed untrue, too unlike her, but there was that stupid newspaper, reporting exactly that.

What the hell had she been thinking?

Patrick's rejection, that's what she'd been thinking.

More guilt surged through her when Zoë came home from work and dinner hadn't even been thought about.

'The beef's still in the fridge.' Libby sipped her tea as Zoë flopped onto the sofa. 'Don't come too close, I think I'm coming down with flu.'

Zoë kicked off her heels, sighing. 'It's okay. I'm fasting today.'

'Fasting?' Oh god, no. This is where it would start, where it always started. First the fasting, pretending to herself as much as Libby that it was part of some 5:2 fad diet, but then would come the obsessive calorie counting, the weeks of eating rock all but coffee and celery. 'What's going on?'

For a minute, Zoë stared at her hands, picking at her nail polish.

'Zo?' *Please, don't stop eating.*

'Apparently, we're prostitutes.'

'I know. I've never been more proud. But there's no reason to... react to it.'

'I had two sellers ask to switch to Adam and... Jonathan's totally pissed off. *"I don't need this kind of exposure, Miss Horton".*'

'Patrick hates me.'

'Where's Paolo?'

'Gone home.'

Zoë nodded. 'The minute I'm out of tax exile, we should get the hell out of here. Maybe we're not cut out to be country folk. Where do you fancy next?'

Libby was about to say anywhere, when the cat flap rattled. Hyssop had finally come home. He padded in, mewing hello as he jumped on her knee. Leaving Gosthwaite meant leaving Hyssop and being able to run on grassy bridleways.

I like it here.

No matter what had happened, Libby wanted to stay in Gosthwaite. She wanted to be happy and she had an odd feeling that this is where it would happen.

'I don't want to leave,' she said, her face resting against Hyssop.

'Me neither.' Zoë thumped the sofa. 'Jonathan's far too good a prospect to give up just because of a little scandal. I'm going to have to make it up to him though.'

'Isn't his wife going to have something to say?'

'It's complicated.'

'Complicated?'

'She's weird. The other day, I was shagging Jonathan and she stood in the doorway, totally perving.'

'How? Where on earth were you?'

'One of their many guest rooms.'

'Zo!'

'He gets off on doing it in his house.'

'That's so wrong.'

'No. Her watching is wrong. Seriously, she's weird, totally out of it on prescription drugs and weed most of the time. Jonathan reckons it's only a matter of time before she loses her job at the vets.'

'She works for Patrick?'

'Not really. At the surgery in Haverton.'

'What do you see in Jonathan anyway? Isn't he about sixty?'

'He's fifty-five and plays a lot of tennis so he's got a great body. He's intelligent, funny, considerate and he likes buying me shiny trinkets. Best of all...' Zoë's grin grew. 'He's the most amazing shag. He's into BDSM.'

'What, you let him hit you?' Libby stared, repulsed, but Zoë laughed.

'Jesus, no. He's the one who likes being tied up.' Her eyes twinkled. 'I am the mistress of all his fantasies and oh my God, does he have some filthy fantasies. Needless to say, it's not his Times-reading wife's knitting bag, at all.'

Libby opened her mouth, but finding herself speechless, she closed it again.

'Your face.' Zoë stood up, laughing. 'Anyway, I was thinking we could try Kendal next. A little less *Deliverance* than here.'

Libby watched Zoë leave, frowning at the heels she had in her hand. Well, Jonathan Carr's sexual preferences and trinket buying explained Zoë's addiction to the metal-studded Louboutins – hardly the getup for a respectable estate agent, but for the dominatrix mistress of the boss? Perfect.

Sometimes she wondered if she knew Zoë at all.

Chapter Twenty-Six

It wasn't her fault. The driver who knocked her off her bike had to take the majority of the blame, and the surgeon who'd left a piece of bone in her back, his hands weren't entirely spotless. Even God, whose benevolent nature she'd been brought up to believe in, he'd let this happen to her.

But it wasn't her fault.

Fee had been left in constant pain, the bone fragment sitting too close to her spine to be removed. She winced as she tried to lift the teapot.

'Let me?' Elizabeth McBride said, taking the pot from her. 'How are you?'

'Oh, you know. No worse than usual.' It's what people expected to hear. They didn't want to know about the ineffective prescription painkillers rattling inside her handbag, or the more effective but illegal drugs she had in her knitting bag.

'And have you…' Elizabeth paused, sipping her tea. 'Have you read the paper?'

Through the fug she'd lived in since Halloween, Fee laughed. The effort sent a bolt of agony up her spine. 'Do you mean about Jonathan and his latest whore?'

For fifteen years, she'd been unable to make love to her husband, not that she'd been overly anxious to do so before her accident. It was only natural that he'd look for his release elsewhere, but how funny that it should be with Zoë Horton. The sense of history spiralling around, always moving on but at times colliding, filled Fee with awe. Maybe God did have a plan.

Maggie Keeley had been Fee's source of a very good anaesthetic: marijuana. News of her death had been a bitter blow and Fee had fallen into a depression, lost without her only source of the drug. She was a fifty-year-old woman. How could she buy *dope*?

Then one day, back in September, Jonathan informed her that Maggie's niece, Zoë, was working for him at the Estate Agent's. She'd considered it fate and invited the girl over for lunch, planning to ask if she had the marijuana plants while Jonathan was out of the room. What she hadn't planned on was Jonathan being overly-familiar with the twenty-something girl who bore more than a passing resemblance to her great-aunt. And he'd barely managed to eat his salmon, too busy staring at the girl's cleavage. Fee had merely poured more wine, pretending she hadn't noticed.

Zoë refused to sell the plants, but as recompense, did promise a regular supply of marijuana. The girl was so reliable, the skunk so effective, Fee stopped caring that Jonathan had taken to making... no, what they did could hardly be described as *making love*. Jonathan had taken to fucking his little whore in their guest room, just like he had Maggie.

The doorbell rang, returning Fee to Elizabeth's polite, but banal chatter.

'Should I get it for you?' Elizabeth asked.

'No, no. Jonathan's here. How's everything at the surgery? I am sorry to let you down.'

Elizabeth smiled. 'Fee, you need to look after yourself. Please, don't worry about work. Everything's fine. Grace is helping out.'

The silence stretched between them, *the Archers* filling the space.

'Did the police ever catch anyone for the break in?' Fee toyed with the glass vial in her cardigan pocket.

Elizabeth shook her head. 'Patrick was devastated, blames himself, and Grace feels just as bad, the poor wee thing, but she swears she'd switched the alarm on.'

'Poor Grace. Dreadful business.'

Jonathan popped his head around the door. 'Fee, I'm heading out for an hour or two. Squash.'

Fee smiled, not believing a word of it. 'Have a nice time, dear.'

'Night, Jonathan.' Elizabeth gave a little wave.

Fee sipped her tea, longing for Elizabeth to leave so she could let oblivion take over. She'd take a little more tonight, in case Jonathan brought his whore back to the house again.

In the darkened room, with Vivaldi playing quietly in the background, Fee's pain eased. Her arms and legs were floating as she glided along the sand towards the sunshine, leaving her ravaged body on the bed. She glanced back. When had she grown so old?

'Are you okay, Fee?' God stretched out a hand, stroking her hair.

I'm fine. Happy. But why did you do it?

'Do what, Fee?'

Hurt me, God.

'I didn't hurt you, Fee. That was Mr Simmonds in his BMW. Remember?'

She wandered on along the beach, glancing behind her, at the single track of footprints. *Are you really carrying me?*

'Of course I am.'

Is it time to let go?

'Only if you want to Fee.'

I want to. It hurts so much. Every day, it hurts so much.

'Then just stop.'

But who'll look after Jonathan? Who'll wash his clothes, make sure there're always bananas in the house?

'He'll be fine. Don't worry.'

Fee smiled as she breathed out.

Her mind simply forgot to breathe in again.

* * *

Tears splashed from Jonathan's face onto the bed. Relief, grief, he had no idea which. He stroked his wife's hair. She'd looked so beautiful on their wedding day. He'd loved her so much, but he'd let her down. He'd selfishly let her sink into prescription drugs so she wouldn't care that he was indulging in his own addiction.

No, it wasn't like that. He'd tried so many times to help her, but the pain had been too much for her to bear.

But not anymore. She looked so peaceful, with her gentle, kind smile. Had she died happy, finally free from pain? He took her hand, bringing it to his lips, but a small glass bottle fell to the bed. He lifted it to the lamp, peering at the label.

Ketamine? Where the hell had she got Ketamine from?

Chapter Twenty-Seven

A staff meeting was not the way to start the day after his worst day ever, but Patrick dutifully sat in the Haverton waiting room, the only space big enough to house the McBride Veterinary Clinic staff. With him and his parents were Fergus and Kate, his fellow vets, plus Grace, Hannah and the two other RVNs. He was fairly sure the two nondescript brunettes were called Sarah and Susan, but which was which, he had no idea.

'What's going on?' Grace whispered as she sat down next to him.

'Did you cancel everyone?'

She nodded. 'I bumped Manor Farm to eleven and Mrs Dawson to five. Sorry, I know, but you'll never get away from Tom's 'til after lunch. What's happening?'

Patrick leant in, so the others couldn't hear. 'Fee died last night. Maybe an overdose, maybe natural causes. I don't know.'

Grace stared at him, her eyes filling.

'Oh for Christ's sake, Grace. You're worse than Libby for crying.' He regretted the words the minute they came out. Grace bristled, sulking at his mention of her arch-nemesis, and he couldn't help wondering how Libby was after their fight yesterday. He'd been harsh.

'But I called her a prescription drug junkie...'

'Pull it together,' he hissed. 'She *was* a prescription drug junkie. Everyone knew it.'

'So is that why they've got us all here, to tell us?'

Patrick sucked in his cheek for a moment. 'Partly. And I reckon they're going to talk about reshuffling.'

'What?'

'Gracey, they need a practice manager here. You know I don't want any of these muppets working for me. Christ, I've traded Hannah for you once already, but it'd be a promotion.'

She shook her head. 'That's not why I do it. I don't want to spend my time working out rotas and payrolls. I want to look after animals.'

'Look, I don't even know if this is what they're thinking.' He crossed his fingers behind his back. 'But think of the money. You wouldn't have to work at the pub.'

'No, I'd just work stupid hours here, instead. Forget it. They can find some other idiot.'

He tried not to grin. 'That's what I said you'd say.'

She glanced around, trying not to laugh. 'How much money are they offering?'

He shrugged. 'But please don't take it. Ever.'

As predicted, his parents stood before the staff, his mum wiping her eyes, speaking of their sad loss. Fee had died quietly at home, after a long battle against her spinal pain. Their thoughts were with her husband, Jonathan, and their two grown-up sons. Grace caught Patrick's eye and they both struggled not to laugh.

Rather than recruit an irreplaceable Fee, Malcolm stressed his desire for his other staff to step up to the role. He struggled not to look with hope at Grace, but she had her arms crossed, fascinated with the floor.

Good girl, Gracey. Don't sell out.

By ten o'clock, the majority of the staff tears, platitudes and excitement about potential promotions had calmed down. He had an hour until he had to be at Manor Farm, so he wandered down to the local coffee shop for a decent caffeine hit.

Fee, dead. If he were honest, he'd never really warmed to the woman. She twittered and fussed, always worrying if the biscuit barrel was full. Who the hell cared? His job was to look after the health and welfare of animals. But still, she was dead. Oh, he knew she'd struggled with back pain and prescription drugs, his mum had told him that, but an overdose? Sad.

He was standing in the queue, silently cursing the office junior ordering coffee for the entire team of accountants down the road, when a familiar ex-ballerina walked along the opposite pavement.

She had on her trademark mini-skirt, but in deference to the bitterly cold weather, she wore leggings and chunky work boots. The long turquoise coat and bright purple scarf he'd not seen before. She suited the vibrant colours. He smiled. Her pink hair streamed behind her as she struggled with a large canvas. Was that *the Broken Ballerina*?

'What can I get you?' the barista asked.

He had no intention of going out there, no intention until Libby ducked into the Haverton Animal Rescue charity shop. What was she doing? He smiled apologetically to the barista then ran out of the shop. Two buses blocked his way and when he crossed the High Street, she'd gone. He scanned the street, but couldn't see the turquoise coat.

He swore, stepping into the charity shop. The canvas, still wrapped, stood propped against the checkout. Where the hell had Libby gone? The woman behind the counter, not a day less than eighty, stopped her clearly pointless struggle with a tagging gun.

'Can I help you?' she asked.

'The girl who donated this picture,' he said. 'Where's she gone?'

'Out dear.' She pottered around the desk, reaching down to take the paper from the canvas.

'No.' Patrick grabbed her hand. 'It's just... I know she's going to regret giving it away.'

The woman tore the paper and her smile grew. This was going to cost him.

Ten minutes and fifteen hundred pounds later, after he'd locked the painting in his car, he headed back to the surgery. If he was really unlucky, there'd be some of Hannah's piss-poor coffee still available. Could his day get any worse?

He got his answer as he approached the front door. Two police officers climbed out of their car and pulled their hats on. One of them was PC Andy. Patrick paused, swearing at the sky.

'What?' he asked.

'We'd appreciate it if you could come with us to the station,' Andy said, sounding genuinely apologetic.

'Why?'

'It'd be better to talk there.'

Patrick refused to be riled. This was fine. Helping with enquiries. This wasn't news. He got into the police car as quickly as he could, hoping no one had time to take a photo, and rang his dad.

'Dad?'

'Yes.'

Patrick took a breath. 'I have to go to the police station.'

'So I believe. There are another two officers questioning your mother. Grace has already been taken to the station. This better be nothing to do with you.'

Patrick rested his head against the glass window. Even his own father didn't trust him.

The police processing actual criminals meant Patrick was kept waiting in an interview room for over an hour. Surely this was unreasonable. For the eightieth time, Patrick fidgeted in his chair and wished they'd get on with it. He'd been arrested enough times to know the score. They weren't arresting him, merely questioning him.

The door opened, and Andy came in with Dave Hardy, another local lad.

'What's going on?' Patrick asked, focussing his question on Andy, his childhood friend.

Andy held up a plastic evidence bag containing a bottle of Ketamine, the same brand they used at work.

'Is that part of the batch stolen from my surgery,' Patrick asked.

Andy nodded. 'It was found in Fiona Carr's hand.'

Patrick stared. 'Is it a coincidence?'

'That one of the surgery staff ends up dead after shooting up, no doubt k-holing from your missing drugs?' Andy smiled. 'Yeah, a coincidence is one theory.'

'Another theory,' offered PC Hardy, 'is that your surgery wasn't actually robbed. Maybe you, or Grace, helped yourselves to the drugs. It's easy done. Money to be made.'

'Leave Grace alone. She's done nothing wrong,'

Andy held up a hand. 'She's just helping with enquiries.'

'So what do you want to know?'

Andy rested his elbows on the table. 'Mrs Carr had three of these bottles.'

'So she got them from some dealer in town?'

'Mrs Carr worked at the vets. Would she know the alarm codes, have keys?'

'No.' Stay calm.

'Who does?'

'My parents, Fergus, Grace and me. We changed the code when I took over a couple of years ago.'

Andy nodded. 'So there's no way, none that you can think of, for Mrs Carr to obtain a batch of your stolen drugs?'

'No.' Patrick leant forward. 'Now, get to the point.'

PC Hardy took the lead. Andy merely watched.

'Mrs Carr was found this morning by her husband, Jonathan. She was dead and probably had been for several hours. She was holding a bottle of ketamine. I'm fairly sure the autopsy will show that's what killed her.'

'And?' Patrick asked, still failing to see what the fuck it had to do with him.

'We asked Mr Carr where Mrs Carr might've obtained this ketamine. He said she couldn't have got it from work because she'd been off sick for almost two weeks.'

'And?' Patrick sighed, weary from the routine stupidity.

'And Mr Carr said she'd received a package from a courier.'

Patrick shrugged. 'It's nothing to do with me, or my surgery.'

'Where were you on the night of the burglary?'

'Having dinner with a friend until I went home about eleven. My dad called my landline just after.'

'And this friend will confirm that?' PC Brady said as he scribbled on his notepad, clearly disappointed.

'Yes.'

Andy leaned forwards. 'Mr Carr said the package was delivered on Halloween between nine-thirty and quarter to ten. Where were you?'

'At home. Tom from Manor Farm rang just before ten. I went round there at half-past.'

'And before you were called out, you were at home?'

'For fuck's sake, Andy. What are you getting at and what do you want to know? I didn't kill Fee, or sell her any drugs, but I'm more than happy to help you find out who the hell did.' Patrick kept his breathing slow and steady. He would not get riled.

'Half the village was at that party. Why weren't you?'

'I was on call, so I was at home, sober.' How many times did he have to tell them?

Andy sighed. 'Paddy, mate, the bottom line is we need to know what the hell you were doing on that Saturday night between nine and ten. You had plenty of time to get to the Carr's house in Haverton and be back before Tom rang.'

'I was at home, watching TV.'

'Any witnesses?'

Patrick paused. 'Yes. Olivia Wilde.'

Andy frowned. 'Libby?'

'She came round. About quarter to. I reckon it's pretty difficult to get back from Haverton in fifteen minutes.'

'And what did Libby come round for?'

'She wanted to know if I was coming to the party.' Patrick didn't drop his eye contact. 'Andy, mate, the bottom line is Libby came round and I have a witness who can confirm I wasn't in Haverton at half-nine.'

'And the name of friend you had dinner with the night of the burglary?' PC Hardy asked.

Patrick's smile grew. 'Olivia Wilde. Now, get off my case and let me get back to work.'

Andy shook his head. 'With your previous, sunshine, until your slate's crystal clear, you're not going anywhere.'

You bastard. Patrick sat back in his chair, his anger rising.

* * *

As ever, Libby started her shift, cursing the night staff for never bothering to refill the fridges. They always claimed to have been too busy. On a Monday night, really? But bitchy staff were the least of her problems. Everywhere Libby went, people slyly pointed her out, whispering. Even the old woman in the charity shop had raised her eyebrows, clearly recognising her. People seriously believed she was a prostitute.

With her black gloom threatening to engulf her, Libby went out for a cigarette, hating herself for smoking. She'd vowed to give up after the party, citing the fell race as the reason when Zoë asked. The truth was Patrick hated smoking. If she did ever get the chance to kiss him, she didn't want him to be put off by her fag breath.

'Libby?' Megan said, hovering in the doorway. 'The police are here. They need to ask you a few questions.'

'What on earth do they want to talk to me about?'

'Maybe it's about the brothel you've set up,' Megan said, as she headed back inside.

The door shut in Libby's face. How much more could she take? By the bar, Sheila's eldest son, PC Andy and another officer stood waiting.

'What's up?' she asked.

The other officer, PC Hardy, explained how a woman called Fee had died, most likely from an overdose of the ketamine stolen from Patrick's surgery, and Libby sat on a bar stool, more confused.

Andy finally looked at her. 'We're trying to rule out a few suspects. Patrick said–'

'Patrick's a suspect?'

'We need to confirm his whereabouts on Saturday evening.' Andy took a deep breath. 'He said you went round to his.'

Libby couldn't stop her blushes. 'I… Yes. I went round, about quarter to ten, to see if he was coming to the party. He didn't want to.'

'But he was at home?'

She nodded. 'I was there for about five minutes then I went back to the party. Zoë and Clara saw me go and come back, if you need them to confirm the time.'

'And the night the surgery was burgled,' said PC Hardy, 'a witness saw someone at the back of the surgery around eight o'clock. Can you confirm Mr McBride's location?'

Libby's blushes worsened. 'Patrick was at my house. We had dinner and sat out in the garden getting drunk. He left around eleven.'

PC Hardy nodded. 'Thank you for your time, Miss Wilde.'

'Is that okay?' Libby asked. 'I mean, Patrick's not in trouble?'

Andy shrugged. 'We'll have to see. You're not what we'd call a reliable witness.'

'What?' she asked. Of course, she was a reliable witness. 'I'd never lie, even for a friend.'

With a disdainful expression, PC Andy looked her over. 'Wouldn't you?'

Andy stalked off, leaving her staring at the floor. Patrick hated her, the police didn't trust her and she'd brought it all on herself. She'd left the door wide open for Michael Wray to embellish her life into front page scandal, but no more. What had been Patrick's advice? Don't get up to no good, and when your name's trashed, don't go getting wasted and making things ten times worse. That's exactly what she'd done with Jack at the party. Why hadn't she listened?

Well, no more. From now on, she'd remember the values her mother had instilled in her, and to hell with anyone who thought her morals were a little too stuffy. There was nothing wrong with being nice.

For the rest of the afternoon, Libby threw herself into her work, scrubbing shelves, rewashing seldom used glasses, welcoming the lunchtime rush that distracted her from her thoughts. But by six o'clock when she was getting ready to leave, there were no more distractions. She'd have to go home, back to Gosthwaite, and deal with the whispering and pointing.

'Libby?' Simon, the campest barman in town, came skipping in, fizzing with excitement. 'You have a delivery. I'm totally green.'

On the bar sat a vast bunch of flowers. The peach roses smelled as pretty as they looked. Peach roses. Libby's fingers shook as she opened the card. *Thank You. P.* Patrick had bought her flowers. And not just any flowers, he'd remembered these were her favourites. Oh please, let this mean he wasn't cross with her anymore.

'Who are they off?' Megan said, eyeing the flowers with blatant envy.

Libby held her head high, flashing a smile. 'One of my regulars. You know, from the brothel.'

Chapter Twenty-Eight

Mourners stood around Oscar's Bar and Bistro clutching glasses of wine or pints of beer as waitresses circulated with trays of canapés. Fee had been a popular and respected lady, it seemed. Patrick scanned the room, spotting Grace waving from a table at the far side. Good girl. The last place he wanted to be was near the bar where Libby was pulling pints. She had her pink plaits pinned over her head and he couldn't help a little smile. What the hell was it with her?

Okay, so he fancied her, a bit anyway. If he could change a few things about her, like everything about the way she looked, then maybe next June, when his twelve months' probation was over, then... well, maybe.

'Is that the wee lassie who was in the paper?' His father scowled towards the bar.

'She's called Libby and she's very nice.' Patrick loosened his tie, craving a pint. Funerals unnerved him.

'Aye, but she's trouble, mark my words, and don't you forget you're wearing a black tie.'

Patrick fought the urge to answer back and his father wandered away. Would he ever trust him or give him the benefit of the doubt? For months, Patrick hadn't broken a single rule and he didn't intend to start because of Olivia Wilde, no matter how cute she looked with her Heidi hair.

He slumped in a chair next to Grace, gratefully taking the coffee she pushed towards him. 'So, on a scale of one to weird?'

'Definitely off it. I daren't not cry at the crem in case people thought I did sell her the Special K.' Grace sipped her orange juice. 'And is it me, or is it bloody inappropriate for the girl who copped off with the dead woman's husband to be here? Fabulous shoes though.'

Zoë sat on the other side of the room, chatting with a couple of girls Patrick assumed were from the estate agents. The others wore cheap suits and struggled to even totter on the polished wooden floor in their high heels, but from her neat bun and pearl earrings to her five inch sling-backs, Zoë screamed respectability. Patrick wasn't fooled and he hadn't missed the fact that Jonathan Carr couldn't keep his eyes off her, or that Zoë looked as if she hadn't slept in a week.

'Give her a break,' Patrick said. 'She's here with the other estate agents. It would've looked just as bad if she hadn't turned up.'

'Where's your mum?'

'Using the dogs as an excuse not to be here. She's upset.'

'Where do you think she got the ketamine? Fee, I mean.'

'No idea. But if it's someone I know...' He looked her in the eye, checking for the hair twiddles and pauses in conversation Libby had taught him to watch for. 'Jack wouldn't–'

'He couldn't turn off an alarm if you stood there giving him directions, let alone override it.' Grace sighed. 'And he wouldn't do it. Neither would Sparky or any of the other Gosthwaite lot. They're all too scared of you. Plus, Ket's nasty. Jack and I did it last year.'

'You better not have got it from my surgery.'

She shook her head. 'You ever do it?'

'Probably the only thing I haven't.'

'I totally thought I was talking to God. Had the whole out-of-body, floating down the tunnel experience. Couldn't move. Just lay there like a bloody cabbage. Never again.'

Patrick picked up his coffee, looking towards the bar. A man walked away with a pint and Libby turned to her next customer, flashing a polite smile, but there was no sparkle. She looked up, catching Patrick's eye. Shit. He stared, regretting shouting at her, regretting blaming her for dragging his name into the paper. How many times over the last week had he wanted to pop round, to take a bottle of wine and apologise? They were friends, they had been friends, and he wanted it back, but his dad was right, Libby was trouble.

'It's your round,' Grace said and knocked back the rest of her orange juice. 'And since you're driving. I'll have a vodka and fat free Coke.'

He took out his wallet and dropped a twenty on the table. 'You go.'

'She's your bessy mate. You go. She'll probably spit in my drink.'

'Do me a favour, Gracey, and make friends with her?'

'Bugger off.'

'Come on, you'd like her.'

'Hating her will give me a competitive edge in the race.'

'Okay, then after the race.'

Grace tipped her head to the side, studying him. 'If she's so ace, why are you trying to avoid her?'

He snatched up the money and headed to the bar.

* * *

Fee Carr's funeral was a day Libby had tried to avoid, but she'd swapped so many shifts to have the party weekend off, that the rota was starting to resemble a spider diagram and irritated her manager every time he consulted it.

Firstly, she wasn't sure if she could face Jonathan Carr without giggling. Very inappropriate at his wife's funeral, but the man got off on being spanked with a riding crop. He was fit though, somewhere between George Clooney and one of the guys from *Mad Men*. Shame she couldn't dismiss an unpleasant mental image of him with a ball gag in his mouth.

The second issue was that Fee had worked for the McBride Veterinary Clinic, which meant Patrick would turn up. Libby hadn't seen him since he'd told her that whatever was going on in her pretty little head was never going to happen. She hadn't even had the chance to say thank you for the roses. She hadn't dared go round, but she could've sent a text at least.

He'd arrived with an older man Libby suspected was his father. None of the women sitting with Grace looked old enough to be his mother though.

The first time she'd looked over to where he sat slouching in a chair next to Grace, Patrick had been looking her way. He didn't smile, he just sat there staring until she'd overfilled the pint glass and spilled Cumberland Ale all over her hand. Genius. The other seventy-nine times she glanced over he'd been looking anywhere but at her. He still hated her.

She faux-smiled her way through the afternoon, praying for six o'clock. She'd agreed to wear ballet pumps instead of her usual boots for work and as a result, her feet were covered in beer – most of it spilled by Simon, who was the sloppiest – and campest – barman in town.

'I hate funerals.' Megan hovered next to him on her way out with canapés. 'Half the people get pissed and cry and the other half get shit-faced and start fighting. Look at that bloke in the corner. He's been knocking back whisky for an hour. Hammered.'

'Fit though.' Simon shrugged.

The guy was Ed, Jonathan's youngest son. Who could blame him for getting drunk at his mother's funeral? Crikey, Zoë's Mr Coffee Shop was fit. All Jonathan's good-looks, but in a dark-haired, thirty year-old package. Worryingly, for the fifth time, Libby had caught him staring at Zoë. Megan was right. Booze and fraught emotional times never went well together.

'Hi.'

Libby turned, her welcoming smile faltering. Patrick perched on a stool, determinedly staring at the oak bar.

'Hi,' she replied. 'What would you like?'

He barely looked up as he ordered a coffee and a vodka. Nothing had changed. He still hated her. She focussed on her job, making the best damned coffee Oscar's had ever served, but wasn't this her chance to build bridges?

'Thank you for the flowers. They're lovely.'

He nodded.

She put his coffee on the bar. 'Diet Coke? Can or cheap crap that comes out of the pump?'

'Can.'

'Ice?'

He nodded.

Building the Panama Canal had required less negotiation. 'Anything else?'

He shook his head and handed her a twenty. He was supposed to be the one she'd summoned, her true love, her Somebody. Had the spell not worked? Tears stung her eyes, but her own problems faded when she realised Ed was walking up to Zoë, and from his bitter scowl, it would be anything but a pleasant conversation.

Arse. Libby headed over to the till, eavesdropping on them. Zoë wasn't in any fit state to deal with him. The 5:2 fasting had become 4:3, but even on the non-fasting days she appeared to consume nothing more than celery and black coffee. It was as worrying for Libby as it was wearing, with Zoë turning into a jittery, anxious bitch.

'Sorry about your mum,' Zoë said, folding her arms.

Sorry? Libby frowned. In fourteen years, she'd never once heard Zoë utter the word.

'Of course you're sorry,' Ed replied, looking Zoë over with undisguised disdain. 'Just devastated.'

'Ed–'

'Get out of here, Zoë.'

Her cheeks flushed with guilt and her shoulders sagged as she nodded. 'Sorry.'

Two sorrys? Libby stared. What was it with this guy? If Zoë was prepared to apologise to him, why wouldn't she admit she... bloody loved him?

'Ed...' Zoë asked, defiantly raising her chin. 'Who do I look like?'

'What?'

'You said you knew, the minute you saw me, because I look like *her*. Who did you mean?'

'You don't know?' Ed laughed and downed his whisky. 'His first bitch. She was a total dominatrix apparently, and you look just like her. *She's* why he gave you a job.'

'Who?' Zoë whispered.

But from her pale face, she'd already guessed. Libby prayed for it not to be true. *Please, don't say it, Ed.*

'Your great-aunt Maggie.'

Oh God, no. Libby dashed from behind the bar, but Zoë was already striding across the room. A couple of elderly gents hampered Libby's interception and Zoë made it to Jonathan.

'You had an affair with Maggie?' Zoë hissed.

Jonathan stuttered through a half-hearted denial as Libby reached them.

'Zo,' she said, 'not the time.'

'She was a hideous old bitch.'

Jonathan stared at Zoë. 'No, she was–'

'You gave me the job because I look like her.'

'No.'

Zoë slapped him.

The room gradually fell silent around them.

'Zo,' Libby grasped her arm. 'Let's go.'

Outside, Zoë lit a cigarette, her hands shaking, and paced up and down.

'He fucked her,' she muttered. 'And he wanted me as some... replacement fuck. For *her*. Christ, I feel sick.'

'You'll be hungry. I bet you haven't eaten all day, have you?'

Zoë shook her head. 'I'm fine. It's a fasting day. I need to get out of here.'

But there was no point trying to talk to Zoë when she was like this and Simon was beckoning Libby back inside. 'You can escape through the side lane. Will you be okay? I'll be home as soon as I can.'

'Expect me to be shit-faced.' Zoë kissed her cheek. 'Later 'gator.'

'While 'dile.'

Libby sat for a moment, watching Zoë stride away. Jonathan and Maggie... who'd seen that coming? Had Fee known about it? Had she been another wife hell-bent on revenge?

'It's a never-ending drama around you.' Patrick came out, perching on the table. 'What the hell was that about?'

God, he looked good in a suit. He'd loosened his tie and undone his top button. 'It seems Jonathan had an affair with Maggie. Zoë's not too pleased.'

'I can imagine. Hell of a slap.'

'I wouldn't worry. He probably enjoyed it.' Libby giggled, miming flicking a whip. 'He's into a bit of that.'

'The Silver Fox? Wow.'

They both laughed for a moment, but then an uneasy silence fell.

'Patrick... I'm really sorry about the paper, but I honestly have no idea what happened with Miss Haverton. What was it?'

He pushed his hands in his pockets. 'I was doing lines of coke off Miss Haverton. She was lying on the bar.'

'*Off* Miss Haverton?' Libby laughed. 'Oh, is that what everyone thinks Jack was doing? For the record, it wasn't coke. It was salt. We were doing tequila body shots.'

'I was shocked, Miss Wilde. You're supposed to be *nice*, remember?'

'And look at the trouble I get into trying not to be.' She stood up. 'I ought to get back inside before I get sacked.'

'How is work?' he asked.

She shrugged. 'I've been thinking about living up to my appalling reputation and introducing *Coyote Ugly* style dancing on the bar. If I could get any of the other girls to talk to me, I could teach them the routine. We'd make a fortune in tips.'

'An interesting career plan. Why aren't they talking to you?'

She wrapped her arms around herself and explained, before bravely facing him. 'Look, I'm really sorry about... Halloween.'

'Don't be. Just don't do it again.' He looked at his feet, fighting a grin. 'At least it proves I do have an off switch.'

'Are we... friends again?'

He looked up and nodded slowly.

'Thank you.' She didn't bother to hide her smile. He'd forgiven her.

'Thank you for saving me from twenty to life.' He grabbed her hand, bringing her wrist to his face. 'What on earth is that perfume?'

She swayed, unaware of anything other than the proximity of his lips to her wrist. 'My *Chloe* got smashed at the party. I'm blaming Grace. This is Zoë's *Guilty*.'

'It stinks.'

She snatched her hand away, blushing. 'That's the sweetest thing anyone's ever said.'

He laughed, holding the door open for her, but his smile faltered as he saw his father standing before them, scowling.

'So, can I get my change now?' Patrick asked Libby, his tone frosty.

Libby still held his twenty. 'Sorry, yes. I won't be a minute.'

There were no more smiles, no more lips hovering near wrists. He took his change and headed off with his drinks, muttering a thank you. *Whatever you're imagining in your pretty little head, it's never going to happen.* The card had said *Thank You*, not *I love you*.

* * *

The waitress, holding out a tray of pointlessly small, beef and horseradish sandwiches flashed Patrick the flirtiest smile. *Megan*, her name tag said. One of the bullying bitches making Libby's life hell. He looked Megan over, making sure she fully understood how little he thought of her, and as she scuttled off he glanced over at Libby. She forced yet another smile for yet another customer and Patrick swore under his breath. This place was killing her.

'Gracey,' he said, 'does Rob still want me to look at Sambuca?'

She nodded. 'But you're chocka this week.'

'Set it up for tomorrow. Bump a few people, or I'll stay late. Whatever.'

Patrick nursed his coffee, trying to ignore Grace's astonished face. If working until six meant he could make Libby smile again, so be it. Because if he didn't do something, she'd leave. Though why he felt he had to prevent that from happening was still a mystery.

The next day at Low Wood Farm, Patrick stooped to pet Cromwell, hiding his amusement as Robbie's latest groom came out of a stable leading Cleo. Robbie didn't even begin to hide his annoyance.

'Naomi, that's not Sambuca. Sammy's the bay *gelding* in the end box.' Robbie shook his head. 'Two months and she hasn't a bloody clue.'

'She's no worse than the others who've worked here,' Patrick said. 'Except for one. The problem is, your expectations have been raised.'

Robbie sighed, kicking a pebble. 'How is she?'

'Unhappy.'

'You'd better not be contributing to that.'

'Don't worry. I have no intention of messing around with Libby. She's *Off Limits*, remember?'

'How's she getting on at the bar?'

'How do you think? The male staff are hitting on her and none of the female staff trust her. All they know is she screwed the owner's sons. Plural.'

Robbie shook his head, muttering under his breath.

'I was there yesterday,' Patrick went on. 'Libs said she's dying to live up to her reputation and introduce *Coyote Ugly* style dancing on the bar. What are you going to do about it?'

'Me?' Robbie raised his eyebrows.

'Yes, you. She's a nice girl who you shouldn't have dragged into your fucked up marriage and she shouldn't have lost her job over it.'

'I know, but–'

'She deserves her job back.'

'There's no way Van's letting her set foot on the yard. You can't blame her.'

'No, but then this mess is partly her fault.' Patrick folded his arms. Why wasn't Robbie even trying to help? 'Come on, Rob. You've never been able to resist playing the hero. Do you think you can be Libby's hero without getting divorced?'

'Naomi,' Robbie bellowed, his scowl growing, 'you need to get on him. Today preferably. I can't do it to Van. It'd crucify her.'

Bollocks. 'If you can't give her a job, there is something else.'

'What?'

'Did you see this?' Patrick took a folded up page from his pocket. 'It's from the Guardian the other week. It's the *Broken Ballerina* story.'

'Yeah, I saw... Jesus, that's not Libby is it?'

Patrick nodded.

'I knew she used to be a ballet dancer, but...' Robbie frowned at him. 'Has she told you about it?'

'Yes.' Patrick turned his attention to the bay horse the clueless

Naomi was struggling to clamber onto.

'When?'

'When it was in the paper. Look, what I know is irrelevant. What you need to do is persuade Clara to get Libby to her mum's dance studio.'

'Why me? You ring Clara.'

'Because Clara will assume something that isn't happening. Besides, she does anything you ask.' Patrick frowned as Sambuca shifted under Naomi's weight – but the girl couldn't weigh more than eight stone. 'I think Libby might be right. It's his back. We should scan it.'

* * *

Libby pushed open the doors to the community hall, fighting the urge to go home and hide under her duvet. No. Failing to attend Pilates was unacceptable. It only ran at term-times on a Thursday. She couldn't miss it just because a few people might point and whisper. Besides, Pilates was as good for the soul as it was the body. Okay, it wasn't yoga or grounding, but it worked for her. The gentle stretches were more calming than running, or even dancing. And being realistic, it was the only good thing in her life. That and Hyssop.

She smiled at the yummy mummies and waved to Gladys, the trendy granny, happy that none of them seemed to be snickering behind her back, but her smile vanished when she saw the glossy black bob of Vanessa Golding. Oh God, no.

Sheena the instructor opened the doors, inviting them in, but Libby couldn't move. Robbie had told her the Haverton Community Centre had a Pilates class. How would he have known, except for his wife being a regular? Libby had lost her job and her friendship with Robbie, surely Vanessa couldn't take this from her too.

She needed to leave, to go to Paolo who rang every other day, or to see her parents, who hadn't rung for months. Libby staggered away, tears already falling. Paolo, parents... it didn't matter. She just had to pick a destination.

'Oh crikey, don't. You'll have me set off.' Vanessa grabbed her arm and before Libby could protest, led her away to the little café. 'The hot drinks are bloody awful, but they do a fantastic can of Diet Coke.'

Libby stared at her.

'You don't like Diet Coke?'

'Actually, I quite like the tea they do here.' Libby wiped her eyes. 'Your accent. You're Welsh.'

'Yes...'

'He told me so much about you, but he never said you were Welsh.'

'Oh.' Vanessa's foot jiggled under the table. 'So he said you came here, but now I've been coming for years–'

'It's a big hall and I don't have anything else. Can't we share, just this?' Tears rolled down Libby's face and she craved a cigarette, but she lacked the energy to run away.

'I'm not here to... I wanted to say sorry.'

Libby looked up. 'What?'

'And thank you.' Vanessa paused. 'He told me everything, how you always said I would come back. Thanks for doing that. I think if you hadn't... maybe he'd never have had the guts to ask me to come home.'

'You're welcome.' Libby wiped her eyes. 'Don't do it again.'

'I won't.' Vanessa sat on her hands, jiggling her feet. 'Do you love him?'

Libby shook her head. 'But I do miss him. He was a good friend.'

'I think he misses you too.' Vanessa took a deep breath. 'He's asked me if you can come back to work. I said no. It's too much to ask, right now.'

Libby's heart surged with hope. '*Right now*? You mean–'

'Maybe. I don't know. Just maybe. But I will try, like socially. Just... stay away from Rob.'

Tears pricked at Libby's eyes again as she nodded. 'You really are the nicest person in the world. Everyone said so. I didn't think anyone was this nice.'

'I'm not a saint, Libby.' Vanessa tucked her hair behind her ears. 'And if I ever think that–'

'You won't. I promise.'

'And I've a favour to ask.'

'Anything.'

'Rob wants to make sure you're okay. He worries.' Vanessa took a deep breath. 'And I hear you're at a bit of a loss, now that you can't dance. I need you to do something about that.'

'Why?' Libby frowned, dubious.

'Because if you don't, Rob won't be able to stop himself from rescuing you and that'll kill my marriage.'

'I...'

'Rob was concocting some charade with Clara, but I think honesty is better.' Vanessa handed her a business card. 'You're supposed to be there at four on Monday.'

Libby stared at the card. *The Keeley Dance Studio.* Oh God. 'I'm sorry, I–'

'If you're about to tell me that you can't, look me in the eye and do it.'

Libby couldn't. Instead she stroked the ballerina on the business card. 'I just don't know if–'

'Being here is the hardest thing I've ever done, so you'll damn well look me in the eye and tell me you can't do it.'

Libby raised her head, her jaw clenched. 'I'll be there.'

* * *

'Jane rang. Libby hasn't turned up,' Robbie said, sighing down the phone.

Patrick sipped his coffee, taking his time. He knew Libby hadn't turned up. She was sitting on the churchyard wall, staring at the dance studio opposite. He knew she'd balk. He just hadn't been sure what he'd do about it. 'And?'

'And aren't you at the Haverton surgery today? Can you see if she's outside, or something?'

'Oh for Christ's sake, I'll see if I can find her.' Patrick hung up and gestured to the waitress. 'Two more espressos. I'll be back in a minute.'

The ground floor of the Keeley Dance Studio housed a dancewear shop and a small café where a group of young girls in pale pink leotards were drinking Coke. Libby was staring at them, oblivious to his presence.

'If you sit there for much longer you'll get arrested for perving at underage girls.' He sat next to her, elbowing her ribs. Despite the black streaks, make-up and chunky work boots, she looked cute huddled in her turquoise coat, her nose pinker than her hair from the cold. 'What are you doing?'

After she'd explained, he took her arm and led her to the coffee shop. He sat her outside and ducked in to get the two espressos, as if he'd not had them premade, as if he'd not sat watching her for the last ten minutes.

'You are going in there,' he said.

'What if…'

'What if what? What's the worst that can happen? You'll get upset that you can't dance professionally and cry? So cry, do some dancing and get over it.'

'Wow, you're so kind and compassionate. Why is it you don't have a girlfriend?' She sank half her coffee.

'What are your options?' he asked, trying to sound a little more understanding.

'Aren't you supposed to be castrating cows or something?'

'Monday afternoons I have to work at our practice here.' He pointed to the surgery down the road. 'I hate it. It's all small animal crap. I'd just dealt with another mangy mongrel when I saw you about to get arrested for weird behaviour. I'm glad of the chance to escape. So what are your options? How can you get ballet back into your life?'

'Mangy mongrel? Do you actually like being a vet?'

'You're avoiding my question.' He downed his espresso in one.

'Do you think Fee found out about Jonathan and Maggie, bumped her off then crippled with guilt, did herself in? Shame we'll never know. Unless she told Jonathan. Zoë still won't speak to him, but I bet she could torture him to find out if Fee confessed.'

'And how would Fee kill Maggie? Push her down the stairs? Fee could barely walk most days. If it wasn't her back, it was Xanax.' He shook his head. 'You are the queen of question avoidance.'

'I shouldn't be here. You know it's the fell race on Saturday? I should be training.'

'Stop changing the subject. Ballet. What can you do?'

Her brow furrowed in a tight knot as she sat on her hands, glancing longingly at the lad at the next table who'd lit a cigarette.

'You're not smoking.'

'I've given up. Two whole weeks now.'

'Well done. Ballet?'

'I…'

'Come on, Libs.'

'I could dance for fun, just take the odd class, or I could teach, but I don't know…'

'Well, start simple. Go in there and say hello to Jane. Her and my mum are friends.' He wanted to push the fringe out of the way and wipe off half the black make-up. 'The kids call her Mrs Knightmare, but she's very nice, not too fond of me though.'

'Why?'

'Bit of a fling with her daughter, Juliet, last year.'

'Clara *and* Juliet? You really are appalling.' She sank the last of her coffee.

He smiled. 'You ready?'

He took her hand and dragged her across the road into the studio. When she pulled back, trying to flee, he tightened his grip. The girl behind the counter directed them upstairs where Jane Knight was in the office, doing paperwork.

'Hi Jane, this is Libby.' He gently pushed Libby in front of him, his hands resting on her shaking shoulders.

'Sorry I'm late,' she whispered.

'It's okay. Clara explained.' Jane stood up, eyeing him with suspicion. 'Hello Patrick.'

And this was why he hadn't intervened until Robbie rang. Jane, like Clara, would put two and two together and make up the rest.

'What would you like to do, Libby?' Jane asked, but Libby was already staring into the studio, mesmerised.

'Can I go in?'

She didn't wait for an answer, but walked into the studio, gazing around as if she'd found Kansas again. Patrick watched through the round window in the door, smiling as she started peeling off layers to reveal she was already dressed in the *Flashdance* black leotard.

'Is she what's keeping you on the straight and narrow?' Jane asked.

'She's nothing to do with me, just a friend.' His phone rang. Grateful for the excuse, he walked away.

By the time he was off the phone, rescued from an afternoon with small animals by a lame bull, Libby was dancing. Jesus Christ, she really was a ballet dancer. Even though he'd seen the photos he'd not really believed it, not to this extent. For a good ten minutes, he stood mesmerised as she leapt and twirled on the tips of her toes, as graceful as a fairy.

'She's very good. Out of practice and her feet will hurt tomorrow, but very good. I have friends at the English National Ballet and I made some enquiries. She had great potential, would have made principal. She's a turner.' Jane smiled at his confused expression. 'Her speciality is turning, doing pirouettes, manéges, fouettés, just like that.'

Libby's skin glistened with sweat, her muscles taut as she span through twenty or so turns. Then suddenly, she stopped dead and burst into tears.

No, no, no. Don't cry. This was supposed to fix you.

'You don't look as though she's nothing to do with you,' Jane said. 'And about time too. Your mother worries about you.'

'I have to go,' Patrick said, still loitering. 'Don't tell her I watched.'

Jane smiled, clearly amused, but went into the studio.

'Miss it?' she asked Libby.

Libby nodded. 'I need to start dancing again. I know I'm crying, but I'm actually happy. I can't believe I've avoided it for this long.'

'You needed some time. I stopped for five years after Juliet was born.'

'Please, can I come to class?'

'Of course.' Jane studied her. 'What else? Do you want to teach?'

'I don't know.'

'We're putting on the Nutcracker next month. I could do with some help marshalling the girls around. Would you like to help?' When Libby nodded, Jane smiled. 'Good. Now, I'll let you off for today, but if you want to dance here, you will look like a ballerina. The eye make-up has to go and a fringe that long will need to be pinned back. You were a professional dancer so I expect you to set a good example to the girls. Barre?'

Libby nodded, wiping her eyes, and Patrick left her to it, his good deed done.

* * *

Libby knocked on Patrick's door, her smile still in place from the forty minutes of punishment Jane had subjected her to. Between Jane and Xander, she'd end up fitter than ever.

Patrick answered, his expression blank, as if he had no idea why she might be standing on his doorstep. Libby's smile fell. He'd gone out of his way to help her, but now he shoved his hands in his pockets, clearly not inviting her in.

'I just wanted to say thank you, for today.'

He didn't react.

'I'm... I'm going to start class again and help out with the ballet they're putting on at Christmas.' She blushed, she shouldn't have come. 'Anyway, sorry to... just, thanks.'

Her cheeks burned as she walked away, but she held her head

high. What was wrong with him? Clearly he didn't like her, so why did he keep being nice?

* * *

'But all she does is run.'

The frustrated voice, the high-pitch of the last word did little to alleviate Michael Wray's worries.

'You don't have anything?'

'No.'

'Her and McBride?'

'He really doesn't like her.'

'Pity. They'd be big money. Readers love her. Readers love him. Get the scoop on them and it'll be double what it was for the Goldings.'

Chapter Twenty-Nine

Fifteen miles.

Libby lay in a field behind the Miller's Arms in Gosthwaite Mills, the panorama surrounding her line of vision took in almost the entire route – the climbs, the descents, the streams, the walls.

Fifteen miles. Twenty-five kilometres. Seven check points. Five peaks.

And two thousand metres of climbing.

It all added up to approximately three hours and forty-five minutes of sheer hell. Less if she wanted to beat Grace's record. Xander's record was three hours twenty, but he wasn't looking to beat that this year. His goal was to help Libby round in a new women's record time – he wanted to punish Grace for the newspaper quote as much as Libby did.

Positives. The weather was perfect. Cool, but not freezing. Barely any wind. Overcast skies, so no need for sunglasses. She was fitter than she'd been in years, if not ever. Her ankle and core muscles had never felt so strong. She glanced down at her stomach, where she'd pinned her number. Twenty-four. Her age. Perfect.

Ninety-three entrants, fifteen women, but only one mattered – Grace. She stood chatting to some of the other members of the Haverton Harriers, all easily identifiable in their royal blue running tops.

'How's life now you're dancing again?'

Libby opened her eyes to see Patrick standing a few feet away holding an ancient collie on a lead. Not Patrick, not now. She didn't get him. Hot, cold, hot, cold. How could he go out of the way to drag her into the dance studio then not speak to her later the same day?

'It's good.' She held out her hand to the collie, who limped towards her, licking her hand.

'This is Baxter.'

'Hello, Baxter. You have a dog?'

'Sort of. How were you the next day? Jane said your feet would hurt. I'm not surprised. Standing on your tip toes like that can't be right.'

'It's called *en pointe* and my feet were agony, but bizarrely, I miss the pain.' She frowned at him. 'You watched?'

'Only for a bit. I got called away,' he admitted. 'I've never seen a ballet dancer in real life, impressive.'

'Well, thanks for making me go in.' She didn't get him, didn't get him at all.

'You're welcome.'

'Now, why couldn't you have said that when I came round? Two words? Anything would've done. You're so bloody rude sometimes.'

'I had company. It wasn't a good time for a doorstep chat.'

Was that his best apology? Company? Some girl no doubt. 'Whatever. I need to focus.'

'You look worried.' Patrick crouched down, stroking Baxter. 'It's only a race, Libs.'

'It's fifteen miles of uphill struggle.'

'You know you don't have to finish. Or win. No one will think any less of you.'

'If you think it's the taking part that matters, you clearly didn't listen to the ballet story.'

He smiled. 'You've never done this before. Grace has.'

'You don't think I can do it.' Libby sat up, appalled. 'God, not since my dad thought I'd never... Screw you. I will do this.' *Or die bloody trying.*

At the start, Libby's desire to throw up intensified. Grace stood six feet away, looking calm, focussed and every bit the professional fell runner. Like Libby, she had her hair in a single plait, her fringe pinned off her face. Grace was probably carrying a stone more than Libby, but all of it as muscle. How the hell had she got so fit so quickly?

Xander rubbed her shoulders. 'Stop looking at Grace and relax. Once you start running, you'll be fine, Wilde.'

Libby stared straight ahead, trying to focus on the race organiser wittering about checkpoints and full body cover, but the blood pumping in her ears drowned out his words. The pistol fired.

She ran.

Once the start melee thinned out, Libby and Xander were where they wanted to be, in the front quarter of the pack. From here Xander's plan was to chip away, using their quicker pace to put a gap between them and Grace. Libby would need it. She and Xander could maintain a faster pace for longer, but he'd warned her Grace always upped her pace at the end and if Libby was less than half a kilometre ahead of her when she reached Lum Crag, Grace would win. Xander had it all worked out.

One, two, three. One, two, three. The carefully chosen music on her iPod worked to keep her pace even. She'd maintain the same rhythm, only changing the length of her stride to match inclines. How could Patrick think she couldn't do this? Because he knew she'd failed before. Well, not this time.

The lactic burn in her thighs wasn't the worst it'd ever been, but heading up Black Fell, it wasn't far off. Eight other runners were in front of Libby and Xander, but Grace was the required half a kilometre behind. Ten miles had gone. Libby had mud splatters up to her knees and a graze on her left elbow from stumbling over rocks. She checked her watch – still on target and feeling good. She could do this.

She leapt up onto a stile, vaulting over the top and landing on the grass, already running. Behind her, Xander swore. He bent over, clutching his side.

'What happened?' she asked, switching her iPod off.

'Stitch. And it isn't going away.' He jogged on, his face set in a grim frown.

Their pace slowed but they ran on, heading up to the peak of Black Fell towards the fifth check point. A patch of scree slowed them further, twice making Xander mutter under his breath.

'Are you okay?' she asked.

He didn't answer, but glanced up at the cairn. Fifty metres to go. A runner overtook them.

'Xand?' she asked, concerned by his increasingly pale face.

'Just get to the checkpoint,' he said through gritted teeth. 'I'll have to retire. I can get a lift from here.'

Libby's nausea returned. 'But–'

'You keep running.'

'I can't do this by myself.'

'Yes you can. You know the route. You're on time.'

Libby shook her head. 'Not without you. I'll get lost. I'll never find the right route down from the Crag.' Twice she'd buggered it up in training, not spotting the gap in the rocks that led to a wall gap where the drop on the other side was only a couple of feet instead of ten. Instead she'd had to detour to reach the stile.

At the summit, Xander struggled towards the checkpoint, looking ahead to the runners already on their way to the fourth peak.

'Okay, new plan. See the Haverton Harriers runner, three in front of us?'

Libby narrowed her eyes, but nodded. 'Isn't that Mike Robb, last year's champion?'

'Go catch him up.'

'I can't—'

'Yes, you can. You're faster uphill. He'll leave you for dust going downhill, but if you can get somewhere near him going up the Crag, you'll be able to follow his route to the wall. Watch him.'

The checkpoint loomed. She could retire too.

'Wilde, you can do this. You have an hour left. You got the legs?'

She nodded.

'Don't kill yourself, but catch him up. You can get the guy in front of us by the time you get to the bottom of the Pike. Then focus on the guy in front of him. Aim to catch Mike Robb by the top of the Pike. Stick with him across the ridge to the Crag.'

'I'll get lost and die.'

'You've got your GPS watch on. I'll track you on Daisy's laptop.'

She paused, sticking her dibber into the reader and thanking the marshals.

'You can do this, Wilde.' Xander kissed the top of the head. 'Now go. Grace will up her pace at this point and she's less than half a K behind you.'

Libby hesitated.

'For fuck's sake, Wilde. Run!'

Shit. She strode away, switching her iPod back on as she focussed on the lime green vest of the runner in front of her.

Your ass is mine.

The ground disappeared under long, easy strides as she enjoyed the gentle, grassy descent. The lactic burn eased and she took a small drink, her confidence boosted by the quickly diminishing gap between her and the lime green vest.

She'd prove Patrick wrong. She'd prove Grace wrong. She'd prove she wasn't a quitter. Not anymore.

She passed the first runner way before the bottom of the Pike, and target two was only twenty metres in front when she started the next uphill. A glance down to her left showed Grace sprinting down from checkpoint five. Xander's stitch had slowed Libby down, giving Grace the chance to make up some ground.

She's going to catch me.

Libby ignored the runner ahead, instead focussing on her main target, Mike Robb, fifty metres away. Her legs burned as her pace increased, but the gap shrank. This might kill her, but Xander had given her a strategy and she wouldn't let him down.

Ten more minutes to the top of Lum Pike, then five down along the Ridge, ten up to Lum Crag, then ten down to the valley bottom. The last ten minutes would be flatter, but with more obstacles – streams, walls, and mud.

Mike didn't look remotely pleased to see her, but she stayed at his heel up to the checkpoint. As Xander predicted, Mike left her on the downhill, his experience allowing him to run with more confidence over the rough terrain, but on the way up to Lum Crag, Libby once again sat on his heel, sticking her dibber in the checkpoint the second he'd taken his out. Grace was half a kilometre behind. Libby could do this.

For the first time, her hope soared. She'd done the climbs. She'd done the majority of the miles. Twenty minutes stood between her and victory. Instead of letting Mike get away, she ran faster than she'd ever dared, determined not to lose him or her way down to the wall. Once she was at the wall, she could let him go.

Twice she slipped, but she kept running. Adrenalin took over, her instincts kicked in and she found she was smiling as she sped down the mountain. She was fell running with the best. Grace would never catch her now.

Mike led her to the wall and Libby relaxed. Familiar territory. Safe territory. She eased up a little, no longer needing the tour guide, but coming back to her usual pace, letting her feet match the music. She placed a hand on the wall as she stepped onto it, but the stone moved and she stumbled. Unable to control her landing, her foot hit a rock, twisting her ankle. She yelped, landing in a heap.

Oh God, no.

Mike Robb glanced back, but she stood up and waved, telling him she was fine. Just keep running. She jogged on, but each step sent a bolt of agony through her ankle. Behind her, Grace was at the top of the Crag. In two minutes, she'd be at the wall. There was no way Libby could win, but she'd finish if she had to walk over the line.

If only Xander were here... He'd be at the finishing line. She couldn't let him down. She couldn't walk across the line – she had to run across it. The two runners she'd overtaken earlier dashed past, followed by another two. Grace was next.

'Stick to ballet,' she called, laughing as she ran like a gazelle past Libby.

No. Libby would not be beaten, not like this. She'd danced on worse. Grace had no idea what Libby could do.

I can out run her. I'm faster.

Libby ran as she'd danced in Swan Lake, ignoring the messages her ankle was sending to her brain. In the woods, she caught Grace, but didn't overtake. She'd wait. Five minutes to go. Grace's pace steadily increased as they leapt streams and boulders.

The woods disappeared and the Miller's Arms came into view as Libby prepared to make her move. Around the next bend the track opened out onto a grassy fell. The final half-kilometre. At full stretch, Libby could do it in just under two minutes. Crikey, they were within the record time.

She pulled to the right, lengthening her stride.

'Oh no you don't.' Grace kept pace.

Libby refused to glance around or answer back. She had to run faster. Pumping her legs, focussing on breathing, she ran as though she hadn't run twenty-four kilometres already. Grace was right behind her, cursing her, wasting her breath, as Libby turned onto the bridleway.

Just keep running.

She could hear the cheers and applause for the runners ahead of them. Her legs moved faster. Xander would be waiting. Patrick would be there. She had to win. Her ankle had numbed to one searing burn and she turned into the field with no idea where Grace was – on her heel or by her side.

At the end of the fenced off route in the field, Xander was shouting at her to run, pointing to the clock. She would beat Grace's record by five bloody minutes. From the excited cheers, she knew Grace was behind her, the spectators cheering on the sprint finish. Zoë, Patrick, Daisy, Robbie, Vanessa… familiar faces flashed by as Libby pushed harder, her legs burning, her lungs on fire.

Twenty-five metres… ten metres… five.

She crossed the line.

Xander helped guide her hand to the dibber sensor and once her finish time was logged, Libby raised her arms to the sky. She'd done it.

'You are totally amazing,' Xander yelled, lifting her off her feet.

She wanted to thank him, but as he put her down, pain shot through her ankle. Using his arm for support, she hopped to the official's booth and handed in her dibber. It was over. She'd won the women's race.

Grace slumped against the booth as she handed in her dibber. 'When you fell at the wall... you could barely walk. Were you faking it?'

Libby glanced down at her right foot, which she was still holding up from the floor, and shook her head. 'Can't walk.'

'Respect.' Grace held out her hand.

Libby's lip wobbled as she shook it.

Two hours later, after a shower, a vast bowl of pasta and copious amounts of orange juice at Xander and Daisy's, Libby had returned to the Miller's Arms, still limping, still exhausted, but feeling almost human again. The same Mumford & Sons tribute band played folk classics in a mini-marquee out the back, the pub barbeque was churning out burgers, but pretty much every runner she'd seen had eaten nothing more than chips and crisps.

And people were dancing, people who'd run that day. She admired them. Even if her ankle hadn't been strapped up, she'd never have the energy to jig around.

In her favourite purple t-shirt and ancient jeans, with hiking boots for walking home later, Libby sat curled up in the corner of the snug, happily drinking her very first pint of real ale – a ritual Grace insisted on. The first mouthful hadn't been the nicest thing she'd ever drunk, but encouraged by Patrick, who was also drinking the Cumbrian beer at the bar, Libby persevered. And it wasn't half bad.

'Oh for Christ's sake...' Zoë killed the beeping on her phone and drained her Bacardi and soda. 'That's the sixth time that bastard's called today. Does he think I'm going to forgive him, just like that?'

'Are you?' Grace asked.

Libby half-hoped Zoë would forgive him. It'd been over two weeks since Fee's funeral and Zoë's obsessive fasting, like the frequency of Jonathan's calls, hadn't diminished. Maybe if she'd talk to Jonathan, she'd get over his affair with Maggie. Something had to change.

'Never,' Zoë said, switching her phone off.

'Never say never,' Libby said, repeating Zoë's mantra.

But Zoë just laughed and kissed Libby's cheek. 'I'm going for a fag.'

Zoë left, giving Libby her first opportunity alone with Grace. After the handshake, there had been no more animosity, but they'd never had a chance to talk. Grace picked at her cheese and onion crisps, smiling at her.

'Out with it.'

'I wanted to say sorry.' Libby took a deep breath. 'I never would've messed around with Jack while he was seeing you. Never, ever. It's not my style. But even if the elderflower wine thing hadn't happened... well, if it hadn't happened, I'd have gone out with him. I'm sorry for that. It's always felt like a betrayal.'

Grace merely nodded.

'You don't fancy giving it another go with Jack?'

Grace shrugged. 'I don't know. Maybe it's time to move on. Someone new.'

Libby reached into her back pocket, taking out a small, yellow silk pouch. 'I made this last night. For you. Patrick said... well, I'm assuming you know what it is.'

'A retribution spell?'

Libby nodded. 'Everything I've done to you, will come back to me, times three.'

Grace shook her head. 'I can't take it. We both know you didn't do anything.'

'Then nothing will come back at me, times three.' Libby held out the bag. 'Please.'

Grace took it, her hand shaking. 'Blessed be.'

'Blessed be.'

Inside the bag was the little amulet of the naked woman holding up an offering, the one to promote new beginnings. Grace clipped it to her charm bracelet, still smiling. 'I think this might be one of the most honest, nicest things that anyone's ever done for me.'

To Libby's surprise, Grace leaned over the table and hugged her. Libby clung to her, the relief at making friends with Grace greater than finishing the fell race.

'Oh hello,' Patrick said as he stood in doorway, holding another three pints. 'Scott, check this out. Libby and Grace are questioning their attraction to men.'

Libby threw a beer mat at him, but couldn't help laughing as he sat next to her, grinning like a fool. Scott, Clara, Robbie and Vanessa joined them, cramming into the little snug.

'Who's for poker?' Scott asked.

Patrick bent his head to whisper in her ear. 'For half your winnings, I won't tell him about your spooky mindreading skills.'

She had to press her lips together to suppress her grin. 'Did you bring your wallet, Scott? I hear you get paid the big bucks.'

Scott shook his head. 'We play for matchsticks, sweetheart.'

Libby leant up to Patrick, whispering. 'The deal's off.'

But Patrick laughed, his breath tickling her neck. 'Ah, but those matchsticks we cash in for beer tokens. Play your cards right and we can drink for free off this lot.'

Who cared about winning at poker when Hot Patrick was sitting next to her, whispering to her, his lips accidentally brushing her ear? Was this bliss, or did attention like this only make Cold Patrick harder to deal with? Bugger it. She'd take ten minutes of Hot Patrick any day.

Across the table, Scott watched her, smiling as though he knew what she was thinking.

Arse.

* * *

Under clear skies and a full moon, a gaggle of drunken revellers left the Miller's Arms, heading back to Gosthwaite. Patrick had to jog to catch up to them after being delayed by Steve the landlord to discuss his pet pig's balding skin.

Up ahead, he spotted Libby zipping up her thick down jacket, shivering against the frosty evening.

'Cold?' he asked, slowing to walk beside her.

'A bit. I'll be okay once I get walking.'

'Here,' he said, pulling his woollen hat over her hair. 'You should've got a lift back. How's your ankle?'

'It's fine.' She had that angelic smile. 'Thanks.'

'Sorry for annoying you this morning.'

She tried to pout, but only made him laugh. 'I can't believe you doubted me.'

'I didn't doubt you could do it. I was worried that if you didn't win, you'd think you'd failed.'

'I would've.' She smiled. 'Obsessive, I know. Anyway, it was a handy motivational tool so, thank you.'

'Glad to be of service.' He ambled along, his hands in his pockets. 'Where's Zoë?'

'Buggered off with Sparky. Poor guy.' She smiled as Scott ran past, giving a giggling Clara a piggyback. 'Where's your dog?'

'Home. He lives with mum and dad. He's old.'

'But you don't have any other pets?'

'Yeah, I've got a cat.' He tried not to smile as she elbowed him.

'I'd like a dog. Someone to run with.'

'So get one.'

'I can't. Not while I'm living with Zoë.' She frowned down at the track. 'Though how long we'll be here is—'

'You're leaving?' She couldn't leave, not now.

'Well, no. I mean, I don't know. Zoë's nearly served her tax exile time, so she's putting the house on the market. It depends on how quickly it sells.'

'You could share with Grace,' he suggested. 'She's always skint. Has two bedrooms.'

Libby laughed. 'I think it's a bit soon to suggest moving in together. We're only just on speaking terms.'

'At least you'd still be in the village. Hyssop would have to live with me, of course.'

She elbowed him again, but this time he was ready and grabbed her arm. For a moment he held her close, preventing her from hitting him. Roses and sweet peas. Christ, how did she... She gave up the fight and looked up at him. If a dozen people weren't with them, he would've kissed her. And she knew it. He let her go and she got in one playful arm swat before he pushed her away, still laughing.

'Now, what's this about Jonathan Carr being into a bit of—' He mimed brandishing a whip.

Libby giggled, checking for who was nearby, but the nearest person was ten feet in front of them. Her sore ankle proved the perfect excuse for walking slowly and Patrick couldn't care less. As Libby explained, their pace slowed further. If only the walk were ten miles, not two.

All too soon, they'd reached the village and her garden gate. He mustn't kiss her. Absolutely, mustn't kiss her. Anyone could be watching. With a camera. He stood four feet from her, with his hands in his pockets.

'Night then,' she said, pausing.

'Night.' He stepped towards her and tugged the hat off. 'I'm glad you won, Libs.'

Oh Christ, that smile. He kissed her forehead and left, not daring to look back. If he did, there was every chance he'd turn round and kiss her properly. It was going to be a very long seven months until June.

Chapter Thirty

How quickly things had changed.

Three weeks earlier, Libby had been researching flights to Sydney – she'd had a job she despised, a feud with Grace, Patrick hated her and she was afraid to walk into a charity shop for fear of the octogenarian staff whispering behind her back. Now, everything had changed. And sixty faces stared expectantly, cross-legged, chins on hands, waiting.

Oh god.

'Are you ready?' Jane whispered.

Why am I nervous? Libby closed her eyes, taking slow steadying breaths. This wasn't the Coliseum. It was the dance studio in Haverton. The audience weren't middle class dance aficionados, they were ballet students aged five to eighteen. So why did she have clammy palms?

'Okay, let's do it.' She flexed her feet one last time as Jane pressed play.

The music began and years of rehearsals took over, moving Libby's feet without her having to think about the steps. It had been Jane's idea, to inspire the students, to show them first-hand what they could achieve if they worked hard. Libby had been doubtful. Show them what a failed ballerina was like? But they didn't know she'd failed. They didn't know she should still be on stage. All they saw was a grown up, someone way, way older than them. To them she was the dream come true.

It ought to have depressed her, but their little faces stared in wonder and she tried not to laugh. That's probably what she looked like when she first saw the Sugar Plum Fairy. Libby floated through the moves, feeling more appreciated than she had in front of several hundred people at the Royal Opera House. Bugger keeping her smile restrained, she let it grow.

For the first time in four years, her future felt... hopeful.

She had ballet. She had a tentative new friendship with Grace. And then there was Patrick. God, why did one night sitting next to

Patrick playing cards still make her smile? He'd kissed her forehead, nothing more, but before she'd come to class, he'd been at the coffee shop, just like the previous week. They'd had espressos and he'd laughed at her nerves, but when he wished her luck, he'd tugged her plait, smiling. Okay, he didn't kiss her or ask if she'd like to go out for dinner to celebrate, but hope, she had hope.

After her dance, Libby sat in a corner, relaxing in her warm-up clothes, planning to watch the rest of Jane's classes. What she wasn't planning was to be joined by six of Jane's students. They sat around her, most simply gawping, but the newest recruit, Matilda, broke the ice by clambering onto Libby's knee.

'Libby, can I plait your hair?' asked Amelie.

'Oh, and me,' piped up Ella.

They're just people – really short people. Braving a smile, Libby let down her bun. 'Okay.'

* * *

Something had to change. He had to talk to his parents. Patrick wandered into their house, lifting the large canvas above the marauding pack of wagging tails and exuberant paws. He didn't go into the kitchen, but poked his head around the door. Bacon frying, coffee brewing, mum nose deep in the Guardian – Saturday morning.

'Mum?'

'Hello, darling. Coffee's fresh.'

'In a minute. Can I have a word?'

She followed him into the dining room, where he propped the painting, still covered in brown paper, against the table.

'Oh, a present for me?' She laughed. 'It's not my birthday.'

'I've... look, you can't tell anyone about it, especially Jane. You know what she's like. Promise.' After his mum nodded, Patrick tore away the paper and her eyes widened.

'Is that... the original?' she whispered.

'Yes. I know her.'

'This is the ballerina you took to Jane's? The girl from the Green.'

He nodded.

'Why's she so sad?'

Patrick explained, never taking his eyes off Libby's mournful face.

'You like her?' his mum asked.

He took a deep breath, folding his arms. 'Maybe.'

'Well, she's trouble.' His father stood in the doorway, his hands in his pockets.

'Dad, she's not like that. She's a really nice girl.'

'She could be the next Mother Theresa, but if you're seen with her, getting up to no good, you'll be on the front page of the paper.'

'But dad—'

'We have an agreement and if she's such a nice girl, she'll wait 'til June. Or you'll deal with the repercussions.'

'Mum?' Patrick implored her. Be reasonable.

She shook her head, wrapping her arms around herself.

'Fine. You can keep the painting and just so you know I'm going out tomorrow night. Drinking. But I've taken Monday off, swapped with Fergus. I take it that's within the rules?'

He strode out, pushing past his dad. Why couldn't they see that he'd changed? He slumped against the front door, resenting them. Sod it. He'd just do what he liked. He'd go out with Libby and to hell with their bloody rules.

'No, Elizabeth.' His dad's voice carried through the ancient single-glazed windows. 'The boy hasn't learned a damned thing. He can't always have his own way—'

Patrick climbed in his car. *I've never been so ashamed to call you my son.* Did he really want to risk seeing that look in his mum's eye again, even for… even for what? Would he risk everything, his mum's respect, for a few months with Libby? She wanted to get married, have kids. It'd never work.

Well, it might. Could he risk everything on *might?*

* * *

As birthdays went, Libby's twenty-fifth didn't hold much hope for being the most exciting. Her boss, pressured by Robbie no doubt, had given her the day off, but aside from a leisurely run with Xander and going to the Alfred with Zoë later, she had bugger all planned.

And if she were honest, the last place Zoë needed to be was a pub. Weeks of constant drinking, late-nights shagging Sparky – and the odd blast of coke no doubt – were taking their toll on her. She called in sick more than she went to work and her skin, once glowing with peaches and cream, was grey and dull. Her jeans hung off her hips but Libby was at a loss to help – Zoë wouldn't even contemplate talking about Jonathan, or Ed.

But for three hours, she could run with Xander and forget all about the world.

She lay on the floor, stretching and smiling as sunlight streamed through the window. And on the plus side, it was such a beautiful day, she could merrily potter around the garden, and maybe if Patrick passed by after his usual Sunday morning bike ride she could invite him in for a coffee. That's what happened most Sundays. They did little more than read the papers, but Libby adored his company. Maybe this week she could ask him to stay for dinner. Okay, it wouldn't be a Zoë extravaganza of lamb with red wine *jus*, but there was a chicken in the fridge and who didn't like roast chicken?

The doorbell ringing almost brought her back to reality, but still daydreaming of kissing Patrick over roast potatoes had Libby answering the door, smiling like a loon.

Xander stood leaning against the porch. 'Happy birthday, Wilde.'

His baggy shorts and bike helmet tempered her smile. 'You're cancelling on me?'

'Slight change of plan,' Xander said. 'We're going for a bike ride.'

Libby shook her head. 'I don't like bikes.'

'Tough.'

'I don't even have a bike.'

'You're right out of luck because Daisy has a bike she's used once and clothes she's never worn.' Xander handed her a bag. 'Go and get changed.'

'But I hate bikes. I haven't been on one in years.'

'It wasn't that long ago,' Patrick said as he pulled up. 'Challenge yourself, Libs.'

Oh god, he was coming too? What was the lesser of the two evils, looking like a chicken in front of Patrick, or a turkey when she fell off the bike?

Bugger it.

Ten minutes later, she headed back outside, looking every bit a pro-biker in Daisy's clothes. All the gear and no idea. To her horror, Robbie, Vanessa, Clara and Scott were all standing around, chatting excitedly in their biking gear. They offered raucous Happy Birthdays, Vanessa even gave a cheery wave, but Libby's trepidation grew. She'd look like an idiot in front of them all. How would Patrick ever like her?

'Xand, I'm not sure I can do this,' she whispered as he tinkered with Daisy's bike.

'You'll be fine, Wilde. You can ride mental horses and run the socks off me so you're pretty fearless and fit. It's easy.'

She fiddled with her plait. 'I'm not–'

'Seriously, this is what Rob and I used to do before the restaurant, take people out doing extreme sports. We know how to look after people. We're not going anywhere tricky.'

'Do I have to put my feet in the clippy pedals?'

'Yes, but you're going to have a quick lesson with the best instructor in the world. Rob taught Daisy and she's a pain the arse to teach anything. She acts like a three year-old when she can't do something. It'll be fun, Wilde.' Xander handed her the bike. 'Rob?'

Robbie beckoned her towards the lane at the side of the house and Libby followed reluctantly, shooting Vanessa a nervous glance.

'I don't want to do this,' she muttered, dying to run away.

Robbie smiled, taking hold of her handlebars. 'I didn't think you did scared. Besides, it's definitely easier than riding Dolomite. In fact, it's a lot like riding cross-county. Your knees and ankles are your suspension, your arms too. You just need to stay loose.'

'Cross country?' She took a deep, confidence-soothing breath. 'I'm listening.'

While he patiently explained how the gears, brakes and clips on her shoes worked, she tried to pay attention, but no matter how much theory she took in, the thought of having her feet trapped, tethered to the pedals, terrified her. As they completed lengths of the lane, up and down like a swimmer, Robbie jogged alongside, reassuring her, talking her through everything, holding her up when she slowed but couldn't release her feet quickly enough.

'I can't do this.' Frustrated with failure, she struggled not to cry.

Robbie held her face with both hands. 'Do you trust me?'

More than anyone she'd ever known. She stared into his reassuring brown eyes and nodded.

'Here's the thing, Lib. You're going to fall off. It's half the fun of the ride. You're going to forget about your feet being clipped in and you'll fall over. We all do it. Just enjoy it. I'd never let you get hurt.'

Galvanised, she pushed her reticence to the side and they practised stopping and starting several more times, until finally, she got it. Her foot hit the ground and he didn't need to catch her.

She paused at the end of the lane. 'Rob, please look after me?'

He kissed the top of her head. 'I promise.'

* * *

Libby and Robbie were friends. Just friends. Rob was just showing her what to do. He knew it was nothing more, but Patrick stood astride his bike, leaning on his handlebars, wondering what was taking them so long. Beside him, Vanessa watched the lane between the houses, just as anxious as he was.

'Libby is absolutely terrified,' Xander said, pulling up the other side of Vanessa.

Really? Patrick stood up. Maybe he shouldn't have agreed to this ride out. Maybe he should tell her to forget it. 'Will she be okay?'

Xander grinned, that smug fucking grin. 'Of course, because you're going to look after her.'

'Why isn't your wife here? I'd look after her.'

Vanessa swatted them both. 'Play nicely, you two.'

Patrick opened his mouth, but then Robbie and Libby appeared. Finally. He relaxed. He relaxed for three seconds until Rob kissed Libby's head.

Vanessa gave a little squeak.

'Van, stop it,' Xander said, putting his hand on her shoulder. 'It doesn't mean anything and you know it.'

'Yes, well it's not nice to see.' She looked up at Patrick. 'Is it?'

Patrick bent down, pretending to adjust his brakes. *No, it's not.* 'I'll look after Libs and keep her away from Rob.'

Libby's face was set with determination as she slowly cycled over, wobbling a little as she took her feet out of the pedals.

'If I die,' she said, 'you get full custody of Hyssop.'

Patrick laughed. 'Told you I wasn't going to rely on plying you with booze.'

And the grim determination fled. She smiled. 'I hate these shorts. It feels like I'm wearing a nappy.'

'You'll appreciate them later.' He leant over, tightening her chin strap. 'Come on, you'll get nervous waiting for this lot to arse about. They can catch up.'

She swore under her breath, but followed him tentatively down the road. 'Don't go too fast.'

'Speed is your friend.' He slowed, pottering next to her. 'And stay away from Rob. You're making Van nervous.'

She frowned underneath her helmet. 'I hardly think looking like a four year-old learning to ride without stabilisers is a fabulous seduction technique.'

Oh, I don't know. It looks pretty cute to me.

He turned off the road, onto the bridleway into the woods, smiling as she squealed going over a tiny pothole.

Might. Was *might* worth risking everything?

Twenty minutes later, Libby waited at the top of the first hill. She'd overtaken them all, her fitness and Daisy's top-of-the-range bike proving their worth.

'Who the hell invited you?' Patrick said, catching her up. 'You're supposed to be at the back, being rubbish with Clara.'

Her face paled as Robbie and Vanessa whizzed past, speeding down the other side. 'Uphill, I could handle, but that just looks bloody scary.'

'Just go steady to start with,' Xander said. 'You'll get the hang of it.'

'Sod that, Libs. Follow me.' Patrick set off. 'Remember, speed is your friend. And stay loose.'

The grim determination came back, but she followed him, swearing and squealing most of the way. By the time the track bottomed out, her relief was palpable, and her smile was back in place.

'Okay,' she said, breathless with adrenaline, 'if I don't die, this might be fun.'

Good girl. He pedalled on, absurdly pleased. Why, because he was proud of her attitude or because if she liked this, then maybe she could go on ride outs with him instead of running with Xander?

From that point, she stayed behind him. He picked out the easiest side of the track, never going too fast and always glancing behind him. After the first hour, the grim determination disappeared, replaced by a huge smile, though she still squealed her way down most of the hills. She rode along, occasionally talking with the others, mostly Xander, but unlike Clara, she never asked how much further and unlike Vanessa, she didn't constantly need to duck behind a wall for a wee.

'OMG, I hate this bit. Can I go round?' Clara whined.

'What bit?' Libby stared at the track in front of them. 'Jesus Christ, that's not a hill. It's a cliff. It just drops off.'

'I'll take you round, Clara,' Xander offered. 'Wilde?'

Don't bottle out. Patrick coaxed her nearer the edge. 'Ready for an adrenaline rush?'

'No.' She glanced from him to Xander as Robbie, Vanessa and Scott hurtled down the steep hill.

Patrick frowned. 'Okay, it's a bit–'

'Vertical and a bloody long way down?'

'But it's just grass. No rocks, or tricky bits. You just point your bike down and go. Back brake on, careful with your front. Don't lock it up.'

She had her bottom lip tucked between her teeth, watching as the racing trio reached the bottom.

'It's okay, Libs. You don't have to do it. You can go with Clar–'

She'd gone for it. Fucking hell, he loved this girl. Well, he didn't but… Christ, she made him smile. As she gained speed her squealing grew louder, but she kept going. He laughed, his weight adding to his momentum and taking him flying past her.

'You bugger… Oh shit!'

He glanced back to see her wobble, losing control. 'Don't lock your brakes up!'

She reached the bottom, still out of control. The front wheel hit a rut, sending her over the handlebars. Patrick was already off his bike sprinting towards her, Robbie not far behind. Libby didn't get up.

Don't be hurt, Libs. Please, don't be hurt.

Her eyes were wide open, staring at the sky.

Oh Christ, she's dead.

As he stood over her, her eyes moved and she flashed him the biggest smile.

'Ohmigod, can we do it again?'

He fell to his knees, struggling for breath as he waved to the others to say she was okay.

'Seriously, can we?' she asked. 'That was awesome.'

Okay, maybe he did love her.

* * *

Three hours after leaving the Green, Libby unclipped her feet from the pedals for the last time and lay down on the pavement outside the Alfred. She'd made it alive. She'd had five minor incidents after the first off, the most spectacular of the day, but she'd made it alive. The others had all dashed inside, desperate for a pint, the toilet or both, but Patrick stayed outside, fiddling with his bike.

'I have scabbed knees, a bruised elbow and my legs feel like jelly,' she said, smiling up at him.

'I'm sorry, I can't hear you. My ears are still ringing from all your screaming.' He glanced at the pub. 'Come on. I'll buy you a birthday drink.'

'Oh for a cup of tea.' She let him pull her to her feet.

'Christ, you know how to live. It's your birthday.'

'Tea then wine.'

'Real beer then whisky.'

They were still debating what she should drink when he held open the door for her.

'Happy birthday!'

Libby stepped back, startled, but Patrick's hands were on her shoulders, pushing her into the pub, now filled with her friends. They launched into a rousing chorus of *Happy Birthday to You* and Zoë appeared with a vast cake, the assumed twenty-five candles turning it into a veritable inferno.

As the singing finished, Libby blew out the candles, laughing, smiling and almost crying in shock. Everyone she knew, at least the ones she cared about, were all there. The mountain bikers, plus Grace, Jack, Sheila, Jane, Daisy and Sparky.

'You didn't really think we'd just go to the pub for your birthday, did you?' Zoë bear-hugged her.

As Zoë cut up the cake, Libby sat at the bar, inundated with congratulations, drinks and gifts, the latter which she stashed on a table while she soaked up the goodwill. Her co-dancers at the ballet would never have done this for her, or her random friends in Manchester.

'Surprised?' Patrick asked as he perched on the stool next to her, handing her a mug.

Surprised? Still reeling. Libby smiled, taking the tea. Hot tea, Hot Patrick. He'd been Hot Patrick all day, never leaving her side. It might actually rate as one of the best days of her life. The laughs, the adrenaline, the company. Why did he change everything?

* * *

Patrick sat at the bar, watching as Libby flitted around, saying hello to everyone. His mood deteriorated slightly when she reached Sheila and Jack. Stay away, Libs.

'Pint?' Scott asked, joining him. 'You see the rugby yesterday?'

They discussed England's dismal performance, but Patrick knew his old friend well enough. A team talk was on the way. Sure enough once Dave behind the bar handed over their drinks, Scott dragged him over to an empty table in the window.

'What's going on?' Scott asked.

'With what?'

'You and Libby.'

'Nothing.'

'Come on. It's pretty fucking obvious.'

'We're just friends.'

'The question is why?' Scott leaned forwards, speaking quietly. 'It's not like you.'

To explain, or not to explain.

'Well?' Scott asked again.

'Look, she's nice but that's it.'

'Nice?' Scott laughed. 'Try again, mate. You look like you're in love with her.'

'Piss off.'

'You haven't left her side all day.'

'Someone had to look after her. And it couldn't be Rob.'

Scott shook his head, laughing. 'Do you know why I gave up the shit-hot job in London? Because Clara cried. It was the day her dad died. She hated that twat, but she cried her eyes out and that was it. You ever seen Libby cry?'

Patrick closed his eyes, remembering her sitting with her head on her knees the day she lost her job. And the day that bastard Jack threatened her. He nodded.

'And I bet you never want to see her cry again. You'd do anything to keep her safe and happy. Sound about right?'

So he'd sorted out a few things for her, like taking her to the ballet, but that didn't... Christ, he'd even paid a small fortune for the Broken Ballerina because he knew she'd regret giving it away. Was Scott right?

'I'll take your silence as a resounding yes. You're totally into her, mate. Now, why the hell aren't you doing anything about it?'

Patrick slumped back in his seat. 'Because if I go out with her, I could lose everything.'

Libby moved on, accepting a glass of wine from Daisy, and Patrick explained to Scott about the ultimatum.

'I tried to talk to mum and dad yesterday, but they're adamant. Dad really doesn't like Libby.'

'Shit. Well, it's better than having HIV. Clara's convinced that's why you're not shagging Libby.'

'Bitch.' Patrick flicked a beer mat at the wall. 'She'd better not be spreading that around.'

Scott glanced across to Libby. 'Tell her.'

'I can't.'

'Why?'

'She'll leave. And she'd blame herself.'

Scott nodded, leaning forward on his elbows. 'Thing is, mate, I've seen how she looks at you. If you don't do something about it, she might leave anyway. You think she's going to sit around waiting for seven months?'

Patrick stared at him.

'Tell her. You can work something out. Just keep it quiet, no bad behaviour until June.'

'It's a big risk and I don't even know...'

'If you like her that much?' Scott grinned. 'We wouldn't be having this conversation if you really doubted that.'

'She wants the whole marriage and kids thing.'

'And you don't? You might like it.'

'You're always knackered and Vanessa pissed off with a violin player.'

'Viola, and you still might like it.'

'A big risk.'

'You're an adrenaline junkie. Suck it up.'

With appalling timing, Libby excused herself from Daisy and headed over to her pile of gifts. Scott shot him a grin.

'Off you go.'

Fuck.

She opened a card, smiling at the joke on the front, but her smile grew when he joined her. 'It's from Paolo.'

'Here,' Patrick said, handing her a purple gift bag from the pile. 'Happy birthday.'

She frowned, blushing a little. 'You got me a present?'

'I got you a present.' Okay, this was about as excruciating as life could get. He stared down at his feet as she tore off the striped paper some shop assistant had spent five minutes neatly taping on.

'It's my Chloe perfume.' She gazed up at him. 'Thank you. Really.'

No, this bit of his life was definitely more excruciating. Maybe he should do this another time, at her house, in the garden, away from prying eyes. 'At least you won't stink anymore.'

She tipped her head to the side, as she sprayed on a little of the fragrance. 'I reckon about fifty percent of the time, I really hate you.'

He laughed, breathing in her familiar floral scent. 'And the other fifty percent?'

'Then you're just slappable.'

He relaxed next to her, enjoying her uncomfortable blushes as she picked up another gift. This would be okay. She liked him. He liked her. They'd work it out.

'Libs, I need to talk to you about something.'

She nodded, but became distracted by the little yellow bag she'd unwrapped, weighing it in her palm. She peeked inside and gasped. 'Oh god, no.'

'What?'

'I gave this pouch to Grace after the fell race,' she whispered, staring at him. 'It was a Retribution Spell. You can use them to punish someone, or you can use them to promote forgiveness. The idea is that the bad things you've done, you get back times three.'

He frowned. 'But you didn't technically—'

'Then technically, nothing will come back to me.' Libby shook her head. 'The point is I gave this bag to Grace. I stitched our initials on, see? Where is she?'

'She went home a couple of hours ago, said she wasn't feeling too well.'

'She wouldn't do anything stupid, would she?'

'Why?'

Libby delved inside the bag and lifted out Maggie's emerald pendant.

Patrick bolted.

Chapter Thirty-One

Patrick sprinted from the pub, praying it wasn't true. Not Gracey. Please, don't let it be Gracey. Libby had to be wrong. What the fuck would he do if she wasn't? What if Grace admitted it? He loved Gracey. She'd been his best mate for the last two years. No. Grace wouldn't kill Maggie. She wouldn't. Grace wouldn't hurt a fly. Literally. She yelled at him for swatting a wasp back in August.

It couldn't be Grace.

Libby ran alongside him, but held back as he reached Grace's house. He knocked. They waited. The ghost of Grace answered the door, her skin pale and her eyes red. She didn't speak, but headed back inside, leaving the door open for them to come in.

Oh Christ, Grace. What have you done?

She sat curled up in an armchair and wrapped herself in a grey cardigan.

'Gracey, what's going on?' he asked quietly, praying for a rational explanation that didn't involve murder. 'Did you give Maggie's pendant to Libby?'

She burst into tears, nodding and he sat heavily onto the sofa. Libby perched on the windowsill, frowning at him.

'Gracey, how did you get the pendant?' *Please tell me Maggie gave it to you.*

'I didn't hurt her, I swear.' Grace wiped in vain at her tears. 'I went... at the festival, she wasn't feeling well. I got back about two and went to check on her. I don't know why. I just felt I had to. And she was there. Dead. I didn't know... I should've called... but I didn't. She had the pendant in her hand. And I took it.'

Her body shook as she sobbed. Should he hug her or call the fucking police?

'Why?' he asked.

'I wanted it for a spell. It's an ancient Egyptian amulet, really powerful.' Grace picked at a loose thread in her cardigan.

'The inscription looks like hieroglyphics,' Libby said. 'What does it mean?'

'*See the Truth. Seize the Power.*' Grace sniffed.

'What did you want it for?' Libby asked. 'A summoning spell?'

Grace nodded. 'I'd asked Maggie if I could borrow it, but she said no, because if Jack really wanted me, he wouldn't be shagging around in the first place. She could be such a bitch, always wanting to be in control. I just wanted to do one spell.'

'But you'd stolen the emerald, so its power backfired on you.' Libby rolled the stone in her hands. 'It sent Jack away.'

Patrick shook his head. 'Enough of the Wicca crap. Did you push her down the stairs, Grace?'

'No!' She started crying again.

Oh for fuck's sake.

'But you left her,' he said. 'Why did you leave her there? You could've taken the pendant and still called for help.'

'I... I was scared.' Grace wiped at her eyes. 'People might know I took it.'

How could this be happening?

'What do we do now?' Libby asked, her voice so quiet he barely heard her.

Grace's eyes implored him, begging him to pretend none of it had happened. Libby's moralistic frown said the opposite. Oh Christ, this wasn't the time for Libby's honesty. He loved her moral values and her innate desire to do the right thing, but not when it came to Grace. How often had Grace bailed him out, covered for him? Was this his chance to repay her?

'Look,' he said, hoping Libby would understand, 'she didn't hurt Maggie. She just took the pendant. You can give it back to Zoë. No harm done.'

'But you can't just ignore—'

'Grace isn't a bad person.'

Libby turned to face out of the window, clearly unhappy. 'This is wrong.'

'I'm sorry,' Grace sobbed. 'After you gave me the retribution spell, I couldn't keep the pendant any more. And look what happened with you. The summoning spell backfired big style. I give up.'

'What the hell's a summoning spell anyway? Is this to invoke the devil or something weird?' Patrick asked, but Grace went back to picking at the loose thread and Libby carried on staring out of the window.

All this over a stupid spell? None of it was even real. Libby stepped onto the table underneath the window, still peering outside. Oh Christ, now he had two deranged women on his hands.

'Libs, what are you doing?'

Libby pointed to the other side of the Green, towards their houses. 'The angle's not quite right, but this is where the photos were taken from, the ones of me with Xander and Robbie.' She turned to Grace. 'Did you take them from upstairs?'

Grace blanched.

Libby stepped down, staring at Grace. 'You gave them the evidence to call me a prostitute. Why?'

Grace raised her chin. 'You shagged Jack.'

Libby shook her head. 'This started before then.'

'Money. I have a hefty mortgage and Wray pays well. You and Jack were only worth a hundred quid, but the ones from Halloween? Five hundred. You and Xander, two hundred. You and Robbie, four.' Grace glanced from Libby to Patrick. 'There's a grand for a photo of you two together.'

Fuck. 'Did you take photos of me?' Patrick barely dared ask.

Grace nibbled her thumbnail, but nodded. There were no more tears.

'The ones with Miss Haverton in the park?'

'No. That was one of Miss Haverton's friends. Emma somebody.'

Emma? No wonder he'd been smiling at the camera. She'd joined in five minutes later. 'But the others? Tabitha Doyle? Lucy Errington?'

Another nod. 'What I don't sell to him, or he didn't dare print, I... put on the website.'

The website? Patrick leapt to his feet, backing away from Grace, scared he might hit her.

'You're the fucking Wraydar?' *You've ruined my life. I might lose everything because of you.*

'Why did you do it, Grace?' Libby asked.

'I just told you.'

'No. Why did you do it to Patrick? You two are friends.'

Grace stared at her.

'Grace?' he whispered.

'That's right.' She laughed. 'Friends.'

His heart stopped. *Please don't let this be about me.*

'Who did you really want to summon with the emerald?' Libby asked, her arms folded. 'Was it Jack, or was it someone tall, dark and good with animals?'

'Yeah, well,' Grace spat. 'It backfired, didn't it?'

Patrick slumped against the wall, his eyes closed, his head in his hands. Ten minutes. If he'd just had another ten minutes with Libby... Why did she have to open Grace's stupid gift? They could've been on their way to his house, or hers, and this wouldn't be happening.

No. This was his fault. This was his fault for something that happened almost a year ago, on Christmas Eve. The thing was, though he'd woken up in Grace's bed, he hadn't the faintest idea what that something was. He could make a pretty good guess, but they'd been so wasted, he couldn't remember a thing and on Christmas Day, they'd agreed to pretend nothing had ever happened.

'Libs, can you–' He glanced up but she was already heading out of the door.

'Just go with her, Patrick.' Grace said, wiping her eyes.

'Come here, you idiot.' He pulled her to her feet and wrapped his arms around her, resting his head on hers.

* * *

Libby closed the front door and walked away, her heart hammering. Grace loved him. Why hadn't she seen it before? It was so obvious. She'd do anything for him. How long had poor Grace loved what she couldn't have? *Poor Grace?* The cow had sold her out and left Maggie in a heap at the bottom of the stairs. That's right, poor, poor Grace.

Libby marched back to the pub, resisting the temptation to bolt home. She owed it to her friends, the ones who'd planned a surprise party for her – she owed it to them to put on a brave face and enjoy her birthday party.

What if Patrick loved Grace? Grace was pretty, sexy and one of his best friends. What if he was kissing her, discarding her cardigan, peeling off her top?

In a corner of the bar, Zoë and Jack were chatting. Perfect. Libby joined them.

'Where did you and the hot vet go?' Zoë asked, raising her eyebrows.

'Nothing like that, thank you. I have a gift for you.' Libby stole a sip of Zoë's Bacardi and soda before holding up the emerald pendant.

'Fuck me, is that Maggie's?' Zoë snatched it, her eyes sparkling for the first time in weeks. Maybe this would get her over Jonathan. 'Where did you get it?'

'Found it in the garden.'

Jack gave a derisory laugh. 'Liar.'

'Let's just say, someone borrowed it and now they want to return it.'

'Who?' Zoë asked, still eyeing the stone as a mother would a newborn baby.

Libby paused, watching for Jack's reaction. 'Grace.'

'Did Grace *borrow* it out of Maggie's cold dead hands?' Zoë's eyes narrowed as she studied Libby.

'Yes.' Libby frowned. Jack hadn't even flinched. 'You knew?'

Slowly, he nodded. 'What are you going to do?'

'Nothing,' Zoë said firmly. 'There is no crime. I lost it and now I've found it. Didn't Sheila say this thing was worth twenty-five grand?'

Libby nodded.

'Then it's settled.' Zoë held up the emerald, her eyes flashing with pound signs. 'If the police get involved, this baby will be tied up forever and it's so going on eBay tonight.'

'But Zo–'

'Bloody ugly thing. Are they hieroglyphics?'

Libby nodded, despairing. Why was it that no one ever wanted to do the right thing?

'I'll be back in a bit,' Zoë said, already standing up. 'I have to know if monstrosities like this actually sell.'

Appropriating Zoë's abandoned drink, Libby sat back and sighed. 'How messed up is this Maggie thing?'

'Very. Some kind of birthday this is turning out to be for you.' Jack chinked his glass against hers, shaking his head. 'Is he still with Grace?'

'Yes.' She glanced at the door, willing Patrick to come back. 'They've a few issues to sort out. It turns out she's…'

'Been in love with him since they started working together?'

'You already know?'

'Last Christmas…' Jack frowned. 'I'd gone on a stag weekend. They ended up in here, E'd up.'

'Did they…' The tea, wine, Bacardi and birthday cake churned in her stomach as Jack nodded.

'And sure enough, he fucked off the next day like it'd never happened.' He frowned at her, utterly serious. 'Don't mess around with him.'

Libby wanted a cigarette more than she had in the month since she'd given up. Patrick had slept with Grace and now he knew Grace was in love with him. Was that why he hadn't come back? Was it time for round two?

* * *

One thousand pounds for a single photo.

Patrick left Grace's at nine o'clock, as Scott and Clara were leaving the pub. He glanced through the window, but couldn't see any candyfloss pink hair. In fact only Zoë and Jack remained in the pub from the birthday party. At least Libby hadn't buggered off with him again.

'Where the hell have you been?' Scott asked.

'Grace's. Had some–' He shook his head, dragging Scott away from Clara's gossip-mongering ears. 'It doesn't matter. Where is she?'

'Gone home. It's fair to say she was shitfaced.'

Patrick swore. 'What happened?'

'She drank a lot of wine. Did you know she can play the piano? She also does a very good Lady Gaga impression and can do pirouette things with a shot of vodka in each hand and one on her head. That girl has some top party tricks.'

Patrick perched on one of the outside tables, staring at the dark windows at Maggie's cottage. 'When did she go?'

'Hour ago. Xander had to carry her home.'

Patrick folded his arms, desperate not to show his jealousy. Bloody Xander.

'Did you tell her?' Scott asked.

'Didn't get chance.'

'Well, you've missed your opportunity tonight.' Scott clapped his back. 'Gotta go.'

'Night, pal.'

Patrick wandered across the Green. One thousand pounds. A grand for a photo. Grace wasn't the only source of Michael Wray's photos, which meant she wouldn't be the only person looking to catch him and Libby together. Even if they kept it quiet, they'd get busted sooner or later. People got lax. Look what happened to her and Robbie. It couldn't happen.

He had to leave. There was nothing in the rules about where he had to be. He could go to Sam's, keep his head down and come back in June. Maybe she'd wait, or maybe she'd have moved on, but that was a risk he'd have to take. He wasn't prepared to risk his entire life.

He wandered past his own house, down the lane to her garden. Maybe she'd be sobering up with a mug of tea. She wasn't. Sod it. He crossed the lawn. Okay, this was borderline stalker territory. There were no lights on in the house. This would be classed as breaking and entering. Or checking she's okay, not choking on her own vomit. A public service really. He smiled at himself. No, this was stalking. He wanted her to be awake.

'Libby?' he called softly, not wanting to freak her out. 'Libs?'

In the living room, she lay curled up and unconscious on the sofa, her hair covering her face. Trust Xander to do a half-arsed job of taking a girl to bed. Hyssop sat at her feet, watching over her as Patrick lifted her hair off her face. Still breathing. Still wearing her biking gear. Christ, that seemed a week ago. He should go, but he rubbed Hyssop's chin. Libby didn't look very comfortable. He could put her to bed.

This had to be the lamest tactic ever. When he picked her up, would she wake up?

'Libs?' He gently shook her shoulder. 'Libs, you need to go to bed.'

No response. She wasn't waking up. He sighed, disappointment coursing through him, but scooped her up. She was as light as a feather. Carefully, he picked his way around the furniture and headed upstairs. Her head lolled against his shoulder. How the hell did she still smell... pretty? She hadn't had a shower after the ride. Neither had he, but he bet he didn't smell like an English summer's day. There was something odd about the roses.

A stair creaked and she stirred, wrapping her arms around his neck. Oh, this was a bad idea. Her fingers laced into his hair at the back of his neck. A very bad idea.

'...must be dreaming...' she mumbled.

'Yes, you're dreaming. Go back to sleep.' Was this the kind of dream she had? He quite liked it.

It wasn't difficult to tell which bedroom was whose. The first one he came to smelled of that bloody awful, cloying perfume Zoë wore and high heels were scattered around the floor. In the other room, several books were piled up on the bedside table, photos of horses were stuck to the dressing table mirror and it smelled of roses and sweet peas.

He laid her down, drawing the line at even the idea of removing any clothes to make her more comfortable. Gently he stroked her hair back.

'Night, princess.'

He kissed her, barely brushing his lips against hers. But sleeping beauty didn't wake.

She was a habit. An addiction.

Chapter Thirty-Two

Wrapped in a thick ruby red cashmere blanket her mother had sent for her birthday, Libby curled up on the bench in the garden, trying to read *The Crucible* by the light from the kitchen window, but her only real mission was to survive until bedtime. Her headache had gone, but her slightly queasy stomach remained despite a bowl of Zoë's all-curing chicken noodle soup. Eight o'clock, surely she could go to bed at nine.

'You have a message.' Zoë came out, carrying Libby's phone.

Libby struggled not to giggle, or die of relief. After over a month of malaise, her Zoë was back. She'd cocooned her hair in a conditioning treatment, her face was smothered in a mud mask – it was as if the emerald had worked some kind of magic.

'It's from your boyfriend,' Zoë added, blatantly reading the message.

'I haven't got a boyfriend.'

'Okay, your friend who's a boy, you know the one you don't get to shag, it's from him. *Need a drink. You busy?*'

Libby snatched the phone. Crikey, it really was from Patrick. What was wrong? What on earth had happened the day before? All day, she'd not been able to dismiss a silly thought that he'd carried her home. But it was wishful thinking. Xander had carried her home. She vaguely remembered that.

Just in garden. Come round?

How many minutes did she have? Two, ten, twenty? She sprinted into the house already stripping off her tatty old exercise clothes, her comfort clothes. What to wear? With no idea how long she had, she couldn't waste time choosing. Jeans, a snug black jumper, a squirt of perfume and two layers of mascara on top of the three she'd applied that morning. Sadly, the oversized beanie she'd been wearing all day had made her fringe stick out at seventeen different angles. She clipped it back and pulled the hat back on. She'd have to do.

With only seconds to spare, she sat back down on the bench and picked up her book.

'Why are you sitting out here? It's freezing.' Patrick stood leaning on the gate, a bottle in his hand. 'You do realise that book's upside down.'

Arse. 'Come in. I have a new, super warm blanket.'

'This...' he said, holding up the bottle, 'is totally against the rules, but I've had a very, very bad day.'

The bottle wasn't wine. It looked like whisky. 'What's up?'

'I'm prepared to drink straight from the bottle, but since it's a thirty-one year-old Laphroaig, we ought to give it the dignity of a glass.'

We? Libby couldn't bear the thought of a glass of wine. Neat whisky might actually make her sick. She didn't like the stuff at the best of times. As Patrick wandered across the lawn, she ducked inside for two tumblers, hoping to avoid drinking any of the rancid stuff.

'Sorry for just turning up,' he said, 'but I don't drink at home and with a thousand pound bounty on my head–'

'*Our* heads. You're only worth five hundred by yourself.'

He gave a hollow laugh as he added an inch of amber liquid to each of the glasses. 'I'm fairly sure you're hung-over to hell and really don't want this, but as hair of the dog, it kicks arse.'

'I'll give it a go, but I'm not promising anything.'

He remained leaning forwards, his elbows on his knees. 'Do you ever just watch TV?'

'Never have. Too busy dancing or thinking about dancing or talking about dancing. I'd rather read a book out here.' She curled up. 'What's up?'

'Once, you asked if I liked being a vet. Well today, I don't.' He rubbed his forehead.

'Did something die?'

'Baxter, my dog.'

Oh, the friendly collie.

'I was sixteen when I got him as a puppy. He was my dog, but he ended up living with Mum and Dad when I moved back here. I was too busy having fun to look after him.'

Libby put a hand on his back, comforting him. For a second, he glanced back at her, his eyes sparkling with tears.

'I put him down this afternoon, Libs.' He took a deep, shaky breath. 'He was old and in pain. Dad was in Kendal and Fergus was on call, so I told them I'd do it. There's no way Mum could have. I said it wasn't a problem; I said I could do it. I could and I did, but I shouldn't have because it *was* a problem. I feel like I've murdered my own dog.'

Without stopping to think, she pulled him to her, wrapping her arms around his shoulders. His head rested against hers, his eyes firmly closed. Silence filled the air, but he didn't pull away. For minutes, he let her hug him and she mindlessly twirled one of his curls around her finger. God, he had lovely hair.

'Have you tried the whisky yet?' he asked, apparently not worried by her obsessive twirling.

'Is it compulsory?'

He nodded. 'It'll warm you up. It really is freezing out here.'

She laughed, throwing the blanket over their legs. It was like being in bed together – a massive step forward. 'Okay, I did say I'd give it a go.'

The neat alcohol burned, but the taste was smoother than she'd expected and even with her raging hangover, not unpleasant.

Patrick smiled at her then stretched out his legs, relaxing back, his shoulder resting against hers. 'Christ, it's been a fucking awful day, and not just Baxter. That was just the icing to finish it off.'

'Grace?' Libby asked, braving another sip for something to do.

Patrick nodded.

'Jack told me what happened last Christmas.'

Patrick knocked back the rest of his whisky. 'Yeah, so this is partly my fault, but I had no idea that all this time, she's... Anyway, she wants to take the practice manager job at the Haverton surgery, Fee's old job. It's the right thing. She'll get the promotion she deserves and they'll get the person who should've been doing it for a year. The downside is I get stuck with Hannah, who can't make coffee to save her life.'

Libby laughed and pulled her feet up to sit cross-legged. It didn't sound as though he was seeing Grace. If he was, he'd be sitting in her garden, not Libby's. Why was he here? Why come here when he had a bad day? She shifted slightly, her knee now almost touching his thigh. He refilled his glass.

'What happened last night?' she asked.

'I'm sorry she ruined your birthday.'

'It wasn't ruined.' *But it would've been a million times better with you there.* 'I had a great day. I loved the bike ride. Thank you for looking after me.'

He smiled down at her, her knee now touching his leg. Had he moved his leg, or she her knee?

'You should be very proud,' he said. 'You had your eyes open the whole time.'

Thank God, it was dark and he couldn't see her blushing. 'Maybe not the whole time.'

'I'm sorry I didn't get back to the party.'

Libby shrugged. 'You two needed to talk.'

'Well, mostly, I needed to delete every photo she had in the house and get the passwords to take that fucking website down. The Haverton Eye is now offline.' He shook his head. 'The photos she had of people, on her phone, on her PC, they're unbelievable. She actually has a camera on a tripod in her bedroom.'

He was in Grace's bedroom? Libby drained her glass. Was he here because he and Libby were *friends* now? 'You two get along very well. Aren't you tempted to give it a go?'

'With Grace? Are you kidding? Libs, she almost ruined my life. She still might. Besides...' He laughed into his glass before taking another sip.

'What?'

'I'm not interested in Grace.' He turned away, fighting a smile. 'And I never will be.'

Did that mean her liked her? Trying to hide her own grin, Libby held out her glass. 'It's working. The whisky.'

'What on?'

'My hangover.' She swatted his arm. Unadulterated, blatant flirting. 'And it actually tastes... okay.'

'Good girl.' He added a little more to her glass. 'So, did you give the emerald to Zoë?'

'Of course.'

'And did you tell her it was Grace's?'

She nodded. 'But Zoë couldn't care less who borrowed it. She's got it on eBay already. The *Buy It Now* price is twenty grand.'

'Thanks. Seriously, I could kill Grace right now, but she's saved my neck more than a few times. I owe her.' Patrick relaxed again, his body edging closer still to hers. 'Now, what's this I hear about you playing piano and doing party tricks?'

She groaned, but couldn't hold back a smile. When she'd woken that morning, memories had flooded back and she'd wailed into her pillow but now, sitting with Patrick, she laughed, uncaring, because her knee was resting on his thigh and his arm lay on her knee. He refilled her glass and she explained how, after a few too many glasses of wine, her tendency to show off stopped being quite so latent.

'Get another glass,' he said, nudging her. 'I want to see the three-shot spinning trick.'

She laughed. 'Not a chance. I'd fall over if I tried it today.'

'Spoilsport.'

'Hey, so Daisy said I could keep her bike for a while.'

'Want to go for a ride sometime?'

'Promise not to kill me?'

He pulled a face. 'There is the custody issue, but okay.'

Snuggled under the blanket, they relived the ride, laughing at the time she forgot to unclip her feet and fell sideways, taking out him and Scott. Libby sat back, still giggling, her head against the sofa. Hot Patrick was here. This was it, the night something would happen.

An hour later, Libby put her empty glass down. She'd managed to knock back three refills. Her hangover had vanished, but now she was a little tipsy again. Patrick turned to her. She smiled at him. He smiled back.

'It's late. I'd better go.' He screwed the top on the less than half-full bottle and handed it to her. 'So I don't get tempted to drink the rest.'

Though clearly cold, he'd never once suggested they go inside. Instead, he seemed happy to sit in the garden, huddled under the blanket with her.

'Do you really want to go?' Her words were barely more than a whisper, but they made his smile disappear.

Slowly, he shook his head and pushed a strand of her fringe back under her hat. Libby gazed at him, a smile teetering as the distance between them shrank. He kissed her. Patrick kissed her. His lips lingered and without hesitation, Libby kissed him back. Slow, deep, it was gentle for a second, but demanding the next. And he could demand all he wanted, because she was prepared to demand right back. She clutched his jacket as he held her face, his fingers brushing her neck.

Why were they doing this outside where it was bloody freezing? They should be inside, wearing a lot less clothes. No. Robbie always told her to play hard to get. This was one occasion she would stick to her morals. Her morals evaporated when Patrick's hand drifted down, stroking a thumb down her neck, making her tip her head back, catching her breath.

'Do you think,' she said, still gripping his jacket, 'if we send Michael Wray the photo ourselves, he'll still cough up the thousand pounds?'

Patrick's hands dropped and cold air replaced his hot body.

'It was a joke,' she said. *Kiss me again.*

He simply stared at her, his emotions unreadable.

'Patrick?' Oh why did she stop kissing him?

He leant forwards, resting his elbows on his knees, not looking at all like he wanted to kiss her again. Was this the ultimate in Hot and Cold? Kissing her then regretting it? But god, he'd just kissed her and she wanted more, much more. Didn't he?

'What?' she whispered.

'I can't do this,' he said, still staring at the floor. 'I've got to go.'

He was leaving? He kissed her like that and he was just leaving? 'Why?'

'I'm sorry, Libby. I think you're... but I can't do this. I can't be your distraction.'

She blinked. 'Déjà vu.'

He closed his eyes, swearing. 'I thought you were asleep.'

'It was real?' she asked.

He cringed and nodded. It wasn't a dream. He really had said he couldn't be a distraction. He really had kissed her.

'You kissed me, but after that,' she whispered, 'you avoided me for weeks.'

'I had my reasons.'

She stifled a scream as she stood up, striding across the patio. 'And last night? Was that a dream?'

With his eyes still closed, he shook his head. 'I wanted to make sure you were okay. Scott said you were wasted. I just carried you upstairs.'

He'd come into the house. He'd taken her up to bed. Was he some weird pervert? 'And then what?'

'Nothing.' He held up his hands, finally facing her. 'I was trying to be nice. It's like I can't stop looking out for you.'

She raked her hair back. 'I can't take any more of this.'

'Libs...'

'Four months you've been doing this, four bloody months. You'll be my best-friend one minute, kissing me when you think I'm asleep, taking me to see Jane, hanging out in the garden, all the nice things that made me think... And then bam! You walk out of the pub, and refuse to speak to me when I come to say thank you, and...' *What about Halloween?* 'But this has to be the showstopper in your hot and cold routine.'

He stared at the floor, but her tears loomed. He'd rejected her, twice.

'Your best friend told me to stay the hell away from you,' she said, trying not to sob. 'I should've bloody listened.'

She headed for the door, but he jumped up, grabbing her arm.

'Libs, please don't run off.' He dropped his head to whisper in her ear, 'I'm sorry if I've fucked you around.'

'Then why do you keep doing it?' She stared straight ahead, determined to resist him, but his lips were against her cheek.

'Because I'm finding it impossible to stay away from you, and I have to.'

'Why?'

'Look, I have my—'

'Don't you dare.' She spun around, pressing her hand against his chest to keep him away. 'Don't you dare say you've got your bloody reasons. I don't care about your bloody reasons. You had your chance, you blew it in October. I'm really sorry about Baxter and Grace and I'm sorry you're having a really bad day, but...' She leaned up to whisper in his ear, using the words he'd crucified her with on Halloween. 'Patrick, you need to leave. Please.'

And just like he'd done, she pushed him away.

'Libs...'

'Whatever you're imagining in your pretty little head, it's never going to happen.' She ran into the house, slamming the door, her tears already falling.

Why did he keep doing this to her? Why couldn't they go out together? What was so wrong with her? Was he ashamed of her? He couldn't like her, not really. If he did, he wouldn't mess her around like this.

Slumping against the hallway wall, she willed him to come in, to explain. Had she overreacted? Probably. But one minute they were laughing over her squealing down the bridleway from Lum Crag, the next he was kissing her. God, that had to be the all-time greatest kiss. She closed her eyes, reliving every moment. How his hands held her face, his fingers in her hair, his stubble on her skin, and when his thumb brushed down her neck. She shivered. If she hadn't stopped the kiss, they'd have ended up in bed. They could be in bed. Why the hell had she stopped kissing him?

She'd overreacted. She should go back out. Apologise.

Whatever you're imagining in your pretty little head isn't going to happen.

No, this was self-preservation. He didn't want to go out with her. He just wanted a sympathy shag because he was feeling down. That's how much he thought of her. She was just another Grace. Hadn't she learned anything? She'd been warned, told that he was trouble, that he'd break her heart, and oh look, job done.

No, he'd said he couldn't stay away from her. He liked her. She knew he did, but he had to stay away from her. She stifled another sob. If he had reasons not to want to be with her then he wasn't her Somebody, because her Somebody would forget their reasons. She'd forget all rational thought for him.

The chicken noodle soup, whisky and desolation churned in her stomach. She bolted to the bathroom just in time to throw up.

* * *

He could go after her, make her listen, but listen to what? He couldn't tell her what he was prepared to tell her the day before. He couldn't tell her about the ultimatum anymore. He couldn't tell her the truth because several other people had their fingers on a shutter button, dying to catch the two of them together. And if they got a photograph, Wray would make up a story and they'd be front page news. He'd lose his job, his parents' respect, everything. All for a thousand pounds. He'd pay five grand for anyone with a camera to piss off and leave them alone.

Why did he have to kiss her? Kissing her had screwed up everything. Fuck. He'd kissed her because the woollen hat had hidden the pink fringe and the dark had disguised the black eye make-up. She'd sat there looking more than pretty. She looked adorable, beautiful and, Christ, she tasted even sweeter than she looked.

The girl was amazing, but if they went out, they'd be busted by Wray's trigger happy fortune hunters. He rested his head against the door. Did it matter? What would he rather lose, everything or Libby? This was crazy. How could he be thinking of sacrificing everything for a girl with pink hair and a teenager's wardrobe?

Christ, he'd never seen her angry. Had he really messed her around that much? *Whatever you're imagining in your pretty little head isn't going to happen.* Yeah, he'd messed her around that much.

The kitchen was in darkness, no movement inside. He wanted to apologise, but he had no idea how to make it better. He knew it would be a mistake coming here, but he'd wanted a shoulder to cry on and there was nowhere else he wanted to be.

Jesus, did he want to go out with her, to have a *relationship*? He shuddered at the word. No. This was a mistake, a fucking big mistake. He should never have listened to Scott.

Sod it. He kicked a gnome off the patio steps and strode away. The worst day ever had got much, much worse, but he'd left the whisky on the table. Why could no one see that he'd changed?

Chapter Thirty-Three

On stage, Annalise as the Sugar Plum Fairy paused in an arabesque before sinking into a low curtsey to rapturous applause. Hardly a flawless performance, but impressive for a sixteen year-old. Libby longed to kick her off the stage and show them all how it should be done, but that wasn't her job. She ushered the girls off the stage, telling them to shush, while Jane sent on the next batch.

Twenty years ago, Libby had been in her first ballet. She'd played a mouse and watched the Sugar Plum Fairy with awe. That was what made her want to be a ballerina. Did she really want to teach *Good Toes, Bad Toes* to five year-olds? This wasn't how her life was supposed to be. She was supposed to be on stage, executing thirty-two perfect *fouettés* in her role as Odile. She wasn't supposed to be babysitting five year-olds.

And yet she couldn't stop smiling.

The second act flew by all too quickly and soon she was sitting downstairs, surrounded by the four to six year-olds she'd been coaching, all trying to sit on her knee, play with her hair and find out how brilliant they were.

'You were awesome,' she said to them. 'You all tried really hard and should be super-duper proud of yourselves. Now, get your coats on, quick quick.'

They really had worked hard and they'd maintained their concentration for a whole ballet, which was more than could be said for a few of the dads in the audience who'd slept through most of the second act, Robbie included. When the last of the kids had been collected, abandoned ballet slippers and scrunchies tided into a box, Libby quickly changed from her practical backstage clothes into a slinky black top she'd appropriated from Zoë's wardrobe, faux-leather jeans and high heels. With another three layers of eye shadow and two of mascara, she was ready for a night out in Haverton.

'You look fabulous,' Jane said, poking her head around the door. 'Now come on. They want to lock up.'

After a final squirt of perfume, Libby followed Jane through the empty auditorium, her hand brushing over the seats as she passed them.

'Do you miss it?' Libby asked. 'Performing, I mean.'

'I used to, but it's over thirty years since I last danced on stage.' Jane smiled. 'These days I get a much bigger kick out of watching girls I've taught since they were four performing a lead role with confidence.'

'Annalise was brilliant.'

'You know, we don't always do the Nutcracker. Maybe we'll do Swan Lake next year. You'd make the perfect Odette-Odile.'

'Aren't the students supposed to dance?'

'Technically, you are a student.'

'I'm a bit old compared to the rest.'

'Experienced. Maggie made me perform it when I came here.' Jane checked her watch. 'Do you need a lift? My friend Liz will be here in a minute.'

'No, I'm going to Oscar's for Xander's birthday. A well-earned mojito is on the cards. Do you think she died happy? Maggie I mean.'

'Happ*ier*, maybe.' Jane tightened her scarf against the biting cold. 'She was a bitch to work for, but I've a lot to thank her for. She helped me get out of an abusive marriage and she mellowed as she got older, accepted things the way they were.'

'That she couldn't perform anymore?' Was there hope for Libby too?

But Jane gave a quiet laugh. 'She wasn't bitter because she couldn't dance. She was thirty-five when she had that accident. Her career was already over. It gave her a massive payout and the opportunity to move up here.'

And be with Seamus. Libby hesitated, wanting to know more. Didn't Daisy say that Jane, like Clara, loved to gossip? Libby decided to play dumb. 'Why did she want to move up here? It is a bit of a cultural leap from Covent Garden.'

Jane's eyes glinted, the bait taken. 'Well, not everyone knows, but between me and you, she's had the most passionate affair with Seamus Doyle.'

'The poet?' Libby widened her eyes, pretending to look shocked.

'Went on for over forty years.' Jane checked her watch again. 'He was living up here, and when she moved up, she assumed he'd leave his wife. He didn't.'

'Poor Maggie.' Seemed the right answer.

'That's why she was bitter. She blamed the world for him choosing Lucinda, but eventually they settled into this odd relationship, together as much as his marriage would allow. I think he truly loved her and she accepted that a little of him was better than none. It was the only weakness I ever saw her show. At least he was there the day she died.'

Libby tucked her hair behind her ear, desperately trying not to look shocked. 'He was?'

Again, Jane's eyes twinkled with gossip. 'I'm sure it's nothing, but Maggie did say he was staying the week. No one seemed to see him in Gosthwaite after she died though. I suppose he must've left the day before...'

Had Seamus been there that night? Libby flashed a smile, hiding her intrigue. Wouldn't it be interesting to have a chat with Mr Doyle? 'I heard Maggie said Gosthwaite's where ballerinas come to die.'

Jane laughed. 'I've always said it's where we come to live. I've made a good life here, Libby, and so did Maggie. You can too, if you want to. You just need to work out what you want to do.'

'I *think* I want to teach.'

Jane smiled. 'You're a natural. The kids love you.'

'It's funny. Not long ago, little kids terrified me.'

'At the moment it'd only be late afternoons and early evenings, but the pay's not bad.'

Jane was offering her a job? Libby didn't know how to react. Surely if she were to teach she'd do it in London, with real dancers? That's where she belonged.

'But the studio's empty in the mornings.' Jane waved as the lights of a Land Rover came into view. 'Clara's always saying I should do adult dance classes. You could run those?'

Back to Ballet for yummy mummies in the morning and *Good Toes, Bad Toes* in the evenings – was that really how she wanted to spend the rest of her life?

'Think about it,' Jane said as the car pulled up.

'I will,' Libby said. *I really will.* 'Thank you.'

Libby hugged Jane goodnight, as the driver wound down a window. The woman had untidy dark grey hair and glasses perched on her head.

'Hello, Libby,' she said, smiling.

Libby blinked, trying to work out if she knew the woman.

'Oh, Liz, this is Olivia Wilde. Libby, this is Elizabeth McBride.'

'It's nice to meet you, finally,' Liz said, holding out her hand. 'I've heard so much about you.'

Scottish accent... McBride... Was this Patrick's mother? Libby managed a smile. Had Patrick told his mother about her?

'Jane's always telling me how marvellous you are. I'd love to see you dance.'

Jane had told her, not Patrick. Libby's forced smile grew as she stepped away. 'I'm retired, I'm afraid.'

The temperature outside might be near freezing, but inside a tinsel and bauble festooned Oscar's Bar and Bistro, it had to be twenty-five degrees. Libby stripped off her coat, wishing she'd worn a skirt, not leather bloody jeans. Zoë's text said she was in the Judge's Chamber, a side room where Xander was holding his cocktail party. What Zoë's text failed to mention was that she was sharing a jug of Long Island Iced Tea with Robbie, Scott and Patrick. Arse.

Twelve days. Twelve days since he'd kissed her and she'd seen nothing of him. Back to cold Patrick. The pattern was easy to spot now, but she missed him. They were friends and just when more looked promising, he ripped the crazy paving from under her.

Sitting on tall stools around a high table, they overlooked the rest of the room, clearly the best seats in the house, but then Robbie practically owned the place. Libby hovered in the doorway. Clara, Daisy and Vanessa were behind the bar, being shown how to mix cosmos by Tom the barman. She could scarper and send a message saying she'd gone home, citing a headache. Too late, Xander spotted her and yelled her name. Arse. As he released her from a bear hug, Libby eyed the table.

Which side of Zoë should she opt for, the one by Robbie, risking pissing his wife off, or the one by Patrick, risking... god only knows what? Robbie gave a huge grin as she walked up, but Patrick focussed on his pint, his jaw twitching. Robbie it was.

'Why are you doing this to me?' she whispered, hugging Zoë hello.

'I bumped into Scott on my way in,' Zoë whispered back. 'He insisted.'

'Can we not bump into them on the way to the bar?'

'Oh, get over it. Patrick looks hot. You should so fuck him.'

'It's all I'd get to do.' Libby wiggled her fingers, waving at Vanessa, who watched with a worried frown from across the bar. 'Can we sit somewhere else?'

'No,' Zoë snapped, checking her watch.

'When you've finished whispering,' Robbie said, smiling and pushing a vast highball glass towards her. 'Careful, it's rocket fuel, but after sitting through seventeen hours of ballet, I bloody deserve it.'

Libby swatted his arm. 'It was only ninety minutes.'

'The longest ninety minutes of my life.' Robbie shot her a wink, making her laugh and Patrick finally looked up, but with no hint of a smile.

In a beautifully ironed, black and grey striped shirt, he looked like some girlfriend with excellent taste shopped for him – a far cry from the threadbare jeans and tatty t-shirt he'd worn on their non-date. Nice jeans too. And shoes. Libby turned away, looking for a distraction.

She found one.

Bugger.

'Zo, Silver Fox at five o'clock.'

Zoë's head shot around, but Jonathan loitered at the bar, merely watching her. Libby admired his composure.

'You okay, Zo?' Libby asked as quietly as she could over the chattering crowd.

Zoë flashed a sweet smile. 'How was the ballet?'

'Good. Odd.' Libby frowned, bemused by the hold this guy had on Zoë. It just wasn't Zoë's style. 'I had to stop myself from sabotaging the Sugar Plum Fairy so I could take her place. You should've come.'

Zoë mimed stabbing herself in the heart and Patrick leant forwards, beckoning her closer so he could whisper something. As she did, she put her elbows on the table, a tried and tested trick to make her already fabulous cleavage look like the Grand Canyon. What was worse, Zoë flirting with Patrick or Patrick blatantly appreciating two of the wonders of the natural world?

But Libby's insecurity evaporated as Zoë glanced to Jonathan for the third time in a minute. She took Zoë's arm, tugging her away from Patrick.

'You told him you'd be here, didn't you? And you're flirting with Patrick to make Jonathan jealous, aren't you?'

'No.'

Libby nipped her.

'Maybe.'

She nipped again.

'Okay, yes.' Zoë bent her head to Libby's. 'Look, he messaged me earlier asking to meet up, but I said I was going out and unless he wanted punishing, he'd better leave me alone.'

'So basically, you told him to meet you here.'

'I miss him.'

'Last week you hated him because he'd screwed Maggie.'

'And that's beyond skanky, but...' Zoë glanced across at him. 'Just think what I can get out of him as punishment.'

'Zo, that's not—'

'I miss the sex, okay? The guy's freaking hot. Speaking of which...' Zoë leaned in to Libby. 'Patrick's so hot for you. His face when you came in. You know you're all cigar butts and silk, right?'

Zoë's words faded as Jonathan strode over. Libby sipped her drink, expecting trouble, but Jonathan simply stood against the next table, a few feet from them, watching. Wow. For an older guy, Libby would. And considering his submissive tastes, he had quite a commanding air. Zoë closed her lips around the straw in her glass, slowly sucking until nothing more than crushed ice remained. Jonathan didn't move.

'What?' Zoë asked, stepping towards him and folding her arms.

'I'd like to talk to you, Miss Horton,' Jonathan said.

'Fuck you,' Zoë said, but her words lacked any bitterness.

'I love you.' Jonathan tugged her arms free, pulling her closer. 'And I want you back.'

Libby sipped her drink, trying not to let her jealousy show. Not that she fancied Jonathan, but why couldn't she meet a guy willing to declare his feelings like that. Robbie, Patrick and Scott all leaned on the table, blatantly listening in.

'You've lost too much weight.' Jonathan looked Zoë over, his face filling with concern.

'It's been a tough time... emotionally. Your fault.'

'I'm sorry.' Jonathan said, slipping one arm around her waist. 'How would you like me to make it up to you?'

'I want a present, a small glittery present.'

He held her tighter, his hand slipping down to caress her bum. 'I have the perfect one in mind.'

'Which is?' Zoë asked with faked indifference.

Robbie, Patrick, Scott and Libby all leaned closer, trying to listen.

'An engagement ring. Marry me.'

Libby choked on her drink, mercifully rescued by several

backslaps from Robbie. Surely, Zoë wouldn't consider this. She'd known Jonathan for less than six months. And his wife had just died. And Zoë *really* liked their son.

'Okay,' Zoë said, nodding.

Libby stared at Zoë. Her best friend had just agreed to marry a guy thirty years older than her, and she'd said yes as casually as she would if he'd asked if she wanted parmesan on her pasta. Zoë only betrayed her nonchalant appearance when Jonathan led her away and she shot a triumphant wink to Libby.

It was all Libby could do not to cry. How had everything gone so wrong again? Zoë would move out, sell the cottage and what would Libby be left with? Teaching *Good Toes, Bad Toes* to yummy mummies.

* * *

Patrick watched, mildly amused as Libby drained her glass. Clearly she wasn't happy about Zoë's gold-digging victory, but maybe this could work to his advantage. If Libby were upset, maybe it'd give him the opportunity to apologise, make friends, or something.

Or something? Christ, he could go for a bit of *something*. She wasn't wearing a bra. Not that her perfect breasts needed one, but to see the silk top draped over her nipples was distracting to say the least. Robbie had noticed too. And several blokes nearby. Patrick wanted to punch one particularly lecherous arse.

Despite being braless, wearing more black eye make-up than ever, twenty bangles on each wrist, skinny leather jeans and fuck-me heels, she exuded more class than any other girl in the bar. Zoë, in a clinging red dress, looked like a New York hooker in comparison. Patrick raised his eyebrows to Scott, who nodded, getting the unspoken message and dragged Robbie off to the bar.

Shaking her head, Libby grabbed her coat and bag.

'Where are you going?' Patrick asked. *Fuck, fuck, fuck. Don't go. Stay and drink. We'll go later. Together.*

'Home. And I'm not speaking to you.' She flicked her hair off her shoulder, wafting her perfume his way.

His off-switch fused.

Patrick knocked back his whisky fully aware old habits weren't even close to dying in his life and took hold of Libby's wrist, tugging her towards him. Her eyes widened, but she didn't put up a fight or flinch when his hand slipped inside her coat, pulling her closer.

With him still perched on a stool and her in the skyscraper heels, their eyes were at the same level, but she stared determinedly over his shoulder. If they were at his house, he could slip off that flimsy top and see for real what it suggested. Christ, what it suggested looked good.

'Why are you going?' His thumb stroked up her spine.

'It's late,' she replied, arching her back against his hand.

'No it's not. Stay.'

She sucked in a quick breath, glancing down at his hand as it stroked her side. 'I hate you.'

'I know, but stay.'

For the briefest moment, her pale blue eyes gazed into his. 'Why?'

'We'll all go later.' *And you can come home with me.*

A camera flashed.

He whipped his hands from Libby.

Two girls were messing with a phone, snapping each other, but his heart hammered as he struggled to breathe. What the hell was he doing? Yes, Libby was hot. She was hot, pretty, funny and his friend, but would he give up his life for her? Literally, no. Figuratively, no.

Her face filled with despair. Why? They just... Then he got it. *This* was what he'd been doing to her, building her up then letting her down. No wonder she hated him.

'Libs...' He'd tell her everything. They'd work it out.

'Hello Patrick,' said a woman to his right, her voice a predatory growl. Miss Haverton.

Reluctantly, he glanced over, scowling at her ridiculous fake tits. What the hell had he seen in her? 'Not now, Rachel. I'm busy.'

'You're such an arsehole,' she spat, throwing a disdainful snarl in Libby's direction.

But her venom was wasted. Libby had fled.

Why couldn't he get this even a little bit right?

* * *

It was over. The next day, Libby curled up on Zoë's bed with Hyssop, struggling not to cry or look at the Carr & Young *For Sale* sign which had appeared that afternoon. No home, no friends, no decent job. The Gosthwaite Era was over.

'Is this mine?' Zoë asked, holding up a red halter neck.

'No.' Libby picked up her phone and clicked a bookmark she'd not used for three years. 'But it clashes with my hair, so you can keep it. Why are you dressed like a Stepford wife?'

Zoë frowned down at her prim grey shift dress. 'We're going to the golf club. It has a no jeans dress code.'

'All you're missing is a pearl necklace.'

'That'll come later.'

The English National Ballet's website opened, showing photos of their current Nutcracker performance. Would she want to be a part of it, watching from the side-lines? Maybe she could have a small part, maybe in the corps. Or maybe she could dance for a smaller company? She was tougher now, the fell race had proved that. Her feet ached, longing to be *en pointe*. What a distraction ballet would be.

Oh, the irony. She'd come to the Lakes looking for a distraction from ballet and six months later she was looking at ballet for a distraction from the Lakes, from Patrick.

'God, I'm such an idiot, Zo.' She kissed Hyssops purring head. 'Why don't I learn?'

She'd let Patrick do it again – get her hopes up then toss her aside. In the bar, he'd practically begged her to stay, his hand stroking her back, then, *poof*, it was over. The second that beautiful blonde walked up, he dropped Libby as if she'd burned his fingers. The way he'd stared at the girl's fabulous boobs. Libby could never live up to that.

'It's not about learning, Lib.' Zoë shoved another two of Libby's tops into the case. 'It's about knowing what you want and making sure you get it.'

'Is that what you're doing?' Libby asked quietly, and retrieved a black velvet vest she thought she'd lost over a year ago. 'Is Jonathan really what you want?'

'Yes.'

'Really, really?'

'Really, really.'

'What about Ed?'

Zoë flopped onto the bed beside Libby. 'Honestly? Yes, I still fancy him. Yes, I wish... but Ed and I would never have worked. He's too... he makes me forget time and space. That's not what I need.'

What if it wasn't about control? What if it was about letting go? 'Are you sure?'

'I need the security of Jonathan, of being Mrs Carr. It'll be a good life.' Zoë grinned. 'But okay, Christmas Day is going to be Jeremy Kyle levels of weird.'

Libby laughed, but the first of her tears tumbled out. 'I wish I could be so certain.'

'Your problem is you don't know what you want. Do you want Patrick or do you want ballet?'

Libby blinked away tears, trying to focus on the little screen. 'I love him, possibly more than ballet, but he doesn't love me. If I had any sense, I'd walk away before I get really hurt.'

'Then it's time to go back to London, back to the company.' Zoë rested her head against Libby's. 'I know you ran from it because it hurt so much, but you're dancing again, you're in that world again. At least send an email, say hi.'

'I will,' Libby said, her fingers going nowhere near the *new message* icon. 'Definitely.'

'Actually, bugger packing. If I only take the bare essentials, Jonathan will just have to take me shopping, right?' Zoë flipped her suitcase shut with a foot. 'And we should go out in style.'

'An actual orgy, just open the brothel doors?' Libby suggested, but despite her flippancy, her tears tumbled out.

'Christmas Eve at the Mill. Black tie, sit down dinner. Everyone's going.'

Including Patrick? 'There's a reason not to go.' But Robbie had already given her a ticket, part of his *don't tell the wife, overly generous Christmas Bonus*, so to not show up would be horribly ungrateful.

'Here's your plan.' Zoë stood up, grabbing a carry-on bag. 'Wear the sexiest dress you have, that vintage sequin number maybe? And if you seriously want ballet not the boy, then you show him *exactly* what he's missing. Then walk the hell away.'

But do I want the ballet, or the boy?

Several hours after Zoë left, her car loaded with little more than a holdall full of shoes, Libby sat on her own bed, curled up with Hyssop. She stared at the email she'd drafted to her old boss, asking if he might consider her for a coaching job, anything. The idea left her feeling hollow, but she could return to London and her life of routine exercise. She moved the cursor over the send button. She would have professional ballet and be three hundred miles from Patrick McBride.

I have nothing left here.

Hyssop mewed.

Libby took a deep breath, trying to ignore Hyssop's disapproving scowl. How the hell did a cat scowl anyway? She re-read her words for the fifth time, checking for silly errors before she hit—

A clatter at the window shattered the silence and Libby pressed herself against the headboard, her heart hammering. A second clatter – pebbles against the glass – roused Hyssop to jump to the dresser and peer out of the window. He meowed at Libby. What if it were Patrick? Slowly, she crept over.

In the tiny front garden, Grace stood smiling up at her, which was strange, since they hadn't spoken since Libby's birthday. Stranger still, Grace wore a red coat and held a wicker basket over one crooked arm.

Libby opened a window. 'If you're looking for the Big Bad Wolf, he's out on his bike.'

'I see Zoë's selling up.'

'And?'

'And I need a lodger since Patrick killed off my little sideline.'

'I'm leaving.'

'You won't. You belong here.'

'What do you want, Grace?'

'Remember when I said you shouldn't mess with things you don't understand?'

Intrigued, Libby nodded.

'Can you borrow the emerald from Zoë?'

Again, Libby nodded. The emerald, not part of Zoë's *bare essentials*, was left with Libby for safe keeping.

'There's a full moon and the power of two is better than one. Are you ready to mess around?'

Hyssop, practically smiling, jumped off the dresser and scampered downstairs, but Libby paused, frowning at her laptop. *Message sent.* Arse.

After a chilly, but intense grounding exercise led by Grace, they sat cross-legged, facing each other, just as Libby had made Zoë do. The air was still, the stars bright, but the moon shone down, illuminating the garden and turning Grace's hair almost blue. Libby had never seen Grace with her hair loose before. Even at Xander's party, she'd had half of it pinned back. Now, it hung over her shoulders, as long as Libby's, but blacker than the sky.

'What are we doing?' Libby asked, feeling oddly foolish.

'What do you think?'

Between them, Grace had placed the emerald on a dish etched

with a pentagram, but to her right, she'd set out a red candle, several petals and a tell-tale red pouch.

'A summoning spell?'

Grace nodded. 'The ancient ways say you should only perform a spell with an open heart. The night before Maggie died, at the Ostara festival, she told a forgiveness circle that she'd tried to summon her love, a man with a wife and daughter. Her heart wasn't open to who her true love might be. Her spell would never work, not properly. Yours has.'

'Mine?' Libby blinked. 'But it hasn't.'

'I know him, Libby. He's yours. I don't understand why he's fighting it, but the spell's working. What did you do?'

No doubt Grace would find her efforts amateurish, like a teen girl messing with a parlour game Ouija board, but Libby explained, her cheeks heating up as she did. Grace didn't mock, she listened intently.

'You performed an honest spell with an honest heart. It's what I want to do.' Grace closed her eyes. 'I didn't take Jack back after...'

'I'm sorry.'

'I know. I didn't take him back because I thought maybe if I was single, then maybe Patrick... but it didn't make any difference.' Grace took her piece of handmade paper. 'I miss Jack. I want to summon him, but the right way.'

Libby sat quietly, serenely even, as Grace wrote the traits she wished for: *honest, good-looking, good with his hands, hard-working, a family guy*. But Grace wrote each of them fully aware it might not be Jack she summoned.

'That's the risk,' she explained. 'But if you want true love, you have to open your eyes and your heart to whoever that may be.'

Seize the power, see the truth.

Libby watched the emerald as Grace burned the flower petals and parchment, waiting, expecting, well... something. But the candle fluttered out and Grace took Libby's hands. Together they sat, wordless in the moonlight. Libby's legs were tingling from sitting still for so long, but she no longer felt cold. Instead, warmth filled her. Warmth?

No.

Energy filled her.

Libby opened her eyes, already alarmed by the sensations rushing through her body, but what she saw had her backing away, too scared to scream. Grace sat with her eyes shut, a knowing smile on her lips and a shimmering violet haze drifting around her.

'Can you feel it?' Grace murmured.

'Feel it? I can bloody see it.' Libby stared. 'You're... glowing.'

'Do you want to know what's really freaky?' Grace asked. 'I don't even have to open my eyes to know you're glowing too.'

Libby looked down at her own hand, blinking, but it was unmistakable. The same violet shimmer hovered around her fingers. 'Oh... My... God.'

'Calm down. They're just auras. You're finally in tune with the world.' Grace opened her eyes, smiling. 'Blessed be, sister.'

Chapter Thirty-Four

'You're not actually wearing that shawl, are you?' Zoë frowned at Libby as Jonathan helped her out of the car. 'It's longer than your dress.'

'And that's why I'm wearing it.' Libby frowned at the Mill. It twinkled with fairy lights but the mistletoe over the door only increased her apprehension. 'I look like a Soho stripper.'

She'd assumed her little black dress, a vintage sequined number, would be suitable without trying it on. It wasn't. When she'd bought it for an opening night party four years ago, it had been just shy of too big, but now she could barely breathe. The strapless neckline sat far too low but if she pulled it up, the hem showed the tops of her hold up stockings. With no other even vaguely appropriate dress for a black tie event, she'd had to grin and wear it.

'You look incredible.' Jonathan smiled down at her. 'You both do.'

No. In a red satin, full-length column dress, her glossy hair flowing down her back, Zoë looked incredible – a classy 1950s sex goddess. A classy 1950s sex goddess with a vast rock on her left hand.

While I look like a stripper.

'Er… ears?' Zoë pushed Libby's hair aside, scowling at the diamante strands the Dick had given her for her birthday. 'No.'

'But–'

'No.'

Libby took out the earrings and handed them over. She loved those earrings. Zoë hadn't minded Libby wearing them a few months ago. As they approached the entrance, Libby slipped off the shawl and the cold night air bit at her bare skin. She was going to a Christmas Eve party on her own. Could her life get any more tragic?

But not for much longer. In five days' time, she had a meeting with her old boss at the English National Ballet. He'd called her the day after she'd emailed, delighted to hear from her, overjoyed to learn she was dancing again and ecstatic to discover she might want to come back. That's what she should focus on – her future.

Well, her future and bloody good hair. For some reason known only to Mother Nature, an intense conditioning treatment at the hairdressers had actually worked and her newly highlighted hair hung like a silk curtain. A Christmas miracle.

With her bravest smile plastered on, Libby carried her cashmere shawl over one arm, hoping her legs in her highest black heels would distract anyone from checking out her non-existent cleavage. Of course, if she slipped on the polished wood floor, there was a fair chance people would get to see her non-existent boobs too.

'Hello, angel.' Robbie waylaid her, kissing her cheeks. 'You came. I'm glad.'

'I don't know why. I'd rather be at home reading a book.' Especially since her repeated scanning of the room only confirmed Patrick's absence. Not that she wanted to see him.

'You'll have fun.' He handed her a glass of champagne before looking her over as only he could. 'You didn't fancy making an effort then?'

She managed a genuine laugh. 'Don't let your wife catch you looking at me like that.'

He shot her a wink. 'Seriously, you look beautiful.'

Buoyed up by Robbie's compliments, she wandered across to the seating plan, hoping she'd be sitting at Robbie's table with Patrick on the other side of the room. She found her name and closed her eyes for a second. At table nine, she'd be sitting with six people she'd never heard of and Patrick. This was over. She headed for the door.

'Where do you think you're going?' Robbie said, grabbing her arm.

'Can you switch the tables around? Please?'

'No.' He shifted uncomfortably. 'It's Van's idea.'

This was a set up. A horrific, badly planned, ill-conceived set up.

Zoë appeared by her side, giggling at the seating plan. 'Oh, come on. Just get drunk and have fun. I bet he looks hot in black tie.'

Libby had no doubt he would, but that would be the problem. He'd sweet talk her, be nice to her, somehow persuade her to be friends and then… cold. For some reason, he'd back off. She couldn't let him do it again. She had to focus on London, on her old life.

She and Zoë wandered through to the garden, where guests mingled with glasses of champagne, but Libby came to an abrupt halt when she spotted Jack and Grace. Had the spell worked? Did they really work?

Zoë glanced around, sipping her champagne. 'Is it me, or are you shagging men in alphabetical order?'

Libby frowned at her. 'What?'

'A, artist, Paolo.' She narrowed her eyes. 'B, Tristan, the ballet dancer.'

Oh for god's sake. 'Let me guess, Jack is C for carpenter? And how are you fitting Robbie in?'

'D... how about, Maitre D'.' Zoë flashed a pleased smile. 'Patrick could be next. Elephant doctor?'

'Just stick with Egotist.' Libby giggled.

'Zoë?' Jonathan appeared behind them, accompanied by a boot-faced Malcolm and a clearly uncomfortable Elizabeth McBride.

As Jonathan introduced them to Zoë, Libby cringed. Bitching about Patrick in front of his parents. Awesome. To make matters worse, Malcolm McBride had looked Libby over with a distinctly unimpressed frown. Clearly, he thought she looked like a Soho stripper too. She wrapped her shawl around her shoulders and headed for the exit.

* * *

Christmas Eve. He ought to be in a great mood, but Patrick walked into the Mill and his edginess worsened. Libby would be inside. And his parents. This looked set to be a disastrous evening. He'd pissed off Libby, he'd pissed off Robbie and his parents didn't trust him. He'd fucked up everything and Christ, he missed being able to talk to Grace every morning.

So far, Christmas sucked. The day before, Sam and Charlotte had arrived from Spain, a surprise visit. Cue squealing mother and backslapping father. Patrick played along, happy to see his brother and sister-in-law, but when was the last time he'd seen their parents react like that to seeing him?

Hidden from the guests in the restaurant, Robbie had Vanessa pressed against the reception desk, looking over her slinky green dress. Patrick didn't blame him. She looked every bit the hot model she used to be.

'Put her down,' Patrick said, sounding grumpier than he intended.

'You're late,' Vanessa said, giggling.

'Fashionably.' Patrick scanned the seating plan. Scott and Clara were on a table with Robbie and Vanessa. Where was he... Oh Christ. He turned to Robbie. 'Not your idea, I assume.'

Robbie shook his head. 'And she's not happy about it. She's nearly bolted twice.'

'It's my idea,' Vanessa said. 'Take one for the team, Patrick.'

Could he sit through an entire dinner with Libby in front of half of Gosthwaite? Thank Christ he'd had a joint with Sam earlier. On the positive side, he'd get to hang out with Libby for the evening. Maybe this would be okay. Hell, maybe he could apologise and explain about the ultimatum. Maybe tonight could change everything.

But it was a black tie event, and he mustn't misbehave.

The rest of the diners had taken their seats and waiters scurried around with wine. Scott gave a small salute, but Patrick's returned gesture faltered as he spotted Libby. At a table in the corner, oblivious to the old codgers at the table, she sat writing on her napkin, a shawl wrapped tightly around her shoulders. Libby was hiding her body. Why? And she was blonde again. The fringe and black crap still hid her eyes, but she'd shed the pink, the black streaks and about six inches of hair. As he approached, she glanced up, pushing her napkin under her side plate. She didn't smile. And when did Libby not smile, not even a little bit?

'How are you?' he asked quietly.

'Fine.'

'Refill?'

'I'll take the bottle.'

A whole week later and she was still pissed off. Marvellous.

'You're in a good mood.' He poured her a drink.

'Not the best. You won't have noticed, swanning in here at the last minute, but there's the most horrific set-up going on.'

'I had noticed.' Why was she hiding under a blanket-sized scarf? 'Is it horrific?'

'What, are you thinking of hotting things up?' Her voice was quiet, but her eyes flashed suggestively. 'Back to your place, maybe? We could fuck in the hallway, up against the wall.'

Oh, hello. He raised his eyebrows and shifted in his seat. 'I was going to suggest a coffee and the chance to talk in private, but we could give your idea a go.'

'And what about tomorrow? Will you come over all apologetic and have your *reasons* again?' The eyes lost all suggestion, instead anger, resentment and four months of hurt took over. 'Just another opportunity for you to walk away.'

'You were the one who walked away last.'

'I should go home.'

'You've had an hour to do that, but you're still here.'

'I hate you.'

But you're still here. There's still a chance.

'Okay, enough.' He stabbed an olive, holding it out to her. 'Olive branch? It is Christmas after all.'

She bit the olive off the cocktail stick and he glanced down, hiding his relieved smile. She crossed her fabulous legs demurely under her chair, but nothing more than sheer black stockings and sky-scraper heels covered them. How short was her dress? He had to make friends with her.

'I want to say sorry,' he said, 'so you need to sit nicely and just listen. Pretend we're chit-chatting about your new hair, which looks much better by the way.'

He flashed a smile as a waitress put plates of goats' cheese tartlet and beetroot salad in front of them and as Libby leant back to give the waitress more room, the shawl slipped but she quickly pulled it back into position.

'Spoilsport.' Patrick frowned her. 'Why are you wearing this thing anyway? Not like you.'

As she sipped her wine, not answering him, he tugged a corner of the shawl. One side dropped to reveal the top half of her naked spine and he tried not to grin. That had to be a fabulously small dress.

'You can keep your apology,' she said. 'I've heard it all before.'

'Come on, Libs. I don't like falling out with you.'

'Then you shouldn't have been such an arse.'

'I know.'

She turned to answer back, but he was ready with a little cheese and salad on her fork, holding it near her mouth. Surprisingly, she let him feed her. He hoped it would keep her quiet for a while longer.

'Look, I'm honestly sorry for everything, but after dinner, can we go somewhere and talk?'

As she chewed, she frowned at him then leaned a little closer, taking in a deep breath. 'Have you been smoking weed?'

'Might've been.'

She nodded towards Zoë. 'Have you seen the future Mrs Carr? She's turned all Stepford since he put a ring on it.'

'That's going to make a weird family dynamic. His sons are older than her.'

'It's worse than that. I think she secretly loves one of them.'

Patrick's mouth dropped open for a second. 'That's got Jeremy

Kyle written all over it.'

Libby laughed and he relaxed. While she told him about Zoë moving out, intentionally only taking an overnight bag so Jonathan would buy her a new wardrobe, Patrick demolished his tartlet and Libby's leftovers. Okay, it was time. He topped up their glasses, bolstering himself to tell her about the ultimatum, but the shawl was covering her shoulders again. She might have a polite smile fixed in place, but her eyes were impassive. She hadn't relaxed at all.

'Shit, you just distracted me, didn't you?' He stared at her, confused. Why was she manipulating him? 'Libs, I'm trying to apologise. I want to...'

'I want to... what?' She wrapped her arms around herself. 'What do you actually want, Patrick?'

I don't know. 'My brother's over. He's looking forward to meeting you.'

'Why?'

'Why do you think?'

'Have you seen Grace and Jack?' Libby pointed to the table in the opposite corner. 'They're back together and *totally* loved up.'

'Really?' She could do *so* much better.

'But she's not loving working at Haverton and she said Hannah's cited twenty-three incidents of unreasonable behaviour on your part. Hasn't she learned to make coffee yet?'

'No, it's bloody awful...' Why were they talking about coffee? He closed his eyes, sighing. She'd used her little questioning trick to distract him again. 'Stop it.'

Slowly, she shook her head.

The waitresses cleared their plates, the OAPs shouting about how marvellous the cheese pie was, but silence descended between him and Libby. She shifted in her seat, moving away from him and he twisted his glass around, trying to work out what to say.

Just tell her.

It all seemed so simple when he was with Scott, but the reality was, she didn't want to listen, even to the good stuff – especially to the good stuff.

She flicked her hair back. Roses and sweet peas. What was it with that perfume?

Okay, he'd fucked this up, big style, but if she didn't want to talk about them, or let him apologise, then fine. He wouldn't persevere. Who the hell wanted to talk about *them* anyway?

'What were you doing before?' he asked.

'When?'

'When I arrived, you were writing on your napkin.'

Her cheeks turned through seven shades of red. 'Nothing.'

Oh, that was impossible to resist. He stretched across, blocking her arms and grabbed her napkin. She tried to snatch it back, but he held it out of her reach. A... artist, Paolo. B... ballet dancer, Tristan. C, carpenter, Jack...

He stared at her, as amused as he was shocked. 'An A to Z fuck list by job?'

'You're right out of luck. V's already filled.'

'There's a smutty joke in there. Vicar?'

'I hate you.'

'So you keep saying.' He checked the list. 'Voice coach? Whatever, he can go under C. Jack can go under J.'

'Out ranked by a Jewel Thief.'

'A vet doesn't outrank a voice coach? Thanks.' He tugged her hair. '*You* went out with a Jewel Thief?'

'At sixth form.'

'What?'

Libby swatted his arm. 'Well he wasn't a jewel thief then. He was a dancer. Now, he's a jewel thief. On the run and everything.'

'Good story, but it's cheating.' Patrick handed back the napkin. 'Fill the rest in properly.'

'The rest?' She gave a tiny smile. 'There is no more.'

He studied the list, shocked by the huge gaps. 'It's finished?'

She nodded.

'Libby, there are only ten names on here.'

'I haven't always had an appalling reputation, you know.' She frowned at him. 'I thought ten was plenty. I was pretty wild at sixth form.'

'Whatever, you were a goody-two-shoes. And I still think a vet should outrank a voice coach.'

She didn't drop eye-contact for a second as she dug in her bag and produced a make-up pencil. 'So how bad are you?'

Fuck. 'I know what you're doing. This is one of your distractions.'

'You've been smoking. You're an easy mark tonight.'

'Why don't you want to talk?'

'For B, are you going for Beauty Queen or Barmaid?'

Pushing his frustration aside, Patrick took the pencil.

The waitresses delivered turkey roulade with all the trimmings, and he devoured the lot, including Libby's unwanted potatoes as he completed his list. It took him less than ten minutes. Jesus, that was far too easy. Libby still picked at her vegetables when he started swapping the odd name for one with a higher ranking profession.

'Oh my god, you've finished already?' She took the list, a smile threatening. 'Cow-castrating assistant. Cute. Quantity surveyor, really? You haven't just made that up?'

Sadly no. Needy nightmare, that one, but he could've used Quality Control Inspector too.

'Who the hell knows a zoologist?' she asked.

'A vet, you idiot.' He elbowed her and she laughed, properly laughed. Finally.

Over dessert, they chatted about the ballet, how she adored teaching the little kids at Jane's, and as the waitresses poured coffee, he forgot all about ultimatums and who might be watching. The other guests mingled, swapping seats and heading for the garden, but the two of them remained, loitering over another glass of champagne.

'Are we friends again?' he asked.

Her eyebrows knitted together. 'I'm—'

'We can forget about the fucking in the hallway part, if you like.' He smiled down at his coffee, but couldn't resist a sneaky sideways glance to check her reaction.

The corners of her mouth twitched. 'I can't believe I said that.'

He loved how she turned pink and that the shawl had slipped down her arms, showing her perfect bare shoulders. 'Are you actually wearing a dress under there?'

'Yes.' She glanced up at him, peeking through her fringe. 'There's just not very much of it.'

Fucking in the hallway it was. Maybe he could take off half the black eye make-up when he took off the dress.

'Libs,' he whispered, deliberately letting his lips brush her ear, 'let's get out of here.'

Her smile disappeared along with her shoulders. She'd wrapped the shawl around herself, tighter than ever.

'Libs?'

'No.' She stood up. 'I hate you and I'm not going to let you play hot and cold with me ever again.'

With long, elegant strides, those incredible legs carried her away and for several minutes, he sat staring at the table. *I hate you.* She'd told him enough times. Maybe she actually meant it. He hadn't arsed things up this badly with a girl since... Melody Lawson's sister. What the hell was he going to do?

'You look like you need a drink,' Scott said, patting his shoulder.

Defeated, Patrick followed him to the bar, perching on a stool as Robbie poured three hefty whiskies. He'd never seen Robbie look quite so bad tempered. This wouldn't be good.

'Let's have it.' Patrick knocked back half his whisky.

'We've known each other for twenty years,' Robbie said, 'and I'd say we've been very good friends for the last two. Well, that's in jeopardy.'

'Rob,' Scott pleaded, 'that's not helping.'

'What?' Robbie held up his hands. 'You expect me to sit here and watch while Libby gets used and tossed aside by him?'

'They're made for each other and he's changed.'

'He doesn't even like how she looks.'

Patrick stared at them both. 'I am still here.'

'Libby's an angel,' Scott said, twirling his whisky. 'A sexy, classy, intelligent, funny angel.'

'An *Off Limits* angel,' Patrick replied.

Robbie merely stared at the bar.

'We're not fifteen.' Scott shook his head. 'Come on, Rob.'

'I won't do it again,' Patrick said. He'd nearly lost his friendship with Scott over Clara. He wouldn't make the same mistake twice.

'I just want her to be happy,' Robbie said, rubbing his forehead. 'Forget *Off Limits*.'

Christ, well that was one hurdle down.

'You haven't told her, have you?' Scott asked.

'Told her what?' Robbie's frown worsened. 'You haven't really got HIV, have you?'

'What? No, I haven't.'

'It's just Clara—'

'Clara's going to get throttled. I'm on probation 'til June,' Patrick said. 'My parents will boot me out if I end up in the paper again. Bye-bye job, house, family.'   •

Robbie looked up at the ceiling. 'And Libby's a photographer's magnet.'

'It gets better. Grace was behind the *Haverton Eye*. It's offline now, but she said Wray's offering a grand for a photo of me and Libby. There could be half a dozen people here tonight, ready to sell us out.

It's big risk.'

'Patrick's worried she'll leave if he tells her the truth,' Scott said. 'Is he right?'

Patrick looked up, expecting one answer, but hoping for another from the only person who knew Libby as well as he did. But Robbie nodded.

'She'll blame herself and leave to protect him.' Robbie sighed. 'If your job wasn't on the line, would you have already fucked her and fucked off?'

'No.' He stared at his glass. 'Yes. But it's different now. We're friends because of you.' Christ, maybe everything did happen for a reason.

'So what now?' Robbie asked.

Patrick shrugged. 'I suppose we'd go out. Or something.'

How many times had he imagined it? They'd go out on the bikes and for long walks, though he'd draw the line at running with her. He'd take her to dinner and wander across the Green holding her hand. They'd sit in pubs, getting a little drunk on a Saturday night before going home to bed. And he'd get to go to bed with her every single night.

'Not or something. We'd go out,' he added. 'But what if...'

Robbie drained his glass. 'What, are you worried you'll fuck it up?'

'It's already fucked up. She hates me.'

Robbie sighed. 'Then it's time for an overblown romantic gesture.'

'Like what?' Patrick was wide-open to genius suggestions.

'You know the rules. What I'd do to win her over wouldn't work for you.'

Despite the butterflies now dancing in his stomach, Patrick smiled. The rules: *Do something that'll make her smile and show you're caring, sensitive or romantic.* For a minute, he studied the door to the ladies toilet where she was still hiding, trying to come up with anything that would mean something to Libby. He knocked back the rest of his whisky. This was bloody good stuff. It must be Jura. A slow smile spread over his face. Isla. Libby needed to meet Isla.

'I need to get her back to my place. Taxi?'

'There're a couple on standby outside. But sex isn't an overblown romantic gesture.'

'Have a little faith, brother.'

Robbie leant across the bar. 'If you break her heart, I will kill you.'

'I'll let you. Now, how the hell am I going to get her to come with me?'

Scott patted his back. 'Rob'll talk to her. Won't you, Rob?'

* * *

It took five minutes hiding in the toilets for her to be sure she wasn't going to cry, but she refused to crumble here, not in front of Patrick. Yet again, he'd battered her defences. Wanting to apologise, the *I like you*, the *I want to talk…* all of it raising her hopes, making her think he wanted more, but then when she asked him what he wanted, what did she get? *I want you to meet my brother.* What the hell for, a threesome?

No more.

With her make-up and shawl still in place, she left the safety of the bathroom only to find Robbie hovering by the huge glass doors – between her and escape. Arse. He turned as her heels clipped across the floor.

'Before you run away, can I have a word?' he asked. 'Please?'

Reluctantly, she sat down on the sofa. 'Is it all going well? It seems to be. Doesn't Vanessa look beautiful?'

'Yes, it is and yes, she does.' Robbie sat next to her. 'Now, what are we going to do about you and Patrick?'

Libby picked at a loose thread on her shawl. 'Nothing.'

'I think he's in love with you.'

'He's a funny way of showing it.'

'I don't think he really knew it until tonight.'

'He's stoned and drunk. He's just letting his indulgent, hedonistic side take over. I've seen it all before.'

'Remember on your birthday, I asked you if you trusted me. Do you still?'

She turned to him, frowning as she nodded. 'Of course, I do.'

'Then trust me now. Give him a chance.'

'Why?'

Robbie paused for a moment.

'When Patrick was eleven, he wanted a dog. It's all he wanted for Christmas that year. He'd asked for months and he was convinced he was getting one, a Springer spaniel puppy. Patrick went missing on Boxing Day, just disappeared. His parents rang around, frantic, and eventually Scott and I found him kicking a football at the playground. There was no dog with him. Apparently, his mum and dad explained that because he was away at school, it just wasn't practical. He said he'd go to school here. They still said no. I'll never forget the look on his face. He was devastated that the one thing he really wanted, he'd never get to have.' Robbie nudged her. 'He had the same look on his face when you walked away just now.'

Her heart broke, imagining the eleven year-old Patrick, picturing him with shining eyes, just as he'd had the night Baxter died. 'I don't care.'

'Yes you do.' Robbie sighed. 'Libby, you're in love with him and you have been for a long time. What if he's your Somebody? You can't just walk away and not give him the chance to explain why he's done what he's done.'

'Yes, I can.' Because if Patrick were her Somebody, he wouldn't have behaved so appallingly in the first place.

'But look at all the things he's done for you. Like organising for you to see Jane. And getting Van to talk to you.'

'What? I assumed you... You mean, *he* did it?'

As Robbie nodded, Libby struggled to breathe. Patrick had fixed her life? He'd done those things when he was barely speaking to her. Why? Did he really care? If he did, why did he want to run away the night Baxter died? Why did he ditch her the second that beautiful blonde turned up in Oscar's? Hot, cold, hot, cold.

'I can't do this, Rob.'

She stood up, determined to flee, but Patrick stood ten feet away, leaning against the wall with his hands in his pockets. Slowly, she shook her head. His eyes pleaded with her.

'Trust me,' Robbie whispered, 'and let him explain. He's your Somebody.'

Robbie headed back to the bar and Libby glanced at her escape route. Run. But her legs refused to move. She closed her eyes for a moment, picturing the little silk pouch tucked inside her handbag.

Good looks, 25-35, nice eyes but not brown, English, honest, single, decent morals, good with animals. I want my Somebody.

'I want to talk to you,' Patrick said as he walked over, never shifting his gaze from her eyes. 'No hot, no cold. I just want to talk.'

'What if I don't want to talk?'

A small smile tugged at his mouth. 'Well, there's always your hallway idea.'

He took hold of her hand, linking his fingers with hers, and her resolve withered.

Chapter Thirty-Five

They sat on either side of the taxi, not speaking, not touching. He'd let go of her hand when he helped her into the car and hadn't made a move to take it back. The journey lasted less than five minutes, but the whole time Libby stared out of the window, not daring to look at him. What could she say if she did? Why? It was the only word rattling around in her head. Why, why, why? Why be so nice and then so cold?

By the time, the taxi pulled into the Green, she wished they could drive for another five minutes, for another hour. What was Patrick expecting? A shag? Why did she come out with the fucking in the hallway wisecrack? As if she would. The taxi, with its vanilla air freshener, stifled her and her head swam from the wine she'd drunk. The second the car stopped, she threw open the door, sucking in a massive lungful of air.

Go home.

'Come on,' Patrick said, nodding towards his house. 'I've got a surprise to show you.'

'I'm not sure–' She glanced at Maggie's cottage, needing the security of familiar surroundings.

'It's fine.' He took her hand. 'It's a nice surprise.'

'Why?'

He glanced around the empty Green. 'Why is it a nice surprise?'

'No, why did you get me to see Jane? You were waiting for me, weren't you?'

'Can we go inside?' His fingers linked with hers again, his thumb brushing the back of her hand.

'But you were, weren't you?'

He nodded.

'Why?' She stared into those perfectly non-brown eyes. Did he really care? If he kissed her now, showed her that he cared, she could forget about London. She could settle here, she really could.

Kiss me.

He didn't. Instead, he tugged the shawl. The cold winter air ripped at her skin, but she didn't shiver. Instead, she held her breath as Patrick looked her over. He didn't share Robbie's blatant desire to bend her over the sofa. No, Patrick looked her over with awe, as if he'd never seen a girl in a dress before.

Finally, a huge smile took over his face. 'I was there because you always smell of roses and sweet peas.'

She laughed. 'I smell of what?'

'Come on, princess, I've something to show you.' Still clutching her hand, he led her to his house.

Her heart hammered in her chest, surely loud enough for him to hear, as he unlocked the door. Should she sleep with him or play hard to get? Okay, he hadn't said he loved her, but could he be her Somebody?

Please let Robbie be right.

'What's the surprise?' she asked.

'A cute little redhead I've had my eye on.'

Trusting him to be joking, she followed him down the corridor to a closed door. A strange whimpering came from the other side.

'You keep a cute little redhead locked in the kitchen? Should I run away, screaming for my life?'

His smile grew as he opened the door and a bundle of brown and white fur scurried around his feet, its tail a wagging blur.

'Ohmigod, you've got a puppy.'

'This is Isla.' He kissed the Springer Spaniel's head before sending her off to say hello to Libby. 'And she's a very clever girl who hasn't weed everywhere. Well done, Isles.'

Still smiling, Libby knelt on the kitchen floor showering the puppy with love while Patrick put the kettle on. Was Isla the dog Patrick so desperately wanted when he was eleven?

'How old is she?'

'Twelve weeks. She's the runt no one wanted because she has odd ears.'

Libby examined them. One was only half the size of the other. 'She's adorable.'

'Want to see her party trick? She's better at spinning around than you.' He held Isla's tail near her mouth and they both laughed watching her spin in circles trying to catch it. 'She's why I was so late tonight. I didn't want to leave her on her own for too long.'

'And there's me thinking you didn't like mangy mongrels.'

'Of course I do. Not that she's mangy.'

Libby sat on the slate flagstone floor, laughing as Isla scampered over her legs and turned the hold-ups into a mass of snags and tiny ladders.

'Thank you, Isla. Now I look like a St Trinian's sixth former. It's a great look but I was going for classy tonight.' She kissed the beautiful puppy. 'If it's not the cats and dogs you hate, why don't you like Monday afternoons?'

He pottered around, shedding his jacket, opening a fresh pack of coffee, spooning it into a cafetière without answering her question.

'You'll never be happy,' she said, throwing his words back at him, 'if you don't tell people about yourself.'

He sucked in one cheek, before shaking his head in defeat. 'I prefer dealing with the large animals. The farmers and horse owners around here are a pretty decent bunch, but at the Haverton surgery the people are... Well, the cats and dogs aren't always the best cared for, mostly through ignorance, but I hate it.'

He picked up Isla, laughing as he avoided her doggy kisses, and Libby's walls tumbled. Patrick had the tall, dark and handsome boxes firmly ticked, and although the speed he completed his A to Z appalled her, he wasn't an immoral egotist, not really. He adored animals and he'd gone out of his way to rebuild her life. Surely, he was her Somebody.

The kettle boiled, its click bringing her to reality. No, she had to stop thinking about romantic outcomes; she had to stay focused. With the cafetière filled, Patrick grabbed two mugs and a carton of milk and sat on the floor beside her, their backs against the wall. Isla curled up on his knee.

'Is this how you pull all the girls? Lure them in with a puppy then have coffee on the kitchen floor?'

'This would be a first.'

They weren't even flirting. They were beyond it.

'Do you want to get that apology out of the way?' she asked.

He stroked Isla before taking a deep breath. 'Okay, sod it. I'm sorry for the hot and cold. I'm sorry for walking out of the pub and I'm sorry for not talking to you when you came to say thank you. My parents were round, I think to find out who you were, but that was bloody rude. And Halloween? Unbelievably sorry.'

'I'll forgive you.' She struggled not to grin.

'But I'm not sorry for kissing you, ever.'

'Are you some schizo stalker?'

'No.' He laughed, cringing. 'But I'll admit it's kind of weird behaviour.'

She nodded. 'So why?'

'Why did I kiss you?' He rested his head against the wall, smiling towards the ceiling. 'Because you looked too cute not to.'

She elbowed him. 'You know what I mean.'

Denying her an answer, he pushed the plunger then poured the coffee into two mugs. He handed the first to her. 'A real cup. Not that yours is as bad as Hannah's.'

Libby swatted his arm. 'If I have coffee now I'll be awake half the night.'

He didn't hide his smile. 'That's the plan.'

Libby blushed redder than Isla's wonky ears. 'You're not getting away with it that easily. *Why?*'

'After the Miss Haverton story in the paper, Mum and Dad sent me to Spain. I had to disappear for a couple of months and when I came back there was to be no more trouble. I'm on a year's probation, six months left to go.'

'Okay.'

'There are ground rules. No more drinking on a school night–'

'That explains the whisky being against the rules.'

'No hard drugs, including random drugs tests–'

'Oh my god, and there's me, waltzing in, tempting you to come to party where there's more coke being inhaled than oxygen.'

He laughed and gently nudged her. 'Tempting me. You certainly did that.'

'I'm glad you kicked me out.' No wonder he'd been so cross. 'Sorry, sorry, sorry.'

'Don't be.'

'So I get why you didn't want to come to the party, but why avoid me and not talk to me? And why say you can't be a distraction?' She didn't like the deep breath he took, or the ever lengthening pause. 'Patrick?'

'Because I've been a fucking awful son for the last couple of years and I want to make it up to my mum and dad.' He sipped his coffee. 'The other rules are no more scandals and no more newspaper articles.'

Exactly what I've become. Libby stared at her coffee. *I'm a newspaper scandal waiting to happen. I need to stand up and walk out.*

'You're already thinking about leaving, aren't you?'

She nodded, still unable to look at him.

'Please don't.'

'There's a thousand pound bounty on our heads.'

'I know.'

She picked at one of the snags in her holdups, laddering it. Why had she partied with Jack? Why had she had an affair with Robbie? This was her fault. Stupid, stupid, stupid.

'Look, Libs, I've tried to stay away from you, but I think I've proved that I can't.'

'What are you going to do?' she asked.

He sipped his coffee. 'I have no idea. Do we have to worry about it now?'

Hot Patrick. This was Hot Patrick. Would he be cold again tomorrow? Surely not, not after tonight. She picked at another snag, making it run all the way down her leg.

'I've spent the last seven days vowing not to get dragged into you again,' she said.

'Really? Who were you wearing the dress for?'

She couldn't help her blushes. 'It's just a dress.'

'That's not just a dress.' He picked at one of the snags and laughed as it laddered all the way down to her ankle.

'Why did you even turn up tonight?'

'I knew you'd be there in a killer dress.'

'You know you can't lie to me.'

'I knew you'd be there in a killer dress and a bad mood, I couldn't resist that.' He toyed with another snag, but slowly, making the contact last longer. 'I wanted to prove I could behave in black tie, but I wouldn't have stayed an hour if you hadn't been there. Even if you were sulking and pretending you hated me.'

'I don't hate you.'

His hand rested on her knee. 'I've missed you.'

He was prepared to risk his parents' disapproval for her, to put his reasons to one side for her. He was her Somebody. She put her half-drunk coffee down, her heart thumping as she leaned up to kiss him. Her lips had barely touched his when Isla growled.

Patrick laughed softly before reprimanding Isla, sending her to her basket. 'Think she's jealous?'

Libby smiled at the puppy. 'I was here first, sweetheart.'

Okay, if this was happening, it wasn't happening on the kitchen floor. Libby stood up, not missing Patrick's frown at the laddered holdups.

'You don't like the St Trinian's look?'

He shook his head.

'You prefer angelic don't you?'

When he nodded, she put a foot on the dining chair next to him and peeled off one of the hold ups. He raised his eyebrows and as she switched legs, his smile grew. Slowly, she slid the second stocking down and he stood, running his hand up her leg.

'Do you think it's too early to tell you I'm in love with your perfect legs?' he asked.

Libby laughed, unable to stop gazing at his fabulous lips – utterly kissable and just a few inches from hers. She tipped her head up. No growling puppy would stop her this time. The kiss in the garden, the night Baxter died, had been full of nerves on both sides but showed how quickly things would hot up. There were no nerves this time.

She wound her arms around his neck as he pulled her closer, one hand toying with her hair, just like he had over dinner. An involuntary shiver ran through her body as his hand brushed her bare shoulders.

'We still should've done this on Halloween,' she said.

Patrick tried to smile mid-kiss. 'Are you ever going to let me forget that?'

She shook her head and he paused, pushing her fringe out of her eyes. With their bodies so close, she could feel his heart beating, or was it hers? His breathing was as erratic as her own and this time, when he kissed her, his tongue gently toyed with hers. Play hard to get? Not a chance.

Without taking his lips from hers, he guided her out of the kitchen and they staggered through to the living room. The light from the fire in the wood burner and the fairy lights on the Christmas tree created the perfect setting – as if he'd planned it. Maybe he had. Seeing little point in acting coy, Libby began unbuttoning his shirt, adoring the pleased groan he gave. She eased his shirt off his shoulders and used the pause in kissing to check him out. How many times had she imagined him like this, shirtless and horny as hell? The reality was a lot sexier than her dreams. The mountain biking clearly did one hell of a job keeping him fit. She ran a finger over his perfectly toned abs, gazing up at him with a cheeky smile.

'Enjoying yourself?' he asked, grinning.

Her nails raked over his chest and flicked a nipple, wiping the smile off his face. He flinched and laughed, but flipped her around so she faced the wall and he stood behind her.

'Two can play at that game,' he whispered, his breath tickling her ear.

Libby stood helpless, loving the cool wall against her burning cheek. He pushed her hair to one side and scattered tiny kisses up her spine and neck. Shivers flew down her body as one of his hands snuck around her waist, the other to the zip at her side.

'This dress might look sexy as, but it feels like a cheese grater.'

'Better take it off them.'

His fingers tugged at the zip. It didn't budge.

'What the hell?' He moved back a little, using two hands to check the fastening.

Libby giggled, turning to face him. 'It's vintage. You might have to tug it. Tristan—'

'I don't want to hear about Tristan, thank you.' Patrick scowled before focussing on the zip.

Libby held her arms up, giving him easier access. 'As sweet as your jealousy is—'

'I'm not jealous. He's a wanker who dropped you.'

'Whatever. Tristan always said I was an idiot to waste eighty pounds on a second-hand dress. But you're right. He is a wanker. Well?'

The zip hadn't moved.

Patrick straightened, sucking a nick on his thumb. 'It's stuck.'

'I'm wearing a bloody chastity dress,' Libby laughed.

He pushed his curls back with both hands, laughing.

'It's not funny.' She tried the zip herself, trying not to giggle. 'Can't you just rip it off or something?'

He studied the dress for a moment, then darted out of the room. She leant against the wall, close to the warmth of the fire, listening to him rummaging in drawers. They were going to have sex. Would it be in here, or upstairs? It could be on the bloody dining table for all she cared. She crossed her legs. Hurry up.

What if he found her flat chest a disappointment and her ugly feet repulsive? He'd slept with that beauty queen and Grace. Both had boobs she could only dream of. She straightened her back as he returned with a pair of scissors, but her butterflies worsened when he stopped and looked her over.

'What?' she whispered, panicking.

Slowly he walked over, taking his time to put another log on the fire, and she stared down at him, trying to breathe. What? He didn't look up, but gently stroked her calf and dropped a kiss behind her knee. Tingles shot up her leg.

'You look... You are incredible,' he said as he stood up. 'I don't want... so we don't ... are you sure?'

That I want to have sex, or I want you to cut my dress off?

She nodded.

After taking a deep breath, he carefully cut down the zip. Sequins rained to the floor, but finally, the eighty pound mini-dress fell to her feet, leaving her standing in her purple silk underwear and heels. Libby nervously glanced up at him.

'Utterly incredible,' he whispered, his hands holding her face.

His kiss was deep and slow, lacking urgency this time, but the pulsing between her legs increased. She trailed her hands down, planning to unfasten his belt, but he stopped her, smiling as he shook his head.

They fell onto the sofa and he lay beside her, propped on one elbow, his other hand drawing lazy patterns over her neck, skimming the top of her bra.

'You do realise this has nearly happened three times before now,' he said, his hand slipping around her back.

'It has not.' She tensed as he deftly removed her bra. *Please, don't be disappointed.*

His eyes softened. 'Christ, you're perfect.'

She started to disagree, but his thumb trailed around a nipple and the power of speech left her.

'The first time was the day we met,' he went on, 'after the ride down to the village. I was tempted to talk you into bed that morning. Probably would've done if you'd have said yes to help getting into the house.'

'You couldn't have talked me into anything.' The tingling radiating from her breast had her arching her back, desperate for more.

'Oh come on, an icepack, bit of a massage... would you?'

As if, mister. She shook her head, but he replaced his thumb with his lips, and she closed her eyes, unsure how long she could cope.

'I'll take that as a yes.' His thumb took over again. 'But I'm glad that it wasn't then. The second time was Halloween. You've no idea how much I wanted you to stay. I don't know if I've ever wanted to fuck anyone so much in all my life. Aside from now.'

'You say the sweetest things.'

His hand tailed with agonising slowness down her body. 'But you were drunk so I'm glad it didn't happen then.'

Libby couldn't move, she had no control over her own body, only reactions to Patrick's touch. Mindlessly she raked her nails through his hair as he dropped gentle kisses on her stomach and slid the bought-for-the-occasion French knickers down her legs.

'The third time?' she asked, trying to stay focussed.

His fingers drew ever-decreasing circles, moving up the inside of her thigh and she held her breath, the anticipation of what he'd do next making her squirm.

'Your garden,' he said. 'Things would've got out of hand and you know it.'

The circles hit the spot and lightning bolts shot through her body. Instinctively, Libby tried to press her legs together, but his knee blocked hers. He was in control and his lazy smile confirmed it.

'If I hadn't stopped kissing you,' he said, 'it would've happened then.'

She couldn't believe what was happening. Her body was on fire and Patrick was making it happen. Oh god, this had to go a lot further, a lot quicker.

'No, it wouldn't.' She rolled over, ending his torturous games. 'And I stopped kissing you.'

His smile soon vanished when she pressed her naked body against his. She kissed and teased him until he was as breathless as he'd made her, then set to work removing the rest of his clothes, scattering kisses all over his fabulous body. She knelt over him as he fished a condom from his trouser pocket, but when she tried to take it, he shook his head.

'If you do it, this'll be over in no time,' he explained, grinning, and the second it was on, he flipped her onto her back.

'Control freak?'

'For now.' His leg encouraged hers apart. 'You know you'll have to update the A to Z. A vet should definitely outrank a voice coach.'

'There was no voice coach. I put it in so you didn't get any ideas.'

He stroked her fringe out of the way, smiling. 'With the amount of jobs you've had, you could fill my entire list.'

'Wow, does that mean I outrank everyone?' Her pleased giggle turned to a sharp breath as he officially took his place on her A-Z list.

He is my Somebody.

Chapter Thirty-Six

What he liked about Libby was… pretty much everything. In the last hour, she'd made him re-evaluate every other woman he'd fucked. *Fucked.* Certainly for the last two years that's all he'd done. With Libby it had been a whole different experience. They'd gazed into each other's eyes, for Christ's sake. He'd not done that before. He also quite liked that she'd kept the heels on. How he'd lasted as long as he did was a complete mystery.

But what he really liked about Libby was they'd spent the last twenty minutes, lying on the rug in front of the fire, talking about anything and everything, but she didn't feel the need to discuss them or what would happen next. And for that he couldn't be more grateful, because no matter how fantastic she was, he had no idea what would happen in the morning.

He ought to be going to bed, to get some sleep since he was on call in the morning, but instead, he lay beside her, scattering kisses up her spine and neck, unable to believe how flawless she was. She wasn't asleep, but she had her eyes closed, her head resting on her folded arms, giving him the opportunity to study every inch of her. He pushed her fringe to the side. It was the little things he liked, how her eyes weren't ostentatiously blue and her lips weren't a bee-stung pout. She was just ordinary, but ordinary worked on her. Christ, she was pretty.

His erratic heart rate was back. When she'd first kissed him in the kitchen, he seriously worried for his health. His heart had beat way faster than could ever be natural. He'd put it down to nerves. He'd not been nervous before shagging a girl since he was about twenty, but then again, she'd been to bed with Rob and Jack. He'd heard some tales about those two. Now, after the event, he had no doubt he knew his way around this girl better than either of them, so why was his heart beating overtime again? Maybe he did have some kind of arrhythmia. He kissed a freckle on her shoulder. No, he was nervous.

Breathing in the scent of roses and sweet peas, he tried to relax. This was Libby, the girl whose garden he'd sat in, talked with, drank with, laughed with. She'd ridden down a hill for him, she'd been there when he needed her and she'd cooked him a perfect steak. Was that why he was nervous, because she was perfect and maybe she'd find a reason to hate him?

'Is there any part of you that isn't perfect?'

'I have no boobs.'

He rolled her over, stroking one small but flawless breast. 'Have to disagree. Perfect.'

'And... my feet are awful. Ballet dancers have fugly feet.'

He shifted to sit by her feet, running his hand down her calf, laughing when she tried to pull away. 'Relax.'

'Please don't.'

The rosy firelight only amplified her blushes, but he didn't let her escape, instead he began massaging his thumbs into her sole. 'So that's why you kept the shoes on.'

'To stop you running away in horror.'

'Idiot.' He lifted her foot, looking her in the eye as he kissed her big toe.

'I hate them. When I was in the Company, it was fine. Everyone had battered feet, but when I left, the world seemed full of girls in flip flops with perfect toes. This is as good as they get after years of remedial pedicures.' Her resistance to his hands lessened and she closed her eyes, sighing. 'God, that's nice. Paolo used to call them hobbit feet.'

'Paolo's an idiot too. Your feet are like battle scars and show your dedication to dancing.' He smiled at her doubtful frown. 'Besides, I'll take your squashed up toes, and raise you...' He lifted his right foot.

'Oh my god, you only have four toes. Where's the little one?'

'Never ride a bike barefoot. A lesson I learned age seven. Sam's fault.'

'Your brother?' Her leg relaxed completely.

'He bet me I couldn't beat him down to the river. I could and I did, but I crashed, completely out of control, into the rocks.' He settled down to give her the best foot rub ever. 'They're just feet.'

After ten minutes, she lay with a stupid smile on her face and he finally put her second foot down. Christ, when she looked at him like that, with those pretty grey eyes gazing up at him, he couldn't breathe and her familiar perfume wasn't working this time. *Do I love her?* Oh fuck. Was that why he was nervous?

'Who've you been shagging?' she asked.

'Jesus, where did that come from?'

'I'm just curious.'

'What makes you think I've been shagging anyone?' He tipped his head, amused to hear her answer.

'I can't imagine you not. I bet you've got some bored housewife who's very discreet.'

He laughed. 'I don't, but nice idea. I should get one.'

Libby nipped his leg.

'Ow.' He lay next to her, toying with the ends of her hair, wrapping a lock around his finger. 'Honestly? No one.'

She raised her eyebrows.

'I'm as shocked as you.' He kissed her, gently biting her bottom lip. 'But I fully intend to make up for it. What are you doing tomorrow?'

She shrugged. 'Zoë couldn't decide if she'd be here or not, so there's a compromise chicken in the fridge. Are you going to your parents?'

'Supposed to be, but I'm on call and I'd much rather spend the day with you.'

'Making up for the last six months?'

He nodded.

'Then we'd better pray no cows need urgently castrating.'

He was on call from seven. It'd be just his luck to be called out at five past. He really needed to get some sleep. 'Come on, bedtime.'

Nodding, she stood up, pulling on his shirt which swamped her tiny frame. Cute as. He stayed on the rug, propped up on his elbows, smiling at her. The fringe didn't matter and he no longer noticed the black crap. This was Libby, as classy and beautiful as a girl could be.

'What?' she asked, blushing again.

He stood up, not answering her, but took her hand, leading her into the hallway. The hallway? Unable to resist the joke, he pushed her up against the wall, slipping his leg between hers. To his surprise, her eyes glinted as she pulled him closer.

'You're insatiable,' he said, pushing open the shirt.

She shrugged and wound her arms around his neck. 'It's been a while.'

'Halloween was two months ago. Insatiable.'

'We didn't actually *do* anything.'

'When you were dressed like that? He's such a loser.' Christ, he loved her arms around his neck. 'Just so I don't get my hopes up, only

345

to end up disappointed, you do still have that Alice in Wonderland outfit, don't you?'

He hoped to God she did.

She nodded and like a magician produced a condom from behind his ear. Where the hell had she hidden that? Patrick sent a smile of thanks to the Big Man.

* * *

It was Christmas Day. It was Christmas Day and she was in bed with Patrick. Libby stayed absolutely still, not daring to ruin the moment. Patrick was still asleep, face down, but his arm lay across her. She'd woken a few times in the scant hours they'd been asleep, but each time, he'd have an arm wrapped around her and once, his whole body.

Clearly he liked her and more than clearly, she liked him. The sex alone would keep her addicted to him for decades – the sofa, the hallway, the bed. God, the hallway. When Jack suggested it, it'd been hot because it was bad, but with Patrick it'd been hot because they'd shared the joke. Initially they'd giggled; eventually, she'd been unable to talk.

But now what? Hot or Cold? After the sofa, they'd settled side-by-side on the rug, chatting about nonsense – her work, his work, anything, everything, but nothing about them. It was as if neither of them dared. Ninety percent of her head said, *This Is It*. She'd teach at the ballet studio and she'd go out with Patrick. They'd go on dates, she'd meet his parents, he'd tell her he loved her.

Then there was the other ten percent of her.

It said, *But What If?* What if she could dance again? She really was tougher now. If she could dance professionally, would she really want to settle for the tumbledown farmhouse? Could she have both? They had cows in Surrey. Would he come with her?

But those weren't questions for Christmas Day.

'Happy Christmas,' she said, toying with his curls.

'It's not Christmas for another five hours sleep.' He didn't open his eyes.

'Not a morning person then?' She wriggled next to him, stroking his neck. 'Hot or Cold?'

'Warm, but getting hotter if you keep doing that. Time is it?'

'Ten past nine. Shall I make tea?'

'No, it's too early. Go back to sleep.'

She kissed his neck.

'Okay,' he said, fighting a smile, 'but tea's pointless. I'd prefer coffee.'

'I'd prefer tea.'

'Let Isla into the garden?'

'Will do. You can have ten minutes more sleep.'

Grabbing his shirt from the floor, loving the fact that it still smelled of him, she pottered off to the bathroom, admiring his taste. The black and white tiles, perfectly suited the bachelor pad, but the clever lighting and rich green feature wall, created a cosy haven. Sadly, the lighting wasn't cosy enough to hide how appalling she looked.

Her hair resembled a bird's nest, her fringe stuck out at varying angles and the bags under her eyes weren't helped by smudged mascara. She made do with plaiting her hair and wiping away half her make-up with a wet tissue, but in her rush managed to leave black marks on one of his thick white towels. Arse. She flipped the towel over, hoping he wouldn't notice, and ran downstairs.

Oddly, their discarded clothes sat in a neat pile on the bottom stair. Patrick tidying up during the night seemed highly unlikely, so how–

A drawer banged shut in the kitchen. That couldn't be Isla. As the kitchen door opened and Patrick's mother appeared, Libby quickly fastened a couple of buttons on the shirt. She stared, mortified, but Elizabeth gave a pleasant smile, beckoning her into the kitchen.

'Please don't be embarrassed. I've found much worse in the living room than clothes before now. Two boys, nothing shocks me. Merry Christmas, by the way.'

Libby hovered in the doorway, her arms wrapped around herself. She was naked bar Patrick's shirt, and his mother was chatting as if she did this every day. Maybe she did.

'Merry Christmas.'

Elizabeth put the kettle on. 'Coffee?'

'Tea, if that's okay.'

'I'm sorry for being here. He's almost thirty. You'd think I'd learn to let go, but he's my baby son and I can't help looking after him. Patrick has a nasty habit of going a little wild at black tie events. I like to make sure he's still alive the next day.'

'He is.' Libby crouched down as Isla came scampering in, loving the distraction. 'And he didn't go wild. I think he only had three glasses of wine at dinner.'

'I loved your dress. Very classic. Did you have a nice time?' Elizabeth asked, rummaging in the cupboards.

I've spent the night with your son, what do you think? Nice doesn't cover it. 'Yes, thank you. The food was incredible. Did you?'

Elizabeth nodded, holding a red spotted tea pot. 'It's funny. I feel like I've known you since November. You've been hanging in my dining room for a month.'

'Excuse me?' Libby frowned, ready to run away.

'I have your painting,' Elizabeth explained hastily. 'Patrick bought it from the charity shop. He thought you'd regret giving it away.'

'Oh.'

Patrick had bought *the Broken Ballerina* and he'd given it to his mother. Was that just a bit odd, or way beyond odd? Libby hadn't a clue how to react, but Elizabeth busied herself making tea and putting toast on. She dug out butter, marmalade and jam, arranging them on a tray.

'Well, I'll get out of your hair,' Elizabeth said. 'The toast will be ready in a minute. Will you ask him to let me know if he's still coming to dinner?'

Libby nodded, hoping he still planned not to be. Or ideally he'd invite her to go too. She could meet his brother, Sam, and Charlotte, the wannabe psychoanalyst.

Elizabeth paused as she put on her coat. 'My grandfather used to call me Libby.'

'My middle name's Elizabeth and my little brother couldn't pronounce Livvy for years. Libby just took over. Thank you for making breakfast.'

'Look, you seem a nice girl. Jane has nothing but praise for you and Patrick adores you, but... Well, let's just hope Michael Wray doesn't find out. Have a lovely day.'

'Happy Christmas.'

Elizabeth left.

Utterly nonplussed, Libby popped the toast onto the tray and dashed back up to Patrick, desperate for his reassurance. Happily, the bizarre conversation with his mother faded from her head as Libby took in the sexiest thing she'd ever seen on Christmas Day. Lying on his side, propped up on one elbow with only his bottom half covered by the duvet, Patrick looked her over, his smile growing.

'I come bearing gifts.' She put the tray on the bedside table and knelt over him, running her fingers down his treasure trail. 'Tea, I'm afraid. I don't like coffee in the morning, but there is toast.'

Patrick began unbuttoning the shirt. 'That can wait.'

'Have you any idea how very, very pretty you are without the black crap and the fringe?' Patrick handed her a mug of stewed tea.

Thirty minutes of breathless, intense shagging had left her hair bedraggled and her face sweaty. Pretty wasn't the term she'd have used.

'You might have mentioned the pretty thing once or twice, but I like the black crap. I don't like looking pretty. I like looking edgy.'

'You don't look edgy. You look like seventeen year-old trailer trash.' He sipped his tea. 'Christ, really strong tea might actually be worth drinking. Where on earth did you find a teapot? I didn't know I had one.'

'I didn't, your mum did. Ugh, it's cold.' She put her mug on the side. 'Tea really has to be hot.'

'Hang on, my mum did?'

Libby nodded. 'She was downstairs, tidying up. She'd already done the living room.'

'I wonder what she thought when she found your cut up dress.'

'It was possibly the most excruciating five minutes of my life. I look awful. She must think I'm an awful tramp, but she was very blasé. Has she had many chats with girls making tea?'

'It's usually coffee.' He tugged her plait. 'No, not to my knowledge. And you don't look awful. In fact you look cute as fuck in my shirt.'

Libby grinned. She might wear it all day. 'She said she likes to make sure you're still alive the morning after.'

'Bullshit. She most likely heard we'd left together and came for a nosy. Sorry.' He leant back against the headboard, frowning up at the ceiling. 'I wonder if she'll tell Dad.'

'I know you don't want to let him down, but you're nearly thirty. Surely you're not worried what he thinks about who you're shagging?'

'Of course, not.' The tiny twitch in his eye was back.

Libby sat up, frowning at him. 'Liar. He doesn't like me, does he?'

'Why do you think that?'

'The way he looked at me last night.'

A huge frown took over his face. 'I'm sorry, Libs. He doesn't know you. He'd like you if he did.'

Libby hugged her knees. 'Your mum asked if you'd let her know if you were still going to Christmas dinner. Are you?'

If he invited her along, she could meet his dad and hopefully win him over.

'I thought we'd agreed.' He ran his thumb along her thigh. 'We'd pray my phone didn't ring, while I sit watching crap on TV and you make dinner like a good little wench.'

She laughed, gently punching his arm. 'You have to help. And I'm nobody's wench.'

'Okay, but if Zoë catches us shagging in the kitchen, it'll be your fault.'

'I can live with those terms.' Libby smiled. Who wanted to go to his parents anyway? 'Your mum also told me something else.'

'Go on...'

'The painting?'

'Christ, I'm starting to look a little obsessed, aren't I?'

Libby held her finger and thumb an inch apart. 'Just a bit. I went to get it back the next day, but it'd gone. You weren't even speaking to me then.'

'Do you want it?'

'No. Yes. Maybe one day. How much did you pay for it? I'll pay you back.'

'It's fine.'

'How much?'

He shook his head. 'That's between me and Haverton Animal Rescue. The irony isn't lost on me. I already work for free on Monday afternoons, now I've funded the drugs too.'

One day she'd pay him back, but in the meantime he'd have to make do with a million thank you kisses.

'Enough,' he laughed, fending her off.

Libby sat smiling at him for a moment. *I love you. It's absolutely official.* 'Your mum said something else too.'

'I'm going to throttle her when I see her.'

'She said we'd better hope Michael Wray didn't find out.'

'And? I hope he doesn't.' Patrick stood up, pulling her with him. 'Shower?'

Libby let him drag her to the bathroom, fully aware he was distracting her. 'Why does it matter?'

'If we have a shower? I'll smell a lot better.' He opened the vast glass door to the shower, turning on a deluge of water. 'You still smell of roses and sweet peas, but come on.'

'I'll have one at home. I need ridiculous amounts of conditioner.' And industrial make-up remover or she'd look like Alice Cooper. Roses and sweet peas?

'Spoilsport.'

She leaned against the wall, blatantly perving at his naked body. Crikey, he was confident, but then, he had no reason not to be with his long muscular legs and perfect arse. Maybe she could dive in with him.

'What does it matter if Michael Wray finds out?' she asked. 'We have nothing to be ashamed of. Let them read all about it. Hell, we really should send him a photo.'

The glass steamed up, hiding all but his silhouette. He washed his hair, scrubbed his skin, but still didn't answer her. What if this was a one night stand? A Christmas fling. What if he'd got cold feet?

'You're doing it again,' she said. 'You're ignoring me.'

Again, the silence descended, this time magnified as he shut off the shower. She wrapped her arms around herself, the wait unbearable.

'This isn't a scandal,' she said.

'But he'll make it a scandal and I can't afford for that to happen.'

'Why?'

Finally, he came out, tying a towel around his waist. A wet Patrick, droplets running down his flat abdomen, down to the dark hair half covered by the towel was more distracting than the naked one. Oh god, she should've showered with him. Maybe she should stop wearing the black crap.

'You had your chance, princess,' he said, flashing a cheeky grin.

She gave a little laugh, but couldn't ignore the dread building inside. 'What didn't you tell me last night?'

He swore quietly, as he leaned against the shower door. 'The Miss Haverton story, did you ever see it?'

She shook her head.

'Front page, shagging in the park. My mum actually said she was ashamed to call me her son. I'll never forget the disappointment in her eyes. Libs, they've already tried to make out that you're a prostitute. What will they say if I'm involved?'

'But it'd be made up nonsense.'

'But it'd still hurt my parents.'

'So...' She dared to look up at him. 'Is that it? You're protecting your parents? Don't get me wrong, it's admirable, but they are grown-ups. They could handle the truth.'

'It's not just that.' He let out a slow sigh. 'I can't break the rules.'

'Why? What happens if you do?' She closed her eyes, not wanting to hear the answer.

'They'll kick me out. Disowned. Sacked. Bye-bye house, car and my life in Gosthwaite.'

No. Tears stung her eyes, but she hung her head so he couldn't see. 'Do they mean it?'

'My name being linked to your escapades on Halloween cost me two weeks wages. They mean it.'

'I'm so sorry.'

'Don't be. It's not your fault. It's mine.' He gave a brave smile and pulled her to him, wrapping his arms around her. 'Look, so we can't go out in public, but we'll work it out, Libs.'

'How? I know what it's like to lose your job and your family. You can't risk it.' Her cheek rested against his damp shoulder as she inhaled his fresh-from-the-shower scent. *I love you and I won't ruin your life.* She glanced down, spotting the smudge of mascara on his towel. 'I got the black crap on your towel, sorry.'

He gave a small laugh, relaxing his hold on her as he glanced down.

She darted out.

By the time he yelled her name, she was already running down the stairs. She dashed past their neatly folded clothes, an excited Isla and out the back door, hoping no one saw her leave. Who would see her? The rest of the world would be checking under the tree to see what Father Christmas had left them. For a brief moment, she'd thought all her Christmases had come at once, but in reality, she'd spent six months earning her place on the naughty list.

The bitter winter air ripped through the shirt, but Libby ignored it as she ignored the stones cutting into her bare feet. They were her penance for betraying her better judgement. She should never have even remotely flirted with Jack and god, did she need another reason to regret her affair with Robbie?

She strode into Maggie's garden, wiping in vain at the tears falling down her cheeks, the white shirt cuffs now streaked with black. London was her only option. She'd book a ticket on the first train south.

'Libby, stop,' he called from behind her.

She did, but only to put an end to their odd relationship once and for all. He crossed the gap between them, still pulling on his sweatshirt, his nine toes as bare as her ten. Before he could speak she lifted a hand and laid it on his forehead.

'Whatever influence I hold—'

'Don't give me that bullshit.' He knocked her hand away, and pulled her to him, wiping her tears with his sleeve. 'Please, don't cry.'

'It's not worth it, Patrick.'

'Isn't it?' He still held her face.

'I don't want a half-arsed, secret fling.'

'It'll be fun.'

'Fun?' Seriously, did he say *fun*? 'I've done secret. It's not fun. It's horrible.'

'It's just for six months.'

'I want more.'

His hands fell away. 'What do you mean, more?'

I love you. 'You know what I mean.'

Patrick took a step back. 'What are you expecting? We haven't even been out on a date.'

'And with your genius plan, we never will.' Libby folded her arms, shivering against the cold wind. 'Anyway, it doesn't matter.'

'Why?'

'I'm leaving.'

'I knew you'd do this.'

'Do what?'

'Run away.'

'I'm not running away.' She took a deep breath. 'I have a meeting with the English National Ballet on the twenty-ninth. I'm going to discuss going back to work. I arranged it after you messed me around yet again at Xander's party.'

Patrick shoved his hands in his pockets. 'And were you planning to tell me, or just fuck me then fuck off?'

'Of course I was going to tell you.'

'What about teaching ballet to the little kids?'

'London would be better.'

He stared at the ground. 'And us?'

She mustn't cry again. 'What us? You want a fuck buddy who's not going to get in the way of your idyllic life in the country. You might be a bloody good distraction, but let's face it, you're not ballet.' *And I won't ruin your life.*

His forehead creased as he looked up, his eyes blazing with hurt, anger, frustration. 'I guess not. Happy fucking Christmas, princess.'

And he walked away.

Chapter Thirty-Seven

The Cartier watch on Zoë's left wrist, her best Christmas present *ever*, sparkled as she padded down the stairs to say goodbye to Jonathan. He and his family were off on their annual trudge to the next village for mulled wine and mince pies at his brother's house, but Zoë opted to stay at home, citing culinary reasons. Really, she wanted an hour or two away from his bloody family.

The eldest son Eliot and his drippy wife Paula clearly despised her, while their two feral kids, Harriet and Joshua, had no concept of the word *no*. Twice Zoë found six year-old Harriet rummaging in her handbag, the last time pulling out cigarettes, tampons and using her Chanel lipstick to draw a picture of Granddad. But if they made her life hell, they were nothing compared to Ed.

His vitriolic attitude at the funeral hadn't abated and he used every opportunity to snipe at Zoë. The evening before, when she'd excused herself to get ready for the Mill party, Ed had poured her a glass of champagne, his cold eyes glaring into hers.

'But surely someone like you,' he'd said, 'only needs to throw on an old rag, a little lipstick and the latest diamonds my dad bought you.'

He'd become an obnoxious little prick. How had she ever fancied him?

Smiling, she slipped her arms around Jonathan and kissed him. 'Enjoy the walk.'

'Are you sure you don't want to come?' he asked.

'Too much to do.'

'Actually, dad,' Ed said, wandering down the hall. 'I thought I'd stay and give Zoë a hand.'

'Honestly, it's fine.' Zoë flashed a smile. What the hell was that bastard up to? 'Enjoy your walk.'

But Jonathan slapped his sons back. 'Good man, Ed.'

Zoë clenched her fists, barely restraining her fury as Ed headed back to the kitchen. 'I don't need his help.'

'It's a gesture, Zoë,' Jonathan ran his hands down her arms, trying to pacify her. 'Don't think I haven't noticed the tension between you two. I know it's difficult, but why don't you take some time to get to know him? You'll like him.'

All she could do was smile sweetly.

In the kitchen Ed was leaning on the island, waiting for her, his hands in his pockets, his dark hair contrasting fabulously with his Arran jumper, his blue eyes glittering with contempt. It was all too tempting to throttle him.

Or fuck him.

You'll like him. And wasn't that the problem. He was his father's son. Zoë strode past Ed, hating that his aftershave made her want to tie *him* to a four-poster bed. Ten o'clock, time for Buck's Fizz.

'What do you really want, Ed?'

'I'm just keen to help my wonderful step-mother-to-be in the kitchen. I'm one hell of a cook, you know.'

'Bite me.'

He looked her over, as though he were contemplating just that. 'Oh come on, I just want to talk and you've been avoiding me since I got here.'

'I wonder why. I notice you haven't told your dad about... us.'

'There is no us. And you haven't told him either. Why?'

She opened the fridge, needing the cold air to cool her flushing cheeks, and took out the champagne. 'What did you want to talk about?'

'I'll have one.' He leaned against the island, his eyes narrowing. 'Coincidences.'

Zoë raised her eyebrows as she filled two glasses. Bollocks to the orange juice. 'Coincidences?'

'A few months ago I came to see Mum. She had this amazing skunk. I know she used to score it off your aunt—'

'Great aunt.'

'Your *great* aunt, but Maggie was dead, so who was the new dealer, I asked. Your father's latest whore, she replied.'

Zoë smiled over her glass. 'I considered it a good deed. Your mum had needs and your dad had needs. I'm a facilitator.'

'Oh, come on, you're fucking him for the money, for the Cartier watches.'

'I'm fucking him because he's an amazing man.'

Ed stepped closer, invading her space. 'Is it a coincidence that the whore who supplied my mother with skunk happens to live next door to the vet's where the ketamine that killed her was stolen from?'

'Yes.' Zoë refused to back off. 'Yes, it's a massive bloody coincidence. Is this how you want to spend Christmas Day, accusing me of supplying the ket?'

'Did you supply the ket?'

'The night it was stolen, I was shagging your dad at a boutique hotel overlooking Grasmere.' Zoë tried not to smile when Ed flinched at her words. He was jealous? 'And the night your mother received the ket, I was dressed as the Queen of Hearts, surrounded by half of Gosthwaite. The police thoroughly checked my story after you suggested I was her dealer. Thanks for that.'

Ed leaned in, putting his lips next to her ear. 'Thing is, *stepmother*, I think you're a liar.'

He stood so close she could feel his semi and Zoë turned her head so her lips hovered an inch from his. 'What are you really after, Ed? To play with your daddy's toys?'

His lips curled in a mirthless laugh, his semi growing and pushing against her hip. 'You're a gold-digging whore.'

'What a shame you don't have any gold to dig.'

Their lips met in a hot, breathless kiss, his hands holding her face, and Zoë throbbed, her pants already soaking. Jesus, even Jonathan had to do more than just kiss her. She pulled away, staring at Ed. *I want you, not him.*

He stared back. 'Oh Christ.'

'We can't do this.' She begged him, but her fingers were in his hair. 'We can't do this to him.'

'But you and me?' Ed's eyes burned into her.

'It can't happen.' Zoë shook her head, though she pressed her body tight against his. 'I honestly swear I'm not just after his money.'

'It's wasted on him, Zoë. He fucked around on my mum for years. He'll do it to you too.' Ed's hand reached down, slowly hitching up the hem of her jersey dress. 'You can't marry him.'

Zoë wanted to be sick, repulsed by how much she wanted Ed. She couldn't cheat on Jonathan. She couldn't prove everyone right. But she did nothing to stop his hand. 'You just want revenge. To prove a point.'

'This isn't revenge and you feel the same.' His hand ventured further, gliding across the silk of her knickers. The damp patch had him groaning into her hair. 'Oh God, Zoë.'

She kissed him, sucking on his bottom lip, fumbling with the buttons on his jeans as he pushed her knickers to one side. A finger slid over her clit and she leaned into him, encouraging him, needing him to go further.

'Jesus.' He closed his eyes as his finger slipped inside her and her muscles squeezed, begging for more. He obliged. 'I want to fuck you.'

As she nodded, caving in, he spun her around, bending her over the breakfast bar. Or maybe he wasn't his father's son. Ed pushed up her dress with one hand and pulled her knickers to the side with the other. She ought to hate it, the lack of control, the submission of power, but the thrill of him wanting her so badly had her pushing back against him. She'd never needed anything like this before.

He entered her, muttering the things he'd wanted to do to her since they'd met. Fucking her like this was only the start, he said. They belonged together, he said, and they always would.

Zoë knew he was right.

Ed's fingers teased her clit and his teeth bit into her neck. He marked her, owning her, and she didn't stop him. She couldn't. Her body shuddered, coming around his dick, against his hand and ten seconds later, he cried out, pumping himself inside her.

Zoë collapsed, resting her forehead against the cool marble worktop. It was the first time she'd had unprotected sex in ten years. How had she let that happen? How?

'Sorry,' he whispered, still inside her. 'I'm so sorry, but I had to.'

You can, whenever you want. Her weakness scared her, but the thought of Ed never fucking her again, scared her even more. 'I forgive you.'

'Did you supply Mum with the ket?' His words were murmured against her hair.

She turned, facing him with honesty as his come dripped from her. 'If I had, I... I wouldn't feel bad. She was in so much pain. Your dad said she was smiling when he found her. Maybe she thought it was time to let go.'

Ed kissed her, his mouth gentle and sweet. 'For fifteen years, my mother was a zombie in the living room. Her choice, Zoë. My life's better without her. It's good to admit that to someone.'

Zoë held his face. 'You can tell me anything.'

'I don't mind dad finding someone new. Fuck, he deserves to be happy after nursing her for fifteen years, but if he does have a new wife, I'd like one who'd make a half decent mother, not one who brings out every oedipal bone in my body.'

In his bedroom, one cluttered with sports trophies and writing awards, Zoë sucked Ed's dick while he told her to move to London, and when she lay on her back with him slowly sinking into her, she agreed. There was only one man for her, and it was Edward Carr. To prove his point, Ed made her come four times in the hour they had. The final time, Zoë broke down, sobbing, but Ed held her, whispering he loved her.

What the fuck was she going to do? This wasn't how it was supposed to be. He was destroying her.

Libby's text came at the perfect moment. *Need you, Emu.*

Zoë replied, *I'll be there, Koala Bear.*

Ten minutes later Zoë sat in her BMW, Ed's come still soaking her knickers, and screamed. That obnoxious little prick had ruined everything.

* * *

Curled up on the wicker sofa in the garden, Libby pulled a hat over her wet hair and sipped her tea. Half-twelve. Where would Patrick be now, at his parents? Would his dad give him a hard time for going home with her? For the eightieth time that day, tears rolled down her cheeks.

'Hi,' Zoë whispered as she crept out with a bottle of champagne and two mugs. 'I figured you mustn't be in the mood for celebrating, but it's bloody good stuff. The mugs will stop it feeling like a party.'

Libby tried not to sob. 'Thanks for coming. I'm sorry to drag you away from Jonathan.'

Zoë filled the mugs. 'Honestly, I was glad of the chance to escape. Eliot hates me, the grandkids are the spawn of Satan and don't get me started on Ed. They can cook their own bloody dinner. Let's get shitfaced.'

'Have you got cigarettes too?'

'That bad?'

In the grey, frosty light, sipping a mug of vintage Veuve Cliquot and chain-smoking Marlboro Gold, Libby explained about the twelve hours she'd spent with Patrick.

'Zo, I'd give up anything, *everything* for him. I really do love him, but I can't risk him being disowned by his parents. And what if when I go to London... what if I still love ballet more? He won't come with me.'

'He might.' Zoë's hand shook as she took a long drag on a cigarette. 'He loves you, Lib. I saw it the day he came to ask me for Hyssop. He's scared. Give him a break.'

'I don't want to sneak around for six months.'

'Do you really want to go back to the company?'

'If I can't have him, definitely. If I can have him... I don't know, but I have to find out.' Libby wallowed in her own misery until she realised Zoë's furrowed brow hadn't eased. In fact, her nervous blinking had increased, as had the rate she was knocking back the champagne. 'What's up?'

'Nothing.'

'It's after one, there's a chicken in the fridge and you've not made a move to cook it.'

Zoë lit another cigarette. 'Not hungry.'

Libby's own worries waned as concern for Zoë took over. If Zoë didn't want to cook, it meant she didn't want to eat. Again.

Libby put her arm around her. 'Six months on and we're more miserable than when we left Manchester. I'm leaving for London so I don't ruin my not-boyfriends life, but you, young lady, with your fabulous new fiancée, you look more depressed. What happened?'

'I fucked up, Lib.' Zoë cried like she had the day she met Libby fifteen years ago. 'Please don't hate me.'

'As if. We've survived too much.'

Zoë's hands shook as she lit another cigarette. 'This morning... I fucked Ed. I've never known anything like it. I couldn't stop myself.'

Libby bit back every lecturing word on her tongue. 'Do you love him?'

'Obsessive lust maybe, some physical and emotional bond. I lost control and I need it back.' Zoë took a long deep breath. 'What the hell do I do?'

'Surely, if you find something this powerful, you jump on it.'

'Not with him.'

'Why?'

'He's a fucking penniless writer, a waiter to pay the bills.'

'Zo, it's not about money. It doesn't make you happy.'

'Aside from you, it's the only thing I can rely on.' Zoë dragged the back of her hand over her eyes. 'And first thing tomorrow, I need to find a chemist that's open. I need the morning after pill.'

Libby's mouth gaped open. Zoë never had sex without condoms and had regularly lectured Libby for relying on the pill with Paolo.

Zoë refused to take the pill, claiming it made her fat, but really she didn't want to get pregnant and condoms put her in charge of Mother Nature.

'Completely out of control,' Zoë sighed, staring at the decking. 'Have you got a spell to help with that?'

* * *

The second the clock struck seven, his shift on call over, Patrick half-filled a vast wine glass, ignoring his father's disapproving frown. Would Libby be eating roast chicken with Zoë, or sitting with only Hyssop for company? Twice he'd almost gone round. The first time he arrived at the garden to see her halfway down the bridleway with Grace, starting what would turn out to be a two hour run. The second time, Zoë rocked up with two bottles. In the end, he'd decided if he couldn't talk to Libby, he may as well go to his parents' and get drunk with Sam.

'Okay,' his mum said, banging on an imaginary dong. 'Dinner is served.'

He told Isla to wait in her basket and to his delight, she curled up obediently, earning herself a biscuit.

'You'll spoil that dog,' Sam said, patting his back. 'I like her ears.'

Patrick laughed, ushering his brother and Charlotte in front of him. They could all get stoned after the parents had gone to bed. That one pleasant note to his otherwise appalling day fluttered out of the window as he walked into the dining room and Ms Olivia Wilde stared down at him, her eyes filled with tears.

'You've got to be fucking joking.'

'Patrick!' His father glared at him over his glasses.

This is your fault. You and your ridiculous ultimatum. 'Can we take it down?'

'Don't be silly, darling.' His mum pushed him towards his usual chair, the one facing Libby's portrait. 'I'm surprised you didn't bring her. I nearly invited her myself, but I wasn't sure if you'd be cross or not. Where is she? She doesn't have family around here, does she?'

'She's packing her bags.' He knocked back half his wine, trying not to look over Sam's head at the Broken Ballerina. 'She's going back to London so she doesn't land me in the paper.'

The silence descended.

Finally, Patrick turned to his father. 'She's going and it's your fault.

What the hell did you say to her last night?'

'Nothing.' He frowned. 'I barely saw the girl. Jonathan wanted to introduce us to Zoë. They were discussing you, calling you an egotist. Bloody rude, if you ask me.'

'E... is for Egotist. E was empty on her list.' Patrick laughed and stood up. 'I'm out of here.'

'Patrick, sit down,' Charlotte snapped.

Patrick stared at her. Sam stared at her. Their parents stared at her. Charlotte didn't do bossy. Patrick did as he was told.

'The whole world doesn't revolve around you,' she went on. 'We have news. We wanted to tell you yesterday, but then you turned up with Isla. And then this afternoon, we nearly... but you were so bloody grumpy. I'm really sorry about Libby, but I won't let you bugger up Christmas. This should be the happiest day ever. I'm pregnant. You're going to be an uncle and we thought you'd be pleased, but if we waited for a moment when you weren't having some kind of drama, the baby would be born already. Sorry for making a fuss, Liz. Dinner's getting cold.'

But his mum was too busy mopping up tears to care. His dad was the first to move, hugging Charlotte. Patrick stared at his brother across the table. Sam smiled, and they met somewhere behind their mother's chair.

'I'm sorry, man.' Patrick closed his stinging eyes. What kind of selfish bastard had he become? 'Congratulations. Christ, bit of a shock.'

Sam nodded. 'After dinner, Charlotte will fall asleep in front of the TV. Fancy taking the dogs for a walk and getting stoned?'

More than anything in the bloody world. Letting his big brother go, Patrick took over hugging Charlotte, intermittently telling her she was amazing, he was an arse and he couldn't wait to be an uncle.

'All three of them are flat out,' Sam whispered, quietly closing the patio door while trying not to drop a bottle of Jura and two glasses. 'We can walk the dogs later.'

Patrick smiled and took out the joint he'd rolled earlier. 'I feel about fifteen.'

'Me too. Remember that time Juliet Knight and Sarah Barnes came round?'

Patrick laughed. 'And you got caught with Sarah? Christ, we were wasted. I would've got into Juliet's pants if you hadn't broken that window.'

'Ah, the days of behaving badly.'

'Long gone for you, sunshine.' Patrick studied his brother. Two years older, but definitely not wiser. Sam had been kicked out of two schools and got in more trouble with girls than even Patrick could comprehend. But witnessing all Sam's mistakes had taught Patrick to be more careful. 'I can't believe you're going to be a dad. You scared?'

'Bricking it.' Sam took the joint. 'But don't tell Charlotte.'

'I think she'll know from the sheer terror in your eye every time Mum mentions pushchairs and cots.'

'Fuck, don't.' Sam shuddered. 'What's going on with this ballerina girl? Kicking off at dad over her, brave lad. Mum said she met her at yours this morning. Must've been fun.'

'Mum cleaned the fucking house on Christmas morning, just to have a nosy.'

'Who is she?'

Patrick handed his brother his phone, showing him a photo he'd sneakily taken at Oscar's, of Libby braless in the silk top. Not a photo he intended to delete.

Sam grinned. 'She doesn't seem your type, but nice tits. I would.'

Patrick kicked his ankle, taking the joint back.

'So why isn't she here and why are you? Wouldn't be the first time you ditched Christmas dinner to shag a random blonde.'

'She's not a random blonde.' Patrick scowled. 'She's not here because when I told her about the ultimatum, she did what I thought she'd do. She ran away.'

'She wanted a one night stand?'

'No, but she's got a job interview in London.'

'So persuade her to stay.'

'I can't. We'd need to keep it secret and she doesn't want that, not after Rob.'

'Fuck, is she the one who nearly split Rob and Van up? Nice girl.'

'Actually, she is.' Patrick sighed. 'But I think she wants some kind of commitment.'

Sam laughed. 'Aha, here's the problem. Nina mark two.'

'Fuck off, this is different. Libby's alright but I mean...' Patrick took a deep breath. 'How did you know Charlotte was... you know, a keeper?'

Sam shrugged. 'But when I started asking questions like that, I knew she was something else. What's so great about this Libby? Aside from her perfect tits.'

What's so great about her? Patrick explained the last few months – Robbie, the newspaper, the fell race, her birthday, and how he'd pissed her off by backing away once too often.

'It's dad's fault. If he'd just be reasonable–'

'Have to stop you there, little bro. This is your fault. You're the one who fucked the beauty queen in the park.'

'What the... You're supposed to be on my side.'

'I am, you wee fuckwit.'

Patrick sank the rest of his whisky. 'What the hell am I going to do?'

'It's easy. Man up and confess your undying love to her.'

Patrick shook his head.

'Well then, let her go to London, and pray your fucking balls off that she comes back in six months.'

Letting the weed numb his body, Patrick sat back, remembering the perfect few hours he'd had with her. Would she be in bed now? Maybe he could go round. No, this was his hedonistic side coming out. But still, he could go round and persuade her that they could go out in secret. They could go for dinner in some other town. Hell, they could go away for the weekend.

Actually, that wasn't a bad idea. Would a city break work as an overblown romantic gesture? He hated Paris and Rome, most cities in fact. Maybe a weekend skiing? Did she ski? Yes, she and Zoë were supposed to go, but their passports had been stolen and Zoë couldn't find her birth certificate in time. Surely a weekend away would count for something.

He'd talk to her in the morning.

Chapter Thirty-Eight

For Patrick, the morning arrived, not with an internet search for mini-breaks to Courchevel, but helping rescue a pony stuck in a bog. Four hours later he'd barely had chance to shower off the smell of rotting peat, when Becky from across the road called – Snuffles, her guinea pig had broken its leg.

Resigned to a day of appalling coffee and inane drivel, Patrick rang Hannah. She answered immediately, but sounded cagey when he asked her to come in. Maybe she wouldn't show and he could get Sam to assist. Every cloud. He'd prepped the room and had his sleeves rolled up, when Grace came in, carrying the guinea pig.

'What are you doing here?' he asked.

'Hannah can't make it,' she said, pulling her hair into a bun. 'And we need to talk.'

'About what?' He frowned at the unfortunate guinea pig. 'How the hell do you break a guinea pig's leg on Boxing Day anyway?'

'Becky said Snuffles was running around the living room and her mum opened the door on it. Anyway, as practice manager, I'm making some changes. You hate Hannah working here and she leaves every night in tears. She's emailed me, detailing the many, many occasions where you've displayed tribunal-worthy behaviour. She wants to go back to Haverton. I want to come back here.'

'And how's that—'

'The office crap, which it turns out I rather like, I can do at Haverton on Monday afternoons.'

'Out of hours?'

'It's fine.' She pulled on her blue scrubs. 'At least I'll know the in-patients are taken care of.'

'Ah, you don't trust me.' He tried not to smile. He'd get Grace back. 'And what about...' *The minor inconvenience of you being in love with me.*

'I can work with you, if you can work with me.'

'It won't be weird?'

'Has it been for the last year?' Grace glanced out of the window, across at Libby's house. 'Have fun last night?'

'Did you talk to her yesterday? I saw you went running together.'

'She barely said a word. What's going on?'

'It's complicated.'

'No, it's not. The minute I saw her, I knew you'd like her.'

'Why?'

'She's your type.'

'My type?' He had one?

Grace laughed. 'I've listened to you bang on about women for two years. Miss Haverton's slutty underwear, Tabitha Doyle's bitchy attitude, Daisy's innocent looks. I know what you want. You want a nice girl and if you take away her make-up and clothes, that's exactly what Libby is. Plus, you're right. She is like me. That's why you get on so well.'

'It's still complicated.' He bent down to the little brown and white guinea pig, frowning as it scooted along the table, refusing to put its hind leg down. Cute little thing. 'What about you and Jack? Why are you going back there again?'

'I love him. And he puts up with me.'

'He can't keep it in his pants.'

'Jack's insecure and me working with you didn't help. I think we'll be okay now.'

'He knew?'

'I think everyone except you did.'

'Seriously, is this going to be okay?'

'Yep.' Grace peered at Snuffles. 'X-ray and pin job?'

Patrick nodded and let out a frustrated sigh. He wouldn't be talking to Libby anytime soon.

* * *

Libby sat on the edge of Zoë's bed. There was nothing more effective at distracting her from her own misery than the misery of others. On Christmas Day, she and Zoë had got utterly hammered, eventually pulling on little black dresses and heading to the Alfred. Libby had played Christmas classics on the piano, encouraging half the pub to sing along, while Zoë's flirting levels ensured they hadn't needed to buy a single drink all night. Inevitably, Libby ended up wailing on Zoë's shoulder, drunkenly vowing to talk to Patrick the minute he got home – thank god, Zoë had confiscated her phone.

A raging headache thumped in Libby's brain and she promised her lungs she'd never, ever smoke again, but no matter how bad she felt, she'd climbed out of bed. Crikey, she'd dragged her backside into the shower and even managed breakfast, but Zoë hadn't moved. Zoë had been Libby's rock the day before, but now, she lay staring at the wall with tears pouring down her cheeks.

'Zo?' Libby stroked her friend's hair. 'Zo, you can't just shut down. So you fucked up. If you want to fix it, you have to pull yourself together. And to start, you have to eat.'

Zoë flinched.

'Look,' Libby said, 'we both know you don't want to eat because you think control comes from not eating. And we both know why. We've been through this too many times, Zo, and you know I love you, but I'm not prepared for the cucumber, celery and black tea stage. You're a bitch when you go through that bit.'

There was a half laugh.

'So if you want control, take it. Control isn't not eating, or only eating foods with less than one percent fat. Real control is eating just enough. I have real control. Now, sit up.' Libby closed her eyes, praying she wasn't making things worse. 'Now, Zoë.'

Zoë did as she was told. 'I don't—'

'Control.' Libby held up a bowl. The strands of tagliatelle dripped with butter, lemon and chicken jus. 'Real control would be to eat half of this. Not a third, not three quarters, but half. Half, I've calculated, would be a perfectly healthy portion. And by healthy, I mean just a bit less than necessary.'

Zoë hadn't taken her eyes off the dish, but her chin had raised. 'Half?'

Please, Zoë, fight. 'Exactly half.'

Zoë took the bowl.

Libby left, trying not to smile and trying not to be too hopeful. This was Maggie's fault, and for a brief moment, Libby wished could bump off the old witch herself.

Downstairs, she curled up on the sofa, once again succumbing to tears. How desperately did she want to say to Patrick *okay, let's do the secret fling?* She could do it. She'd take what she could have. But then she'd remember how easily a simple hug from Xander could be made to look like a kiss. She wouldn't cost Patrick his job and the respect of his parents.

Taking a deep breath, she picked up her phone and called Paolo.

'It's me.'

'Hey, me. What happened to moving on?'

'Are we still friends?'

'Always.'

'Where are you, can you talk?'

'I'm in my Shoreditch apartment watching Dorothy skip down the Yellow Brick Road.'

'Why?'

'It's a cultural phenomenon I've never seen. What's up?'

Libby skipped through the TV channels until she landed on Dorothy and the Tin Man. It was like she and Paolo were together again. 'I have a job interview on Thursday, with the ballet. I could do with a place to stay.'

The sofa creaked and he took a deep breath. 'Are you going to stay-stay, or just stay?'

'I'm in love with Patrick.'

'Just stay then.'

'If I had any sense, I'd stay-stay. Sorry.'

He laughed. 'You can still share my bed.'

Libby closed her eyes, picturing him as she'd last seen him. His dark hair, slightly curling at the ends, falling to his chin, a little longer at the back. She'd cut it for him once, but the next day he'd shaved it all off, proclaiming her the worst hairdresser in the world.

'Why do you put up with me?' she asked.

'Because I still love you.'

'I'll go to a hotel.'

'No, you won't.' He paused. 'But return favour? I need a date on Wednesday, for a friend's exhibition. Come with me?'

'Of course.' Libby paused for a moment. 'Paolo, do you know Seamus Doyle?'

'The poet? Not personally.'

'I want to meet him. Can you get him invited to the exhibition?'

'Don't see why not. His wife's a massive patron of undiscovered artists. Why do you want to meet him though?'

'I think he might've been the last person to see Maggie alive.' *And I want to know if he murdered her. Or at least if she died happy.*

'I'll see what I can do.' Paolo paused. 'I ought to warn you though. The papers are still looking for you.'

'What?'

'The Daily Mail, the Sun… They want to know who the Broken

Ballerina is. They might guess when they see you. Sorry.'

And if she were famous, then she wouldn't be able to return to Gosthwaite, to Patrick, for six months. No ifs or buts. What would Michael Wray do if he found out if his *Libertine* was the Broken Ballerina? So this was it, her choice: Patrick or ballet.

* * *

As Dorothy found her way back to Kansas, the old Zoë put the half-empty, half-full bowl of pasta on the coffee table. For weeks she'd been wearing conservative dresses, prim skirts and fifties cardigans, anything to fit in at the golf club and not look like a gold-digging whore. But not anymore. In skinny jeans, a slinky red top and the metal-studded Louboutins, she sat on the window sill and applied her trademark scarlet lipstick.

'Why the scarf?' Libby asked, trying not grin.

'Hide the bloody love bite.'

'I take it from the shoes, you're choosing Jonathan.'

Zoë flicked back her immaculately straightened hair. 'Yes. I'm not giving up everything just because I fancy Ed.'

'Fancy Ed?' Libby frowned. 'I thought it was more than that. A physical and emotional bond, you said.'

'It's irrelevant. Real control?' Zoë nodded to the bowl of pasta. 'Real control is walking in that house and never fucking Ed again. Real control is marrying Jonathan and getting everything I ever wanted.'

'Are you sure?'

'Look, I know you'd give up everything for love. But it's not what's most important to me.'

'I suppose this way,' Libby said, flashing the fakest smile, Zoë had ever seen, 'you only have to bump off the old man to get the money. If you chose the son, you'd have to bump them both off.'

Oh Libby, if only you knew how close to the bone you are. Tears rolled down Zoë's cheeks as she returned the smile. 'It'd be worse than that. If I chose the son, I'd have to bump off the dad, the son, the brother, his wife and their two grubby children. Shagging Jonathan requires much less effort.'

Libby enveloped her in a bear hug. 'I'm proud of you. You didn't give in to food.'

'Thank you,' Zoë whispered. 'What are you going to do?'

'Go to London and avoid getting me or Patrick in the bloody newspaper. I'll come back in six months.'

'That's a crappy plan.'

'It's all I have.' Libby wiped her eyes. 'On the upside, I have a date on Wednesday. Paolo's taking me to some fancy-schmancy art exhibition. Though it will mean the papers finding out I'm the Broken Ballerina.'

'Is that a bad thing?' Zoë asked, tapping her phone against her thigh. 'I mean, why hide if you're going back to the company? Why not let the bloody world know you're the Broken Ballerina? Because let's say if the Guardian ran with an exclusive, would it hurt your chances of getting the odd role? That's what you really want, isn't it?'

Libby stared at her.

A slow smile spread over Zoë's face. 'Lib, real control isn't avoiding the press. It's using them to get what you want.'

Twenty minutes later, Zoë arrived at Jonathan's. He'd stood leaning in the doorway as she parked, but strolled over to open her door. Ever the gent, he helped her out, a gentle hand lifting her chin to kiss her. A warmth filled her insides and it wasn't down to some base desire to tie him to the bed. This was the life she wanted; a life of power – power, not uncontrollable lust. A less gentle hand brushed over her breast squeezing it just a little. And Jesus, she did love shagging Jonathan.

'I missed you,' he said, his hands roving over her arse. 'How's Libby?'

'Devastated. She's horrendously in love with Patrick, but she's moving back to London.' Zoë smiled up at him, raking her fingers through his hair. 'Did you have a nice day?'

'We did. Ed finally got into the spirit of Christmas and Paula knocked dinner together.' He leant in, whispering in her ear. 'They're going out for lunch, but I want to make love to you, to worship you for hours.'

Zoë nodded, her insides liquefying. 'Just what I need.'

'You still need to open your present.'

'But I already did.' She glanced down at her Cartier watch. 'I adore it.'

'You have another.' Smiling, he held a hand over her eyes and led her around the side of the house.

Inside the open garage doors sat a brand new BMW Z4 – shiny, black and wrapped in a big red bow. Tears filled her eyes as she turned to him.

'Jonathan, I really do love you.' She held his face. 'And not because you buy me cars and watches.'

For several minutes, she kissed him, whispering how much she adored him and the things she'd do to him when they were alone later.

'Ooh, Granny Zoë, can we go for a drive in your new car?' little Harriet asked.

Granny? Jesus, that kid was priceless. Zoë ignored her, instead kissing Eliot and Paula a happy Christmas. Ed wandered up, his tousled dark hair reminding her of the previous day and creating a dull ache between her legs. More than anything in the world Zoë wanted to feel Ed's dick inside her again, but she did nothing more than politely kiss his cheek.

'Stepmother's home,' she whispered.

Devastation flashed in his eyes and his fingers dug into her arm, but Zoë refused to weaken. Jonathan was real control.

* * *

Knocking on the imposing blue door of Kiln Howe terrified Libby, but she held her head high as the barking of dogs grew louder. Someone was coming. She prayed it wasn't Patrick's father. The door opened and Patrick stooped, holding back two energetic black retrievers. She blinked. It couldn't be Patrick; he was at the vet's.

'You must be Sam,' she said, still staring.

His smile grew. 'And you must be Libby. He's not here.'

'I know.' She tipped her head to the side. Same black curly hair, same nose, same hazel eyes. 'You two look really alike, really, really alike.'

He laughed. 'It's very nice to meet you at last. I've heard a lot about you.'

Libby blushed. 'Is your mum in? I wondered if I could borrow the painting.'

'I can't see why not. It's yours after all.'

'Well, not really. I gave it away. Patrick bought it and gave it to your mum. It's hers.'

'Well, I'm sure she won't mind. Come in.' Sam stood aside, still holding the dogs. 'Mum!'

Elizabeth appeared, promptly followed by Malcolm McBride. Libby cringed.

'Hello, Miss Wilde,' he said.

'For God's sake, Dad, her name's Libby.' Sam shook his head. 'She wants to borrow the painting.'

'Just for a day or so.' Libby daren't look Malcolm McBride in the eye. He probably believed she was a prostitute.

'Of course.' Elizabeth beckoned her in. 'Tea?'

Libby hesitated. Crikey, all she'd wanted was to take the painting, but Sam took her arm, leading her down the hallway.

Malcolm hovered at the door to the kitchen, holding out his hand. 'It's very nice to meet you, Libby.'

Stunned, Libby shook his hand, not missing that Patrick's hazel eyes and thick black lashes came from his father.

'Come on,' Sam whispered. 'We don't bite. But to be on the safe side, I wouldn't take any of the ginger snaps. My wife Charlotte is likely to take you out with a teaspoon.'

Libby glanced up at him, as bemused by his similarity to Patrick as she was with his words.

'She's pregnant,' he explained, ushering her into the warmth of the kitchen. 'They stop her feeling sick.'

Libby couldn't help laughing, and Sam's enormous smile, so like Patrick's, took over his face. 'Congratulations.'

Within minutes, Libby found herself sitting at the kitchen table with a mug of tea and a fat slice of Elizabeth's carrot cake. Malcolm continued filling in his crossword, calling out clues to which the others would suggest answers – Sam and Elizabeth clearly competitive, while Charlotte offered ridiculous solutions.

A sudden longing overcame Libby – a need to be part of a family once again. If she went to London, if she became the Broken Ballerina, would she ever belong in a family like this?

Patrick or ballet.

* * *

After an hour of surgery, the guinea pig was recovering comfortably and Patrick sat down with a well-earned coffee. Pinning a guinea pig's leg was possibly the fiddliest job he'd done in a long time. Thank Christ Hannah hadn't come in – no way would she have been able to get a cannula in the tiny creature. Grace on the other hand, had inserted one in seconds.

'Oh my God,' Grace squealed. 'It's snowing. It never snows at Christmas.'

The minor flurry, against his expectations, settled and developed into a veritable blizzard over the next thirty minutes. Libby's ancient Golf still wasn't parked outside the house. Was she driving? Maybe he should ring her. Grace could watch the patient while he picked Libby up. But if he were alone with her, what the hell would he say? He stared at his phone. What would Robbie do? He'd tell her he loved her and everything would be fine. How did Rob do that? How could he just know a girl was right?

By five o'clock the blizzard eased off and Patrick couldn't help feeling cheered by the snow. It changed the community. The orange glow from the street lamps and multi-coloured lights flashing on the Green's Christmas tree added a cosy warmth. Merry drinkers spilled from the Alfred and three sets of children were building snowmen, but despite the laughter, the Green remained peaceful, muffled under its white duvet.

Creeping slowly up the Green came his parents' Range Rover. Perfect timing. Maybe his mum or dad would keep an eye on Snuffles while he rescued Libby. The car pulled up outside and Sam jumped out, carrying *the Broken Ballerina*.

'What the hell...'

Libby climbed out of the car, jogging ahead of Sam. He took the painting into Maggie's cottage and when he came back out Libby kissed his cheek, thanking him. Briefly, as though she knew he was watching, she glanced at Patrick. Her face as sad as it had been the morning before.

What are you doing, Libs?

She gave him the smallest of smiles. He needed to talk to her. They had to sort this out. The arrival of his parents distracted him for a moment and when he looked back, Libby had gone. He forced a smile for his mum, but the sudden intrusion irritated him.

'Darling, Libby's a sweetheart,' she said. 'How's Becky's guinea pig?'

He let Grace fill his mum in, Patrick turning his attention to his buoyant brother.

'Bro, time for a pint?' Sam hugged him, slapping his back, before whispering, 'I love Libby.'

'What the hell's going on? Why's she got the painting?'

'She wants to borrow it. She stayed for tea and it's fair to say Dad's smitten. It started snowing so we gave her a lift. Left her death trap at Kiln Howe. Thought we'd take you to the pub. Seriously, Dad's smitten.'

Patrick glanced towards Libby's closed door. 'Why does she want the painting?'

'Wouldn't say. She was more interested in your niece or nephew.'

'She was distracting you, getting you to talk about what you wanted to so you wouldn't pry. It's a skill of hers.'

'Who cares? She'd make a great sister-in-law.'

Sister-in-law? Jesus.

'I don't know if you've noticed, bro, but there's snow outside.' Sam's eyes glinted. 'Fight?'

'I get Grace. You can have Charlotte and Mum.'

'Our mother and a pregnant woman? Thanks.'

'As if I'd throw anything at Charlotte.'

Sam merely raised his eyebrows.

Ten minutes later, led by the two McBride brothers, the entire Green became embroiled in a snowball fight.

'It's like when the boys were little,' said seventy year-old Mrs Jenkins, as she and Andrea from number twelve pelted Malcolm with snow.

Despite waging war and orchestrating his troops against Sam, Patrick didn't miss Libby's front door opening. She came out, bundled up in her down jacket, a hat pulled low over her eyes. Sadly, Grace had spotted her too and a white ball smacked against Libby's woollen hat, making her shriek.

While Patrick debated high-fiving Grace or reprimanding her for friendly fire, Libby retaliated, sending a snowball flying towards Grace. She ducked and the missile landed squarely on Patrick's shoulder. Libby's hand went to her mouth, shocked she'd hit him.

My brother loves her, my best friends love her, even my dad is fairly enamoured...

She laughed.

He hadn't seen her laugh, not really laugh, since Christmas Eve. Grinning, he scooped up a double handful of snow. Libby ran.

Still laughing, she dashed behind the war memorial, dodged between cars, but as they neared the surgery her hiking boots failed to grip the snow and she slipped, giving him the chance to catch her. He grabbed her jacket and dumped the snow over her head, sending the ice cold flakes down her collar. She squealed, and with one leg she kicked his legs from under him.

As he fell backwards, his fingers tightened, clutching at her jacket and pulling her with him. He thudded onto the snowy pavement and she landed on top of him. Hidden by his Land Rover from the rest of the Green, they were cocooned in their own winter wonderland and her body relaxed against his.

'How the hell do you do that?' he asked, laughing. Snowflakes dusted her hat, her eyelashes, her nose. Why couldn't it be like this all the time? 'I've missed you.'

'It's been twenty-four hours.'

Thirty-one actually. 'A very long twenty-four hours.'

'I hear you're going to be an uncle.'

'I hear you had tea with my family.'

'You and your brother look so alike, I thought he was you when he answered the door.'

'He likes you.' *She'd make a great sister-in-law.*

Patrick suppressed a shiver and tucked her fringe under the hat, taking his time to just look at her, to breathe in her perfume. *You're not ballet, are you?* Had she really meant that? Her pretty grey eyes gazed down at him. Sod it. He kissed her. Roses and sweet peas.

She kissed him back and for a few blissful seconds it was Christmas Day again. The whole world was new and they could do anything they wanted. A war cry brought him crashing back to reality.

'We can't do this,' she whispered, pulling out of his arms and sitting up.

'I know, but I was thinking... we could escape for a couple of days.' Jesus, he hadn't intended to throw that out there so early. In bed later, maybe.

'What do you mean?'

'Go somewhere. Get away from prying eyes.'

She glanced at her hands, playing with a handful of snow. 'Come to London with me?'

'You're really going?'

'Yes.'

'Why?'

'Because I want to see if... You said I should stop looking for distractions and stop pretending my past didn't happen. You're right. My life isn't ruined. It just needs to be different.'

'But why London? You can teach here.' He sat up, sighing.

'But what if I can have my old life back? If I use the Broken Ballerina to market myself, maybe I might just get another fifteen minutes, maybe I could get a few roles, small solos.'

'You want to dance again?' *You're not ballet, are you?* She did mean it.

'Just for a few months—'

'If you do, you won't come back.'

'Maybe, I don't know.' She took a deep breath. 'But... I hear they have cows in Surrey.'

He stared at her. Was she serious?

'It's okay,' she said, standing up and forcing a smile. 'Whatever I'm imagining in my pretty little head, it's never going to happen.'

'Libs, be fair.' He sat on his heels, leaning against his Land Rover. 'I'm trying to hang on to my life here. I'm not going to throw it all away and move to London.'

She nodded and headed back to cottage.

'Libby...'

She turned back to him. 'Look, I really like you. I think you already know that, but I really, *really* like you and I don't want, I can't cope with the random attention you're willing to give.'

'Lib—'

'Patrick, I love you.'

Why did girls have to do this? 'Can't we just—'

'You might be happy with a secret fling, discreet nights out where no one sees who you're with, but I've tried that and I hated it. I deserve better.' She glanced up to the grey sky, tears shining in her eyes. 'The thing is, I admire what you're doing, I really do, but I don't think this is just about the ultimatum and I have no intention of ending up like Nina, wasting four years of my life, only for you to run two hundred miles because you're scared of commitment.'

And she walked away.

Chapter Thirty-Nine

The camera flashes startled her, but Libby maintained her cool smile as Paolo helped her from the taxi. Several photographers yelled to him, asking for her name. He obliged, but told them nothing more. Together they headed toward the burly doormen, Libby striding out on her highest black heels.

'You look beautiful. A real star,' Paolo whispered. 'You sure you're in love with the vet and his rural dream? This could be us, being fabulous in London and going to all the best parties…'

She laughed, in her element. Here, she didn't worry about not having real world curves like Zoë and Grace. Here, she walked amongst neurotic models and size zero actresses. Here, Libby blended in. Tomorrow, the cannier journalists would discover Olivia Wilde was a ballerina, a ballerina who hadn't danced for four years. Her anonymity would be over and she'd become known as the Broken Ballerina.

Inside the Kensington art gallery, Libby and Paolo drifted around, studying the bizarre paintings and even more bizarre sculptures. Just about everyone they met air-kissed and hugged him. This was Paolo, her destitute ex-boyfriend, who'd lived in more squats than he'd held down real jobs. Now he wore a cutting edge suit and Italian leather shoes. She missed his threadbare jeans and Converse boots.

'Some art I just don't get,' Libby said, frowning at a three dimensional, upside down papier-mâché representation of Van Gogh's sunflowers. 'So which is the artist?'

'Danny's the guy with the red beehive by the bar.'

Libby giggled. 'I'm so glad your art is recognisable.'

With his arm around her shoulders, hers around his waist, they looked like the cosy couple they were trying to portray. Both had little to lose from any newspaper inches.

'You really do look beautiful,' Paolo said, kissing her shoulder.

'Thank you.'

She felt it. The silk top she'd once appropriated from Zoë's wardrobe and faux leather jeans had become her favourite outfit.

When she and Patrick got down and dirty in the hallway, he'd admitted that in Oscar's, it'd taken all his self-control not to reach out and touch her, just to see if her breasts felt as good as they looked.

Libby crossed her ankles, trying to banish memories of the sex, and focussed on a painting of a lilac pony galloping through a turquoise sea.

'Now, that I…' she said, glancing around, but Paolo was chatting to some guy in a kaftan.

Abandoned, she took a glass of mineral water from a passing waiter and wandered over to a trio of peach cows munching yellow grass. Cute, but the lilac horse rocked more. She glanced to the price tags. Seven grand for the cows? Five for the lilac horse? Crikey. Maybe she should take up dodgy arts and crafts. Two vast, snub-nosed pigs peered down at her, one lime green, the other sea-blue.

'Lucy, did you see here?' said a low Irish voice behind her. 'Do they not remind you of Portia and Prudence, Tabitha's old Kune Kune's?'

Libby turned. Seamus Doyle, he'd come. He stood with his head tipped to the side. Lucinda Doyle threw her head back, cooing over the painting, begging Seamus to buy it for Tabitha's birthday. If that woman had it in her to murder Maggie, Libby would eat her faux-leather jeans. Lucinda seemed more likely to drown someone in well-meaning hugs.

'They're cute, but I prefer the lilac pony,' Libby said, smiling at the pigs.

'Ah now, you've a cold, cold heart if it can't be melted by a couple of porcine beauties like these.' Seamus Doyle laughed, his eyes twinkling.

Libby couldn't help comparing him to Patrick – both tall, good-looking and both unwilling to offer their hearts to their broken ballerinas.

'Libby?' Paolo offered her a glass of wine.

She held up her water. 'I have to dance tomorrow.'

'It's Paolo de Luca, isn't it?' Seamus held out his hand. 'A pleasure to meet you, sir.'

Paolo smiled, shaking hands. 'This is my good friend, Olivia Wilde.'

'Friend?' Seamus tipped his head, studying Libby before turning back to Paolo. 'Ah now, it's a shameful thing, but, Mr de Luca, do you have the time to say a hello to my wife? She's your biggest fan.'

Libby poked Paolo who dutifully gave Lucinda his biggest smile.

'So, Ms Wilde...' Seamus led her to the next series of Dani's art works, vast profanities painted with tiny fingerprints. 'Are you really a *friend* of Mr de Luca?'

She nodded.

He laughed. 'Do you know what I'm thinking?'

She raised her eyebrows.

'That you'd be his muse, the elusive Broken Ballerina.'

Libby glanced around, ensuring no one heard. 'What makes you say that?'

'You carry yourself with the grace of a dancer. Or is that just a coincidence?'

She shook her head. 'But please don't tell. Not yet.'

He nodded.

'Actually, I have a confession, my own shameful thing.' She mimicked his accent, making him laugh. 'I'm living in Gosthwaite, in Maggie Keeley's old house.'

'Are you now?' He visibly stiffened, focussing on the WHORE painting in front of them. 'They say Dani made this with the fingerprints of underage prostitutes. The world's a dark place, Miss Wilde.'

'My best-friend, Zoë, is Maggie's great niece.' Libby persevered, turning away from the disturbingly small fingerprints. 'I was a huge fan of Maggie's, not that I ever saw her dance, but I understand you knew her.'

Was it too soon to ask if he was with her the day before she died?

Seamus' black eyes had all the compassion of coal as he turned to her. 'Please excuse me, Miss Wilde, I'd hate my wife to take up too much of your friend's time.'

He strode away. Apparently so.

Arse.

It'd changed. Everything had changed. Okay, the buildings were the same, many of the people were the same, but the staff had changed, the way they did things had changed. Libby wandered through the halls of Markova House, air-kissing old friends, smiling at familiar but less well-known faces. Nothing was the same.

She toured the school, watching rows of determined girls point their toes with precision. Few of Jane's students were of the same calibre, but Libby suspected they had more fun. Not that the students seemed unhappy, they just... well, they wouldn't be allowed to sit on the teacher's knee or plait her hair between classes.

After she'd assisted in two classes, calling instruction in one, her nerves grew. Her own class approached. She hadn't attended a professional class for over three years, and she was sure to embarrass herself in front of the other dancers.

No. If Zoë had taught her anything, it was how to hold her head high.

I'm here to teach, not dance. Right now, it doesn't matter what the other dancers think.

Taking slow, steady breaths, she laced up her ballet shoes and removed her warm up layers, unable to ignore the suspicious and sneering glances of the girls around her. But their animosity flooded over her. A newbie stealing your place in the *corps* was horrific, but to have some *has-been* turn up...

Libby arched up onto her toes, relishing the stretch. Well, this has-been *had* turned up and the other dancers were right to be scared of her.

Because I was good.

This was like the fell race. Libby wouldn't just finish, she'd come first, she'd be the best.

Libby sailed through class, the moves as familiar as brushing her teeth, and when she performed thirty-two immaculate fouettés even the ballet mistress cracked a smile. Libby had suspected so, but now she knew – Jane's formidable lessons were as good as any Libby had endured in the company.

Triumphant and breathless, Libby relaxed from her final arabesque only to realise the legendary Tamara Rojo watched from the doorway. Crikey. Her idol even offered a brief smile before slipping out of the room.

Tamara Rojo had watched her dance.

Carlos, her old coach, applauded slowly. 'I am surprised you are not creaking with rust.'

'I've been taking class with Jane Knight. She was a principal with the Royal Ballet.'

'Yes, she called me.' Carlos tapped his forehead. 'But you 'ave something new, Olivia. You've changed. Technically, you were always perfect, now you 'ave what you lacked back then. Now, you 'ave emotion. I think you be in love.'

'I be heartbroken maybe.'

He laughed, clutching both hands to his chest. 'Ah, you can't know what it is to love 'til you 'ave loved and lost.'

'I'd rather be an ice maiden,' she said, not meaning it. Oh, to sit and eat dinner with Patrick, to simply sit, eat and talk.

'What do you want to do, Olivia?'

What did she want to do? Have steak and dauphinoise with Patrick, knocking back red wine and laughing in the garden, or punish herself for hours every day just to dance in the Coliseum again? Both ideas were far-fetched, but only one seemed remotely possible.

'Teach,' she said, raising her chin, 'and dance, as a guest soloist.'

Carlos laughed. 'But only prima ballerinas get that luxury. We'd all–'

'I'm the Broken Ballerina.'

He pursed his lips. 'We supposed as much.'

'Paolo de Luca's a friend. We're using the painting's notoriety to our advantage. For a few months at least, I'll be a name. You could sell tickets on my name.'

'For a few months at least.' Carlos placed his arm around her shoulders, keeping their chat private from the next class padding in on satin toes. 'It's a lot to ask. You ran away.'

'At the end of the season. I didn't let anyone down. So, can I teach and be a guest soloist?'

'*Sí.*' Carlos kissed her cheeks. 'We start with class, we find you a role and then we send you to the school. Welcome back, *cariña*. You need to speak to Annabelle in HR. She sort the terms. And get your blog updated. You had fans. Get them back. And maybe we should ask Jane Knight to come here too.'

She was back.

With her coat buttoned up and scarf tightly wrapped around her neck, she wandered through a snow covered Hyde Park. London. It was lovely to be back, but London meant no more fell running, no more horse-riding – no more Robbie, no more Jane, no more Patrick. Tears tumbled down her cheeks as she typed out a text.

I got the job so you can relax. I won't be around to ruin your idyllic rural life.

Her phone rang.

'Look,' she said, beyond weary. 'I can't–'

'Miss Wilde? Seamus Doyle. Now, how do you fancy brunch with an aging but seldom drunk Irishman?'

* * *

Christmas had started out pretty poor, but steadily it'd turned to rat-shit. Patrick had finally pulled Libby, but what happened? She ran off to London to be a bloody ballet dancer.

I got the job so you can relax. I won't be around to ruin your idyllic rural life.

Fucking marvellous. Patrick leant on the bar, nursing the remainder of his third pint.

'You seen this?' Grace asked, dropping a copy of the *Daily Mail* on the bar.

Oh yes, he'd seen it. The paper lay open at a page showing several celebrities at an art exhibition in some glitzy gallery. The fourth photo was of Libby and Paolo. In the skimpy silk top and black leather trousers, she smiled at the camera oozing class amongst a page of tarted-up wannabes. Her hand held Paolo's. The sight made him want to be sick.

'How did you do it, Gracey? How did you come to work every day and listen to me bang on about...'

'Who you banged at the weekend?'

He hung his head, ashamed. 'Sorry.'

She leant on the bar, her face sympathetic. 'Hey, at the end of the day, you've been a good friend.'

He bumped fists with her and drained the rest of his pint. 'I'm still sorry.'

'Your drinking buddies are here.' Grace nodded behind him.

Patrick turned, just in time to see Robbie's fist flying towards him. Oh shit. The pain shot through Patrick's jaw as he fell backwards, toppling off his stool. Grace yelled, Robbie shouted, Scott apologised, but Patrick lay there, knowing he deserved it and more.

'What the hell was I thinking,' Robbie yelled, 'asking you to keep an eye on her? I should've kept you a million miles from her. She's *Off Limits*. Forever.'

Patrick closed his eyes.

'Off Limits? You three have some messed up loyalties,' Grace said. 'Robbie, she's not your bloody property.'

Robbie pulled away from Scott's grasp. 'She's actually moving to London.'

Patrick could only nod.

'I said I'd kill you if you broke her heart.'

'And I said I'd let you,' Patrick rubbed his chin. 'But not here.'

Scott held out a hand, pulling him up. 'We need a kickabout. Grace, got a bottle of something and a ball?'

'For you, gorgeous,' she said, adding a wink, 'anything.'

Swigging from a bottle of Glenfiddich, Patrick walked up to the penalty spot on the village playing field. Robbie's turn in goal and he was good, but Patrick was the master. For the first time in three days, the first time since the snowball war, he found himself laughing. Thank Christ for friends. Not that it would last. Scott's team-building exercises were always followed by a harsh truth session and meticulous action plans.

Patrick hammered the ball into the left corner of the tattered net while Robbie was falling to the right. Goal! Three pints and way too much Glenfiddich prevented any modesty on Patrick's part. He ran to the side of the pitch, sinking to his knees and raising his arms to an imaginary, screaming crowd. He'd scored the winning penalty for England – or against them for Scotland. Come the World Cup, his allegiance always wavered.

Scott sat next to him, taking the bottle. 'So you can kick a football, but David Beckham you ain't, my son.'

Patrick smiled, faux punching his friend, but Robbie was on his way over, his jaw twitching with repressed animosity.

'What happened?' Scott asked, quietly.

'She ran away like Rob said she would. I had to tell her on Christmas morning–'

'After you shagged her?' Scott's eyebrows shot up and he thumped Patrick's shoulder. 'Didn't you listen to Rob's master classes?'

Quite frankly, no. Robbie gained all his knowledge from Cosmopolitan and chick lit books. His aim was a good one – to understand what girls wanted, but Patrick had much less noble aims. Once he'd learned about overblown romantic gestures being the way in to a girl's pants – a playlist of nauseating tracks had Melody Lawson eager to give up her virginity and relieve him of his – he'd never looked back.

'I could fucking kill you,' Robbie said.

'You'll never let her go, will you?' Patrick asked.

'Don't you dare.' Robbie shook his head. 'Don't you fucking dare. I love that girl and I've had to watch–'

'You *love* her?' Patrick's head reeled.

Robbie swore at the starlit sky.

'Then why did you get Vanessa back?'

'Because Libby doesn't want a second-hand life.' Robbie sat down. 'Maybe if she'd wanted... I wouldn't have gone to Grassington, but it was the right thing. I love Van more and let's face it, Libby's always chosen you. She chose you when she went out for a drink. She chose you when she told you about the ballet.'

Had she?

'But this isn't just about me,' Patrick said, pushing his hair back. 'Because of the painting, she's got a chance to be a ballerina again.'

Robbie groaned. 'Of course it's about you. She doesn't want to go back to that life. Tell her to come back. It's what she wants. Tell her to hell with the ultimatum and then you bloody well put her first on your list.'

Patrick shook his head. 'But I can't put Libby first, there's my job–'

'Don't tell me you can't risk your job for her,' Robbie said, his voice rising. 'She'll never let you down, or fuck around. She's perfect and you know it.'

Patrick dug his toe into the still semi-frozen turf. She was, but it still terrified the hell out of him. 'I know, but it still doesn't get around the fact that she won't let me lose my job.'

'No, it doesn't,' Scott agreed.

Patrick looked to his friend, hoping for a miracle. 'Ideas?'

'Cut the apron strings and open your own practice,' Scott suggested. 'It's not as if your clients wouldn't go with you, and you have the savings, don't you?'

Patrick nodded. 'But it'd be in competition with my parents.' And the last thing he wanted to do was hurt them more.

'Then we need to get Wray off your back.' Scott's brow furrowed in thought. 'We're going to need some leverage. When's Libby coming back?'

Patrick shrugged. What if she didn't come back? But flanked by his brothers in arms, he had hope on his side.

Back at the Alfred an hour later, while Scott and Robbie played pool, Patrick took out his phone, staring at it for five minutes before he had the nerve to ring her. Sadly, she didn't answer any of his three attempts. In the end, he opted for a message.

- *How's London? You hate it, don't you?*
- *What do you want?*

- *Did you tell anyone you're the BB?*
- *No. Why?*
- *Leverage. Don't tell anyone anything. And come home.*
- *Why?*
- *U know why.*
- *Hot. Cold.*
- *What you doing?*
- *Paolo's drawing me. Nude.*
- *Liar. But thanks for the mental image.*
- *Bite me.*
- *Happily. What are you wearing?*
- *OMG, have you been drinking?*

Patrick sent her a photo of the table in the Alfred strewn with empty pint glasses and the near empty bottle of Glenfiddich.

- *Boys night out with Scott and Robbie. They're fixing everything. Promise you won't fuck Paolo?*
- *Lay off the whisky, you idiot.*
- *Promise?*
- *Promise. What would happen if there was no ultimatum?*
- *You'd be here*
- *Would we go out properly?*
- *Define properly*
- *Holding hands in public, meeting your parents, going out for dinner, walks*
- *Sounds tolerable*
- *Tolerable?*
- *Libs, I think you're amazing. Pretty. Funny. I want to be with you all the time. Sorry about the other day. You freaked me out.*
- *I freaked you out? You're the one who snuck into my house and put me to bed*
- *:) come back and I'll put you to bed every night.*
- *Hot. Cold.*
- *I miss you.*
- *You're drunk. You're letting your self-indulgent, hedonistic side come out. Then tomorrow, you'll back off again. Hot. Cold. Leave me alone.*

Sod it, he rang her again, his heart hammering. Maybe he should do what Robbie would do and tell her he loved her. The call went straight to voicemail.

Fuck.

* * *

Walking into the Dorchester wearing faux-leather jeans and ludicrously high heels on a Saturday morning wasn't weird. Telling the Maitre d' she was meeting Seamus Doyle, even that wasn't weird. And sauntering down the Dorchester's famed Promenade and slipping off her coat to reveal Paolo's *Artists Do It In Oils* t-shirt, that wasn't remotely weird.

What was weird was the amount of people gawping at her. Libby's heart rate rose, her eyes widening in panic as a woman whipped out her phone, blatantly snapping her. It was worse than when she was in the paper as a prostitute. Who knew the Broken Ballerina would be so popular? Three journalists had already set up camp outside Paolo's flat.

'Mr Doyle?' The Maitre d' smiled. 'Perhaps you and Miss Wilde would be more comfortable in a private dining area.'

'Jesus man, then they'd really talk.' Seamus laughed. 'Libby, sit yourself down. Now then, I imagine you're not a big eater, but they do a damned fine breakfast here.'

She sat down, relaxing. 'Actually, I didn't eat much yesterday. I'm starving. Do they do bacon sandwiches?'

'It's the goddamn Dorchester. They do what the feck you like. Tea?'

She nodded, glancing around at the sumptuous hall as Seamus poured the tea. 'Beautiful place.'

'Writing here is an indulgence of mine. I plan to tell the world I'm writing a poem about you. As you know, I admire a dancer's grace. You can be my muse.'

Libby laughed. 'Me?'

'You're Paolo de Luca's, aren't you?'

Flattered by the concept, Libby struggled to focus on the matter at hand. 'Is that why you asked me here, to be your muse?'

'I want to apologise for being rude at the gallery. My wife knows about Maggie, but years ago, we agreed I'd never leave and Lucinda would never hear of it again.' He tipped his head to the side, studying her. 'Did you never meet Maggie?'

Libby shook her head. 'Was it hard, enduring a secret relationship like that?'

'Hard? The only thing hard was that bloody siren of a woman. Ah Jesus, I worshipped her, but Maggie was too rich for my soul, too intoxicating, too demanding. I couldn't live with her, but I couldn't live without her.'

Seamus plucked a photograph from his wallet. It showed him with Maggie at a black tie event. She wore a long red gown, her dark eyes gazing up at him with undisguised adoration. They both looked to be in their thirties.

'When was this?' she asked.

'Twenty-five years ago. For a year or so, I left Lucinda. Maggie and I lived in a cottage by Grasmere. We tried so hard to make it work, for the sake of...'

Libby frowned at the photo, at the twinkling below Maggie's ear. 'For the sake of...'

'Our daughter.'

Libby's head shot up. 'Maggie had a daughter?'

He nodded.

'But why didn't she inherit the house?'

Seamus glanced away. 'She did.'

'Zoë?' Libby's hands shook. 'Zoë's Maggie's daughter?'

'And mine. I haven't seen her since she was one. Maggie had her adopted. The day Maggie died, she wanted me to meet her. I refused. We fought...'

Push her down the stairs kind of fought? Libby watched for any tells, but Seamus' eyes filled with tears.

'The last time I ever saw her and I didn't tell her I loved her.'

Maggie wanted him to meet Zoë? Did that mean Zoë knew Maggie was her mother? Surely if she did, she'd have told... Libby closed her eyes, remembering Zoë lying comatose the previous winter. What were the bets it wasn't caused by the burglary, or because they needed to replace their stolen passports and Zoë couldn't find her birth certificate? What were the bets Zoë *had* found her birth certificate, and with it discovered that the woman she hated was her mother?

'But you went back to your wife?'

Seamus nodded. 'Maggie said she couldn't bear to look at Zoë – she'd just turned one – because she reminded her of me. So she spoke to her niece. Her and her husband desperately wanted a child. It seemed the perfect solution.'

'It might've been if Maggie hadn't made her come to Gosthwaite each summer.'

'The girl could dance. Maggie wanted her to be a star.'

But, Zoë never had the inner strength to be a star. Libby couldn't stop staring at the strand of diamonds twinkling under Maggie's earlobe.

'Seamus, Maggie's earrings in this photo–'

'A gift from me, on the day Zoë was born. I said they'd be an heirloom, to be passed from mother to daughter.'

Libby grabbed her coat and the photo, sprinting down the Promenade, ignoring Seamus calling after her. The earrings were the same ones Libby had worn the day Zoë learned Maggie had died. The earrings Zoë said had been a birthday present from Rich.

What have you done, Zoë?

Chapter Forty

With her shopping bags abandoned in the hallway, Zoë checked her lipstick and removed a smudge of eyeliner before she headed to the drawing room in search of Jonathan. His god-awful family ought to have left already, but just in case, she'd left the paint and wallpaper samples in her beautiful new car. It seemed fairly likely they'd be a tiny bit resistant to her eradicating the previous Mrs Carr from Stonerigg House.

Ed was still there.

Ed was still there, and he was sitting in an armchair, staring at the floor. Why? Zoë wanted to drag her hair off her face, but her hands were shaking too much. Why was Ed still here and why the fuck was Jonathan standing in the great bay window, looking out into the garden?

'Hello,' she said, heading over to Jonathan, purposefully ignoring Ed. 'How was golf?'

Jonathan glanced down, frowning at the hand she'd rested on his shoulder. 'Ed, could you give us a minute?'

Zoë's heart rate increased as Ed obediently left the room. No, no, no. 'What's going on?'

'Ed told me.'

Zoë kept her smile despite the bile rising in her throat. 'Told you what?'

Jonathan reached out, stroking her hair, his eyes scanning her face as if memorising every millimetre. 'You were like a dream. I couldn't understand why I deserved you. People said it was for the money, but I never really believed that. It wasn't that, was it?'

'No–'

'He told me what happened on Christmas Day.'

Oh god, no. Zoë sucked in a lungful of air as her world shifted underneath her.

'You have to forgive me,' she whispered. 'It'll never happen again.'

Jonathan kissed her forehead. 'You have to leave.'

Please, please, no. She held his face. 'But you fucked Maggie and I forgave you.'

Jonathan gently held her wrists, his thumbs stroking them. 'He loves you, Zoë. I can't ruin my own son's chance of happiness.'

'He doesn't have a chance of happiness with me. I chose you, not him.'

'And you have no idea what that means to me.' For a moment, Jonathan let her kiss him, her mouth clinging to his. 'But I can't do this to him.'

'Please, no,' Zoë begged, unable to stop the tears trickling down her cheeks. This was her chance to be happy, really happy. 'I love you.'

'He's my son, Zoë. I choose him, not you.'

Jonathan didn't love her. He couldn't. If he did, he wouldn't turn her away like this, wilfully making her unhappy. Did he really think she'd just say okay and bugger off with Ed? Was that what Jonathan thought of her? Zoë raised her chin and with her last ounces of self-control she took out the keys to the Z4, dangling them in front of him.

'Keep it,' Jonathan said, resuming his vigil on the garden.

She pushed the keys into his hand. 'I've had all the *cars* I need from this family.'

Tears loomed, but she walked upstairs, refusing to run. Yes, the money was good, the toys, the shiny trinkets, but more than that, Jonathan gave her power and respect. Now, it'd all gone – ripped from her, destroyed by Ed.

With every item she threw in a case, she prayed Jonathan would come in, telling her he'd changed his mind, but he didn't. In the end, the shadow that came over the room was Ed's.

'I'm sorry,' he whispered.

Zoë gave a small laugh before striding over and slapping him, making his head jerk and her palm burn. 'You've ruined everything.'

'I had to.'

'No.'

'Zoë, you can't marry him. We have something–'

'I don't give a shit what we have.'

'Yes you do.' He held her face, walking her backwards to the wall. 'I want you to come with me. To London, Paris, wherever the fuck you want.'

'What, so we can work in some boho cafe, being poor and in love?' Her body arched towards him, aching to give in. 'Screw that.'

He glanced up to the ceiling, his jaw twitching. 'Fine. I wanted you to want me for me, but I'm not a penniless writer. Those books I ghost-write? They sold over four million copies last year.'

'You have gold to dig?'

He looked in her eye, his hands on the wall, either side of her head. 'I have gold to dig.'

Tears rolled down her cheeks. How much did she want to nod, to kiss him, to grab a bag and run to Paris? But how could she?

'Do you really think all I want is a good shag with money?' she said, desperate not to touch him. 'I want more than that. I want power and control. You take all of that away from me.'

'Power?' Ed let out a hollow laugh. 'You think that's what he gives you? Tying someone to a four-poster bed and fucking them while their wife's downstairs is not power.'

Zoë shrank back against the wall, too mortified to even blush. 'I–'

'You think you have power over him?' Ed shook his head. 'He knows what makes you tick and he gives you just enough of what you want so you'll do *everything* he wants. He's a manipulative bastard with women. Ask Nikki. Or Max. Or any of the other women in that office.'

Jonathan had screwed all of them?

'You need me.' With a gentle hand, Ed wiped away her tears then kissed her, his hands caressing her neck. 'And I need you.'

But I don't deserve a guy like you.

The realisation sent a chill surging over her skin.

And you really don't deserve a girl like me.

'Ed...' Zoë held his face in her hands, her lips hovering by his. 'I held your mother's hand the night she died. Your dad was a little tied up so I went to check on her. I held her hand and she talked to me. She thought I was God.'

Ed's eyes sparkled as he smiled.

'But I was the one who sold her the Ketamine and when she stopped breathing,' Zoë whispered, 'I did nothing to help.'

Predictably, his eyes lost their sparkle.

'Is that what you *need?*' she kissed him, her lips unlikely to make it all better.

When she strode away, he still stood there, staring at her, not saying a word. How long would she have, the five minute drive to the cottage? Would Ed ring the police himself, or spend an hour plucking up the courage to tell his father? And what would Jonathan do, ring the police or stall while he pondered how this was ALL HIS FUCKING FAULT?

* * *

The taxi pulled into the Green and Libby's heart sank at the sight of lights on in the cottage. Zoë was home? Arse. Why wasn't she at Jonathan's? Libby needed just a little more time to get her head together. More time? She'd had two hours and forty minutes on the train from Euston and twenty minutes in a taxi from Oxenholme to get her head together, but all she'd managed to do was ask herself the same two questions, over and over. Were they the same earrings? And if so, how did Zoë get them?

As the driver processed her debit card, Libby stared up at the light on in Zoë's room and dialled Patrick. Sadly, like the other nine times she'd tried already, it went straight to voicemail. The night before he practically said he loved her. Hot, cold, hot, cold – but what was she always left with? Cold.

Libby stepped into the house, kicking off her heels. A suitcase sat in the hallway. Zoë appeared from the kitchen, dressed but with a towel wrapped around her head.

'You're back.' Zoë sounded pleased, but her tell, the nervous blinking, had never been more obvious. 'I can't believe you get to dance again. Happy?'

Libby nodded. 'I need a wee. Put the kettle on?'

Okay, one step at a time. Were they the same earrings? Libby ran upstairs and tiptoed into Zoë's room, checking in the jewellery box. Empty. Completely empty. Okay, Zoë had pretty much moved into Jonathan's, but she'd only taken her bare essentials, and Rich's birthday present earrings hadn't been one of them. But now, they'd gone. Arse.

Libby went to the bathroom and flushed the loo, keeping up her lie before heading downstairs for the confrontation from hell.

'How come you're back?' Libby said, back in the kitchen.

'Just grabbing some more stuff.' Zoë held up a jug, pouring a second glass of the orange-coloured drink. 'We should celebrate your return to the ballet world. We've got no fizz left, so it's orange and wine. When are you moving to London? Will you live with Paolo or get your own place?'

'I don't know.' Libby took the glass, taking in Zoë's red eyes and letting concern override her suspicions. 'What's wrong, Zo?'

Zoë's lip wobbled, but she took a massive gulp of her drink. 'Ed spilled the beans and Jonathan kicked me out. I'm getting away for a bit.'

Oh god, no. Libby pushed the photo into her back pocket. This wasn't the time to ask about Maggie. 'Where are you going?'

'My mum and dad's.' Zoë wiped her eyes. 'I could do with being looked after for a while.'

'And your mum's chicken soup?' Libby sipped her drink, grateful for the booze to calm her nerves. She had to ask about the earrings, but poor Zoë looked ready to crack.

'I'll be back in a week or so.' Zoë sat in front of a mirror, facing the window as she applied her foundation. 'How was London?'

'Not as good as here.'

'And Patrick?'

'He texted me last night, being nice. Hot. Back to cold today.'

'Tell me all about it. Misery loves company.'

Libby knocked back her drink, explaining about being back at the ballet, being out with Paolo, all the while watching Zoë apply her usual, immaculate make-up – subtle brown eye shadow, a thin line of liquid liner on her top lashes, a hint of peach blusher. The mascara was going on. The job would be finished and Zoë would leave. Libby's heart raced.

'Zo, I need to talk to you about something.'

'Is it important, or can you ring me later? I have a taxi coming in about ten minutes and I still need to do my hair.'

'Yes, it's important,' Libby said, helping herself to a second glass of the buck's *flat*. Her mouth was like sandpaper from nerves. 'The earrings...'

Libby stared at her hand, fascinated by the colour of her lilac nails. So much prettier than usual.

Zoë paused, her mascara wand hovering. 'What earrings?'

'The diamond ones you wouldn't let me wear on Christmas Eve. Where did you get them?'

'Oh, those.' Zoë went back to her mascara. 'Rich. You know that.'

'It's just, I've seen a photo...' Libby's hand left tracing patterns in the air. This wasn't right. This was wrong. Her breath came in quick, short bursts.

Zoë put her make-up away. 'Are you feeling okay? You look woozy. Have you eaten today?'

'No...' Libby fanned herself. '...was meant to have brunch with your dad, but... had to leave when...'

'My dad?'

Libby slumped against the wall, sliding down it. Why could she see red snakes hiding under the towel wrapped around Zoë's head? Libby blinked, trying to focus, but Zoë's head split into a kaleidoscope of shapes and colours. 'Don't feel very good.'

Zoë crouched beside her. 'You were having brunch with my dad, why?'

'He wanted to know how you were.' Libby closed her eyes, shutting out the bright lights.

'Libby...'

'Lib? Libby?'

A dull ached throbbed against her brain, but Libby opened her eyes, flinching at the bright light in the room.

'Libby, drink this. It's water.' A strange girl with scarlet hair pushed a glass nearer to Libby's lips. A thick fringe and glasses obscured the girl's eyes, but what Libby could see seemed familiar.

'Zoë?'

'You're okay. Scared me a bit, but you're okay.'

'What did you give me?'

'Sheila's special edition elderflower wine.'

'You poisoned me?'

'Sedated you. There's a difference.' The new Zoë helped her sip more water. 'Now, I haven't got long. I reckon Ed will have told his dad by now, and Jonathan might be tempted to ring the police.'

'Ed knows you stole the earrings?'

'Of course not, but how do you know about the earrings, Libby?'

'The photo.' Libby summoned enough energy to take the photo from her pocket. 'Maggie's wearing them. You stole them from her, didn't you? I mean if she'd given them to you, you wouldn't have said Rich gave them to you. Why didn't you tell me about her?'

'About who?'

'Maggie. Why didn't you tell me she's your mother?'

Zoë took the photo. 'Who's she with?'

'Did you steal the earrings?'

'Who is he?'

'I asked first.'

Zoë sighed, scowling with frustration. 'Yes. My parents finally gave me my birth certificate and there it was, in black and white. Mother, Margaret Keeley. Father, unknown. The fucking whore didn't even know his name. I came up here, to see her, to know why she gave me away. The stupid cow actually cried, saying she'd wanted to tell me for years. She showed me the earrings, telling me that my father gave them to her the day I was born and that they'd be mine one day.

'How dare she keep the fucking earrings when she wouldn't keep me? She wouldn't tell me who he is. She just kept going on and on about how much she loved me. What a joke? She didn't love me. If she had, she wouldn't have starved me for days on end.' Zoë wiped at her tears, now leaving black streaks down her cheeks. 'Who's this man?'

'Your father. When did you steal the earrings?'

'The night she died.'

'Did you kill her?'

'It wasn't intentional. I went to get the earrings while she was out at that pagan festival. She came back early, and the opportunity was too good to miss. She tripped over that stupid cat. She would've fallen down the stairs without me laying a finger on her, but I couldn't resist helping out. How are you feeling?'

'Like my best friend's poisoned me.'

A little clarity came over Libby, the belladonna cloud clearing, and she studied the girl crouching in front of her. The new Zoë wore black crap around her eyes, Libby's ACDC t-shirt and favourite purple striped tights. In fact, only the ancient Converse boots were Zoë's own. 'You're in disguise.'

'Pretty good, hey?'

'Why's Ed going to ring the police?'

'Because I killed his mother.'

Libby tried to stand, but her legs wouldn't work. 'You murdered Fee?'

'Well, I say *killed*, more provided the ketamine. No one forced the old bag to take it.' Zoë shrugged. 'I only wanted to make sure I could fuck Jonathan in peace. She had a habit of accidentally walking in and watching when she was high. Weirdo.'

'*You* broke into Patrick's' surgery?'

'It's funny, but you were practically my accomplice. You taught me about alarm override codes and kept Patrick entertained. Like Maggie, the opportunity was too good to miss.'

Tears streamed down Libby's face as the belladonna took hold again and the girl with red hair no longer resembled Zoë. Where had Zoë gone? Libby shrank away from the stranger. Why was this girl with red hair and glasses trying to kill her? Zoë. Where was Zoë? No, it was Zoë. She'd dyed her hair. It didn't look like Zoë. Fighting to stop her mind fragmenting again, Libby pinched the skin on the back of her wrist.

'I have to go.' Zoë crouched down, peering into Libby's eyes. 'Who's my father?'

'Please don't leave me.'

'They'll arrest me. I have to go. Who's my father?'

'Seamus Doyle. He's a poet.'

'Thank you.' Zoë took a shaky breath and kissed her cheek. 'I've been abandoned by my birth mother, abandoned by my birth father and my adoptive parents were more than happy to send me off every summer to be tortured by the old witch I now know is my mother. You're the only person who's ever been there for me. I'm sorry, but I have to do this. I just need an hour or so to get away. Just a little to knock you out for a while longer.'

Zoë opened a small bottle, sucking up a little liquid with the pipette. Libby squinted, her eyes swimming in and out of focus. *Belladonna.* She tried to scream and fend Zoë off, but found her arms pinned to her sides. No, this wasn't Zoë. It couldn't be. Her Zoë would never do this. Libby sobbed as two drops fell onto her lips. The non-Zoë held the glass of water to Libby's lips, making her sip.

'I won't let you die. I'll ring Patrick in a bit.'

And the red-haired stranger Libby previously knew as her best-friend walked out of the back door, suitcase in hand. Libby closed her eyes, the light hurting them.

Please, Patrick. Don't let me die.

* * *

'Why are we doing this?' Patrick slumped into a chair, grateful for the coffee break.

'Because it's a good deed and if you can't do a good deed at Christmas, when can you?' Grace handed him a mug of coffee, checking her phone.

'After Christmas?' Patrick yawned.

Freebie cat neutering. A genius idea. Well it was in principle, but when he'd agreed to do it, he hadn't thought Grace meant to do it the day before New Year's Eve. He was supposed to be on holiday and the whole experience was made ten times worse by his father offering to help.

'Ohmigod, a message for you. Check it out.' Grace handed Patrick her phone. 'It's from Paolo.'

'Why does Paolo have your number?'

Grace twittered away about how she gave him her number at the Halloween party, but Patrick struggled to focus on anything but the photo. It showed a painting of Libby, again hugging her knees, but this time she was smiling, her eyes sparkling with blatant happiness. Christ, look at how happy dancing made her. She really did need to be back in London. Groaning, he pressed the phone to his forehead. *London, I need to move to London.* Thoroughly depressed, he tossed the phone back to Grace, but she laughed.

'You didn't read the message, did you?' she asked.

He shook his head.

'It says, The Fixed Ballerina is on her way back.'

What? Patrick jumped up, digging his own phone out of his jacket and switching it on. Shit. Ten missed calls from Libby and two from Zoë. He dialled Libby, but it rang out until the answer machine kicked in.

'When did he send that?'

'Two and a half hours ago.'

Should he just go to Oxenholme and meet her off the train? She could be already on her way. She could be home. No lights were on. *Where are you, Libs?*

Breaking his own rule about keeping phones switched off while they were in surgery, Patrick habitually glanced to his phone, willing it to ring. In the midst of prepping a ginger tom called Lord Marmalade, finally, it did.

'Zoë, where is she?'

'I can't talk, but Libby needs an ambulance. She's at the cottage.' Zoë ended the call.

Patrick stared at the phone. What the hell? 'Grace, I'll be back in a minute.'

He ran from the surgery, jumping down the steps and sprinting to Libby's house. He knocked, but didn't wait for an answer before opening the door.

'Libs,' he called, checking the living and dining rooms. 'Libby?'

He found her in the kitchen, curled up on the wooden floor with Hyssop standing guard over her. Patrick knelt beside her and gently shook her, but her only reaction was to curl up tighter. Behind her closed lids, her eyes flitted around as though she were dreaming.

'Libby? It's Patrick. Can you hear me?'

He glanced around, looking for a cause, some explanation. On the worktop sat a bottle of elderflower wine and a letter addressed to Libby. Swearing, he pocketed the letter and scooped Libby up, begging her to hang on, as he ran back to the surgery.

'Dad, Grace!' he yelled, ignoring the alarmed expressions on the cat owners' faces in the waiting room. Gently, he laid her on the empty examination table. 'Come on, Libs. Wake up.'

His father was the first to arrive. 'Libby? Patrick... what did you do–'

'For Christ's sake, Dad, you've fussed over me all fucking day. When did I get chance to do this?' He paused as Grace came in. 'Gracey, call an ambulance. I think it's belladonna poisoning. Get rid of everyone then go to the cottage. There's a bottle of elderflower wine in the kitchen. Bring it here. You'd better wear gloves.'

Grace stood staring at Libby's limp body.

'Now, Grace.' He picked up his phone again and dialled Zoë. 'Dad, do something.'

'I'm not a doctor.'

'No, you're a vet, so pretend she's a cat. Just check her pulse or something.' The ringing on the phone stopped. 'Zoë?'

'Is she okay?'

'Zoë, what happened?'

'Is she awake?'

'No. Is that the bottle of wine with the belladonna in? How much has she had?'

'About two glasses. One did her no harm in August.'

'Where are you?' He stroked Libby's hair back, but Zoë didn't answer, a garbled tannoy filled the silence. 'When did you leave her?'

'About an hour ago. I thought she'd be awake by now.' Zoë sobbed. 'You will look after her, won't you? And make sure she gets the letter. I have to go, but tell her I love her and I'm sorry. Promise you'll look after her?'

'I promise.'

Zoë ended the call and he tossed the phone aside.

'Libby? It's Patrick. Can you hear me, Libs?' He held her hand, stroking her hair, and her fingers closed around his. Her eyes flickered but didn't open. Gently, he kissed her forehead. 'Hang in there, princess.'

Grace came back. 'They're on the way, but realistically, they'll be at least fifteen minutes. Did she overdose because of you?'

'No. I think Zoë poisoned her, but I have no idea why.' Patrick laced his fingers with Libby's. 'Deadly Nightshade. Dad, what do you think?'

'If she were a horse...' Malcolm shook his head.

'She's not a horse.' Patrick stared at Libby's pale, beautiful face. 'Grace, the Wicca side, what don't I know?'

'People use nightshade as a flying potion. It makes you hallucinate. She'll be tripping her tits off. Maggie taught me to use it medicinally, for headaches and stuff.' Grace took a deep breath. 'She did say, if it went wrong and if it was a real emergency that I should give her physostigmine. Slow IV drip. No more than one mil every five minutes. Max two mil.'

Patrick swore. 'What if it's too much and kills her?'

'What if it kills her not to have it?' Grace asked, chewing her thumbnail.

'Why?'

'Last time, she had a small glass of that wine and was lucid and talking after thirty minutes. This is way worse.' Grace began prepping an IV line. 'I think she's had more, a lot more. If we give her the physostigmine, we might stop any long-term damage and buy her some time 'til she gets to casualty and has her stomach pumped.'

'Dad?' *Tell me not to. Tell me it's a stupid idea.*

'We'll take it slow and steady.'

Shit. Patrick went to get the physostigmine from the drugs locker, praying he wouldn't have to do this, but when he came back into the room, Grace, the only RVN he knew who could put a cannula in a guinea pig, clearly hadn't hesitated or buggered up putting one in Libby's left hand. Fuck, the line and fluids were set up. He couldn't do this. He pulled a chair up, sitting beside Libby, holding her right hand and stroking her hair.

'Libby?' He rested his forehead against hers. 'You need to wake up, right now. Please, princess. Let me know I don't need to do this. Libs?'

Nothing. Her fingers no longer reacted to his and her eyes had stopped flickering.

'Her heart rate's slowed,' his dad said, holding Libby's left wrist. 'Coma?'

Next stage, death. 'Libby, come on.'

'Let me do it,' Grace said, quietly. 'You could get struck off.'

'Or thrown in jail.' Patrick shook his head. 'You're not doing it.'

'Neither are you.' Malcolm took the vial. 'They won't throw me in jail and I'm already retired.'

'No, Dad. Please, let me do it.' Patrick held out his hand. 'You wanted me to take responsibility, right? Well, she's my responsibility.'

'She might be. But my point was that you need to think about the consequences of your actions before you do them. If you do this and she dies... I'll be damned if I let you live with this on your conscience.'

As his father added the drug to the drip, Patrick held Libby's hand, praying his Broken Ballerina would wake up.

Stay with me, Libs. Please.

.

Chapter Forty-One

Libby's eyes began flickering as the first of the blue lights flashed in the Green, but Patrick kept his vigil, holding her hand, smiling a little as her fingers curled around his.

'Come on, Libs,' he whispered, kissing her forehead for the hundredth time. 'Fight through it. The ambulance is here, princess.'

'Actually, it's not.' Grace peered through the window. 'It's one of them ER docs on a motorbike. Fingers crossed for a George Clooney lookalike.'

As Grace went out to meet the doctor, Patrick took a deep breath, but didn't look away from Libby's face.

'Dad?' He cleared his throat. 'If she... when Libby's okay, we're going to go out. Scott's sorting things out to stop Wray printing any ludicrous stories, but people will talk. I can't stop that and if it breaks the Rules...'

'Patrick, now's not–'

'I know it might take some time to gain your respect, but if you do sack me, I was thinking, maybe I could buy the practice. I don't want to set up shop in competition with you, but I'm not giving up everything I have here.' Patrick dared to face his dad.

Please don't hate me.

Malcolm rocked on his heels. 'Obviously, I'd rather there was no scandal, but under the circumstances, if there is...'

'If there is?'

'Well, I can't think of anyone better to take over the practice than you.' Malcolm nodded, his eyes shining. 'You're a hell of a vet, Patrick, but for the last couple of years, you've not been quite the man you should be.'

For the first time since Patrick graduated from Vet School, his father hugged him. Just for a few seconds, but it meant the world.

'I'm sorry for letting you down, dad.'

'It's okay. We could tell when you came back from Spain. You've changed.'

Their smiles and relief were short-lived as Grace showed the motorcycle doctor in, presenting the situation as she would an animal to Patrick. Patrick closed his eyes, pressing his lips to Libby's fingers. There were the expected exclamations of shock, horror, disbelief that a vet would assume they could treat a human. Patrick expected nothing less.

'Duncan, good to see you,' his father said, standing up and shaking the doctor's hand.

Doctor McNamara, a friend of his father's, began his examination of Libby, his equipment saying exactly the same as Patrick's. Finally, he stood back and sighed. 'I don't... You may well have saved her life, but–'

Malcolm shook his head. 'Let's worry about Libby for now.'

Libby's eyes flickered open, her head shaking a little. '...the snakes...'

'Libs? It's Patrick. I know you're seeing weird things, but listen to me. Focus on me. I'm here, holding your hand, can you hear me?'

Libby stirred again. '...can't be Zoë... don't leave me.... where's Patrick?'

'I'm here.'

'... don't like the snakes...'

'Libs, they aren't real. There are no snakes. I promise you.'

'Who is she?' Dr McNamara asked.

'Olivia Wilde. She lives next door,' Malcolm answered.

'Her next of kin?'

'They're in Australia,' Patrick replied.

'But she must have someone here.' Duncan McNamara placed an avuncular hand on Libby's head.

'She has me,' Patrick said, his voice sounding more authoritative than it ever had. 'Do you think she'll be okay?'

Libby babbled a little more, none of it making any sense, but all of it more animated than earlier. Finally, she turned her head, her eyes opening.

'Patrick?'

'I'm here.' He couldn't stop a smile. Okay, she wasn't out of the woods, but the drugs were working. Thank you, Grace.

'Is it really you?' She turned her head, lifting a hand to his face. 'Not Jack?'

'It's really me.'

'Are you castrating cows today, or can we catch up on the last sixth months?'

He almost laughed. 'I think you're still hallucinating, princess.'

'We could fuck in–'

'Shush.' He held a finger over her lips. 'Room full of people.'

'Belladonna can induce quite… provocative delusions,' Dr McNamara explained. 'Libby, can you hear me?'

She nodded, but cowered into Patrick. 'Yes.'

'You're okay, Libs.' Patrick held her close. 'This is Doctor McNamara.'

'Please don't leave me,' she whispered, her eyes widening. 'No cold Patrick. I don't like the snakes.'

'There are no snakes and I'm not going anywhere.'

'Zoë's been taken over by the snakes.' Libby started scratching her arm, shaking her head. 'Big red snakes. They've eaten Zoë. The snakes have eaten Zoë. It's not Zoë any more. She's changed. It's not her–'

'Libby?' Patrick stopped her hands. 'You're safe, with me. Zoë's not here. Just me. Patrick.'

She relaxed again.

'Keep her talking,' Dr McNamara instructed. 'Grace, can you get her some water, please?'

Patrick leant on the table, holding Libby's hand, stroking her hair. 'Remember the night we had dinner?'

She nodded.

'I had a great time and when you're feeling better, I want to do it again.'

She smiled.

For ten minutes, while Dr McNamara monitored her, Patrick kept her awake, calm and semi-lucid with tales of the last few months. They relived the steak and dauphinoise night, the bike ride and the night they made cheese on toast. Finally, he got it. She wasn't a nearly, or an almost, she was a sledgehammer.

And he loved her.

* * *

Libby's throat hurt, her head throbbed and even the dim winter light pained her eyes, but she lifted her head, trying to make sense of her surroundings – antiseptic, beeping machines, a woman in a blue uniform opening the blinds… She was in hospital?

'Sorry to wake you, but it's seven o'clock,' said the nurse, her

403

plump face breaking into a comforting smile as she offered Libby a glass of water. 'They said you'd be thirsty. I'm Katy. Do you know where you are?'

'Hospital?' Libby croaked, in between mouthfuls of blissfully icy water.

Katy nodded. 'There's not much waking him, is there? How are you feeling?'

'Confused.' Him? Libby glanced down. The mop of black curls resting on the bed shocked her more than waking up in the hospital. 'Has he been here long?'

'Long?' Katy laughed. 'He hasn't left your side since they brought you in. It's no wonder the poor lamb's still dead to the world. I reckon he's been up most of the night. If you came round, he'd be there, talking you down from the ceiling.'

'Really?'

Katy smiled at him. 'He's had a few pulses racing, I can tell you. Mine included. Do you remember what happened, love?'

Libby shook her head, sipping more of the water, but fuzzy memories were coming back, the ones of red snakes not fuzzy enough.

Zoë.

Zoë had red hair.

'They said someone gave you deadly nightshade. You're lucky to be alive, love.'

Zoë.

Zoë had poisoned her. Zoë had given Fee the ketamine. Zoë had pushed Maggie down the stairs.

Not Zoë. It couldn't have been Zoë.

'It was in the elderflower wine.'

'Intentionally?' Katy's eyes sparkled, even if she sounded blasé.

Libby looked at the nurse for a second, then shook her head. 'A mistake. She's my best friend.' Why was she defending Zoë?

Katy smiled at Patrick. 'They said she rang him and he gave you the antidote, probably saved your life, but the official line is the motorbike doc administered it. A and E pumped your stomach, then they gave you a sedative and brought you up here. If you need anything, just press your red button. Breakfast will be here in thirty minutes.'

Libby rolled over as Katy left, but Patrick was still fast asleep. Wanting to go back to sleep herself, Libby closed her eyes for a moment, but the snakes leapt into her face. Gingerly, she touched Patrick's arm. He didn't wake. He had to be exhausted if he'd been up all night. She really shouldn't wake him. Then again, she didn't want to have nightmares about snakes. A little less gingerly, she shook his shoulder. Finally, he looked up, his eyes softening, crinkling at the corners as he smiled.

'You okay?' he asked, so quietly it was almost a whisper.

Libby nodded. 'The nurse has been filling me in on what happened.'

'Katy?' he asked through a yawn. 'She has the hots for me.'

'I gathered.' Libby smiled, watching as he helped himself to her water, loving it when he stretched and treated her to a snippet of bare abdomen between his jeans and jumper. 'She also said you saved my life.'

'You know me, can't stop looking out for you.' He leant on the bed again, his chin resting on his folded arms. 'Technically, my dad gave you the drugs, but since you didn't die, I don't mind taking the credit.'

'Thank you.'

'Do you remember much?'

'Too much.'

Patrick nibbled his thumbnail. 'Libs, you said some pretty crazy things last night.'

Her cheeks flushed, vaguely aware she may have suggested a little hallway action. 'I was hallucinating.'

'You were, but...' He took a deep breath. 'Did Zoë steal my ketamine? Did she give it to Fee?'

'Has anyone claimed she did?'

'Yes. You did, last night.'

'Just me?' *Not the police?*

'Just you. What's going on?'

Ed hadn't told anyone.

'Libs?'

She pushed a curl off his face. God, it was good to see him again. At times, back in London, she felt she never would, but he looked so tired. Stubble darkened his chin and shadows blackened his eyes. 'You should go home. Get some rest.'

He shook his head. 'Not happening. Besides, Grace'll only make me castrate the cats I didn't get done yesterday.'

With a weary hand, Libby beckoned him closer and when his face hovered beside hers, she kissed him, her lips gently pressing against his. Just for a moment, he kissed her back.

'You scared me.' He smiled, resting his forehead against hers. 'But you know one perk of this whole drama? The nurses cleaned off the black crap.'

Libby's cheeks flushed. Surely, she must look worse than she felt after a rough night on a cocktail of drugs and having her stomach pumped.

'Pretty Libby.' Patrick stroked her fringe back, kissing her again.

Libby closed her eyes, breathing in the familiar scent of his woody aftershave. Was this Hot Patrick because of the situation, or had something changed?

'Libby? Oh–' Katy stood in the doorway, grinning. 'Put her down, she's supposed to be resting.'

'Katy, your timing's rubbish,' Patrick said, 'but I'll forgive you for a coffee. Libs likes tea.'

Katy pretended to cuff him around the head as she smiled at a giggling Libby.

'He's a cheeky one, but I wish all my patients came with their own nurse. Must be nice having a boyfriend like that. I doubt my Dan would sit with me all night.' She headed for the door, oblivious to the atmosphere she'd created.

Patrick had obediently let go of Libby, but not before she'd caught the fleeting moment of wide-eyed panic flashing in his eyes. *Boyfriend.* He'd freaked at the word. Sighing, Libby sat up, sitting cross-legged. Nothing had changed.

'Oh, that's what I came in for,' Katy said. 'Police are here, so is your lawyer with some journalist. Who do you want to see first?'

'The police?' Libby's eyes widened, staring at Patrick. 'What should I–'

'You want the lawyer. It'll be Scott.'

Libby nodded to Katy. 'Send him in.'

Patrick was right; Scott came in, suited and booted.

'It's New Year's Eve. Don't you ever take a day off?' Patrick asked, back-slapping his friend.

'This is for your sake.' Scott faux-punched him. 'I want Wray to know we mean business.'

'Is he buying it?' Patrick said.

'What are you two talking about?' Libby asked.

'Sorry, Libby.' Scott came over, perching on her bed. 'Clara's coming to see you later. How are you feeling?'

'Like my best friend poisoned me.' She managed a smile. 'Pretty okay, considering. What's going on with Michael Wray? Why's he here?'

Scott opened his briefcase and took out a document. 'Are you fully in charge of your senses again?'

Libby nodded.

'We've a proposal for you,' Scott said. 'Bored housewives around the country are dying to hear about the Broken Ballerina and Michael Wray is prepared to barter for the exclusive.'

Libby shook her head. 'There's no way I'd—'

'It's leverage. You give Wray the Broken Ballerina story and he promises not to publish a single word about you or Patrick for the next six months, including what's happened over the last month. If he does, the *Gazette* has to pay fifty grand to Haverton Animal Rescue. The last part was Patrick's idea. He thought you'd approve. What do you think?'

Oh, she'd sign the contract. Crikey, even if Patrick hadn't saved her life, she'd do anything to protect him, but what did it mean, him asking her to do this? She glanced across to him, but he stared resolutely at the floor. If the coast were clear, could they have a real relationship? She uttered a silent, prayer, as Scott asked for Wray to come in.

And there he was. Michael Wray.

He was a small grey-haired nothing of a man, the kind of man she'd walk past on the street and never notice, but God, did his eyes burn. They were alive, taking everything in. And wasn't that his gift — being able to hide in his own skin but witness everything you did.

'My wife's a huge fan,' Wray said, offering his hand. 'Loves the painting.'

She shook it, but only through ingrained politeness. 'Do you mean it? You won't write about him?'

'I only want stories, Miss Wilde. You're the biggest story right now.'

Libby looked to Scott. 'You've got his back, right?'

Please, promise me you do.

'Always,' Scott said, before his six-figure corporate lawyer eyes focussed on her. 'And you?'

Libby took the pen and signed, but as she did a niggle popped into her head. If Patrick knew he could go out with Libby without worrying about the paper, then why had he panicked when Katy uttered the word boyfriend? Was this the return of Cold Patrick?

As Michael Wray left, a photo-shoot and interview set for two days' time at Jane's studio, Scott fastened the contracts back in his briefcase. 'The police are waiting. They'll ask Patrick to leave while they question you, but would you like me to stay? I'm no criminal defence expert, but–'

'Yes, please,' Libby said, truly grateful.

'Lie down,' Scott instructed her. 'You may as well play up the weak and vulnerable angle.'

For twenty minutes, the two officers asked endless and largely pointless questions. The ones concerning Patrick were easy. Libby could remember little, the little she could remember was fragmented and the bits she could make sense of, she didn't intend to share with the police in case it implicated Patrick in some wrong-doing. The questions regarding Zoë proved trickier. Libby knew she ought to tell them about Maggie, but she kept picturing a seven year-old girl, starving in the cupboard under the stairs.

'Miss Wilde, do you have any idea why Miss Horton might have given you the deadly nightshade?'

'She's my best-friend. I doubt she did it on purpose.' Libby crossed her fingers underneath the sheets, ignoring Scott's valiant effort not to look astonished. 'Her great-aunt would lace elderflower wine with belladonna, maybe there was a bottle of it in the house. Do you know where Zoë's gone?'

Both officers shifted uncomfortably.

'Mr McBride said she sounded like she was at an airport,' one said, 'but there's no Zoë Horton listed on any flights.'

What were the bets that Zoë had a new passport, a new passport using her birth certificate? They'd need to look for Zoë *Keeley*, her original birth name. Libby struggled not to smile and hoping for a distraction, she pressed the tube in her hand against the bed, sending a bolt of pain up her arm.

'Libby, you've gone grey,' Scott said, leaning on the bed. 'Are you okay?'

She turned her head, smiling. 'I'm just a little tired.'

With that, Scott stood up and the police officers thanked her for her time. Libby barely listened as the officers said it sounded like a genuine accident, but when Miss Horton returned from her holiday, they would like to speak to her. Libby nodded, staring out of the window, guilt lying heavily on her shoulders. She should've told them the truth – not just about the belladonna, but about Maggie and Fee. She hadn't just distracted them or omitted a few details, she'd lied. Why?

Because I've got her back.

'You're quiet,' Patrick said.

Libby frowned. 'Says you. That's the first thing you've said to me in an hour.'

He turned the Land Rover into the Green, his jaw twitching. 'You were too busy turning down offers for places to stay.'

A fair point. Her morning had been one steady stream of visitors. Grace had been the first, with a bag of clean clothes for Libby and a repeated offer of a room in her house, swiftly followed by Robbie and Vanessa, who'd brought Patrick's car. They begged Libby to move in with them – an idea Libby laughed off, claiming they only wanted a babysitter.

'So are you leaving?' Patrick asked as he pulled up outside his house. 'Gosthwaite, I mean.'

'Would you want me to stay?'

'Yes.'

'And what would happen?'

'We'd go out.'

'And then what?'

He sighed. 'Why does there have to be a then what?'

Nothing had changed. Libby went to open the door, too tired to cry, but her hand stopped on the handle. Outside Maggie's cottage, sitting on the bonnet of a silver Jaguar, was Seamus Doyle.

'What's he doing here?' Patrick asked.

Libby closed her eyes. How could she tell Seamus that his illegitimate daughter murdered the love of his life? 'Fuck, fuck, fuck.'

Patrick laughed. 'Ooh, Olivia Wilde used the F-word.'

Despite everything, she smiled. 'I think I've used it once or twice before.'

'Like on Christmas Eve?' He raised his eyebrows with fake innocence.

She swatted his arm. 'Look, I really need to talk to him.'

'You really need to talk to me.' He leaned on the steering wheel. At least his twitching jaw had gone if his concerned frown hadn't. 'Should I wait?'

She shook her head. 'Go and put the kettle on. I won't be long.'

Libby climbed out of the car, wishing she could follow Patrick into his house. Maybe he was right, maybe there didn't have to be a *then what*.

'Hello, Miss Wilde,' Seamus said.

She sat next to him, steeling herself. Seamus deserved to know the truth and maybe he'd be the one person who could help Zoë. 'She's not here, I'm afraid.'

Seamus glanced around the Green, not looking remotely disappointed. 'Do you have my photograph, Olivia?'

'The photo?' Libby stared at him, crossing her arms. 'Is that why you came here? You travelled three hundred miles for the *photo*?'

'It means a lot to me.'

'And your daughter? Doesn't she mean a lot to you?' Libby's skin crawled. He didn't deserve to know a damned thing about Zoë.

'It's the only photo I have left of Maggie and me. Lucinda burned the rest.'

'But you have another daughter, right?'

Seamus frowned. 'Zoë has two perfectly good parents.'

Libby stood up, shaking her head. 'She also has the photo. I'd watch my back if I were you, Mr Doyle.'

* * *

Patrick slumped against the front door, nausea taking over his body. Why the hell did there have to be then what? He couldn't do this. He really couldn't. A meow from the living room pulled him back to reality and Patrick went to see Hyssop who sat curled up in front of the fire, where he'd spent most of Christmas.

Crouching down, Patrick stroked him, letting the rhythmic purr relax him. For hours, Patrick had watched over Libby, praying she'd be okay. He loved her. Christ, the day before, he'd seen Paolo's painting, *the Fixed Ballerina*, and come to terms with moving to London, so why did *then what* send him running? He just had to persuade her to stay.

'And I expect you to help, pal.'

After he'd let Isla out into the back garden, Patrick peeked out of the window, checking on Libby. She was still chatting to Seamus Doyle, so he dashed upstairs to brush his teeth. He toyed with the idea of a shower, but made do with swapping his jumper for one he hadn't been wearing for the last twenty-four hours – he had to talk to Libby sooner, not later. He had to make this right.

Doyle's car had gone. Why hadn't Libby come in?

Downstairs, Hyssop sat in the window, tapping his claw against the glass, something he only did when Libby was in the cottage. In the dim light of the cold December day, Patrick could just make out a forlorn figure sitting in the bay window. She shouldn't have gone in there by herself. Whistling for Isla to follow him, Patrick picked up Hyssop and headed over to Maggie's cottage. The door was ajar, but he knocked gently.

'Libs?'

'Come in.'

She sat, hugging her knees, a photo frame in one hand and tears rolling down her cheeks. Even Isla jumping up to say hello didn't raise a smile. Patrick sat beside Libby and handed her Hyssop. If anyone could cheer her up, it'd be the cat. Patrick took the photo – it was one of her and Zoë, in their teens, both in tutus, stood on their toes, an arm around each other's waist.

'What chance did she have?' Libby said, her voice muffled as she hugged Hyssop. 'Her mother gave her away, her parents ignored her pleas to let her spend summers at home, and her father couldn't give a damn. He came here to get a photo I had, not to see Zoë.'

'He's her father? Do you mean–'

'Maggie was Zoë's mother.'

It all made sense. Why hadn't he seen it? They looked so alike, for Christ's sake. 'Libby, what did Zoë do?'

'It's better you don't know.' Libby kissed Hyssop. 'I didn't tell the police. I lied to them. I said it was an accident.'

'Poisoning you, or pushing Maggie down the stairs?'

Libby didn't answer.

'The thing is,' Patrick said, 'I think you told me last night. You told me about Maggie and you told me... about Fee. Was it true?'

She nodded.

Jesus Christ.

'But it's not just black and white, is it?' Libby let Hyssop jump down. 'Like when Grace gave me the emerald pendant. She nearly ruined your life, but you forgave her.'

'This isn't the same. Zoë nearly *killed* you.'

'I know, but not intentionally.' Libby took a deep breath. 'She murdered Maggie, or at least assisted in her death, and she sold the ketamine to Fee.'

'But you're protecting her?' What happened to his moralistic Libby, the one who wouldn't turn a blind eye?

'What difference would it make if I told the police? Nobody forced Fee to take the drugs and Maggie... well, let's be honest, this is all her fault.'

'How is it Maggie's fault?'

'She did this. She damaged Zoë years ago. When our flat was broken into last Christmas, Zoë needed her birth certificate to get a new passport.'

'And she found out Maggie was her mum?'

Libby nodded. 'Can you imagine what that did to Zoë's head? This was the woman who cultivated an eating disorder in her, who used to hit her around the ankles with a walking stick and lock her under the stairs. After you went blackberry picking that time, Maggie didn't let Zoë eat anything for *two* days.'

Patrick leant against the window. Zoë had been seven. It was child abuse and her parents wouldn't listen.

If I'm ever a dad...

Libby looked around the room. 'I used to feel sorry for Maggie. I thought she was this lonely old lady who'd been forgotten by the world. The truth was she was a total bitch. She slept with her friend's husband, she wouldn't help a friend in need and instead of showering a little girl with love, she twisted her until she snapped.'

'You reap what you sow.' He reached into his pocket and took out the letter addressed to Libby. 'Zoë left this for you.'

Libby's hands shook as she ripped open the envelope and while she read, fat tears splashed onto the paper. Patrick put his arm around her shoulders, resting his head against hers as she let him read the letter too.

Lib, I'm so sorry. I never, ever wanted to hurt you, but you wouldn't have let me leave. You're too good, too honest, too right – just what I've always needed in my life. I wish I had your strength.

I never meant to do any of this. Please don't hate me. I really don't want you to hate me because you're the only person who ever cared about me. Jonathan didn't. I loved him, truly loved him. I could've been happy with him, I really could, but let's face it, I don't deserve a man like him, not after the things I've done. But he didn't care, not really.

The oddest twist of fate is Ed might love me. And you'll love this. He's not some penniless writer. He's worth a fortune so the spell worked – a good shag with money. Be careful what you wish for!

But I don't deserve to live happily ever after. You do. Let Patrick make you happy.

I love you.

Zx

Ps. I've sold the cottage. Got £350k for it, but if you look behind the painting, I left you a gift. Later, 'gator.

'In a while, 'dile,' Libby whispered.

The Broken Ballerina stood against the wall and Libby knelt beside it, feeling behind the frame. A smile wavered as she produced the emerald pendant, but she sat twisting the stone between her fingers.

'I want to hate her for what she's done,' Libby said, wiping her cheeks, 'but I can't. She's never been able to rely on anyone, except herself. I tried but even I can't help her now. I've lost my best friend.'

Hyssop meowed, rubbing his head against Libby's hand, but his affection set Libby off sobbing again.

'Oh, what are we going to do, Hyss? It's just me and you.'

Enough. Patrick pulled her to her feet, taking a moment to hug her, to let her cry and to summon the courage he needed for what he was about to say.

'We'll find her, Libs. We'll make sure she's okay.' He rested his head on hers. 'And it's not... It's not just you and the cat. You have me too.'

She shook her head. 'No. I have half of you, the indulgent, hedonistic half.'

This was it, his chance to show she was his first priority. After a deep breath, he took her hand and led her outside, to the bandstand in the middle of the Green.

'What are you doing?' she whispered, gazing up at him.

Christ, when she looked at him like that, with her perfume filling his head, Patrick couldn't breathe and his desire to flee kicked in. It was too much. But he stayed where he was and rested his forehead against hers, trying not to close his eyes. Why was this so hard?

'Not half of me,' he said. 'All of me.'

'But...'

'I'm shit-scared, Libs, but... I love you.'

Her eyes widened. 'What?'

'I love you.' He laughed. Actually, it wasn't so hard. 'While you were in London, Hyssop made himself right at home. He sits in the armchair by the fire and stares at Isla with utter disdain. Why don't you make yourself at home too?'

For what felt like five minutes she didn't smile, or react, she just stared at him. Oh Christ, what if she said no? Gosthwaite, London... did it matter where they were? She just had to say yes.

'Look,' he said, 'I know you need to go back to London and I wouldn't want to do it forever, but I know it's important to you, so... well... I hear they have cows in Surrey.'

'But I don't want to go to London,' she said, her eyes still staring.

'Don't lie. I've seen Paolo's new painting. Ballet makes you happier than anything else. I get it.'

'What painting?'

He took out his phone, showing her the photo of the Fixed Ballerina. At first she frowned, as though confused, but then her cheeks slowly turned pink.

'I'm not happy in that painting because of ballet. Paolo made me talk about the thing I loved the most.'

Patrick's heart officially stopped as she stood on tiptoe and held his face with both her hands.

'He made me talk about you,' she whispered. 'I love you. More than ballet.'

In the middle of the Green, they kissed and he hoped to God someone was watching. This was the love of his life and he wanted the world to know.

'How do you always smell like a rose garden?' he murmured between kisses.

She dropped her head back, laughing. 'I've spent the night in hospital and I really need a shower. The last thing I smell like is a rose garden.'

'It's mental, I know, but you definitely smell of roses and sweet peas.'

'Roses and sweet peas, really?' Glancing sheepishly to the sky, she plucked a little red pouch from her jeans pocket. 'This might sound... but I did this spell in July, to summon my true love.'

He struggled not to laugh. 'We hadn't even met.'

'I summoned someone...' She took a deep breath, turning adorably pink. 'Twenty-five to thirty-five, good-looking, non-brown eyes...'

'That's half the male population.'

'Honest, decent morals, good with animals–'

'Most people are.'

'And English.'

'You're in England. What are the chances?' But he laughed, remembering the Broken Ballerina evening. 'So that's why you freaked out when I said I wasn't Scottish.'

'That's when I knew you were the one I'd summoned.'

'Weirdo. But what's with the roses and sweet peas.'

'They're the flower petals I burned as part of the spell.' She opened the ties on the little pouch and emptied the contents, the ash drifting off on the breeze.

'If you believe in that nonsense, why are you throwing it away?'

'I didn't throw it away. I gave it to the wind. It seals the spell.' She grinned. 'You're mine forever now.'

'Define forever.' He pulled her to him, trying not to grin.

'Oh, you know... marriage, kids, dog, cat, crumbling farmhouse.'

To his surprise, his smile grew. 'Sounds tolerable.'

'Tolerable?'

He nodded to the house where Isla and Hyssop sat, obediently waiting for them. 'Well, we've got the dog and the cat already.'

'He's not your cat.'

'No, he's *our* cat. I told you I wouldn't rely on plying you with booze.'

Chapter Forty-Two

As the monsoon eased, Zoë opened up her laptop and sipped her rum and soda. Bajan rum, was there anything better?

On Facebook, she logged in as *Angelique Balletfreak* and scanned through Ed's latest messages. He was still in Barcelona. He'd found her within a week on Facebook and nearly caught up with her within a month in real life, but for over six months she'd stayed one step ahead. Funny, she didn't need to – she wasn't on the run. Neither Libby nor Ed had gone to the police, it seemed, but keeping Ed at arm's length gave Zoë that all-important element of control.

Libby had uploaded a batch of new photos. The house-warming. Jesus, the farmhouse she and Patrick had bought needed about fifty grand throwing at it, but she could see the potential. Their perfect family home.

The photos showed Robbie, Vanessa, Scott, Clara, Xander and Daisy, the usual faces, even Libby's parents, all smiling and holding glasses of wine in the July sunshine. Zoë paused at a photo of Libby and Patrick. He had his arms around her and his head on her shoulder as they faced the camera. Libby still had the fringe and black eye make-up, but her feet were noticeably bare. Patrick had fixed Olivia Wilde's neurosis. Another photo showed them crouching beside a spaniel while they cooed over that bloody cat. Zoë smiled, tapping his nose via the screen.

Hello, Hyssop. Considering you hated me, you did me so many favours.

'Ms Wilde?' The hotel manager walked up. 'Your guests have arrived.'

Zoë offered a courteous smile to the manager and a hand to the woman who'd agreed to an interview. 'Mrs Doyle, I'm Verity. Thank you so much for agreeing to meet with me.'

Like anyone, even a do-gooding, charitable heiress like Lucinda Doyle wouldn't turn down afternoon tea at Barbados' most fabulous hotel.

After shaking Zoë's hand, Lucinda reached up, gently touching one of Zoë's earrings. 'Beautiful diamonds.'

Zoë gave a suitably appreciative response, but her eyes were fixed on Seamus Doyle. He seemed awfully pale for someone who'd spent the last month in paradise.

Hello, Daddy. It's payback time.

'This way, please,' the manager said leading them down to the Lower Terrace. 'Ms Wilde, your photographer is already setting up.'

Photographer? Zoë's stomach contracted, but she smoothed her hands over her white linen shift. She didn't have a bloody photographer, which meant either *OK* magazine had twigged she'd set up an interview in their name, or he… but he wouldn't just turn up, would he?

Her heels rapped on the pristine marble floor and the *photographer* looked up from the light meter he held, his blue eyes twinkling.

'Nice freckles, beautiful.'

The End

Thank You

My husband opened the first print copy of #*Forfeit* and smiled when he saw I'd dedicated it to him. My daughter opened the second print copy, scowled and said, 'But this one's for daddy too.' Without question, this book's for Lissie. :) My writing partner in training. Love you. (And Daddy too).

I'd like to thank my fab street team for all their Beta Reading, pimping and generally being awesome cheerleaders. Special thanks go out to Amber, Nikki, Lucy, Kirsty and Alyssa for their nit-picky proofreading – ridiculously tight deadlines on a hefty-assed book? Nailed it. You guys rock.

Tay (Chicks That Read), Amber (Cosying Up With Books), Jo and Rachel (Orchard Book Club) – your brilliant book review blogs/pages have been fabulously supportive of me and my books. I'll be forever in your debt.

Laura K – Yeah, so you hit hard with reality, I procrastinate for six months then you pick up the job again and set me straight. I heart you. x

Pezza – If I turned you gay, then my work here is done. ;)

Nat, Janny, Jo – the never-ending writing support crew. Now, if I could just get you all at the same signing at the same time...

And finally, Wattpad's Eva Lau and Caitlin O'Hanlon. If Caitlin hadn't stumbled across Distraction and Eva hadn't given such unwavering support, none of this might've happened.

Thank you all so, so much

Caroline
x

WWW.CAROLINEBATTEN.CO.UK

Lightning Source UK Ltd.
Milton Keynes UK
UKOW04f2323121015

260413UK00002B/20/P